INTERLUDE

AT

COTTONWOOD

SPRINGS

LIZ ADAIR

Though based on family history, this is a work of fiction, and the views expressed herein are the sole responsibility of the author.

Interlude at Cottonwood Springs
Published by Century Press
496 West Kane Drive
Kanab, UT 84741

ISBN: 0-9905027-7-5
ISBN 13: 978-0-9905027-7-7
Printed in the United States of America
Year of first printing: 2015

Cover design by Sarah Beard http://creativecoverart.blogspot.com

Cover photo by Ken Cravillion. Based out of the Midwest, Mr. Cravillion travels the country photographing many amazing places. He loves spending time in the Southwest, having photographed in Zion, Bryce, and Arches National Parks as well as favorite remote areas in Glen Canyon and Grand Staircase Escalante. You can check out more of his work at www.kgcphoto.com

DEDICATION

This book is dedicated to my mother, Lucy Smith Shook, who filled my youth with stories of growing up on a starve-out homestead on the Jornada in New Mexico. Three days before she left this earth, she told me the family secret that no one of my generation knew. That secret grew into this book.

ACKNOWLEDGMENTS

I must acknowledge the gift that my aged uncles, Nate, Clay, and Emory Smith gave me as they told me about life as a cowboy in 1930s New Mexico and about their brother Curtis, on whom this story is based. Nate, in particular, told me two anecdotes concerning Curtis and his wife that I would have had no way of knowing but that I had already written as fiction. That was both spooky and affirming.

Special thanks to two members of my critique group: Christine Thackeray, for telling me that the story, originally published as *Counting the Cost*, was Ruth's story, and it should start with her, and Terry Deighton for taking on the task of editing. I was supported by the rest of my critique group, Tanya Mills, Bonnie Harris and Anne Acton as I wrote new prequel chapters one, two and four.

Beta readers are golden, and mine have proved to be so. Terry Schnepf, Keralee Oblad and Nayna Christensen did yeoman work, and Anne Richardson went above and beyond. Thank you ladies!

As always, thanks to my sweet husband, Derrill, for his unfailing support.

Chapter 1

RUTH REYNOLDS PUSHED through the swinging door to the kitchen of the Park Avenue apartment that was hers for one more day. She carried a bone china cup and saucer and paused at the window as she spied a robin. It sat on a top branch of the budding crepe myrtle in the courtyard below, a reminder that she would miss spring in New York City this year. Her free hand came to her breastbone, and she wondered what caused the mounting pressure there, beneath her fingers. The last time she felt that sickening, elephant-like weight was seven years ago when she was twenty-one and had lost both her father and her fortune.

Bunny Ashton followed her in, setting her own dishes in the sink and hanging her suit jacket and fur piece on a chair. "Tell me again why your maid isn't here."

"She got a new situation. They needed her right away."

Bunny put in the stopper and turned on the hot water. "You're too soft. She should be here to help you today."

Ruth leaned against window, her hair matching the mahogany trim as she watched the robin spread its wings, skim over the fence, and land beside a crumpled paper bag.

"Did you hear me? I said if you're leaving tomorrow, today is the day you need your maid."

Ruth drew her dark eyes away from the bird pecking at the garbage. "I know, but what was I to do? Drag her bodily away?"

"Take away your recommendation. There are probably ten people lined up waiting for that job."

"Fifty. And if I made her come in today, she'd be out of work tomorrow with no prospects." Ruth handed Bunny her cup and saucer. "No. Maggie's been great. She worked extra hours to help get us ready to move, and I'm glad she found another place."

"Who's going to clean for you? Don't think that I'm going to do more than wash this—"

A sound like cymbals crashing came from the living room and Ruth's eyes opened wide. "The Reynolds tea service!" She bolted to the door as fast as she could in her pencil skirt and high heels. Pushing it open, she was reassured by the sight of the man in white coveralls holding a brass candelabrum in one hand and a metal waste basket in the other.

The fellow raised his shoulders sheepishly. "A small mishap," he said. "Nothing broken; nothing dented."

Ruth's eyes swept the room, but everything waiting to be packed still looked intact. She nodded at the man and let the door swing shut.

Bunny picked up a dish towel. "Where did you find your movers? He's a little inept, isn't he?"

"He's an out-of-work architect, doing what he can to keep body and soul together. Here, I'll dry those." Ruth took the towel from Bunny. "He'll be in to pack the china next."

Bunny eased into one of the chairs at the breakfast table. "Let's hope he treats it better than your hollowware. Which reminds me, when did you get the famous Reynolds tea service?"

"Harlan gave it to me for Christmas."

"Really?" Bunny smiled and leaned back in her chair. "I wish I had known. I would have paid money to watch him wrest it away from his mother." She crossed her legs. "Especially to give it to you."

Ruth compressed her lips and turned away to put a cup in a glass-fronted cupboard.

Bunny leaned down to check the seams in her stockings. "What did you give Harlan for Christmas?"

Ruth froze. She didn't turn around, didn't move.

Bunny looked up. "What did I say? What's wrong?" She leaned to the right, so she could see Ruth's profile. "Are you blushing?"

Ruth faced her friend. Her cheeks were pink, but she raised her chin as she endured the scrutiny.

Bunny's laugh tinkled like the entryway chandelier when someone slammed the door. "Let me guess. Your Christmas present to Harlan was that you invited him into your bedroom!"

Ruth put a finger to her lips. "Shh." She pointed toward the living room.

Bunny picked up her purse and opened it. "It's nothing to blush about. Or whisper about. You've been married a year."

Ruth sighed and sank into a chair. "I know. It's just that it's so ..."

Bunny fished a gold cigarette case out of her purse and set it on the table. "I told you not to marry him. Remember? I told you. Not without love."

Ruth raked her fingers through her chestnut mane, pushing it away from her face. "I thought it would be easier. I didn't know it would be so ... so ..." Her mouth twisted like she had bitten into something sour.

Bunny cocked her head sideways. "Surely, at twenty-seven, you knew all that marriage entailed."

Ruth dropped her eyes and didn't answer. She felt her cheeks getting hotter.

Bunny covered her mouth and laughed, not a tinkling chandelier laugh this time but a ribald, dirty-story laugh. "You don't mean to tell me you were a virgin! Oh, that is the funniest thing I have heard in a long time."

Ruth raised her eyes. "Why is that so funny?"

"With your face and figure? And you so modern?"

Ruth twisted the towel in her hand. "I'm also a realist. My only assets were, as you pointed out, my face, my figure, and my virginity. You may not have noticed it, but no man worth anything wants damaged goods."

Bunny sent her a sharp look.

"I mean," Ruth amended, "if there's no accompanying fortune."

Bunny looked inside her purse again, drawing out a silver lighter and a small ebony cigarette holder. "Well, anyway, I warned you not to marry Harlan."

Ruth stood and threw the towel on the counter. "Yes, it's easy for you give advice. Unlike you, my money wasn't in oil." She pulled open a drawer and rummaged around inside. "When the stock market crashed, my father lost everything. I lost everything."

Bunny concentrated on fitting a cigarette into the holder. "Your mother managed to live rather well, as I remember."

Ruth pulled a tablet and pencil out of the drawer. "Yes, Malcolm Newberg had money. He was a sweet man, better than she deserved, actually. He was very generous to let me live with them and give me an allowance." She closed the drawer. "But she was as penniless as I, and when she died, I got nothing." She thought a moment. "I guess my choice wasn't much different from my mother's. I couldn't live without money, either."

"Well, not in a place like this, anyway." Bunny clicked the lighter, lit her cigarette, and inhaled. Leaning back, she blew out a stream of smoke. "I can't get over it. I go to California for three months. I come back, and you're heading west."

Ruth's throat suddenly felt tight. "Yes, it came up quite suddenly. Harlan's uncle told us right after Christmas."

"I don't suppose you had a choice in the matter?"

Ruth shook her head. "There's a Depression on. Harlan's lucky to have a job." She set the tablet down on the counter.

"Where did you say you were going? Texas? I've heard that Neiman Marcus in Dallas is a wonderful store."

Ruth, busy writing, didn't answer. She tore off the bottom of the page and put it on the toaster. She wrote three words on the remaining half sheet.

Bunny pointed with her cigarette holder. "What are you doing?"

"I'm letting the movers know what we're taking and what goes to storage."

"Is the china going or staying?"

Ruth smiled. "Going. Harlan says just because we won't be living uptown, we shouldn't lower our standards."

"Well, I guess the Reynolds silver tea service will serve some purpose." She stood and picked up her jacket and fur scarf. "So you won't come and have supper with Robert and me?"

"No. Harlan's Aunt Gretchen is having us over. I think they want to give us some last minute instructions before we go."

As Bunny leaned over to kiss Ruth's cheek, she glanced at the note on the toaster. "You're not taking my wedding present with you? I'm wounded."

Ruth stood very still. She stared at the small metal appliance and blinked her dark-lashed eyes, willing herself not to care, not to cry. She cleared her throat and traced a pattern on the top of the ceramic tile countertop. "Actually, where we're going is a little bit remote. They have electricity from a light plant, but it's only in the evenings."

Bunny stepped back to the table and sat down, an uncomprehending look on her face. "I don't understand. Where on earth are you going?"

Ruth's chin began to quiver. She folded her arms and clenched her hands until her manicured nails bit into her palms. Against all efforts, her eyes filled, and tears streamed down her cheeks. "We're going to New Mexico," she said, and then she covered her face with her hands and began to sob.

Chapter 2

GRETCHEN HANCOTT LAID her white linen napkin on the table, rose from her chair, and smiled down at Ruth. "Shall we leave the men for awhile?"

Ruth stood as well and glanced at Harlan. Of medium build and precisely dressed, his lowered, black brows and tightened lips told her that he hadn't taken kindly to his uncle's advice about getting ahead in business. Her heart sank. That meant when they got home, he'd be trying to prove his manhood.

Gretchen held the door open. "Let's go to my sitting room. I have something for your journey."

Ruth forced a smile. "I can't wait to see what it is." Turning her back on her husband, Ruth followed the older woman through the foyer and up the broad staircase to a cozy second floor salon. She took a seat in a wingback chair set conversationally opposite an overstuffed rocker.

Gretchen sat and picked up a needlework bag from the floor beside her. She rooted around inside it, pulling out a book-shaped package wrapped in tissue. She set the gift on her lap and regarded Ruth. "Your family isn't old money."

Ruth blinked. Her face must have registered surprise, because Gretchen apologized. "Forgive me, my dear. People keep telling me I'm too blunt, but I have something to say, and I thought if we started with your family, it would help."

"No, that's all right. I just wasn't expecting that. Actually, I do come from old money, just not piles of it. My father had a modest inheritance. He came to the city before I was born and went into banking."

"Where did he come from?"

"Upstate. He was a small town boy, but he did very well."

"Until the crash."

Ruth nodded and looked at her hands, folded in her lap. "He committed suicide."

"Along with lots of others." Gretchen waved the subject away. "That's not what I want to talk about. What do you know about Hancott Land and Cattle Company?"

Ruth paused before answering, searching her mind for any scrap of information. "It's owned by the Hancotts, of course. Harlan works there. And we're moving because his job is taking us away. I'm sorry, I don't know much else."

"Do you know what the company does?"

Ruth felt her cheeks get warm. She brushed a piece of lint off her skirt to mask her embarrassment. "Something to do with land and cattle, I suppose."

Gretchen leaned back in her chair. "Mining and cattle, my dear. And do you know what the secret of success in mining and cattle is?"

Ruth spread her hands, palms up. "You'll have to tell me."

Gretchen began rocking. "It's people. Having good people overseeing the mines and ranches. Having good craftsmen plying their trade on the ground. That's the secret." The laugh lines crinkled the corners of her eyes.

This was a side of Gretchen Hancott new to Ruth. She had only seen her in formal situations, dressed to the nines and making small talk with tycoons and city councilmen. Tonight Ruth noted that, though Gretchen's dress was obviously well made and expensive, it was unadorned, and her shoes were comfortably sensible. Somehow, the at-home wardrobe of her hostess put Ruth at ease, even in the face of her lack of knowledge. "I'm not sure why you're telling me this," she said.

"Because I want you to help Harlan."

"Beg pardon?"

Gretchen smoothed the paper on the gift she still held in her lap. "That's why I asked about your background, my dear. I was hoping maybe your father or grandfather was a self-made man. You know, up from being a cooper or wheelwright."

At Ruth's blank stare, Gretchen went on. "Harlan's father was my brother Philip. He was a good man, but he died when Harlan was a boy."

Ruth nodded. She was familiar with that information.

"Harlan's mother's ideas about ideals and values that should be taught a young man—well, I'll leave that unsaid." Gretchen compressed her lips for a moment and then continued. "On the other hand, my husband's father started out as a blacksmith in Chicago. He built up the Hancott Land and Cattle Company, and he taught his son—my husband, Stephen—the value of hard work and pride in your trade, no matter what it is. Now, Harlan has good instincts for business, but he hasn't yet learned to respect the people who work for him. He doesn't realize that without them, there would be no company."

Ruth leaned forward, understanding showing in her brown eyes.

Gretchen smiled at her. "You know that Harlan will inherit from his mother when she dies?" She paused to wait for Ruth's confirming nod. "He doesn't have any money of his own. I'm sure you've seen how she uses his allowance as a way of controlling him. His job with Hancott means freedom, because I assure you, Mrs. Philip Reynolds doesn't intend to die any time soon."

"We're very grateful for Harlan's position with the company."

Gretchen waved the comment away. "His uncle doesn't expect gratitude. He expects hard work. He'll reward it with promotion if Harlan learns what he's sent to New Mexico to learn."

Ruth closed her eyes and shook her head. "I don't see what I can do."

"You will. I want to tell you about the people you'll meet. I want to make sure you don't look at them and make a wrong judgment because of the way they talk or dress."

"You're starting to scare me. How do they talk and dress?"

"There's nothing to be afraid of. They talk and dress very simply. It's important to realize that they are able to survive, even thrive, in places that are hard and unforgiving. You or I wouldn't last a week in their world."

"But Harlan said we'll be living on the ranch."

"Oh, you might be living on the edges of their world, but you're not doing their work. However, that's not what I wanted to explain."

Gretchen uncrossed her ankles and sat forward, hands clasped on top of the parcel on her lap. "These people face deprivation, even death, on a daily basis. Succeeding in the face of that gives them a sort of independence. The things that earn a man respect here in the city don't stand for a lot out there."

Ruth raised her brows. "Things like ...?"

"Things like money or a college degree."

Ruth smiled wryly. "Or a future inheritance?"

Gretchen returned the smile, her eyes twinkling. "I see you understand what I'm trying to say. Harlan's going to have to earn their respect, but I don't think he's going to realize that right away. It may take a while for him to see through the rough exterior to the sterling characters inside. You can help speed the process, I think."

"I don't know. He doesn't talk much about business."

"Well, maybe when you get out there, and you have to rely on each other more, it will be different." Gretchen picked up the package. "I guess this would be a good time to give you this."

Ruth took the proffered gift and unwrapped the tissue covering. Inside was a small, leather-bound book. She tucked the wrapping beside her and opened it, finding pages filled with handwriting in a delicate, flowing script. Her brow furrowed as she leafed through. "Is this a journal?"

Gretchen pointed to a date on the inside cover. "It's one I kept when I was first married."

Ruth looked up, her brows arched. "Really?"

"Yes. Stephen and I went out west, just like you and Harlan. We were newly married, but instead of going to New Mexico to live on a ranch, we went to Nevada and lived in a mining town. What an experience that was! During the daytime, when Stephen was down in the mine, my next door neighbor, Hulda Gulbranson, taught me how to keep house and cook. I kept careful notes, and I'm going to send this book with you. I want it back, so bring it when you return."

Ruth read the heading at the top of a page, "Cleaning smoky lamp chimneys."

"You won't need that on the Diamond E," Gretchen said. "You'll have electric lights, at least until ten at night. We stayed there last year for a month. It's a hundred times better than the first house I stayed in."

Ruth checked the date in the front of the book. "That was forty years ago. I would hope things have improved."

"You'll have an oil-fired range and a kerosene refrigerator. I had to cook on a wood stove and didn't even have an ice box."

Ruth closed the book and held it on her knees. "Actually, Harlan was saying that there would probably be someone we could hire to come in to cook and clean for us."

Gretchen laughed. "There's a laundry in the nearest town where you can take your clothes to be done. But there's no one who lives close enough to come in and do day work, and the house is too small to hire someone to live in."

Ruth's hand went to her breast. The pressure was starting again. "Oh."

"Think of it as an adventure, a trip to a strange, new land, living among the natives. And what natives they are! There's one young cowboy with dark curly hair and a dimple in his cheek that was so fetching I was tempted to wrap him up and bring him home."

Ruth's eyes grew wide, and she put her fingers to her mouth. "Aunt Gretchen, you surprise me!"

"When I grow too old to appreciate a good looking, manly man, well, you might as well call the undertaker."

Ruth laughed. "I hope we won't have to do that for many a year." She held up the book. "And thank you for trusting me with this. I'll bring it back to you."

Gretchen Hancott rose. "You are most welcome. And now, shall we go join the men?"

It was almost midnight by the time Ruth and Harlan rode the elevator to their floor. Ruth, conscious of Harlan's arm around her waist, didn't want to pull away in front of the elevator operator, afraid there might be a scene. When the door opened, she quickly stepped out and then turned back, letting her husband walk on toward their door.

She pulled a bill out of her evening bag. "Goodbye Andy. We're leaving tomorrow, you know. Thanks for all your good service."

Andy took the tip and touched the brim of his cap. "Thank you, Mrs. Reynolds. I'll miss you."

She waved goodbye and walked briskly to her apartment and through the door Harlan held open. The clink of bottle against glass sounded behind her as she continued down the hall to her bedroom, shrugging off her satin evening coat as she went. In her room, she folded the garment carefully and put it in the suitcase lying open on a stand.

Reaching under her arm to unzip her dress, she turned to find Harlan leaning against the doorjamb, drink in hand.

He motioned with his glass. "Don't let me stop you. I like watching you undress."

She dropped her hand and turned away, sliding into the seat in front of her mirrored vanity table. "I thought the movers packed all the whisky and glasses."

"I made sure they left some out."

She picked up her brush, and as she vigorously raked it through her hair, counting the strokes, she glanced periodically in the mirror. Harlan, eyes dark and smoldering, stood unmoving, save for the rising and falling of his chest. On a downward stroke, she looked up, met his gaze, and saw his Adam's apple move as he swallowed. She turned away and bent down to brush her hair from back to front, counting under her breath, *fifty-five, fifty-six, fifty-seven.*

On *sixty*, she felt his hand caress the nape of her neck, and her reaction was swift and involuntary. She straightened and stood all in one motion, knocking the tumbler from his hand. She remained still for a moment, her back to the mirror, her hair a dark halo around her pale face.

Harlan looked from the wet patch on the knee of his trousers to the puddle soaking into the carpet at his feet.

Ruth bent down to pick up the glass which had rolled to the bench. "I'm sorry. You startled me."

"Obviously." He stepped closer, laced his fingers through her chestnut mane and leaned down to kiss where her shoulder met her neck. "I thought we might ..."

Ruth, trying to quiet her inner flight mechanism, set the glass down and turned away. "It's late, Harlan. We have a long trip ahead of us."

He moved behind her, held her shoulders, and pressed his face against her hair, his breathing heavy, his voice raspy. "It's our last night in New York."

Ruth felt herself beginning to panic. She grabbed a tissue from the vanity and wiped her sweaty palms, pulling herself out of Harlan's grasp as she did so. "I know it's our last night. It makes me sad and weepy. I just want to go to bed and go to sleep and forget it." She walked to her closet.

He didn't move. Head lowered like an angry bull, he stared at her with his heavy brows knotted and his mouth pulled down into a sneer. "All right. Go to bed. Go to sleep." He stalked to the doorway. "But I've got news for you, dear wife. There's only one bedroom and one bed where we're going, and things are going to change."

When he strode down the hall toward his room, she followed him to the door and closed it. With a trembling hand, she turned the key in the lock.

"I heard that," Harlan shouted. "When we get there, things are going to change."

Chapter 3

ABOUT THE TIME that Ruth and Harlan Reynolds were boarding the train for their leisurely trip west, Heck Benham and Mike Eldred rode in from Tucker's Well. Arriving at the Diamond E ranch complex early in the morning, they intended to rest, chew the fat, and eat Shorty's cooking for a day before heading into town for the dance.

Heck was twenty-six, tall and rangy, with sandy hair and blue eyes. Mike, a year younger and a couple inches shorter, had dark, curly hair and an engaging dimple in his left cheek.

They had just finished breakfast when the boss's wife appeared in the cook shack doorway and changed their plans for the day.

Pale and trembling, Ruby Payne sagged against the doorjamb. "Where's Shorty?"

Heck looked behind him. "I don't know, ma'am. He and Dooley were here, but they seem to have gone off."

She sighed. Her chin began to quiver, and tears welled up and slid down her weathered cheeks.

"Oh, here, ma'am. What's the matter?" Springing up, Heck took her arm and helped her to a nearby chair.

She pulled a hankie from her apron pocket and wiped her eyes. "I needed Dooley and Shorty to help get the

17

bungalow cleaned out." Her voice quavered. "I just knew they'd try to get out of it!" Tears began flowing again.

"Me and Heck'll clean it out," Mike offered.

When Heck looked at him in amazement, Mike went on. "Ol' Heck was just sayin' this morning that he's tired of being a cowboy, and he'd like to try some other line of work. And here you are, the answer to a young man's dream. Ain't that right, Heck?"

"That's right, Miz Payne," Heck lied. "I'd dearly love the chance to clean that house."

Ruby brightened. "Will you really help me?"

Heck nodded. "Yes ma'am. But only if you promise to go on home and leave us to it."

After giving detailed directions, Ruby Payne tottered back to her house, and Heck and Mike, instead of swapping stories in the bunkhouse, spent the morning getting the bungalow ready for new tenants.

First, they stowed all the furniture in the tool shed loft. Then they took down the blue chintz curtains, and, with Mike on the inside and Heck outside, they polished the windows, heedless of the stares and gibes from other cowboys riding in.

Next, while Heck scrubbed the kitchen floor, Mike cleaned the bedroom. "Hey, Heck!" he called from the depths of the closet. "Come in here." Mike held a stick at arm's length. "Look what I found in the closet."

Heck brought the mop with him and examined the ebony bump on the end of Mike's stick. "What is it? A black widow?"

"We'll know in a minute." Mike squatted down and flipped the spider over on her back. She stayed there long enough, legs working in the air, for them to see the telltale red hourglass on her belly. Then, Mike stepped on her.

"Well, now you've made a mess," Heck said.

"No, I just did my good deed for the day. Can you imagine the new lady coming face to face with Miz Spider?"

Heck handed him the mop. "Well, she's not going to like it squished on her floor, either. While you clean it up, I want to see how that kerosene refrigerator works."

Mike took the wooden handle. "The way it works is that no cowboy like you will ever have one."

While Heck inspected the refrigerator, Mike finished the bedroom and, by midday, they had the bungalow empty and clean. Ruby's husband, Alan, met them on the porch and rewarded their hard work with a bottle of whiskey.

Mike looked at the label and whistled. "I don't know, sir. That's pretty high-class whiskey for a couple of cowhands."

Alan Payne shook his head. "Stephen Hancott sent me that whiskey. Since he owns the place, and it's his wife's nephew that's going to live here—him and his missus—I figure you boys should have it. I guess you can tell Ruby's having one of her bouts of fever. I appreciate the help."

Heck rolled down his sleeves and buttoned them. "Why'd you have us take all the furniture out?"

"They're bringing their own—should arrive a couple days before they do. I get the idea they're used to something a bit better than what we have here. She's something of a socialite, I gather. Quite a beauty."

The dimple appeared in Mike's cheek. "Well, now, she's bound to find lots of socialness around here. Ol' Heck is about as sociable as they come when he's primed with fine courage like you just give us."

Mr. Payne smiled. "Are you going in to the dance at Hot Springs?"

"Yep. We'd better go purty up, so we can go practice our socialness. Thanks, Mr. Payne." Mike saluted him with the bottle, and the two cowboys descended the porch steps and ambled across to the bunkhouse.

Mike put the bottle in one of his boots while they bathed, shaved, and put on clean clothes. They ate Shorty's stew and cornbread and then sat, chairs tipped back against the cookhouse wall and feet up on the porch railing, as they passed the whiskey back and forth. By late afternoon, they hadn't drunk enough to be ready to face the girls in town, but they were ripe for a lark, and when Mike bragged that he could rope anything, Heck said he bet Mike couldn't rope a pig.

Mike insisted he could and set out to prove it. The only person they knew who had a pig was Ol' Lady Lyons, so Mike got his rope, and they went to find Ras and ask him if they could borrow his jalopy.

Heck held the bottle while Mike drove, and when they got to the Lyons' place, though no one was home, they parked the car and wandered out back to the sty. At the sound of the cowboys' steps, a pig scrambled to his feet and stood grunting, head up and nose working to overcome the deficiencies of porcine eyesight.

Heck eyed the animal. "How you gonna do this?"

"Let's turn 'em out. I'll get on the front of the car, and you drive."

The pig came over and began snuffling around the trough, grunting interrogatives as he nosed in the dirt. Mike stood by the gate with his lasso in his hand. "You get the car, and I'll let him out."

Heck whistled as he walked back to where they'd parked. Getting in, he coaxed the engine to life and drove around the house just in time to see Mike swing the end of his rope and catch the pig smartly in the rear end.

The ungainly animal darted toward the creek bank, its high, keening squeal cutting through the spring afternoon like a rusty razor. Mike jumped on the front of the car, and Heck took off in hot pursuit.

What the race lacked in finesse was supplied by enthusiasm. Heck, urging the old car to its rheumatic limit, drove with his head out the window. Mike, pointing and hollering, tried to direct him along their quarry's devious path until the pig disappeared over the bank at a spot too steep for the jalopy to follow.

Mike pointed south, and Heck drove over sage and bunchgrass to a place where they could make the descent. Mike got his lasso ready, riding the car down the hill as he would a bucking bronc. He lifted his arm to twirl the rope, and just at that moment, the old car backfired.

The pig dropped in its tracks. Just folded up its legs and obeyed the law of gravity. Heck rammed on the brakes, and the car slid on the gravel, stopping just a foot away from the little pink mound.

Heck had seen death enough times to recognize it. He got out and walked around to stand with his hands in his back pockets, looking down at the ridiculous face of the pig, its ears awry and tongue sticking out. He looked up at Mike, still riding the hood of the car. "Looks like we just bought us a pig."

They cut the throat and bled the pig then put it on the fender and drove back to the ranch. Almost sober when they arrived at the bunkhouse, they hung the carcass on the porch to cool overnight and then Heck got a stub of a pencil and a piece of lined paper to figure how they stood financially. He emptied his new-saddle savings out of the Montgomery Ward envelope he kept under his mattress, and Mike shook a roll of bills out of a Prince Albert can. When they got through with their accounting, they had each lost a year's savings.

Chapter 4

A WEEK LATER, Ruth arrived at the Diamond E bungalow. She stood in the doorway and let her eyes wander over the tiny living room illuminated by an inadequate ceiling fixture. The furniture that had graced the Park Avenue apartment hulked in the corners, taking up too much wall space and encroaching on passage areas. The claret color of a Bokhara rug, her only legacy from her father, was a welcome sight, but beyond the rug and through a doorway, she saw the gleaming brass of Harlan's bedstead.

Stepping inside, she pulled off her gloves and laid them and her handbag on the drop-leaf table crowded next to an arched doorway. "You weren't very civil to the Paynes," she called over her shoulder.

"I take it you didn't like me asking him to carry the suitcases to the porch?" Harlan followed her in, and his black eyebrows came down as he looked around the room.

"No, I didn't. He's the manager of Hancott's cattle holdings, not some lackey. "

"And as soon as we're out of this godforsaken place, I will be overseeing all of Hancott's western operations. Alan Payne needs to stay on my good side. You notice he carried the bags."

Ruth turned away and reached through the archway, rubbing her hand on the wall.

"What are you doing?"

"This must be the kitchen, but I can't find the light switch." Touching fingers to the plaster, she walked into the gloomy interior. Something brushed her cheek, and she reflexively batted it away.

Moments later, she realized it was the pull-cord for the single bulb that hung down in the middle of the kitchen. She found the string again, jerked on it, and blinked as the harsh light revealed a small room with a refrigerator on one wall, a sink against a second wall, and an odd-looking black apparatus taking up the third. Leaning over, she read the enameled plaque on the front: *E-Z Wickless Oil Stove*. The appliance stood on tall legs which supported an oven heated by two oil burners. A third burner served as the cook top. There were no cupboards, no counters, no curtains.

Ruth felt tears welling up. She had kept up a brave front in the roomette as they rode the train across the continent. Looking out the window at a landscape that had become increasingly dry and empty, she had spoken in positive tones to Harlan about the opportunities he would have because of their time in New Mexico. She read Gretchen Hancott's journal as they waited for her car to be unloaded at the depot in Cutter, and as they drove to the ranch in the dark, she pictured herself in an apron, supporting Harlan the way his aunt had supported her husband. But this was nothing like that picture. This was a tiny, cramped, tin-roofed house twenty miles out on a dirt road through ugly, barren country. Her neighbors consisted of an anemic-looking older woman and a garrulous younger woman whose fat rear end caused her cheap cotton dress to hike up in the back. Both were married to men who worked on the ranch. Hardly candidates for a game of bridge.

Harlan walked into the kitchen, put his hands on his hips and surveyed the freestanding sink. "I can't believe Uncle Stephen permitted them to put us here."

"He knows what the house is like."

"Uncle Stephen? How would he know?"

She pretended to examine the range, so he wouldn't see she had been on the verge of crying. "This is where they stay when they visit the ranch. Aunt Gretchen just put in this new stove, so we'd be more comfortable."

"That's a stove? To cook on? It doesn't look anything like the one we had."

"That's because ours was electric."

"Oh." Harlan put a finger under her chin and lifted her face. "Are those tears I see? Come here." Putting his hands under her elbows, he pulled her to him. "Don't cry."

Maybe it was because she felt so low; maybe it was because Harlan spoke so simply, but she responded to the offer of comfort and laid her head on his shoulder. She closed her eyes and felt the wetness of tears seeping through her lashes. She drew in a shuddering breath and sighed, and as she sagged against him, she felt his arms slide around her.

"It's going to be all right," he whispered in her ear.

At that moment the lights went out. The low throbbing noise she had been almost unaware of ceased, and a matte-black silence surged over them.

She opened her eyes. "What happened?"

"They must have shut off the light plant. They said it goes off at ten."

She straightened up. "But that's ridiculous. We haven't even unpacked. They could have left it on longer since we just got here."

He laughed and drew her close. "I don't know; it's kind of nice. Improves the look of the place, you know."

As she searched around the room for a glimmer of something to orient herself, she felt Harlan bury his face in her neck.

His voice was husky. "I'll bet I can find the way to the bedroom."

She pulled away and bumped against the stove top. "Really, Harlan. This isn't the time to be thinking about that. We need some light."

"How about fireworks? Shall we make some?"

She felt him grasp the sleeve of her jacket, and she jerked away, moving toward where she thought the doorway should be. A moment later she felt his hand on her shoulder. She tried to get away, but the other hand caught her waist and pulled her in, her back against his chest.

His mouth was next to her ear. "It's been a long time since Christmas." He lifted her a few inches off the ground and half carried, half dragged her forward, but his aim was off in the dark, and they hit the corner of something. The arm that he had around her took the blow, and she heard him curse under his breath.

She had one hand free and felt the coil housing on top of the refrigerator. "Let me go," she said. "I know where we are."

He was panting now. "So do I, and I know where we're headed."

Ruth tried to wrench free. "You promised not to do this. You promised to be patient."

"I'm through being patient." He tightened his grip and moved again towards the archway. This time he was successful, and he wrestled her into the living room. "I warned you that things were going to be different when we got here."

Ruth clawed at his hands, trying to get him to release her. "Let me go!"

"Not on your life." He continued to force her toward the bedroom, but in the pitch black, they bumped into the arm of the sofa. Ruth fell backward over it and pulled Harlan with her. She was underneath as they bounced on the cushions, but she landed on top as they hit the floor. She tried to pull his hands away, but he hung on as they thrashed around trying to regain their footing.

She scratched at his thumbs, trying to loosen his grip. "Let go, so I can stand up."

"You don't need to stand up." He was on his feet now, and he began dragging her backwards with her heels trailing on the floor. He collided with the wall, finding his way with a kind of full-bodied Braille, but moving inexorably toward the bedroom and having his way with his wife.

Ruth, finally able to get her feet under her, arched her back and wrenched herself from his grasp. But he was quick, and as he grabbed blindly, he snared her hair and yanked her off her feet.

"Ow!" She clutched him as she went down and sank her teeth into his thigh.

It was his turn to yell. He still had a fistful of hair, and he pulled so hard that it brought tears to her eyes. She had to let go, but she had discovered a weapon. She grabbed the hand that held her curls, twisted her head, and sank her teeth into his wrist.

Harlan bellowed. He picked her up, one hand still in her hair, the other around her waist. They hit the bedroom door jamb, but he finally lugged her through.

Ruth's heart sank as she felt the bed press against the back of her legs. She tried to stay standing, but his weight was too much for her. They fell together, and then his hands found her shoulders, ran down her arms to her hands, and jerked them up to pin them above her head as he lay on top of her.

They were both breathing heavily. "Please don't," she said. "Please don't."

"It's my right." He moved her left hand over, so he could hold both hands with one of his. She was surprised at how strong he was, and she felt helpless and close to despair.

Still holding her hands in an iron grasp, he turned on his side to fumble with his belt, trying to undo it in utter darkness while still holding her prisoner. As he did so, his left leg slid off her and his right flexed slightly. She felt rather than mentally processed the advantage he had given her in that tiny shift, and it was a visceral reflex that brought her knee up into his crotch.

His reaction was explosive, immediate, and profane. She didn't know what he was doing while he shouted obscenities at her, but she knew he wasn't pinning her to the bed anymore. She scrambled up and fled, feeling for the doorway into the living room, going by memory to the table where her purse lay. She felt around and found it just as Harlan crashed into the bedroom wall.

"I'm going to get you!" he shouted. "You'll be sorry."

Ruth moved instinctively to the front door, fumbling for the doorknob and turning it. Once out, she paused on the porch to reach down and find the luggage, still sitting where Alan Payne had put it. Closing the front door behind her, she pushed Harlan's suitcase in front of it. Then she picked up her own bag and felt her way carefully down the porch steps. The car had been parked to the right of the stairs. She stumbled blindly in that direction and found it just as she heard the door open and Harlan holler her name.

Frantic, she felt along the side for the door handle. She heard Harlan fall over his suitcase, and she heard a sharp crack and then nothing more. She paused, listening, but all was still. Thinking that he may have hit his head on the porch railing, she hesitated, wondering whether she should go back and see about him. But she was afraid if she did, she would never get away, and that little scuffle in the dark had convinced her that she could not continue this marriage. She shivered as she thought of how degrading it was to submit to Harlan pawing her in order to survive. There had to be another way.

She heard a groan from the porch, and that decided her. She reached through the open car window and turned on the lights. With one eye on the inert form at the top of the stairs, she quickly strapped her suitcase to the luggage rack and got in the car. As she searched in her purse for the keys, she saw Harlan sit up. Her heartbeat accelerated as she felt around the recesses of her bag, frantic to find them before he gained his feet and came after her.

At last her fingers touched metal, and she pulled them out. She looked at the porch and saw that Harlan was standing, leaning against the porch railing, staring straight at her. Her hand shook as she selected the right key and tried to get it into the ignition as she kept an eye on her husband.

He was on the first step when she finally found the slot and was able to turn the switch and press on the starter. She found reverse and backed away as he lurched toward the car. The glare of the headlamps must have blinded him for a moment, because he put up his hands, but then she found first gear and drove away.

Before the darkness could swallow him up, she saw Harlan in the rearview mirror. He sank down on the bottom step, and she exhaled and relaxed her grip on the steering wheel.

But where was she going?

The car was hers, a wedding present from her husband, put in her name, so there was no problem with taking it. She had enough money in her handbag for a tank of gas, but since Harlan took care of the bills and gave her only a small allowance, there was no money for lodging. Where could she go? Who could she ask for help? She wondered how much it would cost to call Bunny Ashton if she could find a phone. Even if she could call Bunny, what would she say? *Can I come stay with you? Will you pay my way back to New York?*

Somehow, the thought of that cross-country trip triggered the memory of something she had read on the train. It was an article about the history of the area, and it mentioned a convent in Las Cruces, a town she understood was close enough to drive to. "I'll ask them for help. I'll explain what happened tonight," she murmured to herself. But did nuns even know what went on between a man and a woman? It didn't matter. If they'd give her a place to stay for a while, she'd be able to figure out something.

As she drove past the last of the ranch outbuildings, she saw a light bobbing ahead. Coming closer, she could see a man carrying a bucket in one hand and a lantern in the other. She pulled up beside him and leaned over to roll down the passenger window. "I wonder if you can help me," she called.

The man turned and regarded her for a moment. Then he approached the window, holding the lantern high enough to light the inside. He had thinning hair and gold-rimmed glasses and looked more like he belonged in a bank or a store than on a ranch.

"I need to know how to get to Las Cruces," Ruth said.

"Cruces?"

"Las Cruces. Can you tell me how to get there?" Ruth hoped he wouldn't ask why she was going there in the middle of the night.

The man continued to stare. Ruth looked apprehensively in the rearview mirror for signs that Harlan was pursuing, but all she could see was darkness. "What is your name?"

The man blinked. "Dooley, ma'am."

"Well, Dooley, can you tell me the way to Las Cruces?"

"Yes ma'am."

She waited expectantly.

Finally Dooley spoke. "You head down this road about a mile. Take the first road that turns off thisaway." He motioned to his right. "You'll see another road that turns off thataway, but don't take that one. Wait for the next 'un. Take that one."

"And then what?"

"Keep on a-goin' 'til you get there."

"A mile down this road, take the first road to the right. Thank you, Dooley." She rolled up the window and drove away, leaving him still holding the lantern high, looking after her. The light grew smaller as she drove up the hill beyond the ranch complex. When she topped the rise and dropped down the other side, it disappeared completely.

Chapter 5

EARLY THE NEXT morning, Heck Benham stood in the dooryard of the cow-camp shack at Tucker's Well, listening. In the predawn dusk he could make out the dark outlines of the corral, the windmill and stock tank, the privy, and a pile of fence posts. He stared at the indigo smudge that was the pass between the hills. Presently, a horseman came into view. Heck smiled. "Mornin', Emory."

"That you, little brother?" The man on the horse was broad-shouldered and barrel-chested, and his gravelly voice grated on the quiet of the morning. "I thought you was a ghost. What're you doin' outside in your union suit?"

"I was just on my way out to get my pants. Mike was fooling around last night and got me all wet when he threw out the wash water."

Emory dismounted and looped his reins around the middle rail of the corral. "You got coffee made?"

"I'll make it as soon as I get my pants on."

Emory grabbed an armload of wood from the woodpile. "I don't know how the Diamond E makes any money with lazy hands like you around. The day's half gone and no coffee made."

They entered the shack to find Mike buttoning up his shirt. Emory dropped his burden in the woodbox and

31

clanged around with the stove lids. "I suppose you've been getting your beauty sleep, Michael," he said, "but nothin' can help anyone as ugly as you. You'd best work on being useful. You make the coffee. I'll make the biscuits."

Heck clothed his lanky form in denim pants and a plaid shirt with a hole in the elbow. A ray from the rising sun came in through the window, and Heck took advantage of the extra light and the hot water in the kettle to shave a three-day stubble.

The difference in the Benham brothers was remarkable. Emory was two years older, of average height, with his powerful arms and chest covered with a thick mat of hair. He had slim hips and moved with quick, deft movements. His dark hair curled crisply, and the sun-grins had etched wrinkles at the corners of his blue eyes.

Heck was tall and lean with straight, fair hair that fell over his forehead. He moved with an unhurried grace and spoke with a quiet voice, but he had the same blue eyes as his brother and the same lines earned from gazing long over sun-swept vistas.

By the time Heck's face was clean-shaven, Mike had coffee ready, and Emory had gravy to go over the biscuits. They sat down to breakfast and ate without conversation until, mopping up the last of the gravy with a piece of biscuit, Emory said, "Let's leave Ol' Michael to do the washin' up. Maybe he can throw out the wash water without hittin' anybody this time. Are you buildin' fence today?"

"Yep." Heck pushed his chair and took his saddlebags off a peg by his bunk. Picking up a pair of boots, he stuffed them inside. "We'll finish putting in the posts today and start stretching the wire next week." To Mike he said, "I'm taking my boots to the ranch. I'll bring the block and tackle back and meet you out where we were working yesterday."

"I heard you was the one that cleaned the Diamond E guesthouse out for that fellow Hancott sent from back east. Now you're buildin' fence?"

Heck grinned. "Guilty on both counts. You can blame Mike. He volunteers us for the damndest things." Throwing his saddlebags over his shoulder, Heck picked up his saddle and bridle.

"I hear that fellow wears a three-piece suit."

Heck paused with the door half open, an incredulous look on his face. "He works cattle in a three-piece suit?"

"Nah. He's a pencil pusher. Some cousin or another of the Hancott family. From what I've heard, his wife is a knockout." Emory waved goodbye to Mike and followed Heck out the door. "Are them your new boots?"

"Yeah. Ol' Delgado made them a little tight across the instep. I thought I'd see if someone at the ranch can take them in to Cruces, so he can fix 'em."

At the corral, Heck put his saddle on the top rail of the fence, unfastened his rope, and walked with long, easy strides toward the gate. He stopped with one hand on the latch when Emory said, "I come by to tell you somethin', Heck. Lucy has run off and got married."

"Who was it?" Heck's voice was hardly above a whisper.

"Some fellow she's been goin' around with. Jimmy something-or-other."

"What did Papa say?"

"Oh, you know Papa, Heck. He stormed around and cussed a blue streak but didn't do anything else."

Heck sighed and undid the gate latch. "Where are they living?"

"They're out at Palomas now. Bemis is lettin' 'em live in the little place behind the store."

"What does this fellow do?"

"He works construction."

"Construction! I don't know that I like the idea of that."

Emory untethered his horse. "Well, you know Heck, I don't think it matters what we like."

Heck stood for a moment looking at the toe of one boot. Then he looked up at the hills beyond his brother's shoulder. Taking his hat off, he brushed his hair back with his forearm and set his hat back on his head. "Thanks for telling me, Emory. Maybe I'll see if I can get in to Palomas this week to see them."

Heck swung the gate open and stepped in the corral. Snaking out a loop, he sent it flying over the head of a good-looking sorrel mare. Approaching slowly, he spoke softly, reassuringly, and then led her to the rail to be tied.

"Just bring her in?"

Heck looked around and found that Emory was astride his horse.

"Yep. She's one I used last year, but I swear she forgot everything over the winter. She tries to pitch me off right regular."

"Well, it's good you got your old boots on—in case you have to walk back to the ranch." Emory laughed a hoarse laugh in the back of his throat. Still chuckling, he headed around the corral and back through the notch in the hills.

Heck watched his brother ride away. Then he turned and murmured softly to the sorrel as he approached her with the saddle blanket.

Chapter 6

THE NEWLY-RISEN sun cast long shadows as Heck Benham rode through greasewood and mesquite at a saddle gait on his way to the Diamond E ranch house. He thought about his brother, hard-working and honest, who had made his way alone from the time he was fourteen. Hiring out as wrangler—low man on the totem pole in any outfit—Emory learned the skills needed to be of value to a rancher. By the time he was sixteen, he was working as a cowhand.

Two years after Emory left, Papa had made life so miserable that Heck left home, too. Now Lucy, the little sister Heck had such hopes for, was married at seventeen.

The sorrel shied at a greasewood bush, jerking Heck from his musing. The mare's head went down, and her rump went up, and when Heck pulled up her head, she reared and wheeled. Heck rode through the pitching spell, patting her on the shoulder when she had settled down and speaking softly. "You're a cross-grained old mare now, but you're gonna be a good cow pony."

He spurred her to a lope on a long, gentle upgrade, finally pulling her down to a walk as she began to climb a small knoll. At the top of the hill, he stopped and leaned forward, stroking the sorrel's neck. "That's a girl. You just rest a spell. I'll have a smoke, and then we'll be on our way."

Unbuttoning his shirt pocket, he took out a packet of papers and a pouch of Bull Durham tobacco. Rolling the cigarette, he moistened the edge of the paper with his tongue, twisted the end, and put it in his mouth. As he felt in his pocket for a match, movement in his peripheral vision made him turn in the saddle and narrow his eyes. He struck the match on the seam of his Levi's, cupping the flame in his hands as he studied the figure below him.

That it was a woman, there was no doubt. Down in an arroyo, she stood by a green coupe in the middle of a little-used road, hardly more than a wagon track.

As he smoked, Heck watched. "Now, don't you think that's something right out of Old Tennyson?" he asked his pony. "How does it go?" Heck's brow furrowed.

> *Something, something, something ...*
> *He saw the maiden standing in the dewy light.*

Heck nodded and pointed with the hand holding his cigarette. "Yep. There she is in the dewy light." The mare shifted and blew out a noisy breath. "Hold on, now," Heck said. "It goes on. Let's see ..."

> *Something, something, something,*
> *Suddenly flash'd on her a wild desire,*
> *That he should wear her favour at the tilt.*
> *She braved a riotous heart in asking for it.*

Clicking his tongue, he asked as the mare proceeded, "Do you think she's a fair maid in need of a knight to rescue her?"

He let the pony pick her way to the bottom of the knoll then eased her down the bank into the draw. "I wonder if a cowboy will do," he said under his breath. "One with a hole in his shirt."

The sandy creek bed muffled the sound of the sorrel's hooves, so the lady, intent upon the mirror of a compact that was sitting on the hood of the car, didn't hear them.

Heck stopped the mare and sat still for a moment, watching as she put on lipstick.

Finally, he said, "Good morning, ma'am."

She whirled around, grabbing onto the fender for support, and stared up at him.

Heck had no time to notice more than chestnut hair and large brown eyes. Her startled response spooked the mare, and he suddenly had his hands full of a mount that was trying to pitch him off. When he had the sorrel well in hand, he took a second look.

The lady had one hand spread on her breast; the other was still holding onto the fender. The face she turned up to him was oval, with dark eyes set under arched brows and framed by the longest lashes Heck had ever seen. The nose was straight, and the bottom lip was full. She had a trim figure clad in a chic navy dress.

The mare danced restively, but he held her steady. Heck pushed his battered Stetson to the back of his head, and the corners of his eyes crinkled as he smiled down at the lady. "I must have startled you. I beg your pardon."

She didn't return his smile. "Well!" she declared. "I've certainly had an introduction to this fair country. I've seen the desert at night, and now I've had my own private rodeo." She pronounced it "*ro-day'-o.*"

Heck's smile broadened. "Would you say that again?"

"Say what again?"

"The part about your own private ..." His voice trailed off, inviting her to finish the sentence.

She did. "... *ro-day'-o.*" Her eyes narrowed. "Why should I say it again? Did I say something wrong?"

"Oh, no, ma'am. My brother told me that's the way they say it back east, but you can't always believe everything he says. I guess it's true. We call it a rodeo out here."

The hand that had been on the lady's bosom went to her forehead. She closed her eyes, saying faintly, "You have no idea how grateful I am for this vocabulary lesson."

"I was just telling this sorrel mare, ma'am, that you were in distress, and we should probably help you out."

"Well, I wish you might, but I don't see how you possibly can. Will you just ride to the Diamond E ranch and tell them that Mrs. Reynolds—"

"Were you heading for the ranch, ma'am?"

She stood for a moment, arms crossed, one shapely foot slightly forward. Heck felt her eyes measuring him and wondered if she would answer.

She did. "No. I was going to Las Cruces."

Heck frowned but made no comment. He looked up the arroyo and then turned around in the saddle to look down the other way.

"I made it this far," Mrs. Reynolds explained, "but I couldn't make it up the other side of this riverbed. So, I decided I'd better go back, and when I turned around, I couldn't make it out this side either. Oh, where are you going? Aren't you going to help me?"

Heck had headed the mare down the arroyo. As his pony continued walking, he turned around, touched his hat, and said, "Yes, ma'am."

He made his way fifty feet down the draw to where a good-sized saltcedar tree grew from the bank. As he tied the sorrel there, he whispered, "I think she's just about to brave her riotous heart." Then he patted the pony's rump and walked back to where the lady was standing.

She had her hands on her hips and an edge to her voice. "I had hoped to make it back to the ranch today."

Heck grinned. "Me, too, ma'am. That's why I tied that sorrel mare to the biggest tree I could find." He walked to the coupe and opened the door.

"Can you drive a car?" she asked.

"We're about to find out, aren't we?" Heck stooped to get in, but he straightened up immediately and turned around, blushing. "Do you want to ... um ... your clothes are all out in the front seat, ma'am."

"Of course they are. I spent the night here. In the cold. I covered up with just about everything in my suitcase. You can push it onto the other seat."

Heck looked at the pile of clothing. A lacy slip lay on top, and Heck wiped his moist palms on his pants before gingerly lifting the garments and scooting them to the passenger side. As he got in, he noticed the faint scent of lavender.

He turned on the key, shifted to neutral, and stepped on the starter, letting the engine warm up for a minute. Then he backed off the road and down the draw. He found first gear and gunned the motor, and the little car flew at the bank and charged up but traversing rather than trying to go straight. The wheels spun, grabbed, spun again, and finally it was out. Heck stopped and dug around in the clothing for the hand brake, finding it under a crimson scarf. Setting the brake, he stepped out of the car as the lady came scrambling up the embankment.

"Yep," Heck said.

Mrs. Reynolds stopped a few paces away. "What did you say?"

"Yep," he repeated.

"I don't understand what you mean."

"You asked me if I could drive a car. I think what you meant was, could I drive it out of this gully. I didn't know if I could or not."

She stood with arms folded, one foot tapping in impatience. "I meant exactly what I said. I know you can do all sorts of nineteenth-century things like ride a horse and rope a cow, but this is the twentieth century. I didn't know if you were part of this age or not."

"Yes ma'am." Heck worked hard to keep the smile off his face.

The lady's chin came up, and she turned and marched to the car. Before she could wrench the door open, Heck did it for her, closing it gently after she was in.

Slamming the car in gear, she drove away so quickly that he was obliged to shout his question: "Do you know the way back to the ranch?"

The car braked suddenly and came roaring back. She leaned out the window. "What did you say?"

"Do you know your way back to the ranch?"

"I just stay on this road until I hit the main road to the ranch."

Heck shook his head. 'You have to turn off to the right up a couple, three miles."

"Are you sure? I only made one turn last night, off the main road."

"Was it dark?"

She nodded.

"You must not have noticed the crossroads. Keep a sharp lookout. The road you turn on's not much better'n this one. The main road to the ranch is another five or six miles. Turn left when you get there, and it's maybe a mile further."

She tossed reluctant thanks over her shoulder and took off again.

Heck stood looking after her. He lifted his hat, smoothed back his hair, replaced his hat, and set off down the arroyo. The sound of the car had died away by the time he reached the saltcedar tree. As he checked his cinch, Heck said, "Now, that was a lady! And here I am with my elbow hanging out."

He untied the mare, mounted, and turning her head down the draw, spurred her. After a while, he slowed his pace and reminded the sorrel, "She said *Missus* Reynolds. She's a married lady."

Heck continued on, now at a lope, now at a saddle gait, until he came to a place where the road dipped again into the arroyo. He found a spot where a few tufts of grass were growing and tethered the mare, saying, "She won't be pleased to see me, you know."

Walking back to the shade of a cottonwood, he hunkered down and made himself a smoke, glancing now and again at the way she would come. A locust buzzed above him. A fly droned by. Silence. Then the locust buzzed again, and when it stopped, Heck was certain he heard the sound of an approaching car.

Chapter 7

DRIVING ON THE dusty wagon track, Ruth scolded herself. "He was just helping you out. You may have no place to go except back to Harlan, but that's no reason to take it out on all men."

All the previous night, as she had sat in the car and shivered through the chilly hours, she had examined her options realistically. She realized it was ridiculous to think that the nuns would take in someone like her. She wasn't Catholic. She didn't even believe in God. That might not count against her if she were pregnant and unwed, but showing up in a dress by Mainbocher? Fleeing from a man whose family had practically built the Catholic cathedral in Goshen, New York? Fat chance.

She'd considered selling her car but knew that she'd never get what it was worth out here in this wilderness, and she was loath to part with the freedom it gave her. Just before sunrise, she'd faced the bleak fact that, since she had no money and no marketable skills, she was dependent on Harlan Reynolds for everything. As degrading as it was to let him touch her, she'd made a bargain with him. Maybe she'd better try again to keep her side of it.

Now, driving back toward the ranch, she felt the sickening, familiar weight on her chest. Determined not to think about it until she had to, she thought instead of the cowboy who had rescued her not fifteen minutes before. She ruefully remembered him correcting her pronunciation and felt bad that she had been rude. *I'm as bad as Harlan*, she thought, wishing she had a chance to apologize. *What would I say? I had a sleepless night? I'm always grumpy before I have my coffee? I was leaving my husband?*

She braked as she came to the top of another arroyo. It looked steeper than she remembered, but she had made it both down and up last night. Why should it be any different this time?

She put the car in gear and drove slowly over the bank, following the tracks she'd made on her last passage. When she hit the bottom, she gunned the engine and hung onto the steering wheel, and as she bounced over rocks and ruts, the clothes inside tumbled around. With the accelerator pressed to the floor, she started up the other side, but the car didn't have the power or momentum to make it over the rise. Her heart sank, and she backed a crooked path down and across to the far bank. She revved the motor, revved it again, ground into first, and released the clutch. As she shifted to second, she hit a bump, and the crimson scarf flew up and covered her hand. She waved it out of the way, sending it out the window.

She tried to traverse the slope as the cowboy had done, but the ground was soft, and she didn't make it as far as she had when she had stayed on the road. The rear wheels started spinning, and she quickly backed down to the bottom, turned off the engine, and got out.

A breeze blew her hair out in front of her face, and she impatiently brushed it back. She walked to the back of the car and climbed the rumble seat steps to get some height. Shading her eyes, she looked up and down the draw. Nothing. Shoulders drooping, she climbed down again.

A movement from the shadows caught her eye just as she gained the ground, and she saw the cowboy step from the shade of a cottonwood tree, as if had been waiting for her. At first, she couldn't say a word but simply stood, lips slightly parted, one hand still holding onto the car.

As she watched him approach, the weight that had been pressing on her chest turned into a drifting, fluttering feather. She felt, rather than saw, the strong jaw line, the tall, lean frame, the suntanned hand raised in greeting. He was close enough now that she could feel the heat of his presence, smell the scent of leather, dust and sweat.

When she spoke, her voice was barely above a whisper. "I was leaving my husband."

He stepped back a pace. "Ma'am?"

Her eyes broke away from his, and she turned her head away. "I'm sorry. I don't know how I came to say that. Only, you were so helpful and polite, and I was so rude, and I've been thinking all the way that I needed to explain."

The cowboy dragged the hat from his head and held it in front of him, his eyes moving from her to the car to his feet. He swallowed. Finally, he asked, "Ma'am, are you thirsty?"

She looked up quickly. "Do you have some water? You certainly are heaven-sent! Yes, I'm dying of thirst."

Replacing his Stetson, he walked to the back of the car, unstrapped the suitcase from the luggage rack, and carried it to the shade. Kicking a mound of dirt away to level a space at the base of the cottonwood, he set the suitcase down. "If you'll sit here, I'll go get it. The sorrel's in some grass just down the way."

Ruth sat as directed. She leaned against the trunk of the tree and watched the set of his shoulders as he strode to where the mare was tied.

The cowboy returned with a canteen. "I'm sorry I don't have a cup. The only one that's drunk out of this is—"

She smiled as she reached for the canteen. "I know. You and the sorrel. I don't care."

She tilted her head back and took a long drink. Screwing the lid back on, she noticed that the cowboy was staring. When she met his eyes, he turned away, took off his hat and brushed back his hair. A moment later he turned back, making only the briefest of eye contact.

He put his hat back on, hunkered down, and looked up the arroyo. "Ma'am, I've been puzzlin' at how you could have ended up out here if you were going to Las Cruces."

He wouldn't look at her, but she couldn't keep her eyes off him as he rested with his forearm on one knee, his shirt pulling tightly to reveal the muscles in his back. "You mean this isn't the road?" she asked.

The cowboy looked up. "To Las Cruces? No, ma'am. The same highway that brought you from Hot Springs goes on to Cruces. This road goes up to North Range. It's probably only used a couple times a year when we work cattle up there."

Ruth frowned. "Well, I'm sure I followed the directions I was given."

"Who gave you the directions?"

"Someone at the ranch. Dudley? Something like that."

"Dooley?"

"Yes, Dooley. That's it."

He shook his head. "Ma'am, don't ever put stock in what Dooley says."

"Well, I certainly won't after this. How could he have done that to me?"

He pushed his hat to the back of his head. "You have to understand that he didn't mean any harm. Dooley was in the war, and he came back ... well, different. He's not simple. He just doesn't know everything he used to. Things aren't in the same place in his mind that they used to be."

Ruth said dryly, "Little things like Las Cruces?"

The cowboy smiled. "Not to Dooley."

"Well, thank heavens you came along! I could have died out there!"

"Oh, I don't think so, ma'am. We could have tracked you easy enough."

She shrugged. "If anyone cared that I was gone. By the way, what are you doing here?"

"Well, I figured you'd have trouble at this place. This is the same draw. I just followed it down and waited for you."

"I didn't have any trouble through here last night, but coming down is always easier than going back up. It's pretty steep." She stood. "Can you drive me out of here?" She smiled. "Or, do you want to try before you answer that?"

He stood. "No, ma'am. You were doing just fine. I think if you try again, and I get up on the bank, I can step in and ease you over."

"Let's do it, then! Thank you so much." She held out her hand. "I don't even know your name."

"Heck Benham, ma'am."

When he took her hand, she forgot about Harlan, forgot about life as she knew it before that moment. She felt the roughness of his palm and the strength in his clasp as she looked up into the blue eyes of this man who had watched over her. She saw the way they crinkled at the corner when he smiled, and she wanted him to smile at her that way forever.

It was Heck who broke the connection. He dropped her hand, picked up her suitcase, and echoed, "Let's do it!"

Feeling a little like she was leaving a safe haven, she got in the car, started the engine, and watched in the mirror as he put her suitcase on the rack. With her head out the window, she backed to the far side of the arroyo while he headed toward the bank she had to scale. When he was almost there, she saw him bend down to pick up something. There was a flash of red just before he put it in the pocket of his Levis. Then he climbed to the top of the bank.

He waved her on, and she came bouncing across the dry riverbed and careened up the slope. Like the first try, she petered out at the crest, but Heck stepped behind the car, set his back against it, and pushed. Ruth kept the throttle open, and, all of a sudden, she was over and on her way.

She stopped, found reverse, and backed up to him. "Thank you again. Are there any more creek beds?"

"No. It's pretty flat the rest of the way to the ranch." He raised his hand in farewell. "Good luck."

Thinking of what she had to face when she got to the Diamond E, she felt suddenly very alone. She blinked to keep the tears at bay as she waved goodbye. Then she put the car in gear and left the cowboy standing in the dust of the road.

All the way back, Ruth tried to rehearse what she'd say to Harlan when she saw him, but each time she began to frame a speech, the image of the tall, fair-haired cowboy intruded. By the time she finally drove down the hill into the ranch complex, she had given up trying to prepare. She would have to take things as they came.

No one was around when she parked in front of the bungalow. She looked at her watch. Was it only nine o'clock in the morning? She sat in the car for a moment, watching for signs of movement inside the house. When no one emerged, she grabbed an armload of clothes from the passenger seat, opened the door, and climbed out, looking around to see if she was being observed. The curtain on one of the neighbors' windows moved, but the sash was up, and it might have been stirred by a breeze. Ruth quickly ascended the porch stairs and entered the house.

She closed the door and turned around, surprised to find Harlan sitting on the couch, still in his traveling clothes. His suit jacket and vest lay on the floor, and his tie was undone. Black stubble shadowed his jaw, and the eyes he raised to her were red-rimmed and empty. A purple welt swelled above his left eyebrow.

She set the clothes on a table at the end of the couch. "Hello, Harlan."

His face crumpled and he slid from the sofa, walking to her on his knees. He flung his arms around her and buried his face in the folds of her skirt. "You're back," he said, and he began to sob.

"Don't, Harlan. Please don't." She put her hand on his shoulder and tried to push him away.

He only held on tighter and spoke into the area between her arm and her waist. "I'm so sorry. So sorry. I'll be good, only don't leave."

"Shhh. Don't cry. I'm not going to leave." She looked down at the abject humility of his position and tentatively patted him on the back.

He stopped sobbing, but still he clung to her. "I'll be patient. I'll wait. You can have the bed, and I'll sleep out here. Promise me you won't leave me."

Ruth put her fingertips to her breastbone. She tried to take a deep breath because the feather lightness she had felt with the cowboy had turned back to lead. "I won't leave, Harlan. I have nowhere to go."

Chapter 8

TWO LITTLE WHITE puffs hung over the Sandia Mountains, and a yellow sun warmed the air on its climb toward noon. Heck Benham stopped on the ridge above the Diamond E ranch complex to let a dust devil go by and then sat astride the sorrel in the eddying air to survey the scene below.

There were three proper houses. One was large and white, an adobe house with a flat roof and *vigas* sticking out at intervals along the front. It had a screened-in porch that covered the entire width of the house. Some distance away, two wooden bungalows with pitched tin roofs and railed front porches sat like ugly stepsisters

Alan Payne, the ranch manager, occupied the large house. A successful rancher on his own land in Arizona, he had been lured to New Mexico by the Hancott Land and Cattle Company. Mr. Payne was not only well-liked, he was respected. He knew cattle; he knew the country, and he knew how to handle cowhands. His wife, Ruby, being childless, mothered all the young cowboys.

The ranch foreman, Bob Goodman, lived in the first bungalow. The hands took assignments from him willingly because they knew he knew the loneliness of the lonely work and the danger of the dangerous work. They knew he wouldn't ask them to do anything he hadn't done himself.

Bob Goodman was married to a very silly woman. Sally had been pretty at some time in the past, but self-indulgence and an unfortunate draw from the gene pool had changed her from a pert little blonde to a small mountain of flesh. The cowhands said that her tongue ran on wheels.

The second bungalow was the one that Heck and Mike had cleaned for the fellow in the three-piece suit.

Across from the bungalows, about a hundred feet away, stood a cluster of corrals. Some were small, some large, some had chutes for loading, and some had gates that would open to create larger spaces. A windmill stood at the end of the largest corral, and a huge water tank sat high on a trestle beside it. Behind the water tank was the tack room, and next to it was the cookhouse. At right angles to the cookhouse was the bunkhouse; and at right angles to the bunkhouse, across from the manager's house, was the machine shed.

As Heck rode in, he noticed what had been hidden from view before—a green coupe parked next to the first of the smaller houses. The luggage was no longer strapped to the back, and he saw no sign of anyone around the house.

Ruby Payne, out hoeing in her garden patch, waved to Heck as he rode to the corral. He could hear the throbbing of the gas-powered generating plant and knew that she was too close to it to be able to hear anything he might call, so he simply tipped his hat before dismounting. He let the sorrel drink at the trough and then stripped off the saddle, blanket, and bridle and turned her into one of the smaller corrals. He gave her a measure of oats and then took his saddlebags and headed to the cookhouse.

Fritz Gansel sat in the shade of the cookhouse porch, his chair tipped back against the wall and his boot heels caught in the bottom chair rung. Arms crossed and hat tipped over his face, he peeped under the brim. "Howdy, Heck."

"Mornin' Fritz." Heck entered the cookhouse, the screen door squeaking and banging shut after him. He put his saddlebags in the corner and went to the stove and poured an enamelware cup full of coffee.

Dooley smiled to see who had come through the door. Because he was Mrs. Payne's nephew, he was kept on as wrangler, general helper, and relief cook. "Mornin', Heck. You gonna have dinner here?"

"You bet. What'cha fixing, Dooley?"

"Cornbread and beans. Ready in a minute."

"That sounds fine." Heck took his cup of coffee outside and hooked a chair with his foot, setting it beside Fritz's. He sat down and leaned the chair back against the wall, one heel in the chair rung, the other long leg out before him. "I see Shorty's not back yet." Heck took a sip of his coffee then blew on it to cool it. "I believe we had cornbread and beans last time I was in to dinner."

Fritz spoke from under his Stetson brim. "Dooley says it's his specialty."

Heck chuckled. "Yeah, ol' Dooley. Poor old fella."

Fritz pushed his hat back, revealing reddish hair and merry brown eyes. "How's your fiddle playin' comin', Heck? You as good as ol' Dooley yet?"

Heck grimaced. "I've got a ways to go to be that good."

Fritz grinned. "You gonna play at the next dance?"

Heck shook his head. He picked up his cup and took a tentative sip of the coffee.

Fritz jumped as the dinner triangle clanged right behind him. "Hell, Dooley, there's just two of us. We're not deaf."

"Or, we weren't a minute ago," said Heck, putting his chair back against the wall. He followed the other cowboy in, hanging his hat on a peg by the door and washing at a basin set on two powder boxes stacked atop one another. Dooley dished up beans and cornbread into blue enamelware and then disappeared with a bucket of scraps for the chickens.

The two cowboys ate in silence until Fritz got up to get a second helping. "How you comin' with that fence, Heck?" he asked. "You like it better'n house cleanin'?"

"It's all right. If I get back in time to help Mike, we should get the last of the posts set today. We'll take a little break and check on the cattle out east of us, and then we'll stretch the wire next week."

Heck stood, pushed his chair in, and carried his dishes over to the dishpan. "Know anyone going to Cruces in the next while?" he asked. "I brought in my boots to send to Delgado to get them fixed."

Fritz grinned. "Sure. That new fella from back east—Mr. Reynolds. He's going in today. I imagine he'd be right glad to do that errand for you. Why'nt you call by his house and ask him?"

"All right, I will." Heck watched Fritz stroll to the door. He cleared his throat and said, "Ah, Fritz. I need to tell you something."

The cowboy took his hat off the peg. "What's on your mind?"

"I didn't want you to find out from someone else. Lucy's married."

Fritz looked down at his hat, tracing the soft pattern of dents and depressions with his thumb. His brow furrowed and his lips drew into a straight line. Then he shrugged and looked up. "Hell, Heck, what did I have to offer her? What does any cowhand have to offer a woman?" He put his hat on and pulled it low over his eyes. "It's all right, *compadre. Hasta luego.*" He turned and went out, the sound of his jingling spurs fading as he headed to the corral.

Heck got his saddlebags, pulled his boots out, and tried to ignore the fact that breathing had become a chore as he contemplated taking them to the Reynolds's bungalow. Buckling the flap on his saddlebags, he noticed that the palms of his hands were moist. He wiped them on his pants and told himself he wasn't interested in Mrs. Reynolds. He hadn't even known she was alive when he set out this morning. Flinging the saddlebags back in the corner, he picked up the boots and strode out the door.

The screen door banged behind him as he headed behind the machinery shed and across the way to the second bungalow. "And you'd better get used to meeting her without your little heart going pitty-pat," he told himself sternly. "Either that or find a job with some other outfit."

As he climbed the porch steps, Heck reached up to remove his hat and realized that he had left it in the cookhouse. He laughed at himself for acting like a schoolboy, but even so, before he knocked, he stood on one foot and then another, polishing the toes of his boots on the backs of his pant legs. Then he tapped on the door and waited.

Someone walked across the floor inside the house, but no one came to answer his knock. Just as Heck was about to try again, Alan Payne drove up in his Ford pickup. Immediately, the bungalow door opened, and Heck found himself confronting not the lady, but her husband.

He was not at all what Heck had expected. A short man, compactly built, he wore a blue, pinstripe suit. He had black hair parted on the side and slicked over. His eyebrows, dark and straight, grew almost together over the bridge of a hook nose, and he had an ugly bruise on his forehead.

Mr. Reynolds had to look up to meet the cowboy's eyes, and Heck felt the surge of antipathy between them.

"How do. I'm Heck Benham," he said. "One of the boys said you were going to Cruces today, and I wondered if you would be so kind as to take these boots to Delgado's. I've put a note in explaining what I need him to do."

Harlan Reynolds's glance flickered to Alan Payne, who was coming up the walk, and came back to Heck. A sneer played at the corners of his mouth. "Let me get this straight. You want me to do an errand for you? You are one of the, ah, hired help, aren't you?"

Heck's mouth curved into a slow smile. "Yes, sir. I understood that Hancott paid your wages, too, but maybe I was mistaken?"

Alan Payne stepped up on the porch. The only indication that he had heard the exchange was a crinkling around his eyes as he spoke. "Afternoon, Harlan. Heck."

Heck said, "Afternoon, Mr. Payne." Harlan Reynolds merely nodded.

Mr. Payne's eyes fell on the boots. "Are you wanting to send those back to Delgado, Heck? I'd be glad to take them for you."

"Thank you, sir. There's a note inside. He can mail them back to me. I've told him I'd like to have them for when we start the spring work."

Alan Payne took the boots from him and looked at Harlan. "Are you ready?"

Heck, stifling the urge to glance inside, stepped to the edge of the porch. "Thanks, Mr. Payne." Nodding at Harlan Reynolds, he descended the stairs, his smooth, long-legged stride carrying him quickly down the path and across to the tool shed. There, he stood at the door and watched the Ford pickup climb the ridge above the ranch.

Heck allowed one more glance at the bungalow before stepping into the dimness of the machinery shed. He stood a moment to let his eyes grow accustomed.

Inside were scrapers and fresnos and an ancient cement mixer. On one wall hung hames and harnesses for the teams that pulled the machines. There was an old bullwhip, too, that the cowboys played with sometimes but which was never used in earnest. Another wall sported shovels and picks, pulleys, and all sorts of hand tools neatly assembled by category. Heck went to the wall, got the block and tackle, and stepped back into the brightness, his eyes narrowing against the glare.

He walked around the tool shed and stopped by the empty cookhouse for his hat and saddlebags. No one was around the corral as he saddled the sorrel mare and stowed the saddlebags and tool behind the cantle.

As he set out to retrace his path of that morning, Heck paused at the top of the ridge and watched the tiny plume of dust that marked the progress of the Diamond E pickup. He turned the mare toward Tucker's Well and thought about those cold eyes under the straight, black brows, and he heard again Harlan's voice saying, "... one of the, ah, hired help?" He thought about the manicured hands and smooth hair and the pinstripe suit and wing-tip shoes. This was a man who wouldn't survive two days on the Jornada yet who let a lady wander unprotected at night. A beautiful, brown-eyed lady who said with a breathless voice, "I was leaving—"

Suddenly, with a sinking feeling around his heart, Heck realized he was forgetting that this small, sleek, city-bred man was married to the lady. "What you're contemplating isn't honorable," Heck muttered to himself. "What's more, you're beginning to act like Papa."

With that sobering thought, he spurred his pony to a lope, determined to put the lady out of his mind.

Chapter 9

IT WAS THE end of the week, and the chill of the night was dissipating rapidly as the sun climbed above the hills. Standing on the boss's back porch, Heck could see Ruby Payne drying breakfast dishes through the window. He knocked, and she slung the dishtowel over her shoulder and wiped her hands on it as she came to the door.

In her early sixties, she had a tracery of wrinkles on her cheeks. Her ginger hair was liberally sprinkled with gray, and though she tried to keep it anchored in a bun on top of her head, springy tendrils constantly escaped. She tucked one up as she opened the door and smiled.

Heck tipped his hat. "Mornin', Miz Payne. I know this is your day to go into town. I was wondering if I could hitch a ride as far as Palomas."

"Good morning, Heck. Yes. Certainly you can. What time did you get up to get in here?"

Heck took off his hat as he stepped into the kitchen. "I watched the moon set and the sun rise."

"Well, you got here just in time." Ruby took off her apron and hung it and the dishtowel on a hook in the kitchen. "Grab the mail bag. I'll get my hat."

Heck did as he was told and waited by the kitchen door for her to reappear. She did presently, with her purse slung on one arm, a navy hat with perky flowers sitting atop the bun, and a pair of white gloves clasped in one hand. She paused for him to open the door and preceded him out to the Diamond E pickup.

It was Ruby Payne's practice to make the hour's drive to Hot Springs every Friday for supplies and the mail. Hot Springs sat five miles north of the turnoff to the village of Palomas and was the nearest town with paved streets and more than a basic general store. Any cowboy who wished, and who had leave from Bob Goodman, was welcome to ride with Ruby on her weekly trips to town. The hands said you really had to want to go to town to ride with Mrs. Payne. She had a way of holding the accelerator down and regulating the pickup's speed with the clutch. It was hard on clutches, and Alan Payne, rather than teaching his wife a different technique, simply kept a spare. It usually fell to Heck to replace it.

He threw the canvas bag in the back and climbed in beside Mrs. Payne. As she started the pickup and revved the engine, Heck rolled down the window and opened the wing, figuring that the strut gave him something good to hold onto as he sat with his elbow out the window.

They rode in silence for a while, heading into the morning sun. Heck pulled his Stetson down low over his eyes, and Mrs. Payne put down her visor and frowned. "Ruth Reynolds told me how you rescued her the other morning."

Heck glanced at her, but she kept her eyes on the road. He was grateful she couldn't see his discomfort. He could feel his heart pounding, and breathing was becoming a problem, but he had found out her name. He turned away and whispered the word, savoring the way it felt in his mouth.

"It was a brainless thing for her to do," Ruby went on. "I thought she had more sense than that, to go haring off in the middle of the night. Sally Goodman saw her go and then come back the next day, and she's been asking me questions. I haven't given her any satisfaction. I know I don't have to ask you not to say anything about it, Heck."

"No, ma'am."

At that moment, the car dropped into a dip. Heck involuntarily grabbed the window strut and slammed his right foot to the floor.

Ruby laughed and leaned over to pat Heck's arm. "I didn't think you were ready for that one."

"No, ma'am."

"She's quite taken with you, you know," Ruby confided.

"Who? Sally?" Heck asked, knowing the answer.

"No, silly. Ruth. She says you're handsome and wonderful."

He laughed. "And, you told her I was just a long, lean, drink-a-water that's a pretty good bronc buster and passable cowhand?" He tried to keep his tone light and not betray the aching need to hear more.

"Something like that." Ruby's brow furrowed. "I worry about her."

"Why is that, ma'am?"

"Because of who she is, and where she is, and who she's married to."

"Who is she, then?"

"She's a young woman—though not so young—she's almost thirty—who was raised with money but who has none of her own. Her mother was married and divorced a couple of times, always to someone very well off." Ruby paused to tuck a tendril back under the bun. "And then, Ruth's mama died suddenly, and she was left without means of support. Harlan Reynolds had been hanging around her for years, hoping to be noticed. He'll come into money someday. Until then, he's related to the Hancotts and has a built-in position with their company, so she grabbed onto the meal ticket. That's an ugly way to say it, but they're her words, not mine."

"I see. So, that's who she is. And, this is where she is."

Ruby Payne looked at Heck, holding his eyes for a moment. "And, Harlan Reynolds is who she's married to."

Heck met her look squarely. "I know that, ma'am."

"She's lived a different kind of life, Heck. She's from back east, and her mama ..." Ruby's voice trailed off. She shook her head. "I don't know. I just worry."

Heck didn't answer. He sat looking out the window, not seeing the greasewood and ocotillo moving by but seeing instead brown eyes and a cloud of chestnut hair.

A dun-colored crossroad roused him from his reverie. Pointing to it, Heck said, "If you'll let me out there, I can hoof it on into Palomas. Just tell me when you want me here, and I'll meet you."

Putting in the clutch, Mrs. Payne slowed down, finally taking her foot off the accelerator to brake to a stop.

Heck climbed out and closed the door. Looking through the open window, he tipped his hat.

"Never mind meeting me here," she said. "Where are you going to be? I'll pick you up there. I don't know just when I'll be back through."

"I'll be at Bemis's store. Lucy's married and living behind it."

"Lucy married! Well, I'll be. Give her my love, and you can tell me all about it on the way home."

Heck touched his hat again and stood back as the Ford pickup leaped forward, and Ruby Payne, hair springing out around her like a halo, headed on into Hot Springs.

Chapter 10

HECK BENHAM'S MAMA believed in two universal remedies. The first was Epsom salt. Excellent for soaking infected cuts or sprained ankles, it drew out soreness and made stove-up limbs supple again. In addition, a teaspoon of the crystals dissolved in a cup of hot water and taken internally had purgative properties and was supposed to cure everything from fever to a cold, from listlessness to a bellyache.

Mama's other universal remedy was work. She believed it was a balm for a troubled soul, for a bad attitude, for a quarrelsome nature, or for a broken heart. After returning to Tucker's Well from his ride to town with Ruby Payne, Heck seized on his mother's remedy to ease the trouble in his soul caused by his hankering for a married woman.

Heck threw himself into the work of stringing barbed wire onto the posts that he and Mike had already placed. When they had the first strand on and tightened with the block and tackle, Mike went along hammering staples to hold it to the fence posts while Heck grabbed a crowbar and a roll of wire and headed back to the start again.

There was no comfortable way to carry the wire spools. Heck's arms began to ache from the effort, but he welcomed the screaming muscles because they allowed no room for mental images of a mane of chestnut hair, brown eyes, and an aura of sophistication that was as tantalizing as it was daunting.

Mike was still down the way, pounding in staples, so Heck didn't wait until the block and tackle was free. He blocked up the axle of the wagon and, fastening the wire to one of the spokes, he used the inside of the hub as a rude capstan to stretch the wire. By the time it was tight, Mike had trudged up. Without a word, Heck grabbed the crowbar and spool of wire and headed out again, leaving his partner, hammer hanging down at his side, looking at him in wonder.

Over and over, Heck walked the fence line, unrolling miles of barbed wire and pulling it taut for Mike to staple to the posts, stopping long after sunset and driving the wagon home in the dark. The second day, muscles seldom used in working cattle were protesting, but by dint of ceaseless work, Heck was able to keep from thinking of the lady for long stretches of time, able to push out of his mind dark eyes and the whispered confession, *I was leaving my husband.*

On the last morning of building fence, as they were just beginning, Mike picked up his hammer and said, "Can I ask you somethin'?"

Heck bent down and stuck the crowbar through the wire spool. "What's that, Michael?"

"You been eatin' loco weed?"

Heck straightened and shot his partner a quizzical look. "What do you mean by that?"

"You were the one that didn't want to build fence. Now here you are, trying to rupture yourself from toting spools of wire all alone. Not to mention killing me. I got staple-itis I'm sure."

Heck threw back his head and laughed. It felt so good just to stand there, hands on his hips, and let the sound roll out and across the flatland. It made the wagon team jerk up their heads. It made the red whiteface cows standing a ways off stop licking themselves and turn to watch. It made Mike's dimple appear, too, and he laughed along with Heck.

"Well, I hope you've learned not to volunteer us for any more fence building projects," Heck said.

Mike raised his right hand. "My volunteering days are over."

After that, they worked together as a team, stretching the wire and pounding in staples. They finished by midafternoon, and after they loaded up the wagon, Heck heaved a great sigh. *It's all right*, he thought as he climbed in the wagon box and picked up the reins. *I'm over it.*

Chapter 11

IT WAS LATE afternoon by the time Heck and Mike arrived at the cow camp at Tucker's Well. After unharnessing the team and turning the horses into the corral, they heated up the beans they had reboiled that morning and made a pan of cornbread. Heck sliced an onion to go on top of the beans, and Mike made a pot of strong black coffee.

As evening came on, they were driven outside by the monotonous scraping of a cricket somewhere in the shack, so they sat in the front yard watching thunderheads massing on the twilight horizon. Lightning would flash and, after a pause, the muted rumbling of thunder rolled to them.

Mike sat with his chair tipped back against the wall, playing "The Tennessee Waltz" on his harmonica. He stopped and slapped the instrument against the heel of his hand and pointed at the storm. "It's headin' this way. I don't know that I like the idea of sittin' this close to a windmill in a thunderstorm. My Uncle Del was killed by lightnin'."

Heck put his fiddle under his chin as he eyed the storm. "We'll be all right. We've got a while before the squall hits, and we have to go join that cricket inside. Let's try that again. I think we just about had it."

Mike began to play the melody, cupping his hands around his harmonica. Heck, tentatively at first and then, growing more sure of himself, played counterpoint. When they came to the refrain, Heck took the melody, and Mike played rhythmic chords under him.

The sky darkened as the storm came on. The two cowboys sat in the dooryard and played "Cotton-Eyed Joe," and then, by unspoken agreement, they were still, holding their instruments in their laps as they watched the towering black clouds and the snaking flashes of light that rent the sky into pieces as the night closed in.

Without preamble, a wind began to blow, picking up dust and swirling it around them. Both sprang to their feet and grabbed their chairs, but suddenly Heck froze. "Listen!"

"What was it?" Mike asked.

Heck shook his head. "I thought I heard a car."

"You don't suppose Bob has sent Dooley out with the pickup to help us haul things back?"

"Not with this storm brewing. Dooley wouldn't make it through Loco Creek if it's running."

It was full dark now, and as Heck fumbled for the door handle, the whole sky was lit momentarily by a jagged slash of lightning followed by a clap of thunder so loud it seemed to permeate the pores.

Mike pressed close. "Come on, Heck. Let's get inside."

Heck finally got the door open and stood aside while Mike crashed through, knocking his chair against the doorframe in passage. Heck remained just outside, eyes toward the road into camp. The wind was gone now, and a fat drop of water fell on his shoulder. He heard the splat of a second at his feet. Then another, and another, and all at once the rain was pelting down.

Then, through the notch in the hill behind the corral, headlights cast twin beams into the rainy night, and a car crept through.

Mike had the kerosene lamp lit, and as the glow showed through the window, the driver of the car seemed to take heart and came more surely around the corral and into the dooryard.

It was a small green coupe.

Heck had the sensation of freefalling down a well as he set his chair inside and laid his fiddle and bow on it. Standing in the doorway, he muttered to himself, "Now, hold your horses, fella. It might be that oily little runt."

The car door opened, and in the meager light that fell into the dooryard, Heck saw Ruth Reynolds get out. Rain fell in sheets, but she stood for a moment, eyes fixed on him. As Heck stepped outside, she came around the car to meet him. He put out his hand to assist her over the ground in the darkness, but she must have mistaken his intent, for suddenly she was nestled against him as a blinding flash and a simultaneous crash of thunder seemed to rock the world.

As the rain pelted down, he pressed his cheek against the hair on the crown of her head. Called back to himself by Mike hovering in the doorway, he gently put her from him and took her elbow to help her to the shack.

Mike stepped back, eyes wary, as Ruth entered the room. Heck helped her off with her wet jacket and placed a chair for her to sit. She began shivering, and he jerked the blanket off his bed and put it around her.

She smiled her thanks.

Heck poured a cup of coffee and moving the other chair over by hers, sat down. Putting the cup in her hands, he asked, "Are you all right, ma'am?"

She smiled wanly. "I am now. I have never been so terrified in my life!"

A lightning flash illuminated the room, but the thunder was delayed. The pyrotechnics were moving farther north.

"Was it the storm that frightened you, ma'am?"

"The storm and the dark and the lonely, lonely road. I thought I would never get here."

"You mean you meant to come here? You weren't ..."

"Looking for Las Cruces again?" She shook her head. "No. I've been there today. Sally Goodman went with me. I heard what Harlan said to you the other day. I was embarrassed for him—sorry that he would treat you that way when you had been so good for me. I mean, good to me."

Ruth paused and took a sip of coffee. Heck said nothing. Mike sat in the shadows on his bunk.

"I went to Delgado's and picked up your boots," she said. "I wanted to bring them to you—a thank you and apology all rolled in one. Sally told me how to get here, but it was farther than I thought. And then the storm came up so suddenly."

"You brought my boots to me?"

"Yes. Oh! I left them in the car."

Mike stood and stepped into the light. "I'll get them." He didn't wait for assent from the lady but made it from the shack to the car in four giant strides. Wrenching open the passenger door, he grabbed the package sitting on the seat, slammed the car door shut and sprinted back. Laying the parcel on the table, he retreated again to the shadows.

"Thank you," she said, leaning forward to peer at him. "I don't even know your name."

"I'm sorry," Heck said. "This is Mike Eldred, ma'am. Mike, this is Mrs. Reynolds. Now, we've got to get you home, ma'am. Pronto."

"Pleased to meet you," she said to Mike and then turned to Heck. "Are you going to let me finish my coffee?"

"No, ma'am. We need to get across Loco Creek before it starts running." Heck picked up his saddle and blanket and went to the wall where his spurs hung. There, draped on the rowel of one spur, was a crimson scarf.

Heck quickly looked at Ruth to see if she had seen.

Apparently she had. She watched him with luminous eyes and a half smile on her lips as he snatched the scarf and put it in his pocket.

"I won't try to come back tonight, Michael," Heck said. "Depending on how long the draw's running, I should be able to be back in time for breakfast. Your biscuits are better than Dooley's."

He got no appreciative reaction from Mike. Instead, his partner frowned and asked, "Are you sure you can make it in time? Remember last time when we tried to get in, and Loco Creek ..." His voice trailed off, and he cleared his throat.

Heck stood at the door and addressed Ruth. "If you're ready, ma'am, we really need to get whistling."

Ruth picked up her jacket and turned to Mike. "Nice to have met you." Then she passed through the door of the shack, glancing up at Heck with a conspiratorial smile. With shoulders hunched against the rain, she dashed to the car and got in the passenger seat.

Heck strode to the car and stowed his saddle in the rumble seat. He threw the blanket, bridle, and spurs behind the driver's seat and got in.

"I should have brought that blanket for you." he said and reached for the door handle.

"No. I'm fine."

"You're shivering."

"Believe me, it's not because I'm cold. Besides, I have a heater. Let's get going."

Heck turned the key and pressed his foot on the starter. Then he fumbled around on the dashboard looking for the lights.

"It's that raised dial on the steering wheel. Turn it clockwise."

He did, and twin beams bored holes into the blackness ahead of them. He found first gear and wasted no time in turning around. Ruth reached over and flipped a switch above the windshield, and the wipers began sweeping the water away in twin, hanging arcs.

As they bumped along the primitive road, Heck looked over at Ruth. He could see her profile with its straight nose, fine brow and full lower lip. She must have sensed his look because she turned to face him. Her features were dim in the scant light, but he was very aware of her eyes meeting his.

Heck shook his head. "Whatever possessed you to try to come out here? I was coming in tomorrow."

"That wouldn't have been the same. It wouldn't have been full restitution."

"Well, I appreciate it, but I don't know what Sally was thinking of, to send you out here. With a storm coming on, too. I swear, that woman doesn't have good sense!"

"To be honest, she wasn't too much in favor of it, but I said I'd driven in the rain a hundred times after dark. She said the road led straight here; I didn't have to worry about turning off anywhere."

They drove for a moment in silence. The rain was still coming down hard, and every now and then Heck had to let up on the accelerator to let the wipers speed up.

"I've never seen rain like this!" she exclaimed. "Back east it rains a lot, and it often rains hard. But this is different. This is primitive. It's—"

"Nineteenth century?"

Ruth laughed. "Now you're teasing me. I apologize for saying you weren't part of the twentieth century. You didn't look it that morning." As the car skidded around a curve, she grabbed the armrest. "Do you always drive this fast?"

"No, ma'am, but we're in a bit of a race here to get you across Loco Creek while we can."

They rode again in silence, bouncing and sliding as they tore along through the night. She turned to face him, tucking one leg under her, with her left arm on the back of the seat. "Does it bother you for me to talk?"

Heck glanced at her and smiled. "No. I'd like that."

"Well, then, I met your father yesterday."

"Papa? How did that come about?"

"He was by to see Mr. Payne. He and another man. Mr. Plummer?"

"Plumley?"

"Yes. That's it. They came by, and Alan had them stay to dinner and asked Harlan and me over to meet them. I think Alan wants Harlan to find out that there are civilized people here in New Mexico."

"And did you find Papa civilized?"

"I found him charming." She laughed. "He is so very gallant. And well spoken. And well read. And ..." Ruth grabbed the dash and the seat at the same time as the car hit a patch of clay and fishtailed.

Heck steadied the car. "And what?"

"For want of a better word, gentle. I don't mean, like, kind. I mean that one would take him for a gentleman. He has the air." She paused. "I don't believe I'm having this conversation about 'gentlemen' while I'm rocketing through the wildest country I've ever been in, soaking wet."

"Don't forget that it's pitch black."

"On a pitch black night," she added.

Heck chuckled, but he kept his eyes on the road. "Why was the old gent out at the Diamond E?"

"I don't know exactly. It was something about securing a right-of-way for ore wagons. Does that sound right?"

"Yes. Papa and Mr. Plumley have a claim up Coyote Canyon. I guess they want to cut through Diamond E fences and freight ore across Diamond E land."

"So, your father is a miner?"

"No, ma'am. He's a cowpuncher. Works for the Rafter U outfit out south of Palomas. He aspires to be the owner of a producing mine."

Ruth ran her fingers through her hair, shaking her head to fluff the curls. As she extended her arm on the back of the seat again, her fingertips touched the nape of his neck. "What would this mine produce?" she asked. "Silver? Or Gold?"

"Beg pardon? Oh. No, ma'am. Talc."

"Talc? What in the world is that?"

"It's a mineral. A rock. It's greenish in color and so soft you can carve it with a knife. If you shave off some, it makes a powder that feels slick when you rub it between your fingers. Another word for it is soapstone. It's what talcum powder is made of."

Ruth took her hand away to wipe the condensation off her window, but the nape of Heck's neck still tingled. He reached up to turn off the windshield wipers. "Rain's stopped," he said.

They traveled a ways before Heck picked up the thread of his conversation. "Soapstone's not always green, though. I've seen it almost white."

Ruth's voice cut in sharply. "What did you say?"

Heck glanced at her in perplexity. "Beg pardon?"

"You just said ..."

"Sometimes soapstone is white."

"No. That's not how you said it."

"I don't know how I said it. It's not always green. I've seen it almost white."

"Thank the Lord!"

Heck put his foot on the brake and slowed the car. "Ma'am, are you feeling all right?"

Ruth's laugh had a throaty, velvet, quality. She touched his arm. "Yes. I'm perfectly fine. Drive on. I thought you said, 'I seen it almost white,' and I couldn't bear to have you speak that way. I think if I hear another person say 'I seen' or 'he don't' I'm going to scream!"

Heck threw back his head and laughed a big, free laugh. He looked across at his passenger, and in the faint glow of the dash lights, her eyes met his.

"Did you think I was unhinged?" she asked.

"I was starting to wonder. I thought for a moment there you had taken to religion. Maybe white soapstone was a sign or something."

A jackrabbit suddenly popped up in the glare of the headlights and began running ahead of them, zigzagging from one side to the other. Finally, when they were just about to hit the rabbit, it continued its mad dash past the arc of the headlights and was gone.

"Tell me about your boots," she said.

"What do you want to know?"

"Why are the toes pointed?"

"They're pointed, so you can hit the stirrup more easily. Sometimes you have to find your stirrup astride a pitchin' horse."

"Why are the heels so high? I've got several pair of dress shoes with heels lower than yours."

"Well, it's important that you don't put your foot too far in the stirrup. If you should get thrown, and your foot is too far in, you could end up with a broken leg. Or if your horse spooks, you could be dragged and hurt real bad. The heel makes it so you can't put your foot in too far."

"But it's not a big, masculine looking heel," she teased. "It's tapered and graceful-looking. Why would any self-respecting male wear such a thing?"

"Well, I tell you, ma'am. About the time you're afoot and get an eight-hundred-pound yearling steer on the end of your rope, and he wants to pull out ..." Heck peered through the windshield, and he seemed to lose the thread of what he was saying.

Ruth followed his gaze. "What do you see?"

Suddenly, Heck stopped the car, turned off the motor and got out. They had reached the banks of Loco Creek—an arroyo about eight feet deep and a hundred feet across, just one of innumerable gullies threading across the southwest, bone dry for most of the year. Here at the road, the bank had been worn to an easy grade for crossing.

Heck knew that one did not cross an arroyo after a rainstorm without due consideration. He walked to the bank and stood very still. Then he returned to the car. After starting the motor, he said, "Now, ma'am, the creek's running, but from what I can see and hear, I think we can make it through all right."

"But it's stopped raining," she protested.

"It's stopped raining here; but believe me, it's raining upstream still. Now listen to me. It may just happen that we're going to have to exit right suddenly. If so, it'll have to be on your side."

Ruth opened her mouth to speak, but he cut her off, saying, "We don't have time to talk this over. Will you do exactly as I say the minute I say it?"

She reacted to the urgency in his voice and answered in a voice suddenly tight with fear.

Hardly was the affirmative out of her mouth before they were hurtling down the bank and across the gravel. Ahead of them, they could see a stream of running water about twenty feet wide. "That wasn't there when I came through!" she exclaimed.

Chapter 12

THE WATER WAS probably only five or six inches deep, but it acted as a giant brake when they hit it. Ruth braced herself with both hands, face pale and eyes wide.

Heck had both hands on the steering wheel and was saying softly, "Come on, baby, keep going. Come on, darlin', don't quit on me. Just a little more, sugar; don't quit on me."

As the car plowed through the water, Heck tried to remember any holes he had seen when the arroyo was dry. The running stream would have eroded them further. If they hit one and the car dipped far enough for the fan to splash water around, they would stall for sure. They had almost made it out of the stream when he felt the right front wheel drop. The engine sputtered and died, but there was enough momentum to carry the coupe out of the water and onto the gravel.

Heck swore softly and pressed down on the starter. The engine turned over and over but wouldn't catch. He flung open his door and strode swiftly around to yank her door open. Putting out his hand, he said, "Come on, ma'am."

Ruth scrambled out and followed him to the front of the car, frowning in the glare of the headlights as she listened to his directions.

"I want you to run to the bank. Run." He looked down and said, "Oh, hell. You've got on high heels. It doesn't matter. Run! Don't turn back, and don't come back for any reason. When you get to the top, stay off the road. Do you understand?"

"Off the road?" she said. "What are you going to do?"

"I'm going to drive your little green car out of here. By the time I get to the bank, I'll be going like a bat out of hell. I don't want to have to worry about running over you. Now, git!"

Heck watched Ruth as she ran over the uneven gravel bed, hampered by the narrow skirt of her suit and her high-heeled shoes. The lights of the car illuminated her path, but more than once she tripped.

Heck made his way back to the car, got in, and turned off the lights to save the battery. Sitting with the window down, he could hear a difference in the sound of the rushing water and knew he hadn't much time. But he also knew it took awhile for the heat of the engine to dry wet spark plug wires, and he made himself wait before he tried the starter.

Heck rubbed his hands on his Levi's and considered getting out, grabbing his saddle, and hot-footing it for the bank, but he didn't know if he'd make it that way, either. He leaned over and opened the passenger door, just in case he had to get out that way. Then he began counting slowly, telling himself he'd wait until sixty. When he got to thirty, the sound he heard made him step on the starter and mutter, "Come on, baby, come on!"

The engine caught, coughed, caught, coughed. Heck held the accelerator down and sweet-talked that little green coupe. It caught and turned over, coughed, turned over, and suddenly, it was running.

"Yeeeehaaaa!" he shouted and shoved the gearshift into first. He tore across the gravel with the passenger door flapping, and the steering wheel was almost wrenched from his grasp every time a wheel dropped into a trough. He was having a problem seeing the opposite bank when he realized he hadn't turned on his lights. He flipped the switch just as he approached the incline. Rocketing up the slope, he hit a seam of slick, wet clay and the car changed ends. The headlights described a 180-degree arc, and the car fetched up against a greasewood bush.

With the lights now shining on the arroyo, Heck saw a wall of water, almost as high as the channel was deep, move down the wash. It didn't seem to be rushing, but he knew that he could not have outrun it. Pure kinetic energy, it carried an uprooted, full-grown tree as it moved relentlessly past, a foot below the front wheels of the car.

Heck backed the rest of the way up the bank and turned around. Getting out, his eyes searched the darkness. "Miz Reynolds?" he called, a knot forming in the middle of his chest.

"Over here," she called back.

He followed the sound of her voice and found her sitting two feet away from where the water lapped at the bank.

She looked up at him. "I've never seen anything like that. How could you stay down there, knowing what was coming?"

He hunkered down, cowboy fashion, and sat, watching the water with her. "Well, ma'am, I set great store by my saddle, and I wasn't willing to part company with it." He stood and offered his hand. "It's not safe to sit that close to the bank, ma'am. Sometimes parts wash away."

She gave him her hands, and as he helped her up, she moved close to him, as if to embrace. He held her back gently and said, "There are some things we've got to talk over before we get you home, ma'am." Then he led her to the car and opened the passenger door for her.

She waited until he was in and had started the engine. As he set out at a more sedate pace, she asked, "What do we need to talk over, Heck?" Her voice had a breathy quality to it.

"Well, ma'am—"

She put a hand on his arm. "Don't call me ma'am. Can't you call me by my name? Do you know what my name is?"

Heck kept his eyes on the road and waited to reply, finally saying quietly, "I know what your name is. But, no, I can't."

"Why not?"

"There are some things that just are, ma'am. You are a married lady and connected to the Hancotts. I'm a hired hand. If I start calling you by your Christian name and hugging you, there's no telling how it would end."

"Would that be such a bad thing?"

Heck's voice had an edge to it. "Ma'am, we've got hold of something like that flood. It's got a force all its own, and I don't mind telling you it scares the hell out of me. Now, this is the end of you driving out on the range to see me or paying me any particular attention at all." He struck the steering wheel with the heel of his hand. "I've got a good job here, and I like working for Bob and Mr. Payne. But I'll have to leave, ma'am, because I can't handle you looking at me like you have tonight and knowing you belong to—"

Heck wasn't allowed to finish. She almost shouted, "I don't belong to him! I may be married to him, but I don't belong to him. Don't you see? He knew when we married that it was just an arrangement."

Heck didn't say a word. He just looked at her.

Ruth's hands were tightly clasped in her lap, and she said more quietly, "That's not entirely true. I told him I didn't love him, but I said all the things like I'd try to be a good wife, and he said he'd be a good husband, and he was sure that I'd grow to love him. But I knew it wasn't possible.

From the first, I knew." She was silent a moment, and then she said, "We haven't been husband and wife in the real sense since Christmas."

"Ma'am, that's something that I ought not to know."

"I beg to differ with you. You're the one person who should know."

They didn't speak again. Heck silently drove the remaining miles, both hands on the wheel, eyes straight ahead, lips shut tight in a straight line.

As they dropped down off the ridge into the ranch complex, she picked up her purse and found a comb. She tidied her hair and snapped the bag shut, throwing it on the floor as he stopped a ways away from her bungalow.

Heck got out without a word and reached behind the seat for his saddle blanket and spurs. He held the door for her as she walked around to the driver's side, and he closed it after she was in. Then he tipped his hat and went to retrieve his saddle from the rumble seat. Swinging it to his shoulder, he angled toward the bunkhouse, but after two steps, he turned around.

The look in her eyes as she saw him returning just about broke his resolve. Her lips parted, and she opened the door.

"Don't get out," he said, his voice husky. "I forgot to give you this." Pulling the crimson scarf out of his pocket, he moved to where he could hand it around the half-open door.

She shook her head. "Keep it."

He continued to hold out the scarf. He tried to speak once, but the tightening in his throat wouldn't let any air through. Finally, he was able to rasp, "I can't." He dropped the scarf and wheeled around, striding through the darkness toward the safety of the bunkhouse.

Chapter 13

BIRTHING A NATION takes considerable travail. It also takes a lot of money. In 1862, Benito Juarez, midwife to the emerging Mexican government, found himself without the funds to continue the struggle. Facing the possibility of a stillborn nation, he borrowed heavily from other nations, particularly France.

Anyone who borrows from a loan shark finds there comes a time when, if you cannot pay, the shark will send a big, burly fellow who talks out of the side of his mouth and offers to break your thumbs. Napoleon III sat on the throne of France, and it was he who sent troops to Mexico to break the thumbs of Benito Juarez.

Napoleon III didn't reckon on the fervor and ferocity of these scrappy little Latinos. On the fifth of May, 1862, they made a stand at Puebla, a small city about eighty-five miles south of Mexico City. The Mexican forces, few in number and with the dregs of materiel that could be scraped together by the bankrupt government, fought such a furious and canny battle that the larger, better-equipped French forces retreated in disarray.

Piqued, Napoleon III sent more troops. And then more. Until finally, Juarez was driven into the mountains, and Napoleon III found himself with a country an ocean away that needed to be governed—especially if he were to get his money back. He offered the crown of Mexico to Maximilian of Austria, a young prince.

Maximilian was bred to public service in a monarchy. Educated, polished, extravagant and idealistic, he declared that he would accept the emperorship of Mexico but only if the people wanted him. The French troops coerced a demonstration of joy from the Mexican people as Maximilian and his wife, the Empress Charlotte, arrived to begin their reign.

Subsidized by the French treasury and supported by French troops, the new monarchs acted as if theirs was a stable European realm with centuries of civil traditions and a solid economic base instead of a country of hot-blooded, poverty-ridden revolutionaries seething under the oppression of blue-coated foreigners. Maximilian and Charlotte covered the walls of Chapultepec Castle with silk brocade and built the Paseo de la Reforma, a beautiful avenue they could drive down in state.

About that time the United States, emerging from the Civil War, noticed that France was occupying her nearest neighbor to the south. In December of 1866, the U.S. government officially protested to Napoleon III. A month later, the French troops were gone. So was the money.

Maximilian was left without the means to keep order, to combat Juarez, to run the kingdom, or to buy more wallpaper. Charlotte hastened to Europe to plead with Napoleon III for support, and when her mission failed, she went insane. By the end of the next year, Juarez was back in power, and Maximilian had been executed. Charlotte died fifty years later without ever having recovered her reason.

Such a sad little tale. But this sad little tale is remembered joyously every year by people of Mexican heritage as they celebrate Cinco de Mayo with singing, dancing, fireworks and parades. Long before Charlotte died in that chateau in Belgium where she had been stashed away, it had become the custom in southern New Mexico for the spring roundup to begin the day after Cinco de Mayo.

Every year, while the fiestas were yet in full flight, in the early hours of the morning before the eastern horizon began to take shape, when the bats were still flickering through the night in erratic patterns, when the coyote and skunk and other night animals were still making their silent and stealthy livings, cowboys were rising from bedrolls and cots and bunks. They were kindling fires and making coffee and donning boots, spurs and chaps. Jingling through the early morning twilight, they would throw their bedrolls in the hooligan wagon and carry their saddles to the corral where the horses they would be riding that day, or that morning, anyway, would be roped and led to them. Speaking quietly, they would talk to the horses, cursing them good naturedly when they swelled their bellies against the cinches.

The wrangler would gather the herd of horses they called by the Spanish name, *remuda*. The cook would harness the team to the chuckwagon. The nighthawk, perched on the seat of the hooligan wagon that bulged with huge, ungainly canvas-swathed bedrolls, would slap the reins against the broad backs of his team. He was last in rank, last in file, as they slowly traveled across the dry New Mexico landscape, heading for some far-distant water hole.

Nate Benham, aging cowhand on the Rafter U; Emory Benham, working for Ollie Free on the T Bar X; and Heck Benham on the Diamond E—all rode out in the dusky blue-blackness to begin a sweep across range covered by their outfits' brands. Riding up arroyos, checking *bosques* and box canyons, they gathered cattle by twos and threes and tens, bringing them into a herd that swelled like a spring flood as each cowboy drove his four-footed tributary into the whole.

Chapter 14

THE SIXTH OF May found Heck mounted on Spook and riding drag behind a herd of a hundred cattle, mostly cows with calves at their sides. The going was slow, so the little ones, some with shiny white, day-old faces, wouldn't get separated from their mothers.

The sorrel mare was in the *remuda* along with the five other horses that constituted Heck's mount: a roan mare, one black and two bay geldings, and a paint pony. Dooley was wrangling horses. He had been deposed as cook by Shorty, who had returned with rheumy eyes, trembling hands, and his same old stock of stories about punching cattle at the turn of the century. Shorty and the chuckwagon, Dooley with the *remuda*, and Cleveland with the hooligan wagon were on their way north to Los Arboles.

Spook, he of the placid disposition, was a buckskin gelding that was Heck's favorite horse. He could cut a calf out of a herd with no more direction than an indication of which one, and he was uncanny in his ability to outmaneuver any steer who, tail straight in the air, took it in mind to bolt from the herd. In roping, he knew that as soon as Heck let fly with his lariat, he was supposed to sit back on his haunches and stop the critter in his tracks. Heck might be willing to horse trade around with other ponies in his mount, but no one else rode Spook. Heck had gentled him six years ago, and though he legally belonged to the Diamond E Ranch, everyone called him Heck's horse.

As Heck slowly followed the herd, scanning left and right for calves unable to keep up or cows breaking away, he was aware of a tremendous feeling of contentment. Though he had twinges of restlessness when he let his mind dwell on brown eyes and chestnut hair, nonproximity of the flesh did much to restore his equilibrium. So did the fact that the next month or so would be busy and full of purpose. He had an intelligent and responsive horse under him; he had the companionship of good and loyal men, and he was doing what he loved to do in the most beautiful country in the world.

People might come from other milder, moister regions and declare New Mexico to be ugly and drab, but Heck loved the grays and tans of the landscape. He loved the openness of the country, the clarity of the air, and the hugeness of the sky. He loved the purple of the early morning twilight, the indigo of the evening hills, and the smell of greasewood after a rain. Most of all, he loved the freedom—a freedom bought with a knowledge of the harsh laws of the range and a willingness to abide by them.

Los Arboles consisted of a windmill with a tank about fifty feet in diameter for watering stock, two small corrals, and eight huge cottonwood trees in two clumps. Three of the trees were near the stock tank, and five surrounded an L-shaped adobe wall about two feet high—the remains of a one-room house.

When Heck and his comrades, Mike, Hooter, Ras, and Shadow, arrived with their herd, the chuckwagon and hooligan wagon were already parked in the shade by the adobe ruins. Shorty had a fire going with a large enameled coffeepot sitting beside it. Near the fire were two huge Dutch ovens, one sitting on a bed of coals and the other with coals both under and on top. Standing by the fire with a spoon in his hand, Shorty shaded his eyes against the late afternoon sun and watched the herd come in to water at the tank.

As each cow stopped to drink, her calf would begin to nurse, butting his head against his mother's belly as he sucked. Though the press of the other cattle coming in to water might cause him to lose the teat, he would scramble back, butting and sucking until the mother had her fill and would allow herself to be pushed away from the tank. If separated, the calf would bawl for his mother, and she would low for him until, following the sound he knew, he would find her in the noisy, dusty tangle of white dewlaps and rust-colored flanks.

Bob Goodman and four other hands had brought in a herd earlier and rode out to relieve the new arrivals. Heck and the others watered their horses then rode to the chuckwagon and dismounted, stripping saddles and bridles and slapping their ponies' rumps. Dooley, out a quarter of a mile with the *remuda*, rode in to gather their horses and take them out with the rest.

Shorty waved his spoon and shouted at them, "I got biscuits ready fer ya. I seen your dust five mile back." Shorty was small, wiry, and middling old, with a bent leg from a break that had healed wrong and ended his days as a cowhand. Toothless, he carried his false teeth with him everywhere but only wore them on state occasions. His face was brown and deeply lined, but they were merry lines—crinkles at the eyes and grooves from cheekbone to chin.

Heck and Mike sauntered to the chuckwagon and got in line to wash their hands at the basin.

"Fellas at the Tumblin' T got a cook that'll heat water for them to wash in," Mike said as Shorty heaved a Dutch oven up onto the wagon bed.

"He does that so they won't notice his biscuits are heavier'n a salt block." Shorty took the lid off to reveal a great pile of steak that had been simmering all afternoon in rich, brown gravy. His leathery face creased into its delta of wrinkles. "Besides, I always knew the Tumblin' T only hired sissies. None of our boys is so sissified as to need hot water to wash in." Grabbing his meat fork, he slapped a piece of meat on the first cowhand's plate, and the others lined up for supper.

After eating, the men drifted away. Fritz had his pulp magazine. Shadow, a young man out on his first roundup, sat in the shade of one of the cottonwoods trying to learn to play the harmonica. Ras and Hooter played poker at the corner of the adobe wall. Mike, sharpening his knife, offered to do Heck's, too. Heck tossed his knife to Mike then took a book and went to lie in the shade.

Bob Goodman, Dooley, and two of the other hands rode in and ate. The two cowboys joined Ras and Hooter in the card game with Dooley looking on, while Bob lay on the ground under the farthest cottonwood and went to sleep. Shorty bobbed around his kitchen area, tidying up and setting dried apples and apricots to soak for breakfast.

It was about an hour before sunset when Bob got up and walked over to the card game. He told Dooley to bring in the *remuda* and then went to scavenge in the chuckwagon for a leftover biscuit to go with his coffee. As Dooley rode out to the nearby herd of horses, each of the cowboys put away his occupation and got his lariat, uncoiling it as he walked toward the incoming *remuda*.

Spreading out, each man held onto one end of his own rope and the other end of the cowboy's on his left, forming a rope corral. The two men on the side toward the incoming horses stayed wide apart, closing to complete the circle after Dooley had driven in the horses.

Bob shook out a loop and, stepping under the rope held by Ras and Hooter, he asked which they wanted for night horses. Ras wanted old Tinhorn, and Hooter wanted that Roman-nosed bay, only with his harelip, it came out "Woman-nosen may."

Bob deftly roped each in turn and led them over to the first corral where Shorty was manning the gate. Heck said he wanted Snowball, but Shadow interrupted before Bob threw the loop and said to Heck, "Since I've got night guard with you, I'd like to know where you are. If you ride that black horse ..." His voice trailed off, but he half smiled and cocked his head to one side.

Nobody laughed at Shadow. Heck knew each cowhand remembered his first night herd and fighting to stay awake after a hard day's work, remembered being haunted by stories about night stampedes, remembered feeling alone, alone.

Heck nodded to Shadow and said, "I'll take that paint horse, Bob." Bob lassoed the pinto.

When the last pony had been caught and corralled, the cowboys broke the circle, coiling their ropes as they left. Dooley took the *remuda* over to water while he waited for his relief.

Cleveland, the nighthawk, was at least seventy years old and just couldn't let go. An excellent cowhand in his time, he was now willing to do even humble night-herding chores in order to continue working cattle. Dooley helped him drive the *remuda* out to grazing land and then returned and put his horse in the corral.

Ras and Hooter saddled up and went out to take their turn at guard, holding the herd together nearby, and the rest of the cowboys drifted back toward the fire. Heck and Shadow, mindful that they were to have a big chunk taken out of the middle of their night, saddled their horses with loose cinches and tethered them outside the corral. Then they got their bedrolls from the hooligan wagon and found a place to stretch out away from the stories that were wafting around the campfire.

In early May, the desert nights were still plenty cold. Heck pulled off his boots and put his rolled-up jacket on them for a pillow. He folded his quilts on the tarp into an improvised sleeping bag, drew the tarp over himself, and settled down. He lay on his back, lacing his fingers together behind his head and looked up at the stars. He had made his bed many times under the nighttime sky, but he never got tired of looking at it, never got over the feeling of awe. He pondered again familiar questions: *Are there others like me out there? Is there a plan? What is life? Why is life?* As always, grappling with such matters, he drifted off to sleep.

Heck woke in the middle of the night with Shadow's boot in his ribs. "You aimin' to ride night herd with me?" the young man asked softly.

Heck, emerged from his cocoon and grabbed his boots. "Well, Shadow, you've been working here three, maybe four months. I thought by now you could handle it yourself."

Heck followed Shadow to the campfire Stepping into the circle of light, he took the cup of coffee the young man gave him.

"It's blacker'n three feet down a cow's throat out there," whispered Shadow. "I'm sure glad you're on that paint horse."

They sat in silence, drinking their coffee, and then Shadow built up the fire, so they could see their way to where the ponies were tethered. They tightened their cinches and mounted, turning from memory toward where the herd was being held, letting their horses pick the way.

The cattle were dusky lumps, quietly bedded down. Heck and Shadow rode around the perimeter until they saw

Hooter and told him to go on in. He murmured that things were real quiet then rode on around to pick up Ras and head for the flickering beacon.

Heck told Shadow to stay put, and he'd go round to the other side. He rode slowly, and as he circled, he began to sing quietly.

Heck and Mike argued periodically about whether or not low singing and talking helped quiet the cattle. Mike said all it did was make time pass for the cowboy and irritate his partner.

Heck sang and quoted from "The Lady of the Lake" until the sky turned blue in the east and Mike and Fritz came to relieve them. Riding in, Shadow and Heck passed dark figures heading out to help bring the herd in to water. As they tethered their horses at the corral, they could see others around the campfire, homing in on the coffeepot. When breakfast was ready, the cowboys all fell to, consuming quantities of the light, flaky biscuits that were Shorty's pride, covered with salt-pork gravy and accompanied by stewed fruit.

The eastern horizon was beginning to show pink as Heck rolled up his bedroll, explaining to Shadow, "Some of the boys leave theirs out, so they don't have to go to the trouble of putting it away and taking it out again. But I like to know who I'm bunking with, and I don't cotton to scorpions or snakes bedding down with me."

They stowed their beds in the hooligan wagon and were just about to walk away when Shorty hollered, "Heck!"

Heck turned and pushed his hat to the back of his head. "What'cha need, Shorty?

"I need beef," Shorty answered. "Dangdest bunch of cavernous hollow legs I ever cooked for. I want you to get me a nice fat steer tonight."

"All right, Shorty. I'll do it coming on to evening, when it cools off."

Shorty nodded and went back to his Dutch ovens. Heck took the box of vaccinating supplies out of the chuckwagon and handed it to Shadow. Then he took the branding irons, and he and Shadow walked to where two fires were being built a hundred feet apart.

Someone with acute hearing said, "*Remuda*," and all, save those tending fire, left what they were doing to get their lariats and form the makeshift corral awaiting the horses coming in at a rapid trot. As before, each cowboy indicated the horse he wanted for the morning's work, and Bob Goodman roped it and put it in the second corral. Then the night horses were turned out of the first one, and Dooley took them back with the *remuda*.

Heck chose the sorrel mare, figuring she would be good for day herd. He saddled her but tethered her at the corral, as he was flanking calves first.

And, so, the work began.

Five cowboys held the herd together, constantly riding around it to contain the lowing cattle.

There were two four-man teams of cowboys on the ground, each consisting of two flankers, a man to brand and vaccinate, and a man to castrate and notch ears. Each hand wore chaps made of thick leather. Some wore spurs, but Heck preferred to take his off, hanging them over his saddle horn. There was too much work on his knees, and he had caught his spurs more than once in his clothing.

Ras and Bob were on horseback, roping. There was a lithe and linear grace about the way a calf was cut from the herd. The man was a part of the horse, leaning with him as he turned and darted, following the serpentine path of the little Hereford. The rope, sinuous and fluid, was almost an extension of the man as it wafted through the air to settle around the calf's neck or two hind feet, depending on the intent of the roper. Over and over, man and horse and calf danced their set piece, their rite of spring.

Ras, mounted on a good-looking gray, led a white-faced calf to Heck who leaned over and grabbed two handfuls of hair. Lifting the calf, he deposited him on the ground, put one knee on the animal's neck, and doubled up the calf's front leg. With the other hand, he slipped off the rope. Ras turned and coiled his lariat as he headed back to the herd.

Mike sat with one boot heel against the hock of the calf's back foot nearest the ground, pushing it forward and pulling the top leg back to leave a clear field for Shadow, who was standing with a knife in his hand. His face was pale, and the area around his eyes and mouth had a bluish tint.

Mike laughed at him from under his hat brim, but Heck spoke encouragingly. "Get down where you're comfortable working on him. He's not going to move, so don't worry about cutting the wrong thing. Now, you get ahold and feel to make sure they're both down in. Yeah, like that. You're doing fine. Now take your knife and cut quick across, just above where your thumb is. Quick. It'll be harder on him if you go slow. Good man."

Shadow squatted there for a moment with the scrotum and testicles in his hand. Heck nodded toward the fire, and Shadow tossed his handful over into the flames. "Now, put some of that Smear Sixty-six on. Just slap it on. Now, come up and notch the right ear. All the calves from this range get a notch on the inside down right next to the head. Tells us what bull sired him. Then, on the other side, you notch halfway up. That's so we can tell what year he was born. That way, when it comes time to sell two-year-olds, it's easy to know which ones to cut out."

While Shadow was notching the ears, Mike let go and grabbed the syringe to vaccinate for blackleg. At the same time, Fritz branded Diamond E on the left hip. Then he took a stick with a rag wrapped around it and swabbed coal oil on the burn.

By this time, Ras was there with another calf. He had roped this one around the back feet and dragged him to the crew. They walked to where he lay and repeated the procedure: Heck on its neck, Shadow with the knife, only surer this time, and swifter.

As the morning wore on, they branded and vaccinated and notched. In the case of bull calves, they castrated, as well. Shadow got his turn at flanking, branding and vaccinating, too, under Heck's calm tutelage.

When the sun was halfway to midday, Hooter rode over with a message from the foreman. As usual, when he tried to pronounce, "Bob," his harelip got in the way, so it came out, "Heck, Mom wants to talk to you. He's over at the chuckwagon."

Both Heck and Mike looked over at Bob, standing with his pocket watch in his hand looking toward the south. Heck handed the piggin' string to Shadow and strode over to see what the foreman wanted.

Bob looked at his watch again and put it away. He stood a moment longer, looking toward the south and then said, "Heck, I want you to rope with Ras for the next while. There's something I got to do."

It was a prosaic request in an offhand manner by a fellow preoccupied by something to the south, but Heck couldn't help the tingle of excitement he felt. Being asked to rope on a work was an acknowledgement not only of his roping skills but of his skill as a horseman and his ability to penetrate into the herd and cut out a calf without riling the whole bunch. He regretted he was riding the sorrel mare instead of Spook this morning. She was a quick learner and had settled down, but she wasn't as savvy about cattle as

Spook. On Spook, Heck knew he could do a good job. On the less-experienced sorrel mare, there was a chance he could come to grief. But he figured that Bob was ramrod, and he knew what pony Heck was mounted on, having roped it himself.

Heck looked up to find Mike's eyes on him. Mike was a fine roper, and Heck knew that he would like to have been the one Bob asked to rope. Mike touched the brim of his hat with his forefinger—a brief salute—then turned back to the work at hand.

Heck had a long talk with the sorrel while he was tightening her cinch. He told her of his need for her to be a good horse, to be alert and quick. He told her that his reputation was at stake. He said she hadn't pitched once the last four or five times he'd been on her; he'd be obliged if she'd keep that up. He'd show her what to do at first, and she'd pretty soon see how it was done. She was a well-mannered lady and was going to make a fine cow pony.

Saying it again to convince himself, Heck rode out toward the herd.

The mare did surprisingly well. She proved to be good at working in the herd, and as Heck guided her thorough the exercise of cutting out the calves, she became more and more independent of the pressure of the reins. Heck began to relax and concentrate on his roping. It seemed he couldn't make a bad toss. Head or feet, whichever he aimed at, he unerringly snared, and the team on the ground had to hustle to keep up with him.

So engrossed was he in his task that Heck failed to note a black Ford pickup approaching from the south.

Bob Goodman rode alongside, his head bent to hear what his wife was saying to him from the passenger seat. Sally had her head and one plump shoulder and arm stuck out the window and spoke without pause.

Ruby Payne was at the wheel, revving the engine and regulating their speed with the clutch as they pulled into camp. Next to Ruby sat Ruth Reynolds.

The car jerked to a stop, and Sally opened the door from the outside without pausing in her story. She climbed out of the pickup and stood on the running board to have better access to her husband's ear, but she moved down toward the pickup bed to allow Ruth to get out of the cab.

All of the men around the chuckwagon and those at the branding areas stared at Ruth. The minute she stepped out of the truck, without exception and as if it were choreographed, each man put his hand to his face to rub his unshaven chin.

Ruth didn't notice. Standing by the pickup dressed in tan jodhpurs, black boots, and a black, short-sleeved shirt with a crimson scarf tied around her throat like an ascot, her eyes immediately found Heck. She watched him sitting easily astride the sorrel mare as they broke from the herd at a dead run in pursuit of a big bull calf. She put her hand over her heart and felt it echo the thundering of the sorrel's hooves as she watched his demonstration of the roper's skill.

Chapter 15

THE CALF WAS fast and ran a random pattern through the brush. The sorrel mare, on her mettle, was justifying Heck's faith in her abilities as a cow pony. She stayed right on the calf's trail as Heck held his lasso ready, waiting for his chance. He saw it, twirled the loop over his head, and let fly. It was a long toss, but it settled over the calf's head, and the sorrel mare stopped and braced herself. Heck, in the manner of most New Mexican cowboys, used a long rope tied off to the saddle horn.

Once caught, the calf belligerently refused to be led to the branding area. Alternately digging in with all four feet and darting laterally to the end of the rope, he was making Heck and the sorrel fight for every inch of progress.

The pony was doing well, continually backing to keep the line taut each time the calf bolted transversely. But she was completely undone when the calf charged directly toward her. She threw up her head and sidled sideways, but the calf was under her before she realized what he meant to do. She started pitching as she felt him scrape her belly, and Heck could see there was going to be a wreck, so he kicked free of his offside stirrup and got his leg over the saddle horn.

The mare was in the air when the calf hit the end of the rope, and the force of it pulled her on over. That was about the time that Heck and the mare parted company. He jumped forward, so he wouldn't get tangled in the rope or get hit by flailing hooves, for the mare ended up on her side, still trying to pitch but being held to the ground by the rope that ran from the saddle horn, under her, to the straining calf.

One of the cowboys on the ground cut the rope and the bull bolted for the herd and his mama. Freed from the pull of the rope, the mare was able to regain her feet. She stood with sides heaving, blowing big, gusty breaths. Heck had lost his hat when he jumped off and leaned down to pick it up and dust it off. In doing so, he noticed the new arrivals.

He stood there, hat in hand, clad in dusty chaps, work boots and spurs, and a plaid, long-sleeved work shirt that had come untucked. His hair fell forward over his forehead, and he had two days' growth of stubble on his cheeks and chin. He caught Ruth's eye and felt the heat and intensity of the look she sent him as well as the unbidden, ill-advised answer that found its way back to her.

So much for nonproximity of the flesh.

Feeling suddenly deflated, Heck dragged his eyes away from hers. Bailing off a bucking bronc didn't compare to the danger here, and he didn't know if he had it in him to go on with the fight. Wearily, he slapped his hat against his chaps and set it square on his head. Turning his back on Ruth, he walked to the sorrel mare. Shadow rode up to him with a new rope.

Heck took the rope with a word of thanks and looked around for Bob. He saw him on his horse, tipping his hat to Ruth and Ruby Payne as he headed toward the herd. Heck rode to meet him and said, "I figure there's maybe a dozen left to do. One of them's wearing half my rope."

"That was quite a show," said Bob. "You do that just for the ladies?"

"Sure. That was the matinee. Figured to do it again tonight at eight." He touched his hat to the foreman and then spurred his pony to ride away, away, away to the far side of the herd and safety.

Chapter 16

LIKE A LODESTONE, she drew him. Despising himself for his weakness, time and again Heck rode to the near side of the herd to watch the trim, jodhpur-clad figure as she sat on the front fender of the pickup, a spectator as the last few calves were marked and branded.

When the work was finished, the cowboys put away their equipment and gravitated to the chuckwagon. As Heck watched, Ruth evidently called Mike over to her, for she extended her hand to him. Mike stood talking to her, and once, Heck saw him throw back his head and laugh. Then they were obviously talking about him because both their heads turned his way, and Mike even pointed. Heck turned his pony and rode away, burning with discontent.

When he rode back around, she was still sitting on the fender talking to Mike, but this time it was she who threw back her head and laughed.

Heck found himself gritting his teeth as he watched with narrowed eyes. Chafing against the duty that kept him with the herd, Heck forgot that he had sought it as a refuge only a little while before.

Hooter rode up and said, "Mom wants to talk to you. Go on in, and I'll take your place." Like hitting the end of a rope at full gallop, Heck was jerked up short and remembered his resolution to have nothing more to do with the lady, the beautiful Mrs. Harlan Reynolds.

"That's all right, Hooter. I'll stay out a while longer."

"Mom sain you was to come in. Sain you was to get Showty a meef. Metta have some chuck fust."

"Thanks, Hooter, I will." He spurred the sorrel to a lope and rode to the corral. Mike was still beside Ruth. Though she inclined her head to hear what he was saying, she had her eyes on Heck. He met her gaze for the second time that day and hesitated just a moment before he touched his hat in salute. Then he turned and walked to the chuckwagon.

He washed up in cold water at the basin and dried on the communal towel, conscious of the well-modulated voice that floated to him now and again.

He sat away from everyone to eat his steak and biscuits, assuaging the hunger in his belly that he hadn't realized was there. Ruby Payne walked over to where he squatted with his plate on one knee. He stood up as she approached, but she motioned him down again. She had a car blanket over her arm that she spread on the ground to sit on. Heck took her elbow to help her down, and she sat hugging her knees, her feet peeping out from under the gingham skirt. She turned her head and looked at him for a moment. Springy tendrils of hair floated around her ears and at the nape of her neck.

"So," she said. "Are you two planning on taking out an ad in the Sierra County Record next?"

"Ma'am?" he asked, puzzled.

"You and Ruth. The looks that are passing between you could melt marbles."

The corners of Heck's eyes wrinkled as he grimaced, and he shook his head. "I thought it best to keep my distance."

"Wise boy. Sometimes that's all you can do." Ruby picked up a stick and flicked an ant off her blanket. Then she began to peel the bark off the twig. "You understand, don't you, that this is a part of life? A person makes marriage vows, but it doesn't keep them from feeling ..." She searched for a word. "... hankerings for someone else."

Heck glanced at her, but she seemed intent on the stick and spoke without lifting her eyes. "Vows don't make it so someone doesn't hanker after you, either. It's not King's X."

The ant was back, climbing the fuzzy red plaid ridges. All his progress was lost in one flick of Ruby's stick. "It's painful, Heck," she said, "but it's a part of living."

Heck didn't look up, but he inclined his head ever so slightly.

Ruby pushed on. "My brother, Henry, will be here after roundup. Every time he comes, he says he'd like to have you come to work for him again. Have you ever thought about it?"

"Only in the last few weeks, ma'am."

"Alan would know where you were when the time came to hire a foreman."

"It does bear thinking on."

Ruby threw away her twig and stood. Heck stood, too, holding his empty plate. She picked up her blanket, shook it, and patted his arm. "You're a good boy, Heck." Then she went over to where Sally Goodman was holding Ras a verbal hostage.

Ras didn't hesitate. He bolted to the pickup where the lady from back east was holding court. Mike was still there, standing beside Ruth. Shadow was on the other side with two more hands behind him.

And there was Shorty, bobbing around, looking uncharacteristically grim. Suddenly Heck realized that he had in his false teeth. Feeling a rush of pity, Heck thought, *You poor old son-of-a-gun.*

The rifle was in the front of the chuckwagon. Heck got it out and, hunting for a box of shells, he found the can of peaches Shorty always carried for his story on labels. Heck put the shells in his pocket, took the rifle in one hand and the can in the other, and sauntered over to the group around the pickup.

Ruth watched him come. "Hello, Heck"

"Afternoon," he replied. He almost added "ma'am," but his mouth wouldn't form the word. She must have noticed, for a faint smile touched her lips and eyes.

Suddenly Heck startled her and everyone else by shouting, "Peaches!"

Mike stepped solemnly forward and intoned, "Peaches. Yellow cling. Del Monte Reg. U.S. Pat. Off. Contents: peaches—"

Heck was reading the label and shook his head. "No," he said. You've missed it already."

He tossed the can to Mike who held it for Ruth to read as Shorty stood forth and recited everything that was written on the label. When he was finished, he turned to Ruth and said, "Back when I was young and punchin' cows, we never had nothin' to read, come evenin', so we'd memorize labels and then have contests to see who could recite them best. I remember back in '14, a city fella come out ... "

Heck didn't wait to hear more. He tipped his hat to the lady and strode to the corral where the sorrel mare was tied. He put the rifle in the scabbard and checked his cinch.

As he untied the pony, Heck heard the jingle of spurs and looked over his shoulder to see Mike approaching. His friend came and stood by him, one boot on the bottom rail of the corral, both forearms resting on the top rail. He didn't say anything, and Heck stood quietly, waiting.

Mike pulled his hat brim down and rested his chin on his arms, intent on the horizon. "Do you remember when we were cleaning the guest house, getting ready for her to move in?"

Heck had been looking down at his reins, pulling them through his hands while he waited for Mike to speak. He glanced up quickly.

Mike was still regarding the horizon. He went on without waiting for an answer. "We found that black widow, remember? Turned her over to see the red mark on her underside?"

He stopped. Neither cowboy said anything. The sorrel mare shifted her weight.

Mike looked at Heck. "You know what they say about black widows? They mate with the male and then they kill him and eat him." He jerked his head toward the lady. "She'll have you for dinner."

Heck swung into the saddle and looked down at Mike. "Or you, Michael? Maybe?"

He couldn't see Mike's eyes. "No. Not me," Mike replied. "I'm not even on the menu."

Heck regarded him for a moment and then, without speaking, turned his pony. Just before rowels hit hide, he heard his comrade's admonition: "Be careful, *hombre. Cuidado ...*"

Mike's next words were swallowed up in the dust and the distance and the sound of the sorrel's hooves as Heck galloped toward the herd to find a fat steer for Shorty.

Chapter 17

THINGS PROBABLY WOULD have turned out differently if Heck hadn't had a bottle hidden away.

He got it from Old Man Hickock up at Engle. He'd gone up several times last winter to work with a knot-headed mustang, and Mr. Hickock, being the saloonkeeper, had paid him in kind. Heck hadn't given good money for the whiskey, so he felt no obligation to drink it up right then. He took it back to the Diamond E and begged a cookie tin from Mrs. Payne, saying he needed something for his savings. She must have thought he meant money as she patted him on the arm and parted willingly with a round shortbread canister. Heck wrapped the bottle in a rag, put it inside the cookie tin, and buried it in a corner of the machinery shed.

He remembered it as they were bedding down their last herd of the spring work. It was the end of a day that had been hot and oppressive. The cattle, excitable and noisy, had required all the hands to contain them. The flies had been particularly bad, and time and again, a cow that had been stung broke from the herd, generating a small local stampede.

The men had dark wet patches under their arms and down the middle of their backs, and they took off their hats often to wipe sweaty brows on shirtsleeves. They ate in shifts of two, detouring by the *remuda* to catch fresh mounts and lead them in.

The branding was finished. They had spent a month and a half swinging in a great arc from north to southwest, ending up a half-day's ride from the ranch house. They had had no more visitors, and Heck managed to go long stretches without thinking of Ruth Reynolds.

Bob insisted that the cattle be settled down before they left them. He never allowed his men to ride off and leave a moving herd or one that was white-eyed and restless as this one was. All were aware that it was the twenty-first of June and that tomorrow was the dance at Cutter, but the cattle were perverse and refused to be quieted or calmed until late at night when the moon rose and hung huge and orange over the Caballo Mountains, and a cool breeze sprang up out of the east. The milling and bawling subsided bit by bit, and the cowboys slowed down and began speaking more softly. Heck began to sing:

> *Rye whiskey, rye whiskey, rye whiskey I cry*
> *If a tree don't fall on me, I'll live 'til I die.*

It was then he remembered his bottle. He thought about it as he and the rest of the cowboys put their gear in the hooligan wagon early the next morning and saddled up for the ride back to the ranch. It loomed before him like a cloudy pillar as he rode point, pressing ahead of the rest across the wide valley floor and through the pass to the Diamond E.

The ranch seemed deserted when they got there. Payne's big touring Packard was gone, as was the green coupe from beside the Reynolds's bungalow. Goodman's Model T was there, but Sally didn't come out, as she usually did, straight-arming the screen door and trailing a cloud of non sequiturs. She had probably already gone to Cutter with a neighbor.

The cowboys took care of the horses and turned to the business at hand with the same method and lack of overt direction as they had the spring work.

Heck grabbed a blackened number-two tin tub and a metal stand hanging on the side of the bunkhouse and carried them into the dooryard. Mike brought an armload of wood and began building a fire under the stand while Heck and Shadow filled the tub with water and carried it between them back to set over the fire. Hooter built a fire in the stove in the cookhouse and set the flatirons out to heat. Ras set a chair out on the porch of the cookhouse, rang the triangle and declared that the barbershop was now open.

As soon as the water in the yard was hot, the oblong tub was taken down and set in the bunkhouse, and water was carried in in buckets. Mike was first, and, as Heck refilled the tub over the fire, Hooter called out that the irons were ready.

When all were clean, shaved and shorn, they filled the tub over the fire one last time for those still on their way. Ras said he'd wait for the latecomers, and anyone who didn't mind waiting could ride in with him in his car. All the hands said they'd go in early in the pickup.

While everyone else was finishing preparations for the dance, Heck drew Mike outside with him. "I got something to show ya," he said.

He led his friend to the machinery shed, opened the door, and took a shovel from the wall.

Mike put his hands in his pockets. "What'cha doin', Heck? Digging for gold?"

Heck went to a corner and thrust the spade into the earth, pushing with his foot and bringing up shovelfuls of powdery gray earth. "I got something better'n gold here."

Squatting down, he lifted out the tin, blew off the dust, and held it up for Mike to see.

"Shortbread? You buried some shortbread?"

Heck raised his hand for silence, and with a flourish opened the tin, disclosing the bottle nestled in its swaddling of rags.

"Well, I'll be damned." Mike's dimple appeared, and his brown eyes twinkled. "Can I have a piece of your shortbread?"

Heck offered the bottle to his friend.

"Don't mind if I do, thank you." Mike uncapped it and took a drink. "Boy, that's good stuff. Where'd you get it?"

"Old Man Hickock gave it to me last winter." Heck sat on the back of the scraper and took a swig. He felt the fire slide down his throat and hit his chest like an explosion of thistledown. Dang, but that felt good after two months of dusty, hot, dry work. "Nothing like good shortbread just before a dance," he said. "You know, if I had enough of that in me, I might even play my fiddle."

Mike, with the bottle to his lips, choked and coughed and came up laughing. "Well, if I got drunk enough, I might even enjoy listening to ya."

"As I remember it, last time we passed around a bottle before a dance, we ended up killing Old Lady Lyons' pig."

"Yeah, I forgot that you get reckless when you've had something to drink."

"I get reckless!" Heck snorted. "You're the one said you could rope a pig."

The pickup horn sounded. Mike took one last drink. He gave the bottle back to Heck who took a swig, put the bottle back in the tin, and tucked it under his arm.

As they headed out to join the other cowboys, Mike said, "We're just going to a schoolhouse dance. What could happen?"

Chapter 18

CUTTER WAS AN ore-shipping town about fifty miles away as the crow flies, across the Rio Grande and across the Caballo Mountains. The dance was to be at the schoolhouse with a box social beforehand and proceeds going toward a new stove for the school. For an event such as this, people came from fifty or sixty miles in all directions. Those who lived far away would come in the afternoon, dance all night, and go home the next morning, ready to spend another month or two in isolation.

The cowboys gathered in little clusters and knots around the schoolyard. Hands from big outfits and smallholdings alike sat on their heels in the shade of the schoolhouse or leaned against the sawhorses set up in the play yard.

Heck took Shadow in tow and wandered among the early arrivals. As he passed by the corner of the schoolhouse, he saw a mountain of oaken desks that had been removed from the schoolroom and piled outside to make room for dancing. Heck stopped in front of the precarious-looking mass that towered eight feet high. "I'll bet I could find the desk I sat in my last year of school here," he said.

Shadow eyed the jumble. "Probably has your name on it but you'd have a time findin' it in that mess."

"Yep," Heck agreed.

From where they stood, they could see a table set up in the shade. On it rested a growing array of boxes and baskets, some festive, some unadorned, but all containing an evening meal for two that would be auctioned to the highest bidder. The winning gentleman would enjoy not only the meal but also the company of the lady who'd brought it.

"Now, the thing you need to remember about a box social around here," Heck said quietly to Shadow, "is that it's safe to bid on just about anybody's box but the McAllister girls'. They can ride and rope good as you can, but unless you're partial to fried egg sandwiches and canned peaches, you don't want to buy one of their boxes."

"How will I know? I mean, I don't even know them."

"We just stand around here and watch as the ladies bring their boxes over, see who brings which."

Already a crew of school board members and townspeople were putting planks on top of sawhorses, making long tables set in rows in front of the schoolhouse.

"Now, have you been noticing the ladies?" Heck asked. He nodded toward the table. "That tall, redheaded gal is Carrie McAllister. You see she brought her dinner in that flour sack?"

"Fried egg sandwich?"

"That's right. You don't have to worry, though. Emory'll bid on that. You just have to make sure you miss out on Jimmy's."

"Jimmy who?"

"Jimmy McAllister. Carrie's sister." Heck looked around. "I don't see her yet. Just don't bid on any flour sacks."

Heck spied Emory, so he beckoned Spider to follow and made his way to his brother.

Emory saw them coming and broke away from the group he had been talking to, smiling as he extended his hand to Heck first and then to Shadow. "Why, hallo Heck, Shadow," he said in his loud, hoarse voice. "I wondered if you was gonna be here. Last I heard, you was still out brandin'."

"We got in this morning." Heck scanned the crowd. "Have you seen Lucy?"

Emory shook his head.

"I wouldn't think she'd miss this dance. She'll probably be along in a—" Heck broke off as he caught a glimpse of a green coupe cautiously turning off the road into the parking area. He could see two figures in the front, another perched on the rumble seat.

Shadow and Emory naturally looked toward where he was staring, but by then, the car was hidden behind other vehicles. "Uh, I haven't seen her," Heck finished lamely.

"Well, I tell you what." Emory looked around at the people gathered in the schoolyard. "Who do you suppose has a bottle around here? I don't know that I can face a fried egg sandwich without a good stiff belt."

"I had one, but we finished it on the way in," Heck said.

"Let's go to the parking lot. Someone out there's bound to have one. Maybe Old Lady Stevens'll be there. She usually does a pretty good business at these shindigs. Though not as good as before the repeal."

"Problem is," Heck cautioned, "she's still selling stuff that'll give you jakeleg."

"Yep. But it also makes a fried egg sandwich look better. Comin', Shadow?"

Shadow shook his head. "I'm going to keep an eye on the tables."

Emory set off purposefully toward the parking area. Heck ambled after him, tipping his hat to old Mrs. Martin, his former teacher, as he passed. His attention thus diverted,

Heck almost ran into Emory, who had stopped and was standing with his hat clutched to his chest.

"Well, I'll be damned," Emory said in a gravelly stage whisper. "It's the Prince of Wales."

Heck looked around his brother to see Harlan Reynolds picking his way through the powdery ruts of the makeshift parking area. Dressed in his pinstripe suit, he was carrying a picnic hamper in one hand and a five-pound lard bucket in the other. Under his grey fedora, his black brows were pulled down, and his lip was curled in an expression of distaste. Tiny puffs of dust exploded around each shiny shoe every time he put a foot down, and he placed each with such care that, at the moment, it was occupying all his attention.

Emory turned around and asked Heck in mock terror, "Do I bow or curtsy?" Glancing back over his shoulder, he noticed the two figures following Harlan. "Oh-oh. Here comes Sally Goodman. Her tongue wags at both ends. Let's get outta here." Emory slapped his battered Stetson on his head and bolted for the nearest car.

Heck stood his ground. He touched the brim of his hat to Harlan Reynolds, who ignored him, though his careful progress wound down to a halt as the two ladies behind him stopped to talk to Heck.

Ruth Reynolds was dressed in a navy voile dress with a Quaker collar of white lace and a white picture hat with a brim that turned down to mask her eyes. She tilted her head to look up at Heck as she extended her hand to him.

Heck took her hand, smiling down at her until Sally tugged on his sleeve several times. He finally responded, turning his head to heed her, though he had not yet relinquished the lady's hand.

Sally wanted to know about her husband. When could she expect him? Would he be here in time for the auction, or would she have to depend on some handsome young cowboy to buy her supper? She tittered and bridled and said she had made fried chicken and cherry cobbler, and there were cucumbers in vinegar and watermelon pickles.

Heck finally released Ruth's hand. He touched his hat to Sally and answered as best he could in his quiet voice. He was speaking to Sally, but he looked at Ruth when he said, "I'm sure there'll be some hungry cowboy who'll be glad to share your supper with you."

"It's the one in the lard pail," Sally said gaily.

Heck watched her churn her way through the dust to the throng in the schoolhouse dooryard. Looking back over her shoulder, she tossed orders to Harlan as to what he was to do with his burdens. Harlan hesitated a moment or so, but Sally spoke to him again, gesturing with broad movements of her plump arms.

As Ruth Reynolds walked away from Heck, a breeze stirred the sheer, full skirt of her dress and lifted the brim of her hat, and she put a hand up on the crown to secure it. Heck gazed after her until he heard Emory at his elbow. "Who were those people with Sally?"

"That was Mister and Miz Reynolds. The fellow you told me about. He pushes a pencil for Hancott."

"Charmin' fella."

"Yep."

Alan Payne, standing at the edge of the crowd, detached himself from the people he had been talking to and approached the brothers with his hand outstretched. "Hello, Emory. Good to see you, Heck. When did you get in?"

Shaking his boss's hand, Heck briefly told him the status of the roundup, adding that he was sure Bob Goodman would be along before dark. He glanced around at the women visiting in twos and threes and circles of seven or eight. "I don't see Miz Payne. Isn't she here?"

"Her brother Henry came in yesterday, and they've gone up to Soccoro to see their Auntie June. They'll be back tonight. She said she'd probably be here in time to see Emory Benham start a fight."

"I'll hold off until she gets here," Emory promised.

"If she's gone, that means you're on your own for dinner," observed Heck.

Mr. Payne nodded toward where some women were setting up a table. "I'll get something from the ladies' auxiliary."

"Bob Goodman won't be in 'til later. Sally's lookin' for someone to buy her supper," Heck said. "She's got cherry cobbler and fried chicken and watermelon pickles."

"And greased tongue," added Emory.

Alan Payne laughed and then wagged a finger at Emory. "You didn't say that, and if you did, I didn't hear it."

"You didn't laugh, neither," said Emory.

"Most certainly not." Alan clapped Emory on the shoulder as he turned to go. "Unfortunately, I have pledged to support the auxiliary." He waved and walked away to rejoin the group of ranchers.

Ruth waited in the shade of a cottonwood while Sally sent Harlan into the schoolhouse for three folding chairs. She had him set them up several times, but each time he got them unfolded, she found a place that was leveler or more likely to catch a breeze. She seemed not to notice his beetling brows and set jaw, but she must have got the message that it would be unwise to push him any further.

After they were all seated, Sally chatted steadily to Ruth as she fussed with her chair, which didn't seem to be sitting square. Ruth leaned back, her hand on her cheek, and watched Heck from under the broad brim of her hat.

Sally rocked back and forth on her ample bottom and bent down sideways to look underneath. As she did so, a slim young woman with honey-colored hair ran past and flung herself into Heck's arms, turning her pretty face up for a kiss.

Ruth's chest felt hollow as she watched Heck readily comply then stand with his arm around her.

"Who is she?" Ruth whispered to Sally.

Sally was no help. She was bending over with her knees spread apart, looking at the legs of her chair.

By the time she surfaced, the young lady had done a repeat performance with Emory, and Heck was shaking hands with a wiry young man. He had wavy black hair and wore tan pants, a tan shirt, and Wellington boots.

"What did you say?" Sally asked. "Oh, look. That's Lucy's new husband. He works construction."

"Who is Lucy?" Ruth asked faintly.

"The girl there in white with Emory. She's Heck and Emory's sister. I thought you knew. She and her best friend Helen ran off and married a couple of fellas from out of town. Double eloped. It was just a few months ago, and I hear Lucy's already expecting. That's Helen, standing over by that far table, and that's her husband. Skinny, isn't he? I don't think I've ever seen anyone that thin. Looks like a puff of wind would just blow him away."

Ruth didn't even glance toward the other couple. Sally's chatter washed around her as she sat with her hand at her throat and her eyes on her lap.

Presently, Sally jabbed her arm with a plump elbow and pointed at a small, wizened man who had climbed up on top of the table that held the box suppers. "They're ready to start," Sally said. "That's Spike Clawson. He's the auctioneer."

Ruth raised her eyes, looking, not for the auctioneer, but for Heck Benham. Emory and Lucy were standing together, talking. Lucy's husband was beside her, but Heck was nowhere to be seen.

"Ladies and Gentlemen!" The auctioneer's voice was full and resonant. "We are ready to begin."

The crowd quieted, and people gathered close. There was good-natured kidding with the husbands of the best cooks. They usually had to eat with the ladies' auxiliary, not deeming their wives' cooking to be worth what some hungry cowpuncher was willing to pay.

The auction was an unhurried affair. People settled down for an hour's entertainment, commenting freely to neighbors about the boxes, the probable contents, and the probable (or improbable) pairings that resulted. All laughed and clapped when it turned out that Fannie Lou Forrester, who always brought an excellent meal, had had someone else put her box on the table. Hooter had been top bidder for her anonymous supper, and he grinned under his funny moustache at having made such a coup.

Finally Spike Clawson picked up Ruth's picnic basket. A lard pail and two more cardboard boxes remained.

Sally Goodman leaned over Ruth and tapped Harlan Reynolds on the knee. She tapped again, and, when he finally turned his head, she said, "That's Ruth's basket!" Ruth sat with her arms folded, saying nothing.

"Either this is full of goodies, or someone's made some mighty heavy biscuits!" announced the auctioneer. "Who'll give me a dollar?"

Harlan, used to auctions of a more genteel nature, flicked his hand up. Spike missed it and asked again, "Who'll give me a dollar?"

Sally waved her arms in the air and pointed at Harlan, who shrank away from the index finger stabbing at his airspace. Spike acknowledged the bid and asked for more.

When someone bid two bits higher, Ruth looked around but couldn't see who it was.

Spike turned to Harlan and asked for a dollar fifty. Harlan flicked his hand up. This time Spike caught the motion and turned back to the crowd, asking for two dollars. Someone said, "Here," and Ruth recognized the voice. Her heart started hammering, and she willed herself to breathe normally.

Spike looked to Harlan for two-fifty, and he began to look churlish. He scanned the area, apparently looking for his competitor. As he did so, Alan Payne, smiling broadly, raised his hand in greeting.

"Oh, it's Alan," Harlan said, and he shook his head at the auctioneer. He leaned over and whispered to Ruth, "I think it will be good policy to let him have dinner with you."

Spike declared the basket sold for two dollars, and then picked up Sally's lard pail. Hungry cowboys had the bid up to three dollars when Sally poked Harlan and told him he needed to get in on the bidding, or he was going to be left without supper. When the auctioneer asked for three dollars and fifty cents, she again waved her arms and pointed at Harlan. He put up his hands as if to protect himself, and Spike must have taken it as assent. There were no more bids.

Harlan was the proud owner of a fried chicken dinner—cherry cobbler, cucumbers in vinegar, watermelon pickles, greased tongue and all.

Chapter 19

HECK LEANED AGAINST the pile of desks by the corner of the schoolhouse with a picnic hamper hanging from his left hand. He watched Sally jump to her feet and say, "Well, that's over! Let's hurry, so we can get a good place. Harlan, you move the chairs up to the table, and I'll get the bucket."

Harlan did as he was bid, and, while Sally got her lard pail and plunked it down on the table, Ruth drifted toward the schoolhouse.

Heck pushed his hat to the back of his head, and his eyes followed her approach. He said not a word, nor did she, but she watched him from under the brim of her hat with lucent eyes, and she walked with him around the corner and away from the merry, noisy crowd.

The school at Cutter was set at the edge of town. A large, square-frame building set high on a foundation of native granite, the yard around it was packed hard. Though it had been over a month since school was out, you could still see the snaking trails left by spinning tops or the rings where schoolboys with shaggy locks and hand-me-down clothes knelt in the dirt and played marbles.

It was through this play yard that Heck walked with Ruth in the late afternoon sunlight. They skirted the area that was swept daily, so little girls could sit down to play jacks. They bisected the place where the jump rope had beat the ground so hard and shiny that it was more like stone than dirt. Beyond that, the soil turned soft, and sagebrush and creosote bushes reappeared, sweet and aromatic as the lady's sheer blue skirt brushed them in passing.

Ruth and Heck walked apart. Reckless he was tonight, and heedless, admitting to himself the fascination he felt for her. But his outward demeanor was correct. He would not touch her in a way he had no right. That he could control. What he could not control was the hot blood coursing through his veins, the singing in his heart and brain and being, and his eyes, which spoke the things he could not say aloud.

The ground sloped away from the schoolhouse, and they traversed the gentle grade until they came upon some huge boulders. Heck led the way to a space between the giant rocks that formed an entrance to a chamber. Inside were a few smaller rocks, gray and smooth.

Heck set the basket down on one of the smaller humps. Ruth looked at him and then looked around at their sanctuary. Finally, she looked out through the gap in the rocks to the vista beyond where the valley floor spread out to the mountains in the distance. "You're full of surprises. How did you know about this place?"

"I went to school in Cutter for my first six grades. We used to play here." Heck indicated the basket. "While you break out the vittles, I'll gather some wood. It'll be dark before we go in, and I expect you'd like to be able to see."

"Wait," she said. "I brought candles." She opened the hamper and there, lying on the top, were two long tapers with silver candleholders.

"Talk about surprises! What else have you got in there?"

"Ruby said to fix a picnic. I've never done it before, but I have a friend, Bunny Ashton, who used to go on picnics all the time. I used some of her ideas." Ruth put her toe against one of the middle rocks that was low and fairly flat. "We'll sit on the ground and use this as a table."

She took a blue damask cloth from the hamper and spread it out. Handing the candles and holders to Heck for assembly, she set out dinner plates of white china, silver flatware, and blue damask napkins. She unwrapped a dishcloth from two crystal goblets and set them on the table and then spread the cloth on the ground, so she could sit without soiling her dress.

"My mother would be aghast at anyone sitting down to dinner with the candles unlit. It just isn't done, but shall we save them until it starts getting dark?"

"But if it isn't done ..." Heck's voice sounded undecided, but his eyes were smiling.

"We won't tell anyone," she whispered.

"You might not, but I'm going to find Sally right after dinner and tell her you sat me down to unlit candles."

Ruth paused in the act of taking off her hat with both arms above her head as she searched for the hatpins. There was something provocative in her voice as she said, "Maybe I can buy your silence." She swept off the hat, threw it on the ground, and ran her fingers through her chestnut curls.

He didn't ask the question, "What have you to offer?" but it hung in the evening air between them. Her eyes held his for a moment, and then she looked away and began digging in the hamper. He took off his hat and threw it on the ground beside hers.

Ruth emerged with a bottle of wine and a corkscrew, which she offered to Heck. "How about this? Will it save me?" she asked lightly.

"Done! My lips are sealed." He took the bottle and the corkscrew and went to work as she laid out the rest of the dinner. There was chicken baked with herbs and lemon, blanched carrots in vinaigrette, and a beautiful round loaf of crusty bread.

They sat on the ground and ate dinner as the sun went down, streaking the horizon with crimson and lining the clouds with gold. They talked of Cutter, of the roundup, of chicken baked instead of fried.

Heck told her how his papa had homesteaded a section of land on the Jornada—just over there—and had done pretty well at first. But the drought had come, and the water dried up, and the wells that Papa drilled all turned out to be alkali. "I remember," he said, "when I was about eleven, out skinning cattle that had died of thirst. We could sell the hides, so we took them and left the carcasses for the coyotes."

He paused to break off a piece of bread and brush away the flaky crumbs that littered the tablecloth. "Papa lost the ranch. We lived in Cutter for a while, and he worked for the railroad. Then he got on with the Rafter U, and we moved to Palomas. Not long after that, I left home."

Ruth looked again at the place he had shown her. "What exactly is the Jornada? I don't see much difference between it and the rest of the valley floor."

Heck gazed out across the expanse of greasewood and mesquite that the sunset had colored with a rosy wash.

"It's called *Jornada del Muerto*, Spanish for 'Journey of Death.' It's part of the Camino Real, the trail from Mexico City to Santa Fe, that's almost four hundred years old. It's the way Coronado traveled when he came through."

"How can Santa Fe be four hundred years old? The Pilgrims didn't hit Plymouth Rock until 1620."

"Ah, but the Spanish were here long before that. Actually, the trail is four hundred years old, but Santa Fe was founded in 1610."

"Really? Do they teach that in school?"

"I don't know. I didn't go to school that long. I just know about the Jornada. Later on, it was the road for the stage line. They'd change horses at Radium Springs, then Tucson Springs, then San Marcial—all the places that had water."

"Why did they call it the Journey of Death?"

"Because so many people died on it. They say there was one death for every foot of length. I don't know if that's so, but if a fella didn't know where the water was, he wouldn't last long out there. We used to find things when we were out playing—old coins and ox shoes. One time Emory and I found a skeleton that must have been a soldier because we found brass buttons and the remains of an old gun."

The crimson sky faded to charcoal gray as the twilight deepened, and the evening star appeared. Heck struck a match on his Levi's and lit the candles. He leaned back against the rock behind him with his wineglass in his hand and watched as the candlelight highlighted the planes of her face.

"Sometime I'll take you up in the San Andreas—over there—and we'll look down on it. The travelers had horses and oxen, and they ate mesquite beans as they went. They seeded mesquite trees along the way, and from up there you can see the trail quite plainly." Heck paused and then said quietly, "I don't know why, but I can't ever stay long away from the Jornada. It renews me to come back. It's home."

They sat for a moment, neither speaking. Heck was the first to break the silence. "On that first day," he said tentatively, "why were you trying to get to Cruces?"

Ruth looked behind her for a rock to lean on and took time to move over and get comfortable before she answered. "I had heard there was a convent there. I was seeking asylum."

Heck leaned forward to rub away some wax that had dripped on the candleholder. He sat back again and considered her. "Asylum?"

"I have no resources. No family. No money. Nothing except my car and a Bokhara rug that was in my father's office. Something happened that made me decide to leave Harlan, only I couldn't because I had no money to go on and no one to go to. So, I thought they might take me in at the convent."

"But you didn't go, after all."

"No. In the light of day, it didn't seem such a good plan. I've found out since that it's a teaching convent, anyway. A school. I doubt they could have helped me."

The scraping of a fiddle floated out to them on the night air, playing fifths to tune. "We're going to have to go in soon," Heck said. "They'll be starting the dance."

"I brought fruit for dessert. I couldn't find anything more exotic than this in Hot Springs. Catch!"

She tossed him an orange—tossed it high and awry, but he reached out a long arm and snared it then held it to the light. A slow smile spread across his face, and he looked up at her.

"Do you know how long it's been since I've had an orange? What a treat!"

"Are you making fun of me again? I don't always know when you're serious."

"No, really," Heck assured her. "I have an auntie who lives in California, and every Christmas she used to send us a box of oranges. That was before the crash."

"Surely you had oranges other times. Is this one of your tall tales?" Ruth watched as Heck peeled his orange and carefully separated a wedge and put it in his mouth, smiling at her as he savored the tangy juiciness. She softly answered her own question: "I guess not. You make me ashamed."

Heck paused with a piece of fruit halfway to his mouth. "I don't know what shame has to do with oranges."

She looked down as she began to peel hers. "My daddy was a stockbroker. He did very well—not well enough for my mother—but he had a nice little portfolio of his own stocks and one for me that I came into possession of when I turned twenty-one. It was a marvelous little legacy that I enjoyed to the hilt while it lasted." Her eyes glistened in the candlelight as she meditatively bit into an orange slice. "Daddy didn't survive the crash, financially or physically. I didn't survive it financially, either."

When the fiddle began playing a tune, she looked toward the sound and then set the rest of her orange inside the basket. Wrapping her wineglass in her napkin, she held the bundle in her lap and said, "I grieved. But, you know, Heck, I grieved more for the loss of my independence and my money than I did for my daddy. I was sorry I had to depend on my mother and the latest gilt-edged windbag that she had married in order to have everything that I was used to having."

Ruth put her glass in the hamper and held out her hand for his goblet.

He gave it to her and sat back to watch the way her hair swung forward to hide her face as she bent over the basket.

"What did Harlan do," he asked, "to make you think you had to leave him?"

She was on her knees scraping chicken bones into a piece of waxed paper, which she folded and put in the basket. Then, scanning the area as if to see that everything except the candles had been stowed away, she sat back on her heels and looked steadily at Heck. "He wanted something I wasn't prepared to give him. He tried to take it by force."

She blew out the candles. The darkness was instant and complete, covering them, smothering them, blotting out everything but the meaning of her last seven words.

Heck heard her putting the candles and their silver holders in the basket, heard her shut the lid and pick up her hat.

The strains of "Tennessee Waltz" came drifting through the darkness, tempering the paralysis brought on him by her revelation. He cleared his throat. Then he put on his hat and stood. "If you'll give me your hand, I'll help you up." He felt the warmth of her hand in his, smelled her perfume as she stood, but he did not try to prolong the contact. Picking up the basket, he said, "Come. I'll teach you to dance 'Put Your Little Foot.'"

Chapter 20

THE TABLES IN the schoolyard had been cleared of the clutter and debris from supper, and coal oil lanterns had been set here and there to provide light for those who preferred to sit in the night air and visit rather than dance. They were few.

Heck and Ruth strolled by on their way back to the schoolhouse. Heck nodded and Ruth murmured, "Hello," as they passed. Heck put the hamper on one of the tables, and she laid her hat on top of it. He had his hand lightly under her elbow as they paused in the light of the open doorway and listened to the music and laughter spilling out.

"The night is so lovely," Ruth whispered. "It's a shame to go in."

Heck looked at a couple sitting at the edge of the lantern light, and his eyes strayed to the shadows beyond. How sweet it would be to wander with her beside him through that inky portal out to where the stars were hard and bright. He'd lean close and point out the Big Dipper. Then he'd take her hand and trace a line to the Little Dipper hanging from the North Star.

"Heck? What are you thinking?" Her voice was as breathless as he felt.

He looked down at her, but his mouth wouldn't frame the invitation. Instead, he guided her up the stairs.

At the doorway, they paused, and Heck surveyed the room. Chairs ringed the perimeter, and the floor was packed with couples of all ages, sizes, and states of grace. All were waltzing, twirling in counterclockwise journeys around the room. Gray-haired men with weather-beaten faces and stomachs hanging over belt buckles partnered hefty women in homemade chintz dresses. Tall young men danced with slim, vigorous young women. Old, shrunken, bald-headed men and frail, silver-haired ladies made their tentative way around the floor in perfect three-quarter time.

Heck noticed Lucy dancing with her husband. Tonight was Heck's first chance to meet Jimmy Swank. Lucy had described him to Heck as quiet and reserved, and that's the way he danced; his progress was smooth as sweet cream.

In contrast, Emory, dancing with his rawboned, ruddy-cheeked girlfriend, was animated. With knees bent, feet splayed out, and his left arm pumping up and down, he plowed around the line of dance.

Harlan Reynolds wasn't dancing but sat alone in the corner, a small thunderhead in a pinstripe suit.

The music was provided by a piano and a fiddle. A huge bear of a man in a black habit with his hair shorn in the manner of the Order of St. Francis pounded out the rhythm on the bass notes of the piano and, with his right hand, played melody or counterpoint, depending on what his partner played.

The fiddler was a tall, spare man with sandy hair and a red beard that accentuated his hollow cheeks and intense eyes. On the other side of the piano stood Dooley, bobbing up and down in time with the music. His left hand held an imaginary fiddle, and his right arm sawed back and forth with a phantom bow.

Heck hung his hat just inside the door. He took Ruth by the hand and led her into the stream of dancers. His right arm encircled her with his open palm against her lower back. He held his left high, and Ruth placed her fingers against his palm with the heel of her hand resting on his wrist as he swept her along, turning slowly first to the right and then to the left as they circled around the room.

She put her head back to look at him. "I had no idea you were such a good dancer."

"It's a nineteenth-century accomplishment," he said and then wickedly added, "ma'am."

Ruth laughed at him and then closed her eyes. He felt her cheek touch his chest, and he rested his chin against her hair, giving himself up to the heady feeling of holding her in his arms, lightly though it was.

The music stopped, and so did they. A moment later, Harlan stood beside them, extending a proprietary hand to Ruth. Heck released her and said formally, "Thank you for the supper, Miz Reynolds. And for the dance."

He nodded to Harlan and made his way across the room to where Emory was standing with Lucy.

"Where you been?" Emory asked. "I got a bottle stashed outside. Jimmy and I was just goin' out there and wondered if you wanted to come along."

"No. I haven't danced with Miz Swank yet." Heck smiled down at Lucy. "And I promised to teach someone 'Put Your Little Foot.' You go on."

Heck led Lucy to the dance floor, and she looked up at him as they twirled with the ease of longstanding partners. "Where did you go for supper?"

"Out to the castle."

"I wish I'd thought of that!"

Heck smiled down at her. "I'm glad you didn't."

"Well, that's obvious. She needs to act a little less like the cat that got the cream."

Heck's smile faded. "Why do you say that?"

"She's a married woman. She needn't think she's going to get her elegant claws into you." Lucy glanced over at Ruth.

"Doesn't Helen's husband dance?" Heck asked, trying to give his sister's mind a different direction.

"He does, but he's not been feeling well lately. Can't seem to work a full day and then dance at night. I don't know what the matter is, but I'm a little worried about him."

They circled by the band, and Heck nodded greetings to Red Dougherty, Friar Hollis, and Dooley who smiled and blinked behind his wire-rimmed spectacles as he bobbed and sawed.

When the dance was over, Mike Eldred claimed Lucy, and Heck ambled over to see if Helen wanted to dance. She did, and as they conversed in the comfortable manner of old friends, Heck saw Alan Payne enter with Ruby on his arm and her brother, Henry Coughlin, right behind. They waved a greeting.

During the intermission, Heck joined Emory, Jimmy, and Helen's husband, Eddie, outside in the shadows where they passed around Emory's bottle. As soon as the music began, Heck returned to the schoolhouse to partner matrons and young ladies as the evening wore toward morning. He didn't single out any one person for attention, didn't let his eyes stray too often to the lady who sat calmly by her husband or danced with those cowboys—Mike, Shadow, and Hooter among them—who were brave enough to ask her. She danced with Alan and Bob Goodman and other cattlemen. Her husband didn't dance at all.

When the music began for "Put Your Little Foot," Heck excused himself from his conversation with Henry Coughlin and made his way to the Reynolds's corner. He stood in front of Ruth and held out his hand, impervious to the daggers in Harlan's eyes. "I've come to keep my promise," he said. She stood, and he led her to a corner of the room out of the flow of dancers.

"We start out with you on my right, both of us facing the same way," he said. Placing her there, he put his arm around her shoulder. "Now, give me your right hand, here, in my right hand. There you go. Now, I take your left hand like this." Bending his face down by hers, he spoke softly in her ear, talking her through the simple, repetitive steps of the dance, guiding her as she changed from his right side to his left and back again. She learned quickly, and soon they were out among the crowd on the floor.

They ended up near the doorway, and Ruth moved toward it and stood in the eddying air. "Thank you. I feel more at home now."

"At home?"

"Yes. You take these customs for granted, but not knowing makes one feel like an outsider. Will you teach me the other dances?"

When he said, "Yes, ma'am," she looked at him with a playful pout.

"I mean, yes, Miz Reynolds," he corrected.

"That's not much better than ma'am," she said. "Tell me about the band. What an odd assortment!"

"Well, you already know Dooley."

"He's not playing anything," she pointed out. "Does he always do that?"

"Yep. And then, there's Friar Hollis. He's a Franciscan Brother. Lives in the basement of the church in Hot Springs and plays the piano here and there for money to keep body and soul together."

"It looks as if there's quite a bit of body. Is there an equal amount of soul?"

"Yes..." Heck cleared his throat, catching himself before he voiced the offending "ma'am."

"Who is the other fellow? He has the look of an ascetic."

"Nope. Just takes his fiddling seriously."

"And how about you? Sally says you play the fiddle."

Heck chuckled. "Ah, well, yes. But I don't take it seriously."

They were joined by Alan and Ruby Payne. "Hello, you two." Ruby spoke brightly, but her smile seemed forced. She patted Heck's arm. "I saw you teaching Ruth 'Put Your Little Foot.'" She turned to Ruth. "What do you think of your first dance in New Mexico?"

"It's the nicest evening I've ever spent."

The music was beginning again. Ruth raised her eyes to Heck, and without a word being spoken, they drifted together. He took her hand, and she raised her arm to his shoulder, her fingers touching his neck just below the hairline. She pressed closer, and he rested his cheek against her chestnut curls, closing his eyes to shut out the world.

He was vaguely aware of Ruby saying, "Do something, Alan," and then someone clapped him on his shoulder.

Heck's eyes flew open, and he turned around to confront Mike Eldred. "Sorry, Michael. My dance."

"No it ain't. Emory needs you." He jerked his head toward the doorway.

"Oh, hell." Heck glanced in that direction, but all he could see was a crowd gathered there, watching outside. Turning to Ruth, he said, "You'll have to excuse me. There's something I have to take care of right now."

He escorted her back to her chair, thanked her, nodded again to her unresponsive husband, and strode across the floor through the moving throng, matching his stride to Mike's. As they went, Heck unbuttoned his sleeves and rolled them up. Mike spat on his hands and rubbed them together.

Heck nodded to Ruby and Alan Payne as he went by.

"Emory said he'd wait 'til you got here to start a fight," Alan told his wife, chuckling.

"Bless his heart!" Ruby said. "He was just in time."

Chapter 21

IN 1895, WHEN Ruby Payne was Ruby Coughlin and fourteen years of age, she fell prey to a fever that raged for ten days and left her listless and achy, prone to memory lapses, and barren. She fully recovered her physical strength and memory, but every year or two thereafter, she suffered a recurrence of the fever, though not so intense and debilitating.

In 1928, when Alan sold his ranch in Arizona and before he went to New Mexico to manage the Hancott holdings, he and Ruby took a train to Rochester to visit the Mayo Clinic.

The doctors there diagnosed her illness. Five years previously they would not have been able to, for the organism *brucella abortus*, which had been known since the turn of the century to cause brucellosis in cattle, had only been discovered to cause illness in humans in 1924.

Alan sat in the small, sterile room with his hat upon his knees and looked first at the young doctor in his white coat and then at his wife seated up on the examining table with her ginger bun awry as he listened to the diagnosis and prognosis: Ruby had been infected as a child with brucellosis by drinking milk from an infected cow. There was nothing they could do about the fevers. Take her home. Make her comfortable when she felt the familiar onset. Ride it out.

Undulant fever did not seem to be fatal in its chronic form.

So, they did. Somehow, knowing what it was made it easier to cope. Ruby gave in to the fever when it stole upon her, taking aspirin to stave off the chills and being grateful for a husband who was able to allow for the nervous disorder that accompanied the illness.

It was perhaps that nervous disorder that prompted Ruby, that Friday morning after the dance, to stand up on her bed in her nightgown and scream, "Well, that just took the rag off the bush! How could you?"

Ruby had been fretting because it was her day to go into town. To soothe her, Alan had explained that Ruth had volunteered to go. He added that, responding to a request from Ollie Free, he was sending Heck Benham in with Ruth. That's when Ruby stood up and screamed.

Reflecting that this time she was worse than usual, Alan spoke soothingly as he gently eased her down into bed and patted her shoulder.

"Don't touch me!" she had said and turned her face to the wall.

Alan took the mailbag and walked out to the pickup where Ruth was standing. She looked cool and crisp in a short-sleeved white linen sheath with red piping and buttons. Her shoes and handbag were red, and she wore a red straw pillbox hat. The gloves she carried were white.

Alan threw the mailbag into the back of the pickup and said, "Heck will be here in a minute. I saw him ride in awhile ago. Probably stopped to get a cup of coffee."

At Ruth's look of inquiry, he said, "He's going to meet Emory in Hot Springs and ride on out to Guzman with him. I thought you wouldn't mind company on the way in."

"No, certainly not. I'll enjoy having him along." Ruth smiled as she walked around to get in the passenger door.

Ruby was right. The rag was indeed off the bush.

Alan closed the pickup door and said, "You two are quite a pair with those shiners. Yours is looking much better than Heck's. Hardly shows at all."

She touched a mottled yellow bruise on her left cheekbone. "It's still a little tender, but even when it happened it looked much worse than it was."

"Light a lamp next time you get up in the night," Alan counseled. "Or keep a flashlight by your bed from now on. Sorry we can't run the generator all night, so you can just flip a switch."

She smiled. "I'll make sure the doors are either all the way opened or all the way closed before I go to bed." She spied Heck coming around the corner of the machinery shed and got a good view of the deep purple mark on the inside of the bridge of his nose that was echoed in the same dark hue at the outside corner of his eye and the top of his cheekbone. "Oh, my! He does have a good one; doesn't he?"

Chapter 22

HECK TOUCHED THE brim of his hat as he approached his boss. "You want me to go to Ollie Free's?"

"He asked if you could come over and help Emory pull the pipe on the windmill at Guzman. He says none of his boys knows diddly squat about machinery."

Heck smiled and nodded. "Be glad to, Mr. Payne."

"You can go ahead and drive. Ruby won't be going in."

Heck raised his eyebrows, and Alan said, "She's got the fever again."

"I'm sorry to hear that."

"Ruth is riding in with you. You can help her get what she needs and carry it to the pickup. She'll bring it on back after you meet Emory. Ollie said he'd get you home tomorrow."

Heck felt off balance as he walked to the driver's window of the pickup and leaned down to look in. He met her eyes, saw them note the damage, and he smiled a rueful smile. "There's several in the county that look just as bad, Miz Reynolds."

"I don't doubt it! I've seen Mike."

Heck got in, slammed the door, and touched his hat to Alan Payne again. "Give my best to Miz Payne. I hope she's well soon."

"Thanks. *Adios.*"

"*Adios.*"

They were off, rattling over the gravel, ascending the ridge, heading east for a way and then turning south.

Heck kept his eyes on the road as they traveled in silence. After their easy hours together at dinner in last Saturday's twilight when he was half sprung, Heck couldn't think of anything to say cold sober and in broad daylight. As he cast around for some conversational icebreaker, he felt her touch his cheek. She was sitting on her side of the pickup, but she had turned toward him and extended her right arm to gently brush the purple smudge with cool fingertips. It didn't help matters at all.

"What were you fighting about? What mattered so much that you would end up like that?" she asked.

"I don't know. That's one thing I aim to take up with Emory today."

"You don't know!"

"He was out cold by the time I had breathing space to ask him. Haven't seen him since." Heck let his eyes rest on her for the first time since they started out, and he noticed the discoloration on her cheek.

He frowned. "What happened to you? You weren't in the same fight I was; were you? Someone had a wicked left; I remember."

"No, it wasn't I," she said, laughing. She paused, considering him. "Do you really want to know?"

"Of course."

"I've told everyone I ran into a door in the dark. But what really happened was that I paid for my enjoyment Saturday night."

Heck chewed on that a moment, thinking he understood but not believing it possible.

"Harlan has a wicked left, too."

"He hit you?" Heck was incredulous.

"Oh, yes."

Heck was dumbstruck. Speechless. Again and again, he looked searchingly at her as he drove. Each time, she met his eyes coolly, levelly, while the black pickup hummed along, chattering over washboard sections in the gravel road and laying down a cloud of smoky gray-brown dust that hung in the air long after they were gone.

"Bunny Ashton," Ruth said finally, breaking into his troubled train of thought, "my friend who went on picnics?"

Heck remembered the name and nodded.

"She married a man considerably older than herself. She was just nineteen, and he was thirty-five. He was handsome and rich, and she fell in love with his smooth manners and elegant gifts, I think, not him." Ruth put her elbow on the back of the seat and leaned her head against her hand. "She told me that she realized soon after they married that she didn't love him—that she hadn't even known him when they married. But she made the best of the bargain until she met a man that she did fall in love with."

Heck was driving with his left hand on the steering wheel, his right wrist resting atop it. The road was straight and level, and he was able to glance at her often as she told her story.

"Bunny asked her husband for a divorce," she continued, "but he is a devout Catholic and wouldn't give her one. So, she left him and went to live with the man she loves."

"How did she manage that?"

"She just did it. They found an apartment, bought furniture, hired maids."

"Weren't they shunned by people? Here, if you did that, people would cut you direct in the street."

"Oh, some of the high sticklers were cool, but they both come from the best families in the city. Their friends understand the situation. I would say that they haven't cried over any severed social connections. Things of that nature are much more accepted nowadays."

"There."

"Beg pardon?"

"They're much more accepted nowadays there."

"Yes." Ruth was quiet a moment and then said, "Bunny begged me not to marry Harlan. She said I would be sorry. She said I would foul everything up because, when I did fall in love, I'd end up hurting him and a lot of other people."

"Seems like he's done some hurting, too."

"Well, you mustn't think I'm blameless. I say things to antagonize him. I can't seem to forgive him for being what he is. Last Saturday night I goaded him into hitting me. It's a sorry, sorry situation."

They were nearing the turnoff that goes to Palomas.

"The thing about it is," she said, musing, "if I hadn't married him, I'd never have come to New Mexico. I'd never have met you."

Her last phrase took Heck's breath away and changed the plans he had carefully made after the dance in Cutter. He braked suddenly, shifted down, and made the turn toward Palomas in the best Ruby Payne tradition.

"What are you doing?" Ruth cried as she was thrown suddenly against him.

Heck smiled at her. "I have something to show you."

They continued on down the road but instead of entering the village, he turned to the left on a road that paralleled the main street and then climbed a hill. At the top he stopped in front of an adobe building and turned off the key

Ruth looked around. "Where are we?"

"This is Palomas. My folks moved here after they left Cutter. I went my last two years of school in that schoolhouse."

"You went six in Cutter and two here. You only went through the eighth grade?"

"You'll find that's not uncommon. Don't judge a man out here on how much formal schooling he's had. If a man knows how to read, he can educate himself in the ways of books. There are other kinds of education, too, that're just as important."

"Surely people around here don't despise formal education?"

"Not at all." He opened the door and went around to help her alight. "Can you manage in those shoes? It's just a ways farther."

He led her past the schoolhouse to the crest of the hill, and they found themselves in a graveyard. About forty mounds lined up in rows, piled high with the smooth, oval gray rocks that littered the hilltop. There were no markers, nothing to designate whose mortal remains lay beneath the unpretentious cairns. Greasewood grew sparsely, though indiscriminately, both between and on top of graves.

Oh," Ruth exclaimed, "what a dreary place!"

"Do you think so?"

A breeze ruffled her hair, and she looked up at the blue sky. "I don't know how something could be dreary on a day like this. Maybe I should say, 'How monochromatic.'"

Heck laughed and agreed, leading her to a large rock and dusting it with his hat, so she could sit. He squatted beside her, put his Stetson back on, and pointed at the village below.

"That's Bemis's store there, by the church. My sister, Lucy, lives with her husband behind the store. Then, follow the cottonwood trees down to the corner and look to the end of the street. On the left is the post office. That little tiny house, see it? Old Ildefonso Armijo keeps the post office. His father, Epifanio, had it before him, and his father before him."

Heck pointed. "Now, look across from the post office. There's a lady in the yard out back doing the wash."

"Is that what she's doing? I thought she was cooking something. She's got a fire going; I can see the smoke."

"That's to heat the water. I want to tell you about that lady."

"All right." Ruth folded her hands in her lap, eyes on Heck's face.

"It's a bit of a story, but I'll be as brief as I can. She came to New Mexico with her family in 1880. Her mother had consumption, and her father brought them out in hopes her mother would get well. She did, and when she was on her feet, they found out they couldn't get along. She might have been all right to live with while she was sick, but when she got well, she was a witch on wheels. He left and went back to Missouri and took his daughter—that lady—with him."

Heck nodded toward the tiny, diligent figure bending over the tub in the dooryard. "She was nine years old. The father, his name was Henry, left her in the care of a woman named Mrs. Toothman while he went to teach school in the Indian Territories. I don't know how well Mrs. Toothman looked after the little girl—her name was Della—because she married her off at thirteen to a twenty-six-year-old man. He was from Oregon, and he took her there, and they lived with his mother. Della had her first baby when she was fourteen, her second when she was sixteen."

Heck picked up a rock and tossed it down the hill. He glanced at Ruth, but she was looking intently at the figure below, who was now hanging out clothes.

"I don't know what her husband did," Heck continued, "as I've never been told. But his conduct was such that his mother wrote to hers and asked her to send train fare, so Della could leave. She had need of asylum."

Ruth looked at him then and nodded.

"Anna—that was her mother—sent the fare, and she came here to New Mexico. Della hadn't seen Anna since she was nine, and in that time, her mother had become a prosperous woman, owned a hotel and a livery stable. She gave Della a place to stay for herself and her children but required her to work like a dog. Della divorced her husband and lost both her children to typhoid fever. When she was twenty-eight, she married a cowboy, and she had three more children."

Heck picked up another rock and tossed it in his hand. "Her life has not been easy, but she's lived it according to a strict personal code of honor. She is the most honest, most true person I've ever known."

The breeze blew a wisp of chestnut hair over Ruth's cheek. She brushed it away and smiled at Heck. Her eyes were soft. "I'd very much like to meet her."

"That's what I'm trying to get to, but you have to let me tell it in my own way." Heck tossed the rock away, took off his Stetson and smoothed his hair back. Then he replaced the hat and gestured toward the lady below them. "She's my mother."

Ruth's eyes widened. "Why did you tell me this? You're not ashamed of her, are you?"

"No, certainly not," Heck said quietly. "Let me finish. Her husband—her second husband, my father—has not always treated her as he should. He loves honor, with a capital H, like you read about in books, but he has never been able to get a handle on the practical aspects of that virtue. Now Mama, she's all practice." He shook his head and smiled, remembering. "One time I had done something that I thought was clever, only it wasn't honest. I can't even remember what it was. I'd got the best of a trade, doing some sharp dealing; I think. She got wind of it and came down on me like a tornado with a switch in her hand. Only, by that time, I was too big for my britches, and I thought I was above a hidin'. I ran, and she chased me, but she wasn't fast enough to catch me. She was so mad, she sat down and bawled. I'll tell you, that made me feel lower'n a lizard in a wagon rut. The switching wouldn't have been anything, but to make Mama cry ..."

Heck sat quietly for a minute, and Ruth said nothing. Finally, he began again. "I was reading a book a while back— a sort of a history book. In it, the head man of the village calls all the people together, and he tells them that he's sorry because the wives and children, whose feelings are tender and chaste—that's how he said it, tender and chaste—are going to be wounded. He knows they've come to hear him tell them comforting things to heal them, but instead of that, he says he has to enlarge their wounds and place daggers in their souls. You see, the husbands haven't been faithful, and he has to tell them right out that they're not doing as they should."

Heck pulled some leaves off a creosote bush, crushed them, smelled the pungent fragrance and tossed them away. He looked at Ruth. "I understand about that kind of wounds and daggers. I've seen it at home. I swore long ago not to be a party to wounding anyone in that way."

Ruth began to speak, but he held up his hand. "No, that's not all I'm trying to say. That lady," he nodded toward his mother, "my mama, hasn't been valued as she should. Not by her mother or her father or Mrs. Toothman or either husband. I want you to understand, when we go talking about asylum, as I think we're about to, that I could not introduce a lady that was living with me, to whom I was not married, to my mother. I value her so highly that I would not offer that insult to her, even to please a woman I loved."

Ruth's dark eyes were shiny with unshed tears. "You are the most astonishing person I have ever met. You are constantly surprising me."

Heck pushed his hat to the back of his head and smiled ruefully. "Don't tell me I'm the only person's ever dragged you up to the top of a hill and said, 'There's my mama, and you're not going to meet her'?"

"You said that you wouldn't introduce me, even to please ..."

He put his finger to his lips. "I'm not going to say it again. I didn't mean to say it then, only you have to understand."

"I will try to." It came out in a husky whisper. She leaned forward and dabbed the corners of her eyes with the turned-up hem of her dress. She cleared her throat. "Now," she said with a tremulous briskness, "we were going to talk about asylum; I believe."

Heck leaned an arm on his knee and nodded toward Palomas. "Take a look. I haven't much to offer. Asylum means a safe place. I could keep you safe and dry and fed. And, pretty much, warm. I could promise lots of hard work. I can't say I'll take you away because I don't own a car. Hell, I don't even own my own horse, so don't look to see me carrying you off into the sunset before me on the saddle. I'm a poor man, and I'll probably always be poor. Being the wife of a poor man makes a woman old before her time."

"There are certain dangers associated with being married to Harlan, too."

Heck nodded his head. Still gazing at Palomas, he said, "I'm going away. I've taken a job with Henry Coughlin. He's got a spread in Utah just over the Arizona line." Looking up, he saw that her eyes were full of tears again.

"I hadn't meant to talk to you at all before I left," he explained. "I just figured I needed to get away, but seeing that black eye of yours changed my thinking some. I've got no right to tell you how I feel about you, so I won't. But if you need a safe place to stay, you can come to me. I've got some money put by. I was saving for a saddle, but with one thing and another, I've never been able to get it. I'll leave it in an envelope with Miz Payne along with a map of how to get to Henry's ranch."

Ruth bent over, dabbing at her eyes again. "When are you leaving?"

"In a few days. I'll ride the bus to Kanab, and Henry will pick me up there." He stood. "We'd best be getting on. Emory'll be wondering where I am." He helped Ruth up and followed her through the graveyard.

Suddenly, Ruth stopped and stamped one elegantly shod foot. She turned to face Heck and cried, "I can't just walk away from here as if nothing has happened. You've just said you love me. How can you say that and get up and casually walk away?" She stepped nearer and clutched his shirt at the collar.

He felt a pulse in his throat beat against her thumb.

Her words tumbled out. "Don't you want to know that I love you to distraction? Do you know that I spend days at my window hoping just for a glimpse of you riding by? That I lie awake nights thinking of how it felt to have you hold me, even if it was just to dance?" She slid her arms around his neck and pulled his mouth down to hers.

Heck did not, could not, resist. As they stood entwined on that barren, monochromatic hilltop, that repository of nameless dead, the warm moistness of her lips, the scent of her hair, the feel of her body pressing against him sent his pulse racing and his mind cartwheeling through hunger and hope.

A moment later, he opened his eyes and found himself in the same unrelenting sunlight, surrounded by the harsh New Mexico landscape. Sighing, he took Ruth by the shoulders and put her away from him.

He turned away and kicked a rock off a grave so hard that it flew a dozen feet. "Dammit!" he rasped. "I swore I wouldn't do that." He jerked off his hat and stood with one arm akimbo, the other hanging helplessly at his side. As he stared off toward the river, he peered into his own soul, striving to get his arms around what was happening.

Ruth approached him and stood behind, leaning against him with her cheek touching his shirt. "Couldn't I just go with you when you leave?" she asked in a husky whisper. "Or, you go with me? The car is mine, in my own name."

Heck shook his head. "I'd be taking you away from him instead of you leaving of your own accord." His voice was quiet but hard as flint. "It's a tiny difference, but you have to leave me that or I won't be able to live with myself."

He turned around, holding his battered Stetson with both hands in front of him, as if for safety. "You need to understand how people around here feel," he said. "A woman doesn't leave her husband for another man. They don't live together without marrying. If you choose to disregard the unwritten laws, then you choose the consequences."

Ruth looked up at Heck with misty eyes. "I think you're making it out to be more than it is. Even then, it wouldn't weigh with me." She stood on tiptoe and, mashing his defensive hat, kissed him again, her mouth full and soft against his. When his face twisted in anguish, she put a hand to his lips. "No. Don't say it. That was wrong of me. I'll be good, and when I need a safe place, I'll come."

Then she turned and preceded him down the hill. He followed, trying not to think about the fact that he was severing his relationship with the Hancotts. Alan Payne would never come looking for him when he needed a foreman at the Diamond E or any of the other ranches owned by the company.

Not after he ran off with Mrs. Hancott's nephew's wife.

Chapter 23

HECK DROVE RUTH to the post office to get the mail and to the feed store to pick up laying mash and oats. He loaded the sacks of grain and stood by the tailgate of the truck as she came out of the store, putting the receipt she had signed in her purse.

"I'm to meet Emory at the ice plant," he said. "I'll say goodbye now."

Her face fell. "I thought we'd go somewhere for lunch."

He shook his head. "It wouldn't be seemly. Nothing has changed. You're still another man's wife, and I'm a cowhand that's driven you into town."

"With a detour by the graveyard," she reminded him, smiling.

"That wasn't seemly, either." Heck looked solemnly down at her. "What I said stands. I'll be there if you need me." Touching the brim of his hat, he turned and walked down the street.

He didn't look back, but he heard her say, "Silly man." Moments later, he heard the pickup drive away.

Heck made a stop by the assay office to try to talk one of the clerks out of a small piece of white soapstone. The clerk took him to the back room and dug through boxes of ore samples brought in by countless nameless prospectors.

The accumulated years of sacrifice and privation represented in the jumble of rocks in that back room would equal several lifetimes. Some of the years belonged to Heck's papa, Nate Benham.

From the assay office, Heck walked to the ice plant. It was owned by a friend that Emory hoped to see that day, but a sign on the door said he had gone to Albuquerque, so Heck sat on a box on the loading dock and began carving on his soapstone.

Emory arrived about a half hour later. He sat in the pickup with his arm out the window, looked at Heck's black eye, and made tsk-tsking sounds. "Didn't your mama teach you about the peacemaker bein' blessed?" he asked.

"What she taught me was to be my brother's keeper," Heck retorted. He pointed at the sign with his open pocketknife. "Doyle's not here. Went to Albuquerque."

"Must'a gone up to see about them refrigerators he's figurin' to handle here. Gonna go into competition with hisself. Well, get in. I'll catch Doyle tomorrow."

Heck opened the door and climbed in. As Emory headed out of town, Heck rode with one foot on the dashboard, his attention on the piece of talc he was slowly reducing to powder. Periodically he looked up to check on an armada of small thunderheads as they plowed across the sky, dragging their shadows under them like canvas sails thrown out for sea anchors in a storm.

"Danged if I don't think it's rainin' in Engle." Emory pointed at one of the clouds where the black bottom was smudging halfway down to the ground.

"Could be," Heck agreed. "The whole county could use a good rain."

They turned off the highway and bounced along a dirt road, heading toward the range that was Emory's stewardship. Heck got out and opened the gates as they went through, and soon they could see the windmill of Guzman in the distance, sitting in the shadow of a rain cloud.

"What do you think of Lucy's husband?" Emory asked in his gravelly voice.

"I haven't had much chance to get to know him. Saw him for the first time last Saturday. Seems nice enough. Quiet."

"He's shore a good man in a fight. Wiry, you know."

"Was he in it, too? Couple of lanterns got knocked off the table and broke, and it was pretty dark out there. They were Miz Pettybone's lanterns, and she was madder'n a wet hen about it."

"Is that so? Carrie's papa put me in his truck and took me on home with them. I don't remember much past when you and Mike came out to he'p me."

"Say, I've been meaning to ask you. What started you off this time?"

"Ah, hem, uh ..." Emory put his elbow out the window and looked in the rearview mirror.

Heck regarded him in amusement. They were out of sunshine now, driving through the cooler shadow made by the rain cloud, black and gravid, that brooded above them. "Is it something embarrassing to you?" he asked. "Someone say something about your lady love?"

"No!" The word exploded and Emory looked surprised at himself. His eyes avoided Heck's.

"Come on, *hombre*. I was there, too. I'd like to know what I was fighting for."

"One of the Rafter U fellas, that big, beefy one? Name of Hanks? He said something I didn't cotton to."

"What'd he say?"

Emory had the look of one driven into a corner. "He said somethin' about a Benham actin' like a hound dog after a bitch in heat."

"And you swung on him?"

"No sir. I told him he probably knew about bitches since he was a son of a bitch, and he swang on me."

Heck's eyes were dancing as he said, "I see. You need to let Papa fight his own battles, Emory."

Emory looked out the window again. "He wasn't talkin' about Papa."

The light died out of Heck's eyes. His hands sat idle in his lap as he watched a bolt of lightning connect sky and earth beyond the windmill. Then silently, he closed his knife and put it and the stone in his pocket.

All at once, the cloud released its burdensome weight of water, released it in torrents. It was raining so hard Emory couldn't see out of the windshield. He turned on the wipers, but they were useless.

"Hellsketoot!" he hollered. "My beans are gettin' wet!" He stuck his head out the window, and, with his Stetson drooping over his eyes, he herded the pickup in the direction of the windmill. Heck was out and on the running board before they had even stopped. Leaning over, he picked up a wooden box full of flour and coffee as Emory grabbed a sack of pinto beans.

They carried their burdens into the shack that sat at the bottom of the windmill then dashed back to the pickup to get the sacks of cement that were rapidly becoming soaked.

"Ole Ollie would probably rather have me bring the cement in first," Emory said as he dumped his sack in the corner, "but I ain't partial to *frijoles* that're puttin' out roots." He spoke loudly to be heard over the rain drumming on the tin roof.

"Hell, Emory, you soak beans before you cook 'em."

"Not fifty pounds at a time I don't." Taking off his hat, Emory struck it against his leg to get excess moisture out of it.

"I think they'll be all right. It's a small storm. You can see the sunlight over there. When it passes, just put the sack in the sun, and it'll dry out pretty quick."

They stood and watched out the window as lightning struck a ridge between them and the sunlight.

Heck pulled out his handkerchief and wiped off his face. "Ol' Mike doesn't like to be near a windmill in a rainstorm."

Emory shook his head. "I don't know that a windmill'l draw lightnin', but I know it'll draw electricity from the air. If I was you, I wouldn't touch the riggin' right now. I did once in a thunderstorm and got knocked right on my rump."

The shed they were standing in was a ramshackle affair built around two legs of the tubular metal frame that held up the windmill. It was used primarily to house salt blocks and cottonseed cake, but there was a bunk in one corner and a small cook stove in the other. Emory looked out the window at the rain, but Heck watched the water splashing down the holes where the windmill legs came through. "Why'd old Ollie build around the windmill?"

"I donno. I think it's because he'd poured the concrete and thought he'd just go ahead and use it as the floor for the shack."

"Damndest thing I ever saw!"

"Nope. Hooper's Well's crazier by a long shot."

Heck considered a moment. Hooper's Well was pumped by an old one-lunger gasoline engine that was sheltered from the elements by the same roof and walls that sheltered the cowboy put there to tend it. There was a wide hole in the wall for the belt that ran from the pump to the pulley on the engine. One never needed to worry about carbon monoxide poisoning as there was plenty of fresh air coming in from the hole in the wall. In addition to the cook stove, a heating stove tried to compensate during cold weather. It never did.

"I believe you're right," Heck said.

Emory chuckled. "Ole Ollie. Some of his ideas are cockeyed, but it was a lucky day for us when Papa homesteaded next to his place."

The hair on the back of Heck's neck prickled, and he put his hand up to smooth it down. He felt unsettled, uneasy.

Emory walked closer to the window and looked out, shifting from one foot to the other. "We'll soon be out from under this cloud," he said.

Heck could see the sunlight a half-mile distant. He still felt the odd prickling and wondered if it were because of what Emory had said and what he had to say to Emory. Was this how it felt to become estranged from a brother? Was it a physical thing? "Thanks for straightening out that Rafter U fellow," he said, leaving the phrase hanging, so Emory knew there was more to be said.

Emory was still looking out the window. He rubbed his arms and nodded to show he heard.

The tin-roof percussion was less now, and it was easier to talk, but Heck was having trouble finding the right words. Finally, he just said, "I'm gonna marry her."

Emory's head whipped around, and he stared at his brother. "Marry who?"

"The lady in question. You know who I'm talking about."

"You'll have to excuse me. I seem to remember that that particular lady had a husband hangin' mighty close by."

"She's going to leave him. I'm going to work for Henry Coughlin out at Willow Canyon. She'll come there and stay until we can marry."

"You're goin' to Utah?" Emory shook his head. "You fixin' to hire a maid on a cowhand's wages?"

Heck didn't answer.

"You gonna be able to remember to crook your little finger when you drink your coffee and to use them little finger bowls?" Emory made mincing motions with his fingers. "You gonna dress for dinner ever' evenin'?"

Heck rubbed the back of his neck again. He scowled and turned his shoulder on his brother. "At least she'll know to wash the manure off before she makes the biscuits," he said.

Emory grabbed Heck's shoulder and spun him around and struck him so quickly that Heck was caught completely off guard. His head snapped back His arms flew out, and he stumbled backward trying to regain his balance. The last thing he was conscious of was his arm striking the windmill rigging, for at that moment, lightning struck, and he became a conduit for that awesome fury. His feet flew off the floor as his body arched and then fell in a heap on the concrete. The smell of ozone and singed hair mingled with the wisp of smoke that rose from the ring of tiny flames in the middle of his chest burning the cotton fabric of his work shirt.

Emory had been knocked off his feet by the concussion and hit his head on a wall stud. He was unconscious only a second or two, but it took him several moments to realize what had happened. He sat up, saw the stillness of his brother's body and was at once filled with panic and remorse. Crawling over, he pressed his fingers against the fabric to put out the fire.

"Oh, Lord," he said, "don't let him die. Oh, don't die, Heck! I'm sorry. You can have her. Just don't die. Oh, Lord. Oh, Lord."

Heck gave a great, shuddering gasp and began to breathe. Emory dragged him over to the cot and, conscious of his own weakness, wrestled him up on it. Stifling the urge to weep, Emory sat on his heels by his brother and waited for him to open his eyes.

Chapter 24

IT WAS MIDMORNING the next day when Emory stopped Ollie Free's pickup on the ridge overlooking the Diamond E ranch complex. Heck sat beside him whittling on his soapstone, still wearing the plaid shirt with a hole burnt out of the middle of the chest. He had not taken a change of clothes with him, and Emory had no shirt to lend.

When Heck recovered from the lightning strike, the two brothers had spent an enjoyable day together, standing on the roof of Ollie's improbable shack, pulling the pipe on the windmill. They talked of family news: Lucy was expecting in February. Mama was taking in washing for Old Lady Sales. Papa's mining partner was getting cold feet.

The closest they came to speaking of Ruth Reynolds was on the ride back to the Diamond E when Emory said he'd loan his tapaderos to Heck. Emory said Henry's ranch was in brushy country, and his brother would need to wear the hard leather shells over his stirrups to protect his feet. Emory told Heck he should stop by the house and pick them up on his way to catch the bus. Heck thanked him, and that was the last either of them spoke until Emory stopped the truck on the ridge above the ranch.

The place seemed deserted. The afternoon sun created a shimmering blue mirage across the road in front of the bungalows. Both the pickup and Payne's Packard were gone. Heck could see the back of Ruth Reynolds's coupe sticking from between the bungalows, but Goodman's car wasn't evident.

Emory took his cigarette papers out of his pocket, selected one, and slowly made a crease in it. Without taking his eyes from the job at hand, he asked, "Do you remember that flashy chestnut that appeared one day at our place out at Cutter?"

"The one we called Duchess? Sure, I remember. She wasn't a mustang; that was for sure."

"Nope. She was one of them five-hunnerd-dollar horses with a pedigree long as ol' Ollie's face come payday. Papa took his time about finding who she belonged to. I think he figured on gettin' a foal out of her before he went lookin' for the owner." Emory licked the paper and twisted the end of his cigarette. "Do you remember the day he decided to break Duchess to harness?" Lighting the cigarette, he pitched the flaming match out the window and looked inquisitively at Heck.

"Sure, I remember. He had her paired with old Headlight. I was the one that got Lucy out of the way when they bolted."

"I can still see the old gent standin' up on the wagon box, whippin' those horses and cussin' a blue streak, with Duchess all white-eyed, and Headlight—danged if I don't think he was enjoyin' it! They went right over that old windmill fan that was lyin' on the ground. It's a wonder one of 'em—horse or man—didn't get killed."

"Yep, and Mama had her empty fruit jars stored under that windmill. Broke pretty near every one."

They both sat silently, remembering their father standing in the wagon as it pitched and reeled and finally flew through the air as the galloping horses pulled it over the huge silver blades.

Below them, the door of the Reynolds' bungalow suddenly burst open and Sally Goodman sailed out, wading through the phantom pool of the mirage in hasty little steps. Dooley shambled after her, and both of them disappeared behind the machinery shed. Emory started the pickup but didn't put it in gear.

"You know, Heck," Emory said, "I don't think we ever had a better horse to harness than Headlight, but after that, he wasn't worth much."

Heck's eyes twinkled as he held out his hand. "*Gracias, hermano*. I know what you're trying to say. I'm not a horse, and neither is she. Don't worry. It's gonna be all right."

Emory took his hand and shook it, but he couldn't answer Heck's smile. "Just one more thing. If you try to introduce her to Mama before you're married, I'll whup ya."

"I wouldn't do that," Heck said quietly. "You should know that."

"Well, there's lots of things I thought I knew that I don't."

Emory put the truck in first gear, but Goodman's Model A came tearing around the machinery shed, heading up the hill. Emory changed to reverse and backed away, so they could have the right-of-way up the single-lane road. "Sally's in a bit of a hurry," he said.

"She's probably late for a gab session."

When the Model A crested the hill, they could see that Sally was indeed dressed for town, but she looked too grim for a social call. Dooley, seated next to Sally, started pointing at Heck and shouting, and Sally jammed on the brakes so hard it threw him against the windshield and knocked his glasses awry.

She opened the door and scrambled out of the car so fast she forgot to take it out of gear. It lurched forward, almost knocking her to the ground, but the motor didn't die, and the car started putting down the road, driverless. Sally regained her balance and stood flapping her arms in exasperation as Dooley, his glasses hanging across his mouth, looked out the back window at her with round eyes. She yelled at him to move over and stop the car but didn't stay to see if he understood. Instead, she scuttled over to Emory's window.

Sally's face was white, and for once, she seemed bereft of speech. She stood and stared past Emory at Heck for a moment, and then she started trembling. Heck got out, strode around the pickup, and put an arm around her. "What's the matter, Sally?"

She began to hiccup and shook her head as she tried to get a breath.

"Take it easy. That's a girl." Heck spoke soothingly as he walked her around to the back of the pickup and lifted her to sit on the end of the bed. Emory got out and wet his handkerchief from the water bag hanging on the side. He handed it to Heck, who pressed it to her forehead. "Can you tell me what happened?" he asked.

"I don't know," she whispered. "I don't know if I can talk about it. People don't talk about things like that. People don't do things like that."

Dooley apparently had figured out that he was expected to get in the driver's seat and come back because he arrived at that moment, eager to tell his part of the story.

"Naked as a jaybird, he was!" he proclaimed as he slammed the door of Sally's car. "You never seen such ..."

"Hush, Dooley!" Heck commanded.

Dooley's eyes blinked behind his wire-rimmed glasses, and he hushed.

Emory was awkwardly patting Sally's shoulder. Heck stood with his arm around her, waiting until the trembling and hiccupping subsided. Finally, she drew a long, ragged breath and slowly exhaled.

"Can you tell me about it now?" Heck asked.

"Well," she said in a tiny voice, "we were on our way in to the movies. Bob went to El Paso with Alan, and so it was just Dooley and me going in. Ruth was going to look in on Ruby every now and then. We got almost to the highway when Dooley remembered he hadn't brought his money."

"I was gonna buy a new pocketknife."

"Let her tell it, Dooley," admonished Heck.

Sally continued. "We turned around and came back. I drove around to the bunkhouse, so Dooley could just run in and get his money, but he couldn't remember where he put it, so finally I turned off the motor and just sat waiting for him." Sally searched in her pocket, came up with a handkerchief, and blew her nose. "I heard someone screaming. It was a woman, crying, 'Help me. Oh, won't someone help me.' I got out and walked around the shed, and it was coming from Ruth's house."

"Ruth's?" Heck felt his hackles rising. What had that black-browed runt been doing?

"I thought maybe she fell and broke her leg like Mrs. Gibbons did that time when she had to wait two days for help," Sally said, "so I went in without knocking."

"I went in, too," said Dooley.

"She was in the bedroom, lying on the bed. Her hands were tied to the bedposts—one to each one."

Dooley couldn't restrain himself. "Used them fancy neckties, he did."

Sally's chin quivered. "Her clothes were all torn away. She was bleeding at the mouth, and he was standing over her—"

"Buck naked," supplied Dooley.

"Her eyes were—I don't know—kind of hopeless." Sally had been looking at her hands, but now she looked up at Heck. "When she saw me she told me to go and get you."

"Get Heck. That's what she said," echoed Dooley.

"I just turned around and left," Sally said. "I couldn't stay there when he was—with him like that. We were on our way out to Guzman to get you. Thank heaven you're here!"

Heck gave her a squeeze. "Good girl," he said. "Do you think you can come back down with me? She's gonna need your help."

"I'll come, too," Dooley volunteered. "I want you to see him. You've never seen such—"

Heck cut in. "Fine, Dooley. Fine. Just get in the car. He helped Sally to the Model A and went back to his brother.

"You're not plannin' to kill him, are you?" Emory asked.

"Not unless I find he's hurt her worse than I think he has." He extended his hand to Emory. "It looks like this is it. It's not the way I wanted it, but there you go. I'll say goodbye now. There might be some bad blood over this, and I'd just as soon you were out of it."

"Just try to keep me out!" Emory exclaimed. "You're not gettin' rid of me so easy. I'll he'p ya on your way."

"All right, *hermano*. Appreciate it. I'll go ahead and drive Sally down."

Heck drove to the bungalow below and got out. "Wait here. I'll be right back." Striding to the machinery shed, he disappeared for a moment and reappeared, carrying the ancient bullwhip in his left hand. He opened the car door, assisted Sally to alight, and then stalked up the walk to the porch. He held the screen door for Sally then stepped through into the Reynolds's house.

For just a moment, Heck was caught off balance by the richness of the room. Everything, from the sheen of the mahogany table in front of white lace curtains, to the wine-colored pile of the upholstered furniture, said money and substance. For an instant, Heck wondered if he were crazy to think she would want to leave this for what he could offer.

Then Harlan came through the doorway.

Heck felt Emory's hand gripping his arm, and he was glad for it, because he was filled with such a surge of hatred and loathing that he could have throttled the life out of that precise little man and enjoyed doing it.

But he stood quietly beside his brother. Sally was behind him, and Dooley stood behind Emory, looking over his shoulder.

Harlan was completely dressed in shirt, tie, and vest with hair combed and shoes shined. His black brows arched inquisitively, and his mouth curled into a sneer. "I suppose it's too much to expect the locals to knock before entering."

"Did he say 'locals' or 'locos'?" Emory asked in a hoarse whisper.

Heck didn't take his eyes off Harlan. "I think he's trying to tell us how a gentleman would behave."

Harlan's eyes had strayed to the bullwhip in Heck's hand, but they were drawn back to his face as Heck pushed his hat to the back of his head.

Harlan's sneer appeared again. "A gentleman knows to remove his hat when he enters a house."

"Well, now," said Heck, "I had some things to tell you, and I didn't want you to get the idea that I was coming hat-in-hand. So I decided I'd just leave it on." He turned to Sally. "Will you go in and help Miz Reynolds pack? She's gonna be on a working ranch. You'll know what to take."

Sally stepped forward but hesitated, looking at Harlan standing in the doorway. Heck, without taking his eyes from

Harlan, dropped the coil of whip to the floor where it cracked on the shiny hardwood. He didn't spare a moment thinking how he must have looked, a tall, grim cowboy with his shirt partly burnt away, holding the handle of a long, black, vicious-looking whip.

Harlan stepped aside, and Sally slipped by him and into the bedroom.

"Now then," Heck said. "There's a lawyer in Hot Springs, name of Alfred Pettybone. On Monday, you're to go in and see him about a divorce. You can charge desertion or adultery or whatever it takes. You'll have plenty of legal grounds. In a year's time, I expect to be able to marry Ruth. If she's not free then, I'm coming back, and I'll use this whip on you." He took the time to coil it up to give Harlan the benefit of knowing how long it was. "That's a promise."

There was a rustle at the bedroom doorway, and Ruth appeared in an ivory satin dressing gown. She sagged against the doorjamb and her eyes met Heck's. "I heard you say my name," she said huskily.

For a moment Heck could say nothing, could do nothing but stare at the battered face she turned up to him. Her bottom lip was split and swollen. One eye was puffed to a slit, and a bright red patch decorated her left cheek.

Behind him, Heck heard Emory say, "*Ay, chihuahua!*"

Heck gave her a tender look and walked to the bedroom door. Standing close to her, shutting out all who were spectators, he gently put his hand on her cheek. "Hello, Darlin'," he said softly. "I've come for you."

Ruth turned her face to kiss the roughness of the calluses on his hands and fingers as she leaned against him.

Heck looked up to see Sally, frozen in the act of closing a suitcase, watching them. He spoke to her: "Would you help her to dress, Sally?" Then he spoke to Ruth. "We'll leave as soon as you're ready." He felt her nod against his chest.

Sally came to assist, and Ruth went with her, leaning on her arm like a feeble old woman.

Heck turned back to Harlan. His eyes were like flint, though his voice was silky. "When you don't have anything to do of an evening," he said, "you might just mosey over to the cookhouse and listen to some of Shorty's stories about the vigilance committee. You'll find out how the 'locals' feel about a man who would hit a lady."

Harlan folded his arms and said smugly, "You may call her a lady now, but when she walks out that door with you, she'll be a whore."

Heck answered with his right fist. It connected solidly with Harlan's chin, and the arms that had been folded spread and made circles in the air as he was driven backwards. He fell over a footstool and lay for a moment with eyes turned back and legs lying limply flexed.

When Harlan's eyes started fluttering, Emory went to stand over the inert figure. "Come he'p me, Dooley." Pulling his knife out of his pocket, he opened it and tested the blade with his thumb. "You undo his belt and slide down his pants. It can't be much different than doin' a yearlin' calf."

Dooley was stopped in mid-stride by a screech from the front doorway. They all—Heck, Emory, Dooley, and Harlan, still on the floor—looked to see Ruby Payne, pale, her eyes like two burnt holes in a blanket, standing in a long flannel nightgown with her ginger hair in tangles down her back.

"I don't know what's going on here," she said in a thin, breathless voice, "but I think you're carrying fun too far, Emory Benham. Put that knife away."

"Yes ma'am." Emory folded the knife against his leg, put it back in his pocket, and grabbed a straight-back chair from against the wall for Ruby to sit on.

As she sat, Harlan rose, his hand testing his belt buckle.

"Afternoon, Miz Payne," Heck said, taking off his hat. Emory, standing behind Ruby, removed his, too.

Sally appeared in the doorway and said, "I think you'll have to carry her out, Heck. There's nothing broken. She's just all gone." As Heck stepped past her into the bedroom, Sally's eyes widened. "Oh, Hello, Ruby. What are you doing out of bed?"

"I've come to see what all this racket—oh my. What in the world?" Ruby got up as Heck came into the living room with Ruth in his arms.

"She ran into another door," Heck said, jerking his head toward Harlan. "I'm taking her away with me, ma'am."

"Oh, Heck," Ruby moaned. "Oh, dear."

"Just a minute, Heck," Ruth murmured. He stopped and she looked at Harlan through her good eye. "I heard what you just said. I intended to give you back my diamond ring when I left, but I think, being a whore, that I've earned it today."

Dooley clapped and said, "That's the time!"

Ruth looked at Dooley, and the corners of her mouth turned up crookedly. "Would you roll up that rug that's by the window?" she asked. "It's mine. I'll take it with me."

"Yes, ma'am." Dooley sprang to do her bidding.

They all, except for Harlan, followed Heck out to Ruth's car. Emory put his hand under Ruby's elbow, and Sally carried one suitcase and Ruth's purse while Dooley carried the other satchel and the Bokhara rug.

While his brother strapped the bags onto the rack, Heck settled Ruth and closed her door. He turned to Sally. "Much obliged for your help," he said, and then to Ruby, "I'm sorry to distress you, Miz Payne. I hope this doesn't make you feel worse. You'll take her and put her to bed, won't you, Sally?"

"I'll see you off, first," Ruby said. She offered her hand to Heck.

He took her hand and pressed it with both of his. "Goodbye, ma'am. And thank you."

Heck shook hands with Emory. "*Adios, hermano.* Thanks for standing by."

"*De nada.* By the way, what are you gonna do if he hasn't turned her loose this time next year?"

Heck smiled. "Guess I'll have to learn how to use that whip." He shook Dooley's hand then swung into the car, started the engine, and backed out. As he headed toward the ridge, Ruby, Sally, Emory, and Dooley waved farewell.

Heck's saddle and the rest of his outfit were still at Tucker's Well, so he turned in that direction. As they bounced over the uneven road, he kept glancing at Ruth. She rode for the most part with her eyes closed, but from time to time she would touch his leg with her fingertips, and he would close his hand over hers.

The shack was empty when Heck got to the cow camp. He went inside and took two sugar lumps out of the sugar bowl and put them in his pocket. Then he got the Montgomery Ward envelope from under his mattress and took out his savings—seventy-nine dollars. He put the money in his pocket and dropped the envelope in the stove. He changed his shirt and packed the burnt one along with the rest of his meager wardrobe in a canvas bag and stowed it in the rumble seat.

Mike rode in just as Heck was tying up his bedroll. He dismounted and stood holding his horse's reins as Heck carried the bedroll out to the car and tossed it atop the things in the rumble seat. It stuck up above the roof of the car, even when Heck cinched it down as tight as he could.

Ruth called to him from the car, where she still sat with her head resting against the doorpost. He leaned in closely, since her voice was so faint. "What's that in the rumble seat?" she asked.

"That's my bedroll," he said.

"Tom Mix just uses one blanket. I've seen him in the movies."

Heck smiled tenderly, glad that she was feeling well enough to tease him. "The ground's a lot softer in the movies."

Heck stuck his saddle blanket, bridle, and spurs behind the seat and stood, looking at his saddle. There was no more room, but without his own saddle, he was unemployed. So he threw it across the hood of the car and tied it down with a short piece of rope. He took the quirt that was hanging on his saddle horn and approached his friend. "Afternoon, Michael. I'm pulling out now." He nodded toward the car. "Miz Reynolds is going with me. I think she's feeling too bad to say goodbye." He offered the quirt to Mike. "I made this the other week. I'd like you to have it."

Mike's eyes went from Heck to the car where the battered face showed through the windshield. He swallowed. "Thanks, Heck." He had to make a second try because the words didn't come out right the first time.

"I'd be obliged if you'd take Spook. I know you'll take good care of 'im."

"All right, Heck."

Heck reached in his pocket for the sugar and walked to the corral. Spook trotted up and took the sweet morsel from his hand. "Goodbye, old fella," Heck said softly. "You treat old Mike right, you hear? I'm sure gonna miss you. Yeah. Never been a pony like old Spook." He patted him on the neck and turned away, feeling all of a sudden very weary.

Heck got in the car and turned it around, waving to Mike as he went past. He watched in the rearview mirror, but his friend didn't wave back. He just stood there, holding the quirt in both hands as he watched his comrade drive away with someone else's wife.

Chapter 25

IT WAS A strange beginning for an idyll.

At Socorro, Heck stopped for gas and food. The owner of the gas station chewed on a matchstick as he worked the lever back and forth, filling the glass-faced tank at the top of the pump. While he pumped, he stared, first at the bedroll sitting like a huge canvas jellyroll atop the rumble seat, then at the saddle on the hood, and finally at the woman who leaned her head against the back of the seat and closed her eyes, her hair spread in a dusky cloud underneath her head, her dark lashes making black crescents against the bruises on her cheeks. At Heck's request, the attendant rummaged around inside the service station, found a mason jar, and put some coal oil in it. Heck paid him, grateful to be running now on gas that he, rather than Harlan, had purchased.

That evening they stopped at a roadside restaurant, and Heck went in to order. Parked in the shadows, away from staring passersby, they ate hamburgers wrapped in waxed paper and drank Coke from bottles. Then Heck doctored Ruth's lip with the coal oil, rubbing it on gently with his finger.

As evening turned into night, Ruth slept lying on the seat with her head in his lap. The moon, full and bright, trailed behind them, making a gray ribbon of the highway and casting a black shadow that raced ahead of them across the flat and through the mountain pass into Arizona.

They picked up Route 66 in Holbrook and turned west, pulling into an all-night station in Flagstaff at two in the morning. To the north lay an empty two hundred mile stretch across the Navajo Reservation. Driving through the darkness, Heck tried not to think about whether or not he would still be welcome at Henry Coughlin's or about what they would do if he weren't. Battling weariness, he tried to keep a sharp eye out for cattle or wild burros on the road. But his mind kept returning to the time, just a few hours distant, when he'd be standing on the doorstep of Willow Canyon Ranch, and his soul felt as dark as the inky void beyond the headlights.

His mood lightened with the approach of dawn. The cliffs on his right began to be visible, black silhouettes pasted on a blue-black sky, and ahead of him he could make out the hulking mountain that they would have to cross. By the time they had ascended the snaking route to the top of the Kaibab Plateau and were coming down the other side, the sun was up and illuminating the vista in front of them. Miles away, mesas rose in colored stairsteps—red, white, and in the far distance, pink. The beauty of it swept over Heck, and he almost woke Ruth to show her, but he let her sleep. He could show her other vistas just as beautiful when they got to Willow Canyon.

She sat up as he slowed down for the town limits of Kanab, Utah. Blinking, she brushed her hair away from her face and looked at the red sandstone cliffs surrounding the town. "Where are we?"

"This is Kanab. It's the nearest town to the ranch."

"It's prettier than Hot Springs."

"It may be pretty, but you can't buy a drink of whisky here."

Her brows went up and she turned her head to examine the red brick houses with neat lawns and picket fences. "How about wine?"

He shook his head. "You have to go across the line into Arizona."

"How far is that?"

"A couple miles south. How're you feeling?"

"Better."

They were out of Kanab now, traveling north through a canyon where the red sandstone walls were layered, twisted and hollowed into a myriad of shapes. Ruth rode in silence, but when they turned off the highway onto a gravel road, she asked, "What if he won't let me stay? You can't tell him we're married. He's bound to find out different from Ruby."

"No, I'll tell him what happened. It'll be all right."

"How do you know? Maybe his wife will be angry that you've got a kept woman with you."

"You're not a kept woman yet. I haven't had a chance to keep you."

"You know what I mean."

Heck smiled at the frown on her brow. "His wife won't be angry," he said. "And Henry will certainly understand. He married someone that people won't accept." He almost added, "... too," but caught himself in time.

Ruth turned to face him and tucked her legs under her. "Who did he marry?"

"He married a Mexican."

Ruth lifted inquisitive brows.

"Her name is Romelia," Heck explained. "After Henry's first wife died, she came to keep house and take care of the children. He fell in love with her and married her."

"When was that?"

"Oh, I guess it's been sixteen, eighteen years."

"You can't be serious. They've been married for that long and people still don't accept her?"

"Close friends do, but you've got to understand how things are out here."

Ruth picked up her purse and set it in her lap. "Tell me."

"If you're white, you don't marry a Mexican."

"Period?"

"Period."

"Because they're inferior? Because they're bad people? Why?"

"Certainly not because they're inferior. Some of the finest people I know are Mexicans. One of my best friends is Angel Armijo, Ildefonso's son, but I would never think of marrying his sister. And he wouldn't think of marrying mine."

"And yet, Henry Coughlin married Romelia."

"They knew what they were doing. They chose to live a life apart." Heck pointed over to the left. "See the smoke rising over there? That's the ranch house. I'll stop and just tell them I'm here. I won't introduce you 'til you're feeling better."

"Looking better, you mean. Thank you. You're very kind. I mean that."

Heck reached over and touched her cheek. He felt her cover his hand with her own, and then he felt her lips as she kissed his palm. He smiled at her, and she held his hand in both of hers as they drove the last half mile to the Willow Canyon Ranch House

.

Ruth sat in the car and watched as Heck walked to the white stucco house set in a clearing surrounded by stunted cedar trees just under the brow of a red sandstone cliff. She had a brief look at a tall man with stooped shoulders and grizzled ginger hair, who answered Heck's knock and held the screen door wide, so he could come in.

Ruth opened her purse and took out a mirror. She was heartened by what she saw. The split in her lip was scabbed over, and one cheek had a purple bruise, but much of the swelling was gone from her eye. Though her shoulder pained her, and her ribs felt bruised, she didn't have the shocky, unreal feeling of yesterday.

Heck returned, carrying two steaming mugs in one hand and something tied up in a white cloth in the other. When she leaned over to open the door for him, he handed her the parcel. "Romelia sent you some coffee and tortillas."

Ruth peeked inside the dishtowel. "They're still warm."

"She makes them every morning. Have one. We're still a ways from Cottonwood Springs."

Ruth chewed on a tortilla and held her coffee, so it wouldn't slosh as Heck pulled the car back onto the gravel road that ran past the ranch house. "Cottonwood Springs, Willow Canyon. That's a lot of trees."

"You find 'em both wherever you have water. Cottonwood Springs feeds the creek that carved Willow Canyon. It's at the end of the road. Last time I was there, I thought it was lonely. I won't think so this time." He pointed with a rolled-up tortilla. "It's over in that direction, this side of that notch. I'm glad that's where he's put us. It's got running water."

Ruth giggled. When Heck looked inquiringly at her, she said, "I'm just thinking of what Bunny Ashton would say to see me excited to get to my new home. The one with running water." She went off into another peal of laughter, and Heck joined her.

"Henry mentioned something about the stove," he said. "The fire box has rusted through, so ashes sometimes drop down on the bread."

"Oh, but my dear, it improves the flavor."

"And the roof leaks."

She smiled. "Only when it rains; I'm sure. When do you start to work?"

"Today."

"Today! But you just got here. You haven't slept all night. We have to move in. How can you work today?"

"How long does it take to move in two suitcases and a canvas bag? I need to gather the horses I'm gonna use, get my gear ready, check out the corrals. No one's been at Cottonwood Springs for a while, so there's probably lots to do."

It had been ten years since Heck worked for Henry Coughlin. The intervening years had made the shack at Cottonwood Springs into a snug house in Heck's memory. He himself had installed the water system that ran from a barrel sunk in the ground at the spring on the hill behind the house.

He was devastated at what he saw at the end of the road—a tiny, weather-beaten structure with no curtains to soften the stark blankness of the windows. It had a porch of sorts, but one sheet of the corrugated tin that covered it had been blown off and hung awkwardly at the corner, swaying indecisively in the breeze.

They both sat in the parked car for a moment, staring at the two-room shack in front of them. "You did say it had running water?" Ruth asked in a tentative voice.

Heck nodded, mortified.

"Well," she said briskly. "My people missed the Mayflower, but they were on the next boat over. I daresay they were harder put than we. I come from good stock, Heck. I can make a home of it."

He looked at her in wonder. "It's all right then?"

"Yes, but I'm incredibly ignorant. You'll have to teach me everything. You may think you got the worst of the bargain. Shall we look inside?"

Heck got out. As she got out after him on his side, he saw her wince.

"You all right?" He put his arm around her.

Ruth looked up at him and nodded with dark eyes intense and lips parted. He put both arms lightly around her and bent down, touching her lips softly at first then harder as he pulled her closer. As he kissed her, desire—that instinctive drive toward coupling—flashed, flared, threatened to explode within him for want of release.

Heck tasted salt on his tongue and suddenly realized that it was blood. Pulling away, he saw that Ruth's lip was bleeding again, and he cursed himself for being a clumsy fool. "I'm sorry, Darlin'." He pulled out his soiled handkerchief and looked at it dubiously.

She laughed. "I have one in my bag. Will you get it for me?" She cupped her hand under her chin. "Quickly! It's about to drip."

Heck dove into the car, grabbed her purse, and gave it to her. She opened it and took out a lace-edged hanky which she held against her lip with one hand. Then she took his handkerchief and used it to wipe the blood off his face.

The spell was broken. Heck looked ruefully at her as he set her handbag on the fender of the car and jerked his head toward the house. Her eyes twinkled over the white handkerchief she still held to her lip, and together they walked up the two steps to the porch.

"Screen door needs a new spring," he said as he opened it for her.

She stood in the doorway, silent and still. His eyes moved around the room, and he saw the room as she must be seeing it. A black cast-iron cook stove sat against the opposite wall with an empty woodbox sitting beside it. Next to the woodbox, on the wall to his right, were six powder boxes, stacked three high to form cubbyholes. He saw they were stocked with dried beans, sugar, flour, and cornmeal. Above them, two shelves held canned goods, flatirons, mixing bowls and cooking utensils. A small wooden table and two chairs sat in front of the window of the wall facing the porch. Above it was a shelf with crockery and flatware. Next to the powder boxes, about waist-high, was a faucet. Below the faucet, two buckets sat, stacked one inside the other.

"Where's the sink?" she asked.

"Beg pardon?"

"There's no sink. How can you have running water without a sink?"

"There's a dishpan hanging on the wall." He pointed.

"Where does the water go when you're through with it?"

"Out the door."

"Oh." She walked to the door of the bedroom and looked inside. Sunlight, filtering through a grimy window, fell on the double bed with its sagging middle, decrepit patchwork quilt, and two pillows resembling lumpy growths attached to the rusty bedstead. Three of the ever-useful powder boxes were stacked against the outside wall, and there were a dozen spikes in a row high up for hanging clothes. A pair of abandoned Levi's hung alone, limp and forlorn.

Ruth turned and looked at Heck, standing with his hat in his hands, humbly watching her survey what he had to offer.

"And this is the bedroom," she said.

He looked past her to the bed then back to her and nodded.

Ruth walked over to him and kissed him gently. "I love you," she said. "We shall be very happy here." Then she leaned her head against his chest. "Heck?"

"Hmm?"

"I have to bathe."

He didn't say anything.

"I need to sit and soak away every trace of him. I need to do that before ..."

"That's all right, Darlin'. We'll fix you up." Tipping up her face, he took her handkerchief and dabbed away the blood that had seeped from her cut lip. Then he kissed her forehead. "Let's make some coffee first, though."

He went outside to get some wood. "Coffeepot's on the shelf," he said over his shoulder as he went through the door. Detouring by the car, he got the jar of coal oil before loading up at the woodpile.

When he stepped in the house, Ruth had the coffeepot rinsed and prepared. He filled the firebox of the stove, poured kerosene on the wood, and lit it. Then he put the stove lids back in place and opened the damper.

Ruth set the coffeepot on the stove, and Heck rinsed out the buckets. He threw the water out the door and filled them again. "For your bath," he explained as he set them on the stove.

While the coffee was brewing, they moved in. Heck took his saddle and tack down to the shed by the corral while Ruth put away their clothes, marveling at his scanty wardrobe and puzzling at the shirt with the charred hole in it. She checked the sheets on the bed, wrinkled her nose, and stripped them.

She emerged from the bedroom with the soiled linens in her arms to see Heck with a coiled rope in one hand, a coffee cup in the other, and a number-two tin tub at his feet.

He cast the rope on the table and kicked the tub. "I've washed it out for you," he said, and added as she continued looking at the tub with knit brows. "It's for your bath." He dragged a chair over. "You sit on the chair with your feet in to wash your feet and legs. Then you sit in the tub with your legs out to wash the rest."

"I need to wash these sheets," she said.

"Washboard's hanging around to the side. When you finish your bath, take this tub out for your wash water. There's another tub out there you can use for rinsing. Cold water'll do for that." Noting the bemused look on her face, he paused, observing her over the brim of his cup as he took a sip of coffee. "You ever done any laundry?"

"No."

"Ever seen any laundry done?"

"I watched your mother from the hill on Friday. I've seen Ruby and Sally hang out clothes."

"Then come on, Darlin'. I'll teach you how." He put one arm around her and swept her out the door.

"I think if you stand on the ground and put the tub on the porch, it'll be just the right height." He took down the tub and washboard and left them on the porch as he hopped off to demonstrate. Taking the sheets she still held in her arms, he placed them on the dusty wooden planks next to the washboard and talked her through the washing and rinsing process. He told her how to wring them out and showed her where to hang them to dry. Ruth reached up to touch the single strand of cotton rope that ran from the porch to a spindly pole planted in the side yard. Wiping the dust off her fingers, she followed Heck back inside and watched him pour the steaming contents of one of the buckets into the tub.

"This can be your bath," he said. "When you're ready to get in the tub, just add cold water 'til it's comfortable. When you're through, drag the tub out on the porch to do the laundry."

He put the kettle back on the stove and picked up the rope he had left lying on the table. "I'm gonna get me a horse or two. Old Henry keeps cow ponies in a pasture down the way. They come and water at the creek, and he's got a horse-catching corral there. I won't be afoot too much longer." He pushed his hat to the back of his head, leaned down to kiss her on the cheek, and was gone.

Ruth was left with his empty coffee cup and a tub of water that was rapidly cooling. She stripped off her clothing, noting bruises on her arms and upper body. She sat on the chair to wash her feet and legs with the bar of Ivory soap she found in the dishpan. Then, according to directions, she lowered herself into the tub, splashing the water around to lave her breasts and shoulders. Finally, she just sat soaking, contemplating her ancestors who missed the Mayflower and wondering what they did when the rim of the tub hurt the undersides of their knees.

Chapter 26

THE NEXT MORNING, Ruth woke to the feeling of a rough hand on her cheek. She opened her eyes, frowned in confusion, and then smiled as she remembered where she was. Heck, fully dressed, knelt beside her, and she put her hand over his.

"Hello, Darlin'," he said.

"Good morning. Is it morning? It's still dark."

He smiled back at her. "It's early yet. I'll be back in a couple hours for breakfast."

"What shall I fix? There's hardly anything to cook."

"Biscuits and gravy are fine. Same as we had for supper."

"All right. Do you have to go? Last night hardly qualified as a wedding night, with you dozing off in your chair—and how you could fall asleep in a kitchen chair, I don't know."

"Comes from knowing how to nap in the saddle. Besides, last night wasn't our wedding night." He kissed her gently. "Coffee's on the back of the stove. I'll be home in a while."

"Goodbye, dearest," she said softly. She felt the pressure of his hand squeezing hers, and then he was gone. She heard the jingle of his spurs as he passed through the other room, the sound of his boots on the porch, and later, his voice as he spoke to one of the horses he had brought up to the corral.

Ruth lay in bed thinking about yesterday, how, after her bath, she had dried herself with the dishtowel that Romelia had sent tortillas in rather than using the dingy towel that hung on the nail by the faucet. She thought of how she had wrestled with buckets and tubs of water, sodden sheets, and the corrugated washboard that bruised her knuckles. She thought about her introduction to wood stoves, to coal oil lamps, and to outhouses. She thought about the man who had taught her to make biscuits and about the biscuits he made, flaky and light and golden brown, and dusted with grey powder from the crack in the firebox.

Heck had been tired. That was obvious, and she was ashamed that she couldn't provide for him when he came home hungry. He didn't complain, merely saying that he was used to fixing supper for himself.

As they had eaten, he told her about the horses he had snared and what his plans were for the morrow. In the time that it took her to walk outside and fling out the dishwater, he had fallen asleep in his chair.

She had eyed him with dismay and then laughed at herself for expecting more from a man who had been up for forty hours straight. She shook him awake long enough to put him to bed and then sat alone, making a list of things she needed to set up housekeeping, heading the list with bath towels. Finally, she went to bed, slipping in beside him, between crisp, sweet-smelling sheets she had washed and hung out in the sun to dry.

This morning, as the sun rose, Ruth judged she had been long enough abed. She got up and put on a cool gray chambray dress with a full circle skirt. Sitting at the kitchen table, she looked out over the corrals and tin-roofed shed while she had a cup of coffee. Then she put water on to heat, intending to scrub everything in the room. When the place was clean, she thought, she would see what she could do about making it look prettier.

The sun was warm on her neck and arms as she stood on the porch pouring hot water from a bucket into a tub where were gathered all the rags, towels and old feed sacks she had found lying around the shack. At that moment, she heard Heck whooping and hollering and looked up in time to see him careening down the hill on a big bay horse. Across the creek and up to the porch he galloped, stopping in a cloud of red dust in front of her.

"I thought you'd be excited about my biscuits," she said, smiling her welcome, "but isn't this overdoing it a little bit?"

"We'll have the biscuits later," he said. "I've got something to show you. Get on back."

He turned the bay around, so she could easily step off the porch and mount behind him from the near side, but she hesitated.

"I've never ridden a horse."

"All you gotta do is hold onto me. Hurry! I've got something to show you, and it won't last. Hike your skirt up, if you have to, to sit astride."

Ruth did as he bid, holding on around his waist. She squealed and tightened her hold as the big horse broke into a trot but relaxed a little when he hit a lope.

Crossing the creek, they climbed the trail to the top of the mesa and headed east across the flat. At a place where the ground sloped away to a grassy dell, kept green by a seeping spring, they stopped.

"Look!" he said.

Ruth peeked over his shoulder and sharply drew in her breath. There below them, filling the dell and spilling over onto higher ground, flitting, flickering, catching the sunlight and reflecting it, making the morning gay as Mardi Gras, were monarch butterflies, thousands of them.

Heck swung his right leg over the saddle horn and slid to the ground then reached up to help Ruth alight. They stood side by side, looking down at the three-dimensional, black and orange kaleidoscope that shifted and changed its patterns, sparkling and swirling in the early morning air.

Ruth pulled Heck downhill into the middle of the migration then dropped his hand and spread her arms wide, turning slowly through the tiger-colored cloud as it ebbed and flowed around her. She felt the soft brush of wings on her arms and face as they fluttered against her, tickling, tingling, until finally they were gone—Halloween confetti tossed on the wind and blowing north.

Ruth dropped her arms and turned around. "Oh, Heck!" she cried. "It's an omen!" She was going to say more, but she stopped when she saw the look in his eyes. She had seen that look before.

Slowly she went to him. She took off his hat, threw it to the ground, and pulled his mouth down to hers. Feeling his arms around her, feeling his body against hers, she pressed against him and kissed his chin, his cheek, his ear. "Come lie down."

The grass made a soft bed that smelled like hay. She lay and stretched eager arms to him as he paused to take off his chaps. Then, as he sat beside her and unbuckled his spurs, she stroked his back and tugged on his shirtsleeve until, at last, he turned to lie beside her.

His mouth was warm and urgent, and the hot blood that quickened her pulse beat in rhythm with his. Driven by a hunger that demanded satiety rather than pleasure, their union was brief and fleeting as the butterflies. When it was over, they lay back on the grass, and she was wistful to have squandered the moment.

Heck sighed, a great, long, breathy exhalation, more eloquent than words.

Ruth turned her head and kissed him just below the ear. "Was it all you hoped it would be?" she whispered.

He waited too long to answer, and she propped her head on one elbow, looking down at him, half questioning, half smiling.

He reached up and brushed back a lock of her hair. "I hoped it would be married."

She laughed. "Do you think we're living in sin?"

He was up on one elbow now, facing her, his eyes on a piece of grass he was removing from her hair. He didn't respond to her laughter, simply answering quietly, "Yes."

"But who's to say what sin is? How can something that good be sinful?"

"Well now, God pretty much defined it. He didn't say you couldn't do what we've just done. He just said that things had to take the proper order."

She frowned. "Do you think that God is going to send down a bolt of lightning and strike you for committing adultery?"

Heck surprised her by throwing his head back and giving a great shout of laughter. "Hell, Darlin'," he said. "He did that when I announced my intentions. No telling what he'll do now that I've committed the act."

"But you believe he will?"

"Oh, yes. I think it surely will happen."

"And yet you went ahead?"

"Didn't have much choice."

"What do you mean by that?"

"My love for you is greater than my fear of God. I believe in His justice, though, and when the punishment is dealt to me, I hope I'm man enough not to whine." He leaned over and kissed her. "Come on, Darlin', it's time to go. I am a working cowboy; you know."

Ruth looked curiously at Heck as he stood and refastened the clothing he had so recklessly undone a little while before. She rearranged her underclothing and pulled down the skirt of her chambray dress as he buckled his chaps and put on his spurs. Reaching up so he could help her rise, she walked in the circle of his arm back to where the bay horse was cropping grass.

Heck swung into the saddle and kicked free of the stirrup, so she could mount behind him. Then he turned the bay's head toward Cottonwood Springs.

When they got back to their little cabin, Heck stoked the fire while Ruth mixed up the biscuits. As she made gravy, he went to the shed, returning with a stack of empty feed sacks. He sat at the table and patiently began to unravel the bottom seams, watching her at the stove as he wound the resulting pile of string into a ball.

They dallied over breakfast, savoring the morning moments as they ate their plain fare. Heck spoke little, but to her, his glances were sonnets, lilting and lyrical. They conjured up grassy, butterfly-laden dells and spoke of forever as if it were assured.

Finally, he stood to go. He kissed her and lingered over instructions about how to cook pinto beans for supper, and finally he left.

She watched him cross the creek and answered his wave as he rode up the hill. Then she turned to her tasks for the day.

Chapter 27

WITH NOTHING BETWEEN her and the elements but a half-inch of weathered board, Ruth's relationship with the earth went from nodding acquaintance to soul sister. She loved the way the time of day changed the color of the cliffs that surrounded the cabin in a semicircle. Early mornings they were orange or flaming red; evenings they were purple. She loved the astringent aroma of pine or the fruity bouquet of new-mown alfalfa and often thought she could make a fortune if she could bottle the fragrance.

No matter how humble the nighttime errand, stepping outside the shack was an excursion into splendor. Surrounded by stars, Ruth was amazed at their brilliance and abundance and was tilted a little off balance by the incredible depth of space. Living as she had in artificial light, the nighttime sky had been hidden. She was twenty-nine years old and had just found it.

And she found, as well, the treasure of the southwest. Sitting at the spring and watching the icy font that poured from the damp red earth, she thought it was like money in the bank. It was security. No matter how hot the day or how dry the wind, she could think of her spring and know her hankie dipped in it would come out dripping and cool to wipe her arms and face and neck, and she could endure.

She settled into the rhythm of the earth. She rose early with the sun and the birds, fixed breakfast, put water on to heat, set her sponge to rise for bread, put beans on to cook for dinner. Her wash was always done and gathered in by midday. She learned to do her ironing early in the coolness of the morning as well.

During the heat of the afternoon, she sat under the giant cottonwood by the spring and sketched studies of the shack and fences or of the shed and adjacent watering trough. Heck was delighted with her talent though she had never thought much of it except as handy in caricaturing teachers at school. He surprised her one day with a book on line drawing. Coughlin's son, Sonny, had been going into Tucson, and he had him get it. Ruth was touched at Heck's thoughtfulness, but she wasn't interested in studying technique. In the end, he read the book. She laughed at him and teased him at his seriousness in wanting her to learn, but she answered the questions he asked, and they learned together.

Ruth always bathed and changed into a clean dress in the late afternoon before setting the table and putting on her apron to fix dinner. She wanted to be fresh and pretty when Heck came home. Watching out the window at the trail across the creek, she always felt a fluttering in her breast when he crested the hill, and she twirled the soapstone ring that she wore on the third finger of her left hand.

Heck apparently wasn't dismayed to find she was an indifferent horsewoman. Rather than try to teach her to ride well enough to handle one of the half-broken cow ponies he himself rode, he arrived one afternoon leading a chestnut gelding, the result of Sonny Coughlin's first venture into horse-trading ten years ago. Sonny had thought the horse had lots of promise and named him Lightning, but Henry changed it to Plug. Docile and disinclined to do more than shamble along at a fast walk, Plug was just right for Ruth.

She had kept the Levi's she found hanging on the nail in the bedroom. On impulse one day, she slipped them on and found they were a tolerable fit. When Romelia sent up a pair of hand-me-down boots saved from Sonny's adolescence, Ruth was delighted. She put on the pants and boots and was rewarded by a low whistle from Heck.

Putting her thumbs in her waistband, she swaggered across the bedroom. "Don't you think I look tough?"

He pulled her close and kissed her. "Tough as whitleather."

"What's that?"

"Whitleather? It's sinew." When she still looked questioningly at him, he added, "Remember the part of the roast last night that was too tough to eat? That's whitleather."

She put her arms around his neck, murmured, "Well, just call me Miz Whitleather," and she lifted her lips for another kiss.

The part of the Coughlin range that extended from Cottonwood Springs was too rough for a wagon, so much of Heck's work was done with packhorses. With a string of four or five tied together, lead rope to tail, Heck would be gone for a day or two at a time.

Sometimes Ruth went with him. He'd wake her an hour before dawn and take a lantern out to rig the pack saddles while she fixed breakfast and got into her Levi's and boots. They were on the trail by the time the horizon turned blue, riding by the spring, feeling the cool heaviness of the moisture-laden air. Heading east, they watched as the sunrise played out its pageant before them.

They didn't talk much as they rode, but once, sitting on a rock, drinking coffee and eating jerky and biscuits, Ruth laughed to think that she had friends from back east who paid big money to have this kind of experience.

Heck showed her fossils in the shale of mountainsides and cliff dwellings hanging onto craggy bluffs. He showed her dinosaur tracks and petroglyhs under sandstone overhangs. And he showed her sweeping vistas of mesas marching in ranks, growing purple as they faded into the distant haze.

Ruth teased Heck as she watched him work, asking him when he was going to get a real job. She said one shouldn't enjoy a job as much as Heck did. But she was proud of him because Romelia had told her that packing a horse was an art, and it wasn't every cowboy who could manage a pack string. That's why Henry was so glad to have Heck back.

They rode into Cottonwood Springs one midmorning in early August to find a stake bed truck parked in front of the shack and Emory asleep in the shade of the porch with his hat over his eyes. At the sound of their approach, he sat up and rubbed his face with his hand. "By damn, Heck. Can't you come in a little quieter? How's a fella supposed to get some shut-eye around here?"

Heck smiled down at his brother. "Hello, Emory. You lost?"

"Hell, no, but I was afraid you was. Miz Coughlin said you shoulda been back yesterday." Dragging his watch out of his pocket, he looked at it and said, "I was gonna give you one more hour. Then I got to go."

Heck pushed his hat to the back of his head. "Boy howdy, it's good to see you. What'cha doing over in these parts?"

Emory stood and stretched. "Old Ollie bought one of them Brahma bulls from a fella up in Cedar City, and I told 'em I'd come fetch it. I wanted to bring you those tapaderos. Brought your fiddle, too, and there's a bit of news I thought you'd be interested in." He tipped his hat to Ruth. "Mornin', ma'am."

Ruth smiled her welcome. "Good morning."

Heck twisted in the saddle to look back at her. "Would you go make us some coffee, Whitleather? Emory and I'll go take care of the horses."

Ruth got down, handed the reins to Heck and nodded an "excuse me" to Emory before mounting the steps of the porch and going inside.

Emory held his hat in his hands and answered her nod then turned and followed his brother to the corral.

Ruth watched from the doorway as Heck swung down from his horse and shook Emory's hand. Then she whisked around inside the house, making coffee, changing into a dress, combing her hair. She looked critically around the tiny room—at the feed-sack curtains she had tacked at the windows and at the newly painted shelves, table, and chairs. She straightened the frame Heck had made for one of her drawings, and on impulse, went to the bedroom for her rug and put it on the floor in front of the table. Emory was their first visitor.

She kept looking out the window at the men. At first, she was apprehensive that she would not be ready in time. Then she became irritated that they had not yet come in for coffee. After stripping the horses and taking care of feed and water, they stood talking at the corral. Then they went over to the truck and climbed up on the bed to look at the ugly, humpbacked brute inside. From the laughing and gesticulating, she knew the talk had turned from that specific bull to cattle in general. They climbed down and sat on their heels in the shade of the truck and continued their conversation.

Finally, she went to the screen. "Coffee's ready," she called.

Heck looked up and waved, but it was a minute or two before he stood. He signaled Emory to wait there and came in.

"Thank you, Darlin'," he said as he took two cups from the shelf and poured them full. He sent her a happy glance before he strode out, letting the screen door bang behind him.

Ruth sat drumming her fingers on the table as she watched the brothers drink their coffee as they hunkered by the truck. Then Emory got the tapaderos and an old battered violin case from the cab and gave them to Heck. They both walked around to the driver's side where they stood another ten minutes in lighthearted conversation. Finally, Emory climbed into the truck and leaned out the door to shake his brother's hand. He gestured toward the shack and said something, and Heck nodded before he stepped back to let the truck turn around. Emory tooted the horn in farewell, and Heck waved the taps. He stood and watched until there was nothing but a dust trail hanging in the air and the hum of a descent made in second gear.

Whistling, Heck came up the porch steps and into the house. He set the tapaderos and case in the corner and the empty coffee cups on the table. "Emory said to tell you thanks for the coffee."

Still seated at the table, Ruth said through her teeth, "That's white of him."

Heck leaned a shoulder against the wall and folded his arms, looking gravely down at her.

She met his gaze squarely. "So, that's the way it's done out here!" Standing, she shoved her chair in, wrenched the dishpan off its nail, and slung it down on the table. The cups jangled together as she set them in, and umbrage rose with the steam from the hot water that she poured out of the teakettle.

"You're angry," he observed.

"Ooooh, you're so astute. That's what I like about you, Heck. You're quick." She slammed the kettle down on the stove.

"Why're you angry?"

"Why, he asks." She spoke to an imaginary gallery seated in the woodbox. "He's interested in my opinion! I'm not good enough to converse with his brother, but now he wants my opinion."

Heck cocked his head and narrowed his eyes. "I don't understand."

"Your manners. Both yours and Emory's, though I guess you can both be forgiven, since your mother didn't know to teach you."

Heck pushed away from the wall and stood erect, still saying nothing, staring at Ruth with a wooden countenance. Silently, he turned on his heel and walked out the door, down the stairs and across to the shed.

She came to the door, her gaze searing the screen as she watched him emerge with his saddle and bridle. He was maddeningly methodical about his procedure. There was no jerking or haste to betray how he felt inside, but the pony was restive and sidled and danced as he mounted.

As Heck passed by the porch, Ruth burst through the screen door, spooking the horse. "Running's a coward's way." She yelled. "Don't expect me to be here when you get back. At least Harlan stayed to fight."

Heck got the pony in hand and met her challenging look. "Harlan's dead," he said quietly. Then he rode away.

Chapter 28

SHE WAS THERE when Heck came back.

Ruth had beans cooked and cornbread ready to stir up and pop in the oven as soon as she saw him coming down the hill. Had he given her an opening, she might have apologized, but Heck was silent and remote. He washed at the basin, threw out the water, and sat down to dinner without meeting her eyes. After supper, he thanked her in flat tones, picked up the tapaderos, and went down to the shed.

A while later he came back and hunted silently among the things on the kitchen shelf. Finally, he asked if she had seen his awl. She got it for him, and he took it with averted eyes and mumbled thanks and was gone again.

At twilight, he came in to get his fiddle and sat on the top step of the porch, using the last of the daylight to tune it and put rosin on the bow.

Ruth, inside in the darkness, listened to Heck playing a plaintive air and felt a band tighten around her breast until she felt she would suffocate. At last, she could stand it no longer, and she went out to sit a ways away on the top step. She leaned against the roof support, watching his silhouette against the twilight sky.

Heck finished the song and sat holding his fiddle in his lap. "Do you want to talk?"

"Yes." She waited.

He sat quietly as well. As the moments stretched out, he shifted to lean against the pillar next to him and lifted the fiddle.

"No, don't play," she said. "I don't know how to begin."

"Why don't you start by telling me why you were angry."

Ruth folded her arms in front of her stomach and hunched her shoulders forward. "I felt left out. Excluded. Like I wasn't important enough for you to come in and, well, not just talk to me, but at least talk in front of me." She took a deep, cleansing breath. "I don't know how to say it, but it was company. It was company, and he wouldn't even come in to acknowledge his hostess. Oh, I know that sounds stuffy. I can't explain it."

Heck set his fiddle aside and reached for the Bull Durham tag hanging outside his pocket. "Will you listen to me without getting mad? Just believing what I'm saying?"

"I don't know."

"Well, I tell ya, I don't want to spend another afternoon like the one I've just spent. I don't think that pony wants to, either, because I rode him pretty hard." Heck was silent as he built his cigarette in the dark, striking a match to light it, holding it for a moment afterward to look at her.

He sighed and began. "I told you, there at Palomas, how it would be for people living as we are. It isn't done, and people won't accept it. Won't accept us."

"But Henry and Romelia have accepted us. She's been a dear."

"Have you ever been inside her house?"

"Well, no, but there's never been the opportunity."

"Has she come to visit you here?"

"No." She was quiet for some moments, looking inward, paying out her memory. Finally, she said in bitter accents,

"Do you know, it makes me almost physically ill? I see it now. You have, all of you, it so she won't be forced to receive me in her house. How vile! How degrading! What am I, a leper?"

When he spoke, his voice was gentle. "Let me tell you how I see it. Here's my brother, who's driven out of his way to come see me, bring me my fiddle and his taps for me to use. Not only that, but ol' Ollie's tightern'a tick, and he might not look too kindly on the extra miles. I'm right glad to see Emory. I appreciate him bringing those things to me."

Heck cast away his cigarette, a red ember arcing through the air to land a way off and wink at them through the darkness as he continued. "I take kindly to the fact that he's lifted his hat to you and greeted you first, before you spoke to him. There's not a soul that would blame him for doing otherwise. Now, I know that he's doing that because he's my brother. I also know that he'd be uncomfortable coming into a house we're sharing, not being man and wife." He picked up his fiddle and bow. "The reason he didn't come in was because he wasn't invited. I wouldn't put him in that position. Same with Henry and Romelia. How could I do that when they've been so good to us?"

"But you said Henry would accept us."

"He has, but he doesn't condone what we've done—what we're doing."

"All this folderol because of a piece of paper. A piece of paper, for heaven's sake!"

"What paper?"

"A marriage license."

"Well, if it comes to that, seems to me there's some folderol over a matter of walking fifty feet and going in a door. They're both ways people expect other people to act. Emory's uncomfortable because we don't have the piece of paper that says we're man and wife. You're pushed out of shape because he wouldn't come in your house."

It was Ruth's turn to sigh. "You win. Yes. All right. I don't agree. I think it's stupid, but, finally, I will acknowledge that out west people—in their narrow-minded way—do not find people who live together socially acceptable. Fine. I can live with that." Through the darkness, she felt, rather than saw, his smile of disbelief. "Yes, I know; I said that before, too. But, truly, I can."

Heck put the fiddle to his chin and drew the bow across it then put it in his lap again.

"Did you hear what I said about Harlan?" he asked.

"Yes. I thought that was queer."

"How so?"

"Well, why would you say something like that?"

"Because he's dead."

"You mean really dead? I thought you were speaking ... you know, just saying that he wasn't part of the picture anymore. He's really dead?"

"Emory told me."

"How? When?"

"Just last week. Drove the Diamond E pickup off the bridge over the Rio Grande there above Hot Springs. Coroner said it was suicide. He left a note."

"He would," Ruth said dryly. "Well," she continued, verbally dusting off her hands, "that's that then."

That's that then.

Heck raised his fiddle again and began to play a mournful tune in a minor key. A cloud obscured the moon, and the night grew more intense as the refrain hung close and heavy around them, colored dark as sorrow and threaded with the recurring theme of remorse for a man who died because he had no hope.

Ruth sat quiet and pensive long after he had finished. At last, she said, "Heck?"

He laid his fiddle aside. "Yes, ma'am?"

"So, what now?"

"Beg pardon?"

"I mean us." She cleared her throat. "Harlan's dead, and I'm free."

He sat without speaking so long that her throat began to constrict and tears welled in her eyes. She was glad it was dark, and he couldn't see. She had just grasped the roof support to pull herself up when she felt the heat of his body as he moved nearer. She felt his breath on her cheek and then the stubble on his face as he kissed her.

"Well, Darlin', you're gonna have to do some thinking about what you want to do," he said. "I don't have any more to offer you than I did before."

"I don't want anything more."

"Then we'll be married, quick as we can." He kissed her again, this time on the mouth.

She moved close against him, grateful to be in the circle of his arms again and for the end of his chilling remoteness.

Chapter 29

THE NEXT FEW days were busy ones. Heck stayed close to home, splitting his time between working with a horse he was trying to gentle, shoeing all the horses in his mount, and making jerky out of a hindquarter of beef.

Romelia sent up two bushels of peaches, and Ruth tried canning for the first time in her life. Heck showed her how to blanch the peaches, so she could slip off the skins, and talked her through the process as he worked in the kitchen cutting meat into long strips to be dried in the sun. Many times she caught him watching her as she worked, his eyes warm and a half smile on his lips. When she was finished, she called him in, and they stood admiring the jars full of golden fruit and sweet syrup.

One morning, a week after Emory's visit, Heck caught Ruth with a pan of biscuits in her hand and kissed her. "Let's go into town and get married today," he said.

"Careful. It's hot." She set the biscuits on the table and returned the kiss. "I thought you were still figuring how to afford a ring."

"I got that worked out. After breakfast, put on that pretty gray dress, and we'll head out."

"So what did you come up with?" She put a bowl of gravy on the table and sat down.

He took time to break open two of her light, flaky biscuits and spoon gravy over them. "They're having a rodeo in town. I figured to win some of the prize money."

"I've told you I'm perfectly happy with this one." She held up her hand to show the soapstone ring.

He shook his head. "I'd like you to keep that one safe. If you wear it, one of these days, it will break. Besides, we need money for the license, and I'll have to pay the preacher."

They finished breakfast, and while she cleaned up and changed into the gray chambray dress, he put his saddle in the rumble seat. They drove the fifteen miles into Kanab where he paid down fifteen dollars of his saddle savings as entrance fees.

The rodeo was a small affair, held on the north side of town near the schoolhouse. There were no rodeo grounds, just two corrals to hold the stock and an open area where people parked their cars in a big circle to delineate the arena.

Ruth's wedding day was spent sitting alone on the fender of the car, watching a tall cowboy wearing a big number five pinned to his back try to stay astride a series of animals whose only purpose in life seemed to be to cripple and maim those who dared throw a leg over.

She paled as a cowboy on horseback led a plunging bronc into the circle of cars and over to where Heck was standing with his saddle. A man on the ground blindfolded the horse to quiet him while another held one of the animal's ears and then bit it. With the horse thus distracted, Heck put on his saddle, tying the stirrups forward over the bronc's shoulders. He mounted, and when he was settled, nodded to the men at the horse's head. One ripped off the blindfold while the other let loose of the ear, and the bronco came unbuttoned.

Eight seconds seemed like an eternity to Ruth as she watched. She had seen horses pitching before, but it was nothing like the fury unleashed under Heck now. He rode with lighthearted gusto and grace, one arm in the air, spurs constantly raking the angry brute's shoulders. He lost his hat but stayed in the saddle until, at last, the pickup man was there to lift him off and carry him away.

Feeling faint and lightheaded, Ruth discovered she had not been breathing. For an instant, she panicked because she thought she could not begin again. When her involuntary muscles finally took over, she sat, limp as a dishrag, waiting for Heck to come to her now that he was through.

He didn't come. He was out in the middle, earing down a bronc for another man to mount. Seeing the wild flailing of hooves, Ruth felt that it was almost safer to ride than wrangle.

After that, she saw Heck often, not needing the number on his back to tell her which was he but recognizing him by his height and carriage and by the way he wore his hat on the back of his head. She felt alone and miserable.

Misery turned to raw fear when she saw him astride a bucking bronc with no saddle and nothing to hold onto except a surcingle. He was thrown from the horse but was unhurt and back again soon, riding a bull. Again, eight seconds was a century; the pickup man took forever, and breathing was a forgotten skill.

In midafternoon, Heck finally appeared with his saddle over his shoulder. He was tired, dirty, and richer by fifty dollars. He threw his saddle in the rumble seat and said, "All right, Darlin', we've got three things we've got to do now."

"Are you all right?" she asked.

He paused in the act of dusting himself off. "You weren't frightened, were you, Whitleather? Hell, Baby Doll, I was riding tougher ones than that before I was weaned." He drew her in under his arm and walked around to put her in the car. "Now, let's go find a preacher."

As he got in and reached to turn the key, Ruth laid her hand on his. Her eyes were solemn. "Before we marry, I want you to promise that you won't ride in a rodeo again."

Heck leaned back and half turned in his seat, a puzzled look etching lines around his eyes. "You're sure you know what you're asking?"

"I know I never want to spend another day like today."

He took her hand and held it, running his thumb over her fingers. He looked out the windshield at the rodeo still in progress. Then he looked back at Ruth. "There're a couple of things you've got to consider," he said. "I look at you draw, and I can't understand how you can do it so easy. It's a gift. A talent. That's the way it is with me and riding."

She started to say something, but he held up his hand. "Let me explain. I started out rodeoing when I was nine years old. Ol' Man Hickock had a saloon over at Engle, and he'd pay Emory and me to come over and ride wild mustangs in a corral outside his place. Fellows would stand around and drink and watch us ride. He made lots of money off us, and I discovered then I had this gift. I can ride better'n Emory, and that's saying something. Hell, I can even ride better than Mike." He smiled. "And nobody can ride better than Mike."

Ruth didn't answer. She held his gaze, her jaw set.

Heck went on. "Part of my living is made breaking mustangs. That's not a whole lot different from what you saw out there."

"It is different. You work with them and talk to them, and by the time you get on them, they love you."

Heck sat another moment, considering her. "Is this a condition? If I don't promise, will you still marry me?"

"Yes. Of course. Don't be silly."

Heck stared out the windshield again then shifted back around and started the car. "All right," he agreed, not looking at her. "I love you. I love rodeoing, but I love you more. If you ask it of me, I promise." He put the car in reverse and backed out of the circle.

Ruth sighed and wiped away the tears that had welled up. "Thank you," she whispered.

He leaned over to kiss her and then drove to downtown Kanab. "We've got three things to find. We need something to eat, a wedding ring, and someone to marry us"

The town was small, and they hadn't much choice in any of their errands. It turned out they were well satisfied, especially with the rotund Mormon bishop who married them in his grape arbor and refused the money Heck offered him.

The ride home in the twilight was magical. They moved through time and space, but the physical awareness between them added another dimension—a periwinkle enchantment where nothing mattered, nothing existed except the two of them and the road that led to their little place at Cottonwood Springs.

They achieved something that night in their tiny bedroom with the ancient, sagging bed that they never had before, nor ever did again. Lying with him, skin on skin, mouth on mouth, she felt him declare his love for the life they had together. She understood the pride he felt in having her fight alongside him against the elements. As if in vision, she saw him paint the sun and sky, the red rock cliffs and flowing water. Through it all, in the force and cadence of this most physical language, she felt him saying, "I love you. I love you. I love you."

Holding him tightly, arching to meet him, Ruth comprehended and answered in kind. "I know. I know. I know."

At that time, she did know.

Chapter 30

RUTH SPENT MANY days in the Coughlin kitchen while Heck was out on the fall roundup. She had fully intended to bear a grudge against Romelia for not receiving or visiting her before she married Heck. But the hard feelings nourished at Cottonwood Springs wasted away in the benevolent atmosphere of Romelia's kitchen. Could someone who obviously never had a malicious thought be suspected of malice? Could a snub be dealt by someone as calmly and quietly egalitarian as Romelia Coughlin?

Tall and serene, she had smooth, dusky skin, an aristocratic nose and high cheekbones. She wore her hair, black and shiny as obsidian, braided forward and pinned like a tiara on top of her head. Though she wasn't quick to laugh, in repose her countenance showed contentment.

In that kitchen, Ruth learned how to make hominy and *masa* for corn tortillas. She learned to take clabbered milk and cut the curd, heating it gently and slowly on the back of the stove until just the right moment, when it was to be washed and drained, salted, and mixed with sweet cream for cottage cheese. She learned how to churn, adding a little hot or cold water as needed to make the cream release the butter.

One day when Ruth arrived, Romelia was on the porch, her knee on a box, holding down an old broom while she sawed off the end. She smiled a welcome at Ruth and handed her the eight inches of broomstick. "This is for you."

Amused, Ruth held the little round stick in her hand while Romelia put away the broom and saw. "The last time I came you handed me a rock," she observed when Romelia returned, "and I spent the afternoon grinding masa. What delightful activity do you have for me today?"

Romelia's black eyes twinkled as she passed by, but she said nothing until they were in the kitchen. She took two aprons, handed one to Ruth, and announced, rolling the "r" longer than necessary, "Tortillas!"

Romelia showed Ruth how to work on an unfloured surface, turning the broomstick under the palm of one hand to roll in all directions. Her tortilla was almost completely round. She cooked it on a griddle, storing the finished tortilla in the folds of a clean dishtowel to stay moist and warm.

Rolling the dough as Romelia showed her, Ruth ended up with an irregular shape. "It looks like Jimmy Durante," she said. "Look. There are his eyes, and there's his nose." She placed him on the griddle.

Romelia had no idea who Jimmy Durante was. While Ruth explained, Jimmy's nose got an air pocket in it and swelled up to comic proportions. It gave them both a case of the giggles that progressed as they worked. Ruth's tortillas were all odd-shaped, and her natural love of whimsy led her to give names and characters to each. One stayed on the griddle too long and developed huge black spots, which Ruth immediately diagnosed as infectious. This proved to be true when Romelia, called to attend to her work, turned her own tortilla over and found it afflicted with identical symptoms.

As a tortilla-producing session, it was a complete failure, but laughter and nonsense sometimes can bond two people just as strongly as sharing a sorrow.

Wiping tears from her eyes, Romelia took a huge breath and said, "I don't think I have laughed so much since ... since before the war. *Ay qué!* You make even tortillas fun."

One day, helping Romelia wash chimneys from the kerosene lamps, Ruth asked, "Don't you get tired of cleaning these things day after day after day?"

"I like to be able to see at night. A smoky chimney dims the light."

"If you had electricity, you could just press a switch for all the light you wanted and never have to wash another chimney."

Romelia smiled. "Yes, and if I had a tortilla machine I would never have to roll out another tortilla."

"But wouldn't you like to have electricity? You could have a refrigerator and a washing machine and an electric iron ... and a hot water heater. Don't you wish for all that?"

"No, because there is nothing to be gained from wishing. My parents live in town. They have electricity. I know about all those things. If I wanted them bad enough, I could have them, but what would it cost me?" She put a glistening chimney back on a lamp and placed it on a shelf to wait for nightfall. I'll tell you what it would cost me: my life."

Ruth, halfway to the back door with the dishpan, stopped and set the murky water down on the table. "I don't understand."

"This is my life." Romelia held a lamp in one hand and made a sweeping gesture with the other. "Henry is my life. I married a man who must live away from town. I don't know if they will ever have electricity out here. It doesn't worry me." She placed the lamp on the shelf and turned back to face Ruth. "When I think of all the women who have ever lived on the earth, and all of the women who live here now, and when I think of how many of that number have electricity, I don't feel too bad off. I have so much. There are women who have lived their whole life without ever having enough to eat. Or worse, enough to feed their children." She picked up the dishcloth and began wiping up some water that had spilled.

"But isn't there anything you want that you don't have?" Ruth asked. "Something that you'd trade almost anything for?"

Romelia wrung out the dishcloth over the dishpan that Ruth was still resting her hands on. She looked down at the crumpled rag in her hands and spoke so softly that, had she not been standing so near, Ruth could not have heard.

"A son. The sorrow of my life is that I could not give my husband a son."

"But he has a son."

"He has *her* son." Again, it was whispered. Then, as if she had revealed too much, Romelia smiled apologetically. "It's not the same. I love Sonny, but it's not the same as your own. You will know some day." She shook out the damp cloth and went to hang it on a hook by the dishpan.

Ruth carried the water outside, letting the screen door bang behind her. Walking to the bed of hollyhocks that Romelia had growing beside the house, she drizzled the water around the base of the tall, gangly stocks. Picking a couple of spent blossoms, she stood watching a bee nuzzle around inside one of the flowers.

"The sorrow of my life," she whispered to herself.

Then, dropping the withered blossoms behind the hollyhocks to hide their ugliness, she turned and carried the empty dishpan back inside the house.

Chapter 31

HECK WAS GONE for three weeks. When he came back, it was like the closing of a wound, as if a part of each that had been torn away had been restored again.

Their separation had sharpened their desires and delight in each other, and it seemed as though everything around them was intensified, as well. The days marched one after another through a resplendent fall. Lavish in color, bountiful in harvest, the weather itself seemed like largesse, for though it was crisp in the mornings and evenings, the days stretched temperate and mild. The whole world seemed streaked with gold.

As fall moved into winter, and the evenings got too chilly to sit outside, they moved indoors, sitting in the kitchen by the stove. Ruth would do handwork while Heck read aloud, or she worked on a drawing as he played his fiddle. Sometimes he put the instrument down and sang in a soft baritone, and she listened gravely to the song about Joe, the little wrangler who gave his life to save his comrades. Or she smiled as he sang about the cowboy trying to ride the strawberry roan.

They seldom went to dances in town, preferring to be alone. If they sought society at all, they only went as far as Henry and Romelia's.

One afternoon in December, Heck came home early and began carrying in wood. He heaped the woodbox precariously high then stacked more wood on the porch. By the time that was done, it had begun to snow, and there was a stiff breeze blowing. Each time Ruth looked out the window, it was harder to see the outbuildings. It was as though a sheer white curtain had been dropped between her and the world and was flapping horizontally across the window in the wind.

Heck had disappeared into the shed a half hour before. Ruth knew there was nothing to fret about, but she kept pausing to peer through the blizzard, thinking that he should be coming. It was starting to get dark. Finally, she saw his tall, lanky form moving through the obscurity. His collar was turned up, and his hat was pulled low over his eyes. As he came closer, she saw that he was paying out a rope as he walked toward the front door.

The rope stretched down to the shed. He pulled it tight and tied it off to one of the pillars that supported the porch roof. Then he stamped the snow off his boots and came inside. A rush of cold air accompanied him, and Ruth shivered. She watched him shake the snow off his coat before he hung it on a nail behind the stove. Hanging his hat there too, he smiled down at her. "Any coffee?"

She poured him a cup. "What is the rope for?"

"That's to make sure this doesn't last." Holding the cup in his left hand, he lifted the lid of the stove and put in two more pieces of wood.

She frowned. "I don't understand."

Lifting his arm, he invited her in with a motion of his head and pulled her close. "You see, Whitleather, the last time I was here and a blue norther blew up like this one, it caught us unaware. Came up in the night, and when we got up in the morning it looked like that outside." He indicated the window with his coffee cup. "Kept on for three days."

He took a sip of his coffee, and she waited for him to continue.

"We had stock that had to be taken care of in the corrals. Sammy Tinker and I were the only ones here. He was getting along in years, and I told him I'd take care of it. I didn't have sense enough to string a line, so I could find my way back. Hell, I was a cocky young son-of-a-gun and thought I knew my way around. But I got down to the shed, and it was snowing and blowing so bad that I couldn't see the house. I got turned around and was heading off to Kelsey's place—"

"Who is Kelsey?" Ruth interrupted.

"It's just an expression. Means that I was heading in the wrong direction. The creek was frozen and covered with snow, and I crossed it without knowing. I finally realized I was going downhill, and I turned around. I could just barely tell where I'd been though it hadn't been but a few minutes. Luckily, I blundered into old Sammy. He'd tied on a rope and come out to look for me."

"So the rope you put out there ...?"

"If I hadn't put it there, this thing would blow on for four, five days, and I'd be out there heading off to Kelsey's again. But since I did, it'll blow itself out before morning."

They had biscuits and gravy for supper and sat for a while feeling the warmth of the stove at their backs, listening to the wind whistling around the corners, looking every now and then out the window into the hostile grayness on the other side of the pane.

When Ruth carried the lamp into the bedroom, she found miniature drifts of fine, powdery snow forming on the floor, blown in through the cracks between the boards.

At her cry of dismay, Heck took the mattress off the bed and put it in front of the stove in the kitchen. After she was in bed, he stoked the firebox, turned down the damper, and blew out the lamp. He got in, and they curled together.

Ruth looked up through the kitchen window at the flakes that had eased out of the driven currents of air to eddy and float and drift against the pane. "I've seen lots of snow, but I've never been this close to the raw force of winter," she murmured.

"I remember when I was about eleven, and we were living in Cutter," Heck began. His mouth was near her ear, and though his voice was hardly more than a whisper, she could hear him plainly over the wind. "Papa and I had gone over to Engle for something or other, and we were on our way home when we got caught in a blizzard like this. We were out on a big flat, and there wasn't any shelter anywhere, but we came up against a fence and figured we knew which fence it was and which way it was running. The way we had to go was into the wind, and those ponies sure didn't like it. They were wanting to turn around and ride out the storm with their rumps to the wind. Papa or I neither one were dressed for weather like that. I was so cold!"

He paused so long that she turned her head a trifle and asked softly, "What did you do?"

"Kept on going. I sure didn't want to. I wanted to just stop and let the horses turn around. I could have my back to the wind, too, and maybe I could hunch up and go to sleep. I just didn't want to try anymore, but Papa kept me going. He'd poke me and pinch my ear and call me names. Rude names that he never called me before. I'd be thinking I just wanted to give up, and he'd yank on my ear and call me something, and I'd get mad at him. I'd spend the next fifty, hundred feet thinking what an ornery old cuss he was."

He paused, and Ruth asked, "What happened?"

"We got to the Bostick's place. They wrapped us in blankets and put us in front of the stove and filled us full of hot coffee. Wasn't too long before we got thawed out." Heck chuckled softly. "Took me years to figure out that the old gent was making me mad on purpose, trying to keep me upright in the saddle and thinking about something other than how cold I was. I guess he figured that making me mad at him would work better than saying, 'Come on, son, I know you can do it.'"

"Maybe he didn't know how to say that," Ruth whispered.

"Maybe not. Anyway, I'm sure glad I saw this storm coming."

"Me too." Ruth nestled in closer.

They lay watching and listening and savoring their warm, safe haven and the comfort of lying together. Just before she drifted off to sleep, Ruth heard Heck say, "I put hay around your fruit jars out in the shed, so they won't freeze and break."

They woke the next morning to splendor. The sky was clear and blue, and the landscape was littered with diamonds that sparkled in the sunlight. Ruth woke to the feel of Heck's hand on her cheek. At first she was surprised to find herself in the kitchen. Then she remembered and smiled at Heck.

"Good morning," she said softly. Her eyes sought the window, and she blinked at the brightness beyond. "Did it stop snowing?"

"Yep. Put your britches on, Whitleather. I've got something to show you."

Ruth was up in an instant, dressing in pants and boots while Heck took down the rope and coiled it up on his way to the shed. She grabbed an old winter coat, another of Sonny's hand-me-downs that Romelia had given her to wear around the ranch. Pausing on the porch to shade her eyes against the glare, she gazed in wonder at the changed world around her.

Everything was covered with an ermine blanket. There were long, sweeping dunes on the lee side of the outbuildings and poufs of snow on the tops of all the fence posts. The creek had disappeared except for dark patches where the running water had eaten through in a jagged line stretching down the hill. The two saddle horses Heck kept in the corral stood watching her with ears pricked forward and cloudy puffs of steam around their muzzles.

"Whitleather?" Heck called from the doorway of the shed. "Would you get a blanket off the bed?"

Ruth waved to show she understood and went in to pull a quilt off the mattress on the floor. Folding it up, she headed out to the shed. Heck met her halfway, dragging a toboggan he had fashioned out of a piece of corrugated tin.

Ruth looked at his handiwork and laughed delightedly. "What are you going to do?"

Heck grinned down at her. "I'm going to show you what it feels like to ride a bucking bronc. Throw the blanket on."

She did, and he grabbed her hand and headed toward the trail across the creek. Not able to match his stride, Ruth had to take catch-up steps, but she didn't mind. She was so excited she was dancing, anyway.

At the crest, they could look down and see out across the flat to the cliffs beyond. The scrub pine and cedar trees that dotted the flat were dappled with snow, their dark trunks rising out of the sparkling whiteness. The mesas to the north were snow-clad towers pasted on a brilliant field of blue.

Ruth stood in the hollow under Heck's arm, both her arms around him as they gazed at the grandeur before them. Then she gave him a squeeze and tiptoed up to kiss him. "Thank you for this."

He pulled her around to face him and hugged her tightly, putting his face against her hair. "It was the good Lord made it, not I. You'll have to thank Him."

"But you brought me here. I've done things in my life, Heck, that were tremendously exciting. I've done things that were great fun, but I've never had the feelings here," she wiggled one hand up through his arm to touch her breast, "that I've had since you brought me to Cottonwood Springs. Sometimes it's all I can do not to weep … and not for sadness, either."

She sniffed and then smiled wryly. "I need your handkerchief. My nose always runs when I get sentimental."

Heck kissed the top of her head and let her go, pulling his handkerchief out of his back pocket. It was snowy white, folded and ironed. She delicately blew her nose and gave it back to him.

He fished a pair of gloves out of his pocket and gave them to her. "Put these on. Your hands will freeze without them."

The gloves were old and worn and too large, but they were soft and comfortable. Heck pulled the strap at the top to tighten them, so they wouldn't fall off.

She raised one to her nose. "They smell like horse," she said. "That's nice."

Heck placed their corrugated toboggan at the crown of the hill and fixed the quilt, so it was just large enough to cushion two. "You sit here," he directed, "and I'll sit behind you, like this. Put your legs together, so there's room for my feet beside yours."

Sitting down, the hill suddenly looked steeper. "Have you ever done this before?" she asked.

She didn't hear his answer, for he shifted his body and scooted them the two inches necessary to put the center of gravity down the incline, and they were off. Ruth squealed as they began sliding down the hill, gathering speed as they went. She shrieked as they ricocheted off bumps and bushes, bouncing and flying through the air. She screamed as they were flung off the toboggan into a snowbank halfway down.

She lay there for a moment, half-buried, laughing, and letting her inner ear reorient itself. When she looked up, Heck stood over her, brushing snow off. He was grinning, had lost his hat, and his hair was falling forward over his forehead. He began to sing in a rollicking tone.

> *I'll bet all my money*
> *The man ain't alive.*

She joined him from the depths of the snowdrift.

> *Who can stay with old Strawberry*
> *When he makes his high dive.*

Heck helped her up, brushed her off, and spoke with mock solemnity. "Now, the thing that you have to do when you get thrown off is to get right back on. That shows him you're not afraid of him. Shows you you're not afraid of him, too."

"Yes, Papa," she said meekly.

"Now, you go get old Strawberry and take him back up the hill. I'll get my hat, and then I'm going to get a shovel and see if I can even out some of these bumps."

They spent an hour playing on the hillside. Their last run was perfect, an exhilarating plunge that took the breath away and forced the heart up next to the larynx. Ruth heard Heck hollering in her ear, "Yeeehaw! Ride 'em, Whitleather!"

They reached the bottom unscathed and jubilant, and she knew that this was the time to stop.

So they went home. While Heck took the toboggan apart and put the wood and tin back where he'd found them, Ruth fixed breakfast. They sat at the window and looked at the snow and looked at each other and talked about the things that needed to be done that day. Heck told her not to worry if he was late. He might run into stock that was in trouble, might have to bring some in to the corrals, and he could only travel as fast as they could. He rolled a blanket in a slicker, tied it behind his cantle, and put his rifle in the scabbard. Stuffing some jerky and an extra pair of gloves in his pocket, he picked up his hat and bade her farewell.

He was riding the big bay horse. She watched from the doorway as he swung into the saddle and headed across the creek. At the top of the hill, he paused and raised his hand in salute.

Ruth thought, "I will go to my grave with that picture of him etched in my heart." Then realizing that he was gone, and she must turn to her tasks of the day, she got the broom and began sweeping snow off the porch.

Chapter 32

THE IDYLL OF SUMMER and fall stretched on through winter and spring. Though industry and thrift, ingenuity and enterprise were orders of the day at the little tumbledown range camp on Cottonwood Springs, to Ruth it had the feeling of lovers dallying through drifting time. Perhaps it was because of Heck's glances, lingering and tender, that fell on her when his hands were busy with other work. Or maybe it was because his smile, sent to her across a noisy corral, echoed last night's whispered endearments. Whatever it was, it lent an ambience that hung around the place as heavy and sweet as the scent of sage after a rain.

Something happened in January to mar the idyll, though. It was the arrival of a crisp, white, legal-sized envelope of heavy rag bond with the name of a New Jersey law firm engraved in the upper left hand corner. Heck brought it with him when he drove up in Henry's truck with a load of cottonseed cake on the back.

Ruth waved to him from the window as he got out of the truck, but when she saw him pull off his gloves and fish in the pocket of his heavy coat, she came out on the porch. The wind was cold and sharp, and she folded her arms and hunched her shoulders as she waited for him to find what he was looking for.

He stood on the ground and handed it up to her silently. She read the return address, and when she looked up, Heck was walking away. He got in the truck and drove down to unload.

Ruth went inside and grabbed her coat from the nail by the door, pausing only to tie a scarf under her chin before trotting down to the feed shed with the letter in her hand. "Don't you want to know who it's from?" She spoke loudly against the wind and to Heck's back as he carried a load into the shadowy interior.

He answered from inside the shed. "I know who it's from."

"Well, don't you want to know what they say?"

Heck paused in the doorway. "I figure if it's any of my business, you'll tell me."

He was being cool and remote again, and Ruth was nettled by his attitude. She was a little apprehensive about opening the letter. It was official-looking and an unknown quantity, and she would have appreciated comfort and support. Instead, she was standing in a biting wind shouting at a wintry companion. "I thought what happened to flesh of your flesh was your business," she muttered.

Heck was emerging from the shed again. "Beg pardon?" he asked sharply.

"Nothing." Turning, she walked briskly back up to the house. The door was almost torn from her hand by a gust of wind, and she had to pull hard to close it after herself. She threw the envelope on the table, took off her coat and scarf, and hung them up. Pouring a cup of coffee, she stood sipping it and looking out the window at the disappearing pile of cottonseed cake and at the grim-faced cowboy who was ferrying it into the shed.

Finally, she sat down at the table and tore off the end of the envelope. She drew out a sheet of paper with two lines written under the engraved letterhead. Accompanying it was another smaller, personal-sized, sealed envelope. There was no direction written on the outside of the smaller envelope.

Puzzled, Ruth read the scant information on the two-lined letter.

Madam: Mrs. Philip Reynolds desired that we locate you and deliver to you the enclosed envelope.

There was the usual complementary close and a signature, but it was a cold, terse letter.

Ruth picked up the sealed envelope and knew who it was from. She wasn't afraid any longer. *The old bag*, she thought. *Always, always, she had to have the last word.* Running her fingers under the flap, she ripped half the envelope away to get to the folded sheet inside. Opening it, she saw that there was no salutation.

My attorneys advise me that I may not say the things that I want to say to you. However, I will say that I'm delighted that Harlan left a note, so his death has been ruled a suicide and not an accident. Therefore, you cannot collect his life insurance. I would not care to see you profit from his death any more than you already have. That it would have been blood money I know means nothing to you. You were never careful about how you came by what you had. But leave that be.

I have instructed my agent to see that the household items and furniture, together with your personal effects, are put into storage at the nearest available place. As you were still legally Harlan's wife when he died, they now belong to you. The storage will be paid for one year. If you have not claimed the contents at the end of that time, everything is to be given to charity.

The wedding gifts are included—the china, sterling and silver hollowware you will find there—but not the Reynolds tea service. It is a family heirloom, and I have arranged for it and Harlan's clothing and personal things to be sent to me. You may sue me if you wish.

The money in Harlan's account is in the bank at Hot Springs. As you were a signer on the account, it will be accessible to you. I hope you burn in hell.

Ruth scanned the letter quickly at first, went back and read it more slowly, and then she threw back her head and laughed. Looking out the window, she saw that Heck was just lifting the last of the cottonseed cake from the back of the truck. She flew to the door and called to him, but the wind was against her and spirited the sound away. He disappeared into the shed again.

When he emerged, Ruth waved the letter and motioned him in. He nodded to show he understood but took time to close the shed door and latch it. She went inside, poured him a cup of coffee, and impatiently watched his slow progress.

Entering the room, Heck hung up his coat, put his gloves and hat on the table, and took the coffee she offered him.

Ruth could hardly repress the news she had to share, but she decided to take her cue from Heck's quiet manner. Laying the letter on the table, she sat demurely, crossed her ankles, and asked him to sit down.

"Thanks, but I'd rather stand."

"Well, I can't tell you with you standing over me like that," she complained.

He didn't move. "What've you got to tell me?" His voice was soft, but his eyes were wary.

Ruth could contain herself no longer. "Your saddle," she burst out, smiling. "We can get your saddle now!"

Heck's response was certainly not what she had desired. He took a sip of his coffee without taking his eyes off her.

The smile faded as she waited for him to say something. Anything. But he only stood, quietly drinking his coffee, his face impassive and his eyes never leaving her face.

Her smile faded completely. "Did you hear me?"

Heck's gaze finally dropped. He set his cup on the table with a deliberate gesture, a frown of concentration on his face. "Oh, I heard you. It's just that I sent those coyote hides to Denver thinking I'd get the rest of my saddle money from them." He nodded at the paper and envelopes that littered the table, inches from his coffee cup. "I didn't figure your letter was from an outfit that concerned itself with saddles. What I figured was that it was from the Reynolds' lawyers and had something to do with Harlan."

Ruth's eyes lit up. "That's it." she exclaimed, "That's it! Oh, Heck, we have some money! Harlan and I had a joint account, and I get what's left. I don't know how much, but there's at least three hundred dollars there."

Her hands were clasped together at her breast, and she smiled up at him as the words came tumbling out. She sprang up from the chair. "Where's the catalog? Let's look and see what we can buy." She ran into the bedroom and began rooting among the books stacked behind the door, talking excitedly as she jumbled things about. "Oh, Heck! We can get some real curtains—and a bed. Let's get a new bed! Or we could have the other bed shipped out here from Hot Springs. Or let's get a washing machine—one of those you turn with a—"

Entering the kitchen with the catalog in her hand, Ruth was stopped in midsentence by the sight of her husband standing at the door with his coat and hat on. There was an arctic quality about him that took her breath away. In a voice that was almost a whisper she asked, "What's wrong?"

"The devil of it is that you have to be told." He was yanking on his gloves and speaking clipped accents.

She stood with wide, uncomprehending eyes, the open catalog pressed to her bosom. "But what have I done? You can't be angry that I wanted to use that money to help with your saddle?"

"Yes, ma'am, that's exactly it! Now, I'm going to say this once, and then I don't ever want to talk about it again. You're my wife. I'll take care of you. I'll also take care of buying my own saddle. I don't need any help from that outfit." Without taking his eyes from her, he indicated the correspondence on the table with his thumb. "You can hang on to that money if you like, and if I'm not man enough to provide for you, when I'm gone, you can go ahead and use it for anything that happens to take your fancy. But while I'm above ground, I don't want to know about it; I don't want to talk about it; and I'll be damned if I'll touch a penny of it. It's too much like blood money, and my gorge rises at the thought of it."

It was an unfortunate choice of words. Had he not echoed the elegantly penned words of her former mother-in-law, Ruth might not have become so angry, but the harm was done. Her chin came up, and her eyes blazed.

Flinging the catalog away from her, she shouted, "You and your gorge can both go to hell!" The heavy book hit the handle of the water faucet, knocking it, so the tap turned on as the catalog fell into the bucket below.

Heck glanced at the water pouring down over the book and into the bucket.

Ruth was oblivious. "So you won't take the money for your precious saddle. That's all right. I think you glory in being poor, but what about me? Do you know I don't have a pair of silk stockings to my name? Do you know why I didn't want to go to the dance in town on New Year's Eve?

Because I don't have a winter coat to wear. Do you think I'm going to go somewhere wearing Sonny Coughlin's castoff?" Ruth lifted her arm, pointing an accusing finger at the offending coat.

The gesture was lost as Heck strode by her to turn off the water. He picked up the catalog and flung it, dripping, under the stove to dry. Then he went to the door and looked back at her. "Is there anything else?"

Heck's face had taken on the wooden look that he wore when she had wounded him, but she was too mad to notice. Too mad to care. She stood in the middle of the room, ramrod straight, and her eyes listed for him, alphabetically and by category, all the things she felt that her marriage to him had denied her.

Heck met her eyes. Then he looked down at his hand on the doorknob, murmured, "I see," and was gone.

Ruth watched from the window as he walked to the truck. His head was down, and his shoulders sagged, and he didn't look back as he drove away. She turned and grabbed the sadirons from the shelf and slammed them down on the stove. Then she got a pencil and a tablet and occupied an hour pouring through the catalog, making a list of all the things she wanted to buy with her newfound funds. It was a satisfying, if tedious, business, as she had to iron some of the outer pages dry before she could turn them.

The sun was halfway down in the sky when Ruth finished, so she began supper. As she pounded a piece of beefsteak, she thought of how she would greet Heck when he came home. *Hello, dear. How's your gorge? Do you think you could gag down a mouthful or two?*

She took extra pains to make sure she fixed all the things Heck liked, browning the meat and letting it simmer long in rich gravy, cooking potatoes with the jackets on. She would be sure to provide for him well. He should not lack because of any omission on her part.

At midnight the meat looked like shoe leather curled up in a bed of tar, and the potatoes were wizened and dry. Ruth finally gave up waiting and went to bed. Discontent and an unvented spleen made for a sorry night, and she slept hardly at all until just before daybreak.

She didn't hear Heck as he slipped in and out of the house, but a clinking and jingling noise passing by her window just after sunup roused her, and she hastily got out of bed.

She almost tripped over a cardboard box sitting in the middle of the kitchen and shoved it impatiently out of the way, opening the door just in time to see Heck cross the creek. He was mounted on the big bay horse and had his traps tied behind the cantle, along with a blanket in a slicker.

As she stepped out on the porch, Ruth came full awake, not because of the brisk morning air, but because of the flash of pure intelligence that swept through her mind, sending her back to the carton she had stumbled over. Grinding her teeth, she kicked the box and ran back through the door to stand on the porch and scream, "I will not let you be a martyr! I won't accept them. How dare you, Heck Benham. How dare you!"

But he was cresting the hill and couldn't hear her.

She stomped back into the kitchen and slammed the door. Then she kicked the box again. Hearing something clink, she leaned over to look more closely. Inside was a box of silk stockings, some nail polish and remover, hand lotion, bath powder, emery boards, glycerin and rosewater, a box of pastels, a box of charcoal, and a pad of paper. Folded on top was a winter coat.

As Ruth straightened up and swept back the hair that had fallen forward over her face, her eyes fell on the coffeepot sitting on the back of the stove. Heck had made coffee, as he did each morning, and left it for her.

Suddenly, without knowing why, she was weeping. Whether it was from the sleepless night; or the knowledge that Heck had spent his saddle money on the things in the box; or because he wouldn't take her money for his saddle; or because he, like her mother-in-law, had had the last word, she didn't know. She sat at the table with her head down on her arms and wept great racking sobs that left her with swollen eyes and a red nose and feeling no better than before.

Chapter 33

HECK WAS GONE for two days. He came home silent and reserved, and Ruth matched him in cold courtesy. The box sat in the corner where she had placed it, a mute witness of the rift between them.

Even the whitest heat burns down to cold ashes. After a week, Ruth couldn't remember why she had been so angry. The wind had stopped, and the sun was vigorous and golden, promising springtime soon, beckoning Ruth outside. Needing something to warm her spirits after a week of chilly conjugal formality, she abandoned her morning chores, put some bread and dried apples in her pocket, and gathered her drawing things. As she passed the box, she paused, considering, and slowly lifted out the box of pastels. Tucking them under her arm, she headed out the door and climbed to the top of the trail. There she sat in the sun with her back to a rock and sketched the red rock canyon below.

Intent on her work, she didn't hear a stealthy approach behind her, didn't realize she was being observed until she felt hot breath on her neck. She turned around in alarm to confront two liquid brown eyes calmly studying her.

Ruth's alarm turned to delight. Her inspector was a little gray jenny burro with dainty hooves, a white nose, and long ears that were fuzzy on the inside. "Why, you darling!" Ruth exclaimed, reaching out her hand to pet the white muzzle. The jenny tossed her head and backed a step.

"Oh, I see," said Ruth, sitting still and speaking softly. "We haven't been introduced. My name is Ruth."

The burro leaned her head down to sniff at Ruth's shoulder and took a step closer.

"And you're Bunny? Yes, that would be your name. Are you after my lunch? If you eat it, I'll surely go hungry. Well, all right. I'll share."

She took the bread from her pocket and set a piece on a rock beside her. Bunny daintily lifted it off with her lips and chewed it up.

"I'll give you another piece," Ruth said, "but then the rest is for my lunch."

Bunny got it all. Throughout the morning and early afternoon, Ruth doled it out to the gentle little beast hanging close by, alternately grazing and standing in the sunlight, her ears swiveling to catch the sounds that were carried through the still air.

When the bread was gone, Ruth rose and stretched. She put her things away and headed back toward Cottonwood Springs. Bunny came with her, following five paces behind. If Ruth stopped to look back, she stopped too, blinking long eyelashes over her limpid brown eyes.

Coming down the hill, Ruth saw that Heck's horse was in the corral and smoke was coming from the chimney. Her heart skipped a beat, and she consciously had to restrain herself from running down the hill, hollering his name all the way. Forgotten was the vexatious week in her eagerness to show him what she had brought home.

The horses caught the burro's scent and pressed against the near rail of the corral, bobbing their heads, whickering, and snorting. Bunny cast them a glance but ignored their agitated stampings and followed Ruth up to the porch.

Heck came to the door and stood, leaning his shoulder against the doorjamb. His lips weren't smiling, but his eyes were warm.

"Oh, Heck," Ruth said gaily, twinkling up at him, "look what followed me home! Isn't she darling? At least, I think it's a she." Ruth bent over, looking underneath the little donkey. "There's nothing hanging down." She straightened up and looked at Heck with raised brows.

His eyes were definitely smiling now. "Then it must be a she." He strolled across the porch and down the steps to stand by the jenny's near hindquarter. "Where'd you find her?"

"On the top of the hill. Actually, she found me. Her name is Bunny."

Heck worked his way to the jenny's head, patting her rump then stroking her withers. Finally, he stood in front of the burro and let her become acquainted with his smell. "Hello, Miz Ashton," he said. "Glad you could come for a visit."

Ruth giggled. "I didn't think about the name. I named her Bunny because of the ears. Oh dear." She put her things down on the porch and sat by them while she watched Heck make friends with the enchanting little stranger.

When the formalities had been observed, Heck came and picked up Ruth's drawing things. He eyed the pastels for a moment then set them to the back, so he could take a seat by her. "You notice the black band that crosses her withers?" he asked, pointing at Bunny.

"The stripe? I noticed it but didn't think too much about it."

"Well, that stripe across her withers connects to another. Here, I'll show you."

He stood and waited for her to follow then led the way, so he could show her the black stripe running the length of

Bunny's backbone. "It makes a cross. See?" He traced the pattern with his finger. "All burros have them." Bunny nibbled at his arm, so he took her top lip between his thumb and forefinger and squeezed it.

"What are you doing?"

"Teaching her not to nibble. If she does that, pretty soon she'll be biting. It's the way she shows affection, but it can hurt. If you do this, she'll know not to."

"I slapped her nose once or twice."

"If you do that, she'll get head-shy—jerk her head back every time you move your hand. All you have to do is squeeze her lip. She'll learn."

He patted Bunny's neck and strolled back to the porch. Sitting so he could lean against the roof support, he folded his arms, stretched his long legs out in front of him, and watched Ruth as she held the fuzzy face close to hers and spoke sweet nonsense.

"They say that black cross marks the burro as a sacred beast," Heck said.

Ruth looked at him, still holding Bunny's face in her hands. "Sacred?" She stepped back and looked critically at the shaggy little animal and then shook her head. "I can't see it. A lion or a unicorn I could see as sacred but a jackass?" She walked to the porch and sat down by Heck.

"You think about it. In the Bible there was an ass that saw an angel and told his master about it."

Ruth's eyes widened, and Heck nodded and winked at her. He went on: "Then, there was the burro that carried Mary to Bethlehem where Jesus was born. And when Christ came back to Jerusalem the last time, he sent some fellas to get a young donkey colt because that was the way he was supposed to come in. The people put down their coats and tree branches for him to ride over—made a big thing about it."

Heck pointed at Bunny. "They're sorry-looking critters, but they've been in on some mighty big moments. That's why the Lord marked them with that cross."

Ruth's brows knit as she looked at him, not knowing if he were serious or not. "Is that so?"

"What? About the Lord marking the burro? I don't know. The rest of it's in the Bible."

"The part about the donkey speaking, too?"

"Yep."

"How do you know?"

Heck's brow wrinkled in puzzlement. "Why, I've read it. Several times."

"Why several times?"

"Well, the first time, it was because I was way the heck and gone out working a section for ol' Ollie Free. I was fourteen then, and it was the first time I'd ever worked by myself. Lonely? I'd climb the windmill and sit up there for hours, just thinking maybe someone'd come and see how I was doing. I guess I figured if I could see farther, there was more chance for someone to come. Only thing to read in that camp was a Bible. I must've thought that reading the Bible beat sitting up on the windmill."

"And the next time?"

Heck took his hat off and examined the creases in the crown. "I read it three more times for a different reason than the first. I'd like to tell you about that reason ... but I don't think this is the time to do it."

Ruth was just about to ask what the great mystery was, but, unwilling to jeopardize the thaw that had set in, she bit back the question. Instead, she searched in her pocket for the last dried apple. Calling Bunny's name, she held it out.

Bunny was down at the feed shed scratching her shoulder on the corner of the building and seemed uninterested in a lone slice of apple.

Ruth laid the apple down on the porch and picked up her drawing pad. Struck by a happy thought, she turned back to Heck. "I know a story from the Bible," she announced.

Heck cocked his head and raised an eyebrow.

"I had an old lady taking care of me once for several weeks when my mother went on a cruise. She was telling me about my name—how there is a Ruth in the Bible." She paused to see that her facts were straight. Heck gave the smallest of nods, and she could see that his eyes were smiling again.

"She told me how Ruth stood up bravely and told her husband that she wasn't afraid to go away with him to a strange land, that she'd stay with him because she loved him. I still remember what she said. I was only about twelve when I heard it, but I thought it was a beautiful story." Ruth's voice grew soft, and she sat with her arms folded over the pad she held to her breast. She closed her eyes and recited, "Whither thou goest, I will go. Whither thou lodgest, I will lodge. Thy people shall be my people and thy God my God." Her eyes were moist when she opened them to look at Heck.

His eyes were crinkling at the corners.

"What have I said that's funny? Heck Benham, you're laughing at me."

"No, ma'am. I wouldn't laugh at you when you were quoting something so beautiful." He looked away and cleared his throat. "It's just that she didn't say that to her husband."

"Well, of course she did. Who would she say it to? The Bible isn't going to have a story about her saying that to her lover."

"No, ma'am. It was her mother-in-law."

Ruth's face was such a mask of disbelief and revulsion that Heck couldn't help grinning at her.

"It couldn't be her mother-in-law. Heck Benham, you're making fun of me!"

She whacked him with her drawing pad, and he laughed out loud as he put his arms up to protect himself. His laughter made her attack more vigorously, following him as he got up from the porch. As he retreated, Heck grabbed her drawing pad and flung it away. Then he pinned her arms behind her.

Ruth struggled a moment before turning questioning brown eyes up to him. "Oh, Heck, truly? Her mother-in-law?"

He nodded. All trace of laughter was gone now. Tentatively, he bent down and touched her lips with his, letting go her hands as he did so and gathering her into an embrace.

Ruth clung to him, reaching up hungrily to return his kisses and sighing, "Oh, yes," when he scooped her up and carried her up the steps and into the house, kicking the door shut behind him.

Chapter 34

SITTING ON HIS heels in front of a campfire, Heck used the last rays of daylight to read Emory's letter aloud to Ruth for the second time that day.

> *Hermano,*
>
> *Como sta? Got your letter saying you was married.*
>
> *I figgered maybe I'd do the same so I went and got that redheaded gal and took her up to Hillsboro and we got hitched. Shore is nice having someone to cook the beans and warm the bed. And flank the calves.*
>
> *Old Ollie didn't take too much to me getting spliced. You know he'd skin a flea for its hide and tallow and didn't want to put out the extra groceries, I think. I told him he was getting another hand and that helped. He had me out at Hooper's Well, and Carrie said she'd stay there awhile, but she wasn't going to bunk with that old one-lunger forever. So I got old Ollie to let me tear down that place over at Bitter Well and bring the lumber over to build a better house at Hooper's. It's all stacked and ready to start to build.*
>
> *But the thing is, Heck, that I got the chance to get a place of my own. I was in the bank the other day and some old coot come in and flung a bunch of papers across the*

room and said they might as well have it now since they'd get it in the end. There was papers floating down all around me, so I picked them up and it was his mortgage papers. I held onto them and me and Carrie's dad went to see the banker. We're going in together and see if we can take it over and make the place go. Course me and Carrie'll do the work and her papa is supplying the credit. It's a small place, but it's got good water.

Fella was from back east and didn't know cattle. Didn't know the Jornada.

Ollie's going to need a good man. He said if you want to come you can. He'd put you at Hooper's Well. I don't know how your lady would feel about the housing situation, but there's lumber there to build something else. I have to leave before the spring work, so you would need to be here for that.

Lucy had her baby. A boy. They named him Emory Heck. They call him Little Emory. Mama and Lucy think he's pretty, but I don't know. Seems to be a happy baby, and all the plumbing works just fine.

Helen's husband died. He had T.B. They no more than found out that was what was wrong with him than he got numonia and died. Everyone's taking it pretty hard. Especially Jimmy. He don't say much at the best of times, but you can shore tell he's hurting.

I don't think I've ever wrote a letter this long before.

You'd better come on back, because I don't think I'm ever gonna do it again. Let Ollie know if you want the job.

Your brother, Emory

Ruth watched Heck fold the letter and tuck it back in his shirt pocket and went back to her chore of brewing coffee as the sun slipped behind the mountains, and night began to press down around them. Looking up from her task, she could see very little beyond the glow of the campfire. "Boy, it sure got dark in a hurry!"

"New moon. We'll have a good view of the stars tonight." He took the cup of coffee she handed him. "Thanks. Come sit by me, and let's talk."

"I can't squat like you do. You'll have to sit down." She put her slicker on the ground and threw a blanket on top of that, spreading it so they could share. When they were comfortable, she leaned against Heck, and he put his arm around her.

She took a tentative sip of her coffee and then set it aside to cool. "You want to talk about Emory's letter, don't you?"

"Yes, ma'am. I can't help wanting to go back home, but I'm trying to think what's best for us, for our family."

"And?"

"Well, I look at the size of the spreads, and they're just about the same. Both fairly prosperous, as small places go. But Henry's got a son that will take over someday. I'll never be more than just a hand. Always be sucking the hind tit."

Heck paused and blew on his coffee. "Ol' Ollie's a bachelor," he went on. "He's clutch-fisted and has some odd ideas, but he's been mighty good to me. He doesn't have any kin, and when he gets older, he would probably want me to take over running the ranch for him. He's not afraid to try things that will make the ranch do better—like buying that Brahma bull that Emory brought by."

"And," Ruth added, "his place is on the Jornada."

"And," Heck echoed, "his place is on the Jornada."

Ruth picked up her coffee and tried it again. Then she held the mug cupped in her hands and looked up at him. "I'm Ruth, remember? Whither thou goest, I will go. Whither thou lodgest, I will lodge."

Heck's eyes crinkled. "Well, in the beginning, we'd be lodging at Hooper's Well," he said. "It's a step down from Cottonwood Springs, but if Ollie is going to let me build another place, I can make it nice for you."

"So we're going?"

Heck sat a minute, staring into the fire as if he were trying to see their future in the flickering light. "Yep. We're going."

Ruth nodded and took another sip of coffee. She had the fleeting impression, not even a complete thought, that her wardrobe and household goods were stored near Hooper's Well in Hot Springs. For right now, she was content to sit in the circle of firelight that shrank as the fire burned down to embers and listen to the night sounds made by creatures venturing forth in a world wakening to spring.

Heck sighed. "I sure feel bad about Helen's husband."

Ruth didn't know Helen, but she nodded.

"He's awful young to die. Leave a young wife like that."

She nodded again, and they sat quietly watching the embers flaring and dimming as the breeze came and went.

"Heck?"

"Ummm."

"Do you believe in an afterlife?"

A coal tumbled out of the fire pit, and Heck pushed it back with the toe of his boot. "You mean, after you die?"

"Yes. Do you?"

"Well, yeah, Baby Doll. Don't you?"

"I don't think so. I've never thought much about it, but when Daddy died, he was just gone." She drew up her knees and rested her arms on them as she gazed into the fire. "We live, and then we die, and that's the end of it. That's why having what we want is so important. We only live once, don't you think?"

Heck took a sip of his coffee but didn't answer.

"What are you, anyway?" she asked.

He chuckled. "What kind of question is that? I'm a cowboy. I'm a New Mexican. I'm your husband."

"No. I mean, are you a Baptist or a Presbyterian?"

"I'm not anything."

"Not anything? Can you believe in God and read the Bible and not be anything?"

"I guess I'll find out. The rest of the family are all Episcopalians. Papa says they're Lewisites because they believe in him rather than the Episcopal Church."

"Believe in who? Or is it whom? Believe in whom?"

"In Preacher Lewis. He's the Episcopal priest for our diocese, and he's probably the best man—the *goodest* man— I've ever known."

"So why aren't you an Episcopalian?"

"I don't believe what they teach about the nature of God."

Ruth turned her head, resting her cheek on her arms, and watched her husband. The timbre of his voice had changed, but in the darkness where everything showed in murky outlines, she couldn't see his expression. "What do they say about the nature of God?"

"I don't know that I can even explain it. When I was ten, Preacher Lewis had me memorize the Athanasian Creed, but it didn't stick. Something like, not three eternals, but one eternal, not three incomprehensibles, nor three uncreated, but one uncreated, and one comprehensible."

"Is that supposed to make sense?"

"I guess it does to some people."

Ruth made no comment, turning back to contemplate the fire. Heck threw some sagebrush on the coals, and the fire flared once more. In the light it provided, he grabbed the white tag hanging out of his shirt pocket and pulled out his bag of tobacco.

"I was reading a book a while back," he said as he began to build a cigarette. "There was one place where this old fella was dying, and he called all his sons to him and talked to them about God. He seemed to have a pretty good feel about who God was, and I remember thinking that I needed to remember what he said." He pulled the string with his teeth and put the pouch back in his pocket.

"What did he say?"

Heck shook his head and said ruefully, "I can't remember." Lighting his cigarette, he tossed the flaming match over into the fire. "The old fella said something about God giving us the choice between good and evil, and that's the reason everything—the earth and all the critters and man—were created. He said—what was it?—if there were no evil, there could be no good. If people weren't good, they couldn't be happy. And if there weren't both things, evil and good, there could be no God. It sounds funny the way I'm saying it, but it made sense when he said it. Like the fact that there is good and evil proves the existence of God."

"I don't think that's a very good argument to prove the existence of God."

"Not the way I say it, but when he said it, it did."

They were quiet again. Heck fed the fire another handful of brush and then leaned back on an elbow. "You see, I have this picture in my mind of how God is. It's something I've been working out for years. I told you the other week—the day you brought Bunny down the hill—that I had a reason for reading the Bible more than once. That's it. I wanted to find out about God." He sat a minute, smoking. "It seems to me that He set up things for us, so we could keep our eyes open, look around a bit, and then say, 'Yep, that's the way God is.'"

"I don't know what you mean."

"Well, for instance, when it talks about 'God so loved the world that he gave his only begotten son,' that's something that people who have children can understand."

"What about those of us who don't have children?"

"Well, we look at it from the other angle. It always seemed to me that God must be like Ildefonso Armijo."

Ruth blinked, thinking she had heard wrong. "I'm sorry. I must have missed something somewhere. Would you say that again?"

"Ildefonso Armijo. Angel's papa. It seemed to me that maybe that's the way God is. You look at Mr. Armijo. He loves Angel. I know it. Angel knows it. But he set rules that Angel had to live by while he was a boy living at home. Told him he'd be punished if he broke the rules. Told him what the punishment was. And you could depend on it. If Angel broke a rule, Mr. Armijo would keep his word. Those rules were mighty worrisome to a boy—chafed him, you know? Now he's a man, he can see why his father demanded certain things of him. I expect he's doing the same for his children."

Heck flicked his cigarette butt into the bed of embers. "So, I think that must be how God is. He loves me, but he sets rules for me, too. Tells me I'll be punished if I break the rules. He's not incomprehensible. He's a father."

Heck lay completely down, taking his hat off and resting his head on the palm of his left hand. "Come lie down with me," he said.

Ruth set her empty coffee cup down and lay beside him, putting her head on his shoulder. He pointed with his right hand. "There's the Big Dipper. See?"

"You're not going to try and show me the North Star again, are you?"

"It's right there. Follow the end of the Big Dipper straight up."

"It's not straight, and it's not bright, and I really don't know why it's such a famous star. If I'm ever lost I'll follow the eastern star instead. I'd rather go to Florida than Alaska, anyway."

They lay and looked at the stars brightly winking above them, holes burned through the black blanket of night. The fire cracked and popped occasionally, but otherwise the only sound she could hear was the beating of his heart.

"You asked if I believe in an afterlife," Heck began.

Ruth moved her head, so she could hear him better. "Yes?"

"I do." His voice had that odd timbre again. "When we die, we go to heaven to live with God. I believe that. But I believe in a life before, too."

He paused so long she wondered if she needed to prompt him, but he went on. "I think we lived with God before we were born. That's why people look forward to going to heaven so much. They're going home. It's a place they know. Familiar."

Ruth lay with her head on Heck's shoulder, looking into the spangled blackness above her and listening to the words her husband was speaking.

"But there's more," Heck continued. "I've spent a lot of time looking up at those stars and thinking about God. I got this idea that, not only did we live with God before we were born on the earth, but we lived with him when he created the earth. We knew about it. More than that, I think we helped."

Ruth frowned into the darkness. "I've never heard anyone preach anything like that. Where did you get this?"

"I worked it out myself. I think of Mr. Armijo. When he had something he was gonna build, he'd gather his kids—and me—and talk to us about what he was gonna do. He'd show us the plans and give us assignments and have us out there working and learning. Hell, I learned how to make 'dobe brick building his shed. I never look at that shed, but what I'm proud of what I did when I was twelve years old. That's how I think it was with us."

"Did you tell this to Preacher Lewis?"

"You're the first person I've ever talked to about it."

She shook her head. "It sounds a little fantastic."

"No, listen. I think that's why some folks love birds, or some folks love bugs. We had this old fellow who came by once, studying beetles. That's all he did was study beetles. He was fascinated by them. Or like me with horses. I can almost know what a horse is thinking. I get a-horseback, and it's almost as if we're the same creature. I think that's because, maybe back when the Lord was creating things, I—"

Ruth couldn't help it. The things that Heck was saying were so outlandish that she got the giggles. She tried to stifle them, but he must have felt her ribcage shaking, and he raised up on his elbow, "What's the matter?"

She had to wait a moment until she could master herself. She choked down the laughter that still threatened to bubble out, took a great breath, and finally was able to speak. "Oh, Heck, you certainly are an original. I can just see it. There's your God saying, *Come cheeldren. I weel show ju how to make sometheeng.*" With her gift for mimicry, Ruth imitated the Mexican accent perfectly. "*We only ha' seex days to do thees, and then we ha' to take the siesta.*"

She went off in another peal of laughter that trailed off when Heck abruptly sat up. He threw another handful of sage on the fire and then stood.

She sat uncertainly as he silently rolled out the bedroll and then sat down to pull off his boots. He got under the covers without saying anything but turned them back as an invitation to her to come to bed. She took off her boots and lay down, wondering, as she drew the covers up over her shoulder, what had happened.

That was the end of the interlude. Although the last month at Cottonwood Springs was a time of easy companionship where they worked, laughed, rode, read, sang, and did all of the things they had done before, Ruth felt it was never quite the same again.

Chapter 35

IF COTTONWOOD SPRINGS was an interlude, Hooper's Well was a penance.

Cottonwood Springs was nestled in a red rock canyon with scrub pine and cedar trees that gave welcome shade on a hot summer's day. Hooper's Well was located on a dry, sunbaked flat where there was nothing to stay the wind that blew through and little to hold down the brown dirt.

At Cottonwood Springs the water, sweet and pure, poured forth from the earth in abundance and flowed by the cabin. At Hooper's Well there was water aplenty, but it sat sullenly deep in the ground and had to be hauled out by force. Off-color, ill-tasting, mildly purgative, it left a residue in the bottom of the coffeepot that had to be chiseled out.

The shack at Hooper's Well was deplorable, a shaky frame with walls and roof covered by odd scraps of corrugated tin that cracked and rattled in the wind and allowed copious amounts of dust to blow in. It was furnished in Early Spartan. The chairs, table, and bed were first cousins to those at Cottonwood Springs, but they were definitely poor relations.

Cottonwood Springs was tranquil. Sounds were all soothing—flowing water, the breeze in the trees, the singing of birds. Hooper's Well was never quiet. The bull that Ollie had put on that section of range hung around the water tank huffing and bawling, advertising his wares and warning off interlopers. Day and night, he swaggered and called until the texture of life, sleeping and waking, was covered with a rust-colored undercoat of sound.

Then there was the pump. It crouched inside the shack next to an outside wall, spitting and popping, its immense flywheel squeaking as it turned over and over and over. A sense of rhythm would have made it more acceptable as a roomer, but it had none. It fired intermittently with never an attempt at a cadence. Even the squeaking of the flywheel and the flapping of the belt were without meter.

Ruth and Heck arrived on a gusty April day when the hills were obscured by a brown haze. If the sight of the house was daunting, entering it was more so. Heck opened the door, and as Ruth went in, a gust of wind followed her, swirling in and around, picking up several layers of powdery sediment and suspending them in the air until it was hard to breathe. Ruth retreated to the car while Heck grabbed a bucket and went to get a pail of water from the stock tank, so they could wet down surfaces to control the dust while they swept and cleaned.

Living there was a marginal existence at best, and Ruth would not have stayed five minutes had it not been for Heck. She had thought him cheerful before—good tempered and easy company—but, being back on the Jornada, Heck became more lighthearted, even merry. He whistled and sang as he did his work, and sometimes, while she was engaged in a task, he would catch her unaware and waltz her around. Every morning, even before he made coffee, Heck would go outside and stand in the dooryard, gazing first east to the Caballo Mountains and then west to the San Andreas. Ruth, still abed and savoring the last minutes of warmth and idleness, would listen to the screen door bang as he went out and the jingling of his spurs as he wandered around, and she knew, for his sake, she had to stick it out.

It wasn't easy. There was no Romelia Coughlin to listen and understand, to teach her the philosophy of a cowboy's wife. There was no running water in the house, and the culinary water had to be dipped from a storage barrel that was filled when the old one-lunger pumped water for the stock tank. The water was always warm, and because of the mineral content, it dulled Ruth's hair and chapped her hands. The cook stove was capricious, sometimes starting easily and at other times refusing to draw.

Ollie Free was different from Henry Coughlin. Tall and stooped and mostly legs, he looked like a frail old crane. He was bald-headed with flyaway sideburns, and he wore wire-rimmed spectacles that magnified his pale blue eyes. One day when he pulled into the yard, Ruth mentioned to Heck that those big eyes made her uncomfortable.

"He can't help how he looks," Heck said. "Besides, he likes you."

"He has an odd way of showing it. He always stays out by his pickup when he comes by, even when I invite him in."

They stood at the window and watched as Ollie unfolded himself from the cab. He stood a minute with drooping shoulders. Then he slammed the pickup door and waited for Heck to come out of the house.

"His piles are bothering him. It's gonna be murder for him out on the work." Heck gave Ruth a one-handed hug. "I'll see if I can talk him out of the stuff to put water into the new house. It'd be better if he wasn't hurting, but I'll do what I can."

"Take him some tortillas. The way to a man's heart, you know." She wrapped some still-warm tortillas in a dishtowel.

"Let's see if it'll get to his pocketbook."

"I think to get to Ollie's pocketbook you have to drill and blast," she said dryly.

She was wrong. Heck came in and reported that Ollie felt she should have water in the house. "He said we could scavenge materials from the place at Bitter Well. And if we need to buy some new things, Ollie says that's all right, too."

April was a busy month. Besides the regular work and preparations for the spring roundup, Heck and Ruth began the new house. It was simple, rough carpentry and went up fast. There was no foundation. They chose a site away from the stock tank, and Heck laid two two-by-twelves down along each of the four points of the compass. Their house would be twenty-four feet by twenty-four feet.

They had made good progress by Cinco de Mayo. Because Heck had to leave the next morning, they pushed late into the evening to get the ridgepole set. They celebrated the holiday by watching a splendid sunset while sitting on top of the western wall.

The sunset went on and on, like an actor who couldn't be persuaded to leave the stage. When the colors finally faded to gray, Ruth sighed and sagged against Heck. "I'm glad that's over! My rear end couldn't take much more."

"You have to suffer to truly appreciate beauty," Heck said in a pious voice.

"I truly appreciated that sunset," she returned, "because I have suffered greatly. In fact, I may have to curtail some of my activities if I don't get movement back in my lower quarters."

Heck leaned over and nuzzled under her ear. "Damn, woman!" he murmured. "What're you doing, jeopardizing those lovely lower quarters?"

She squealed and grabbed onto his arm. "Don't lean over like that. Be careful or you'll knock me off!"

He laughed and said, "Here. I'll help you down. We've got to get me ready to go."

They descended the ladder and walked back to the little tin shack with their arms around each other. Somehow, they didn't get around to final preparations for Heck's going until later that night.

Ruth lay on the bed and watched Heck tie up his bedroll and pack his clothes. "How long are you going to be gone?" she asked languidly, reaching out to brush his hand as he went by.

He smiled down at her. "Probably two-and-a-half, three weeks. Ole Ollie's piles are so bad he'll be depending on me to do a lot of the ramrodding. He won't be able to be in the saddle at all. You be all right here?"

"I'll be lonesome."

"Go on into town. Go see Lucy, or Mama."

"Your mother doesn't like me."

"She's only just met you. How can she not like you? If you're not comfortable at Mama's, go to Lucy's."

"Maybe I will. Don't forget your razor. I want to be able to kiss you when you get back."

Ruth stood in the early morning darkness and watched her husband's tall silhouette against the glare of the headlights as he stowed his gear in the back of Ollie's pickup. Ollie revved the motor in impatience as Heck came back to say goodbye.

"I think goodbyes in the dark are the worst," she whispered as he held her close.

"They're all the dickens. Kiss me, Darlin'. It's got to last a long time."

She pushed his hat back and did her best to give him a kiss that would last two-and-a-half, three weeks. Ollie tooted his horn, and Heck chuckled. "Take care of your lower quarters; won't you?" he whispered. Then he gave her one last hug and turned to join his boss.

"I'll be here when you get back," she called as he opened the pickup door.

Chapter 36

RUTH WENT TO Palomas to visit Lucy as Heck suggested. She had first seen Lucy at the dance in Cutter but hadn't formally met her until the week before Heck left. They had come in from Hooper's Well to celebrate Ruth's birthday by shopping for a bathtub, and afterward they had gone to Palomas, so Ruth could meet the family.

Lucy had been standoffish at first. Ruth figured it was because she had never been around a woman who dared to live with a man outside of marriage, and she went out of her way to overcome Lucy's reserve. By the time the visit was over, the two women were well on their way to being friends.

When Heck had been gone about a week, Ruth did some shopping in Hot Springs and then headed to Palomas, arriving about midday. Lucy had just returned from town too, and Ruth made a joke about missing each other in a place as small as Hot Springs.

Lucy ushered her into her little home behind Bemis's store. "I wasn't shopping; you know. I was taking Little Emory in for his four-month checkup. Please sit down."

"How is he?" Ruth looked at the baby lying on a blanket on the floor as she sat in one of the chairs and put her purse on the table.

"He's fine. The doctor says I'm dressing him too warm." She shook her head as she smiled at the baby. "Isn't that right, son? Too warm. Too, too warm!" Looking back at Ruth, she explained, "He wants the baby to be tough, not a hothouse ..." Her voice trailed off as she discovered Ruth staring at her.

When Lucy raised her eyebrows in question, Ruth said, "I'm sorry. You must think me rude. I was just admiring your dress. Where did you get it?"

"I made it."

Ruth sat still, drumming her fingers on the table, regarding the dress. "It's very nice," she said finally. "Do you have some scissors?"

"Yes, of course."

"May I see them?"

Lucy smiled uncertainly but produced a pair of shears.

Ruth took them. "Come here," she said. "Turn around." She looked underneath a bow at the hip and snipped the attaching threads and then did the same to a matching bow on the shoulder. Leaning back, she admired her handiwork. "Before, it was pretty. Now, it's chic." Her brows furrowed in concentration as she continued to stare. "Where did you get the pattern for this dress?"

Lucy's cheeks grew crimson. She turned away and leaned down to pick up her baby, burying her face in his neck so that he cooed and flailed his arms and kicked in delight. Pulling up the other chair, Lucy sat down facing Ruth and cradled the baby on her lap. "It was yours. I copied it."

"Yes, I can see. The lines are the same." Ruth laid the scissors on the table. "You didn't put the white collar on, and that's why I didn't recognize it at first. And those bows!"

Lucy smiled. "I thought if I put the bows on, you wouldn't guess. Are you angry?"

"My dear, of course not. I think it's terribly clever of you. When did you see the dress? Oh, I know. The dance. You saw it just that once and were able to copy it?"

Lucy blushed again and nodded.

"Show me some of the other things you've done."

Lucy didn't have much to show. Her talent was evident, but raw materials were hard to come by on their slender means. She showed Ruth her wardrobe and a pair of work pants that Bemis had given them that she had made over for Jimmy.

As she spread out the garments, she talked of better times to come. An earth dam was to be built over the Rio Grande below Palomas, and they would be hiring lots of men. Jimmy would be sure to get a job there at better wages than he was making now.

They went back to the kitchen, and while Lucy made lunch, Ruth gingerly held the baby, relinquishing him to his mother with relief at the end of five minutes.

As she got ready to go, Ruth asked, "Could you teach me to sew? I'd like to learn. While Heck is gone, I could come in and help you with your housework. Then you'd have time to teach me."

It was agreed. Ruth collected her purse and, with a smile and a wave, was out the door heading for her car. Before she could start the motor, Lucy came running out of the house with her baby on her hip and a letter in her hand.

"I forgot. This came to the Diamond E, and Ruby sent it over for me to give to you when I saw you."

Taking the letter, Ruth recognized Bunny Ashton's writing. She held it for a moment without speaking then thanked Lucy absently and tossed it on the seat beside her before she backed out and drove away.

Ruth felt like a ghost was riding home with her that afternoon, an elegant lady shade that bounced as the car jolted along the gravel roads—a shade holding a lace hankie to her nose as the dust floated in through the windows, who was appallingly bored with the endless expanses of tobosa grass and greasewood.

It was late afternoon when they got home, Ruth and the ghost. The pathetic little tin house—her home—cast a long black shadow that crawled to the east. The new house stood with its naked ridgepole and hand-me-down-lumber walls, tired and worn before it was even finished.

Ruth sat in the car, considering the letter. A letter from a friend, and yet she was curiously reluctant to open it. Finally she shrugged and picked up the envelope. She ran her fingers under the seal and pulled out the pages that were covered with Bunny's meticulous penmanship.

Off-white, elegant, and expensive, the stationery felt familiar in her hand as she read.

> *Dear Ruth,*
>
> *You naughty thing! What have you been doing? I have been able to get nothing from Agatha Reynolds. But you know she was born with her lips pursed in disapproval. Gretchen Hancott was much more helpful. She says you have run off with some cowboy and are living life au naturel. She says she can't recall your cowboy, but there's one with black curly hair and a dimple that she remembers well.*
>
> *Are you sitting down? I've great news. I'm coming through your part of the country! We're moving to California. Robert's father says there are fortunes to be made there, and Robert's fortune isn't near big enough, so we're off. He's already there, and I'm tying up loose ends here before joining him.*

I'm taking the train and will be making the trip around the middle of April. Let me know if you can see me, and I'll come the southern route. I'd love to see you and your horses and dogies. (Why do they always tell them to get along? Does it mean they're quarrelsome?) I'm dying to meet your man. I told you not to marry Harlan, you remember.

Let me know where you will meet me. I can stay a couple of days with you. We'll go to lunch and do some shopping and talk lots of girl talk. I'll fill you in on what all of the old crowd is doing. Oh, my dear, you won't believe what Catherine Eastwood has got herself into. But that can wait. Let me hear from you soon, soon, soon.

Love, Bunny

The panic that seized Ruth when she read that Bunny intended a visit was followed by profound relief as she realized that the letter had come too late to respond. As the adrenalin drained away, she continued to sit in the car, knowing her knees wouldn't support her if she got out.

She ran her fingers over the engraved monogram before she folded the pages and put them away in her purse. Bunny spent more on one trip to the stationers than Heck made in a month. Tears trickled down her cheeks, and she sagged against the seat as the realization hit her. She was ashamed to have Bunny come and see how she was living.

The sun had gone down when Ruth finally crawled out of the car and crept to the house. Pushing the door open, dropping her purse on the table, she didn't even bother to light a lamp. She whimpered softly as she unbuttoned her dress to loosen it for comfort, slid off her shoes, and crawled under the covers. As she lay in the sagging bed, under the lumpy quilt, she whispered to herself, "What have I done?"

There was no man in the bed beside her, and she had no answer for that question.

She slept badly and woke the next morning with a feeling of unrest in her breast. Making a fire in the stove, she poured kerosene over the wood to start it and made a pot of coffee. Then she sat for a long time at the table, drinking coffee and smoking cigarettes, staring out at the half-finished cabin and thinking.

Her error, she could see now, was taking Heck on his terms. He was talented in many areas, not just as a cowboy. There was no reason why he couldn't go to California and make a fortune, too. The first thing to do was to get him off the range and into a more civilized situation. That might be a problem, as Ollie, disabled by hemorrhoids, was using Heck as ramrod now.

Ruth sat back in the chair and crossed her legs. Holding her cigarette in two fingers, she tapped her teeth with a fingernail. Her eyes narrowed as she remembered her mother laying plans to get a rich admirer to propose marriage. "You can catch more flies with honey than vinegar," her mother would say. Ruth's lips began to curl as she reflected that her mother's schemes always ended successfully at the altar.

"Patience and honey," she whispered. Crushing out her cigarette, she rose, full of purpose. With brisk movements, she stripped off her wrinkled dress and bathed, all the while turning over in her mind possible plans, plans that were long on patience and sticky with honey.

Chapter 3I

"I'VE BEEN TO California."

"When? You never mentioned it." Ruth reached over and pushed the hair back from Heck's forehead as he lay beside her.

"Oh, I've done lots of things I haven't mentioned. I figure I've got lots of time to tell you things about me and lots of time to learn about you."

Heck was home. He had shown up one morning, shaggy and dusty, still dressed in his chaps and wearing a shirt that had a pocket ripped off. He had ridden straight from their last camp and surprised Ruth as she sat at the table picking beans. Because she had been listening for the sound of the pickup, she didn't know he was there until she heard the jingling of his spurs.

He had thrown his hat on the table and leaned against the doorjamb. "Howdy, Miz Benham. You cooking a pot of beans?"

All of a sudden, she was breathless. "I was expecting someone."

Heck had rubbed his hand over his chin. "I shaved this mornin'."

She was up in an instant and in his arms. Feeling his strength, smelling the smell of hard work and horses and dust that clung to him, Ruth had forgotten her honeyed plans of the week before.

But not for long. After the first days of elation at having Heck home, as the routine became grind, and the one-lunger shattered the stillness with its erratic explosions, as the flies in the outhouse multiplied, she began to think that she hadn't the patience to endure the time it would take for sweet persuasion.

Sometimes, in the early mornings after Heck got the coffee on, Ruth enticed him back to bed. He claimed she was corrupting him, that no self-respecting cowboy would come back to bed after the coffee was started. But she would lie there with the covers turned back and a provocative smile on her lips, and he would capitulate.

He had come back to bed this morning, and in the mellow early light, as she had lain with him, tracing patterns with her fingertips on his shoulder, she asked him about California.

"They grow oranges, there," he said. "The nights are warm, and the smell of orange blossoms is so heavy and sweet that it makes a man mighty restless."

"Restless? Like what?"

"I don't know. That's just how I felt out there. Restless."

"What were you doing there?"

"Diamond E shipped a load of cattle out, and I went with them. I stayed a few days to look around. Thought since I was there, I'd take advantage of it."

"What did you think of it?"

"Oh, it was nice. But I was ..."

"Restless." She finished for him.

He kissed her briskly on the cheek. "Yep. Like now. I gotta go." He swept back the covers, swung his legs around, and began pulling on his pants.

Ruth lay for a moment, reflecting that California was not immediately a viable prospect. She should probably lower her sights. Get him off the range first.

She began talking about the dam that was to be built. Jimmy was already working there. The project engineer was a man Jimmy had worked for before, and anyone who wanted a job could probably be hired with Jimmy's recommendation.

Heck didn't seem to pick up on the idea that he could leave Ollie and go to work there himself, so finally one day she asked him if he had thought about it.

He was fixing a broken pane of glass in one of the windows that Emory had brought from Bitter Well. Pausing with his putty knife in hand, he looked at her keenly. "No," he said quietly. "Why should I?"

"They make good money."

"While the work is there, they do. But out of the big money they make, they have to pay for their food and housing. Sometimes the money doesn't turn out to be as good as you think it is." He regarded her silently for a moment longer and went back to his window.

Mrs. Pettybone found out Ruth played bridge and asked her to make a fourth one time, and that turned into a regular weekly outing. Each Tuesday, as she carefully dressed, she thought of the clothes somewhere in storage in Hot Springs that she hadn't the courage to get.

"I didn't know cowboys' wives belonged to bridge clubs," Heck called from the roof of the new house one day as she walked to the car with her purse in one hand and her gloves in the other. He had on a carpenter's apron and stood on the incline with a hammer in his hand.

"If they're good enough players to get asked, they do." She smiled at him, blew a kiss, and was gone.

Though Ruth was single-minded in pursuing her goal, she didn't forget the honey. She was attentive and loving to Heck, making sure his needs were met. Only once did vinegar dissolve the honey glaze.

Heck had found a desert tortoise lying in the trail as he was out checking on the cattle. It was not long dead, so he took his knife and stripped out the flesh, leaving the shell on top of a red-ant hill to let the busy little insects finish the cleaning job. He rode by a week later and picked up the shell. Creamy white on the inside and beautiful in translucent brown tones on the outside, he brought it home to Ruth.

It had not been a good day for Ruth. It was her bridge day, and her hands were so chapped that her fingertips had snagged her last pair of hose as she put them on. Two days before payday, there was no money for another pair of stockings. Then, when she got to town, the ladies of the bridge club all wanted to go to the Jade Room for lunch. She had to make a lame excuse about an appointment because she had no money for eating out. Her explanation was accepted at face value, but she was angry that she had to lie.

When she got home in the late afternoon, the stove wouldn't light. She made several abortive tries with paper and kindling, but finally she had to go to the shed and get a can of kerosene to pour on the wood to get it started.

Heck had built Ruth a little evaporation cooler to keep food cool. It consisted of a frame covered in burlap that had moisture wicking down through from a pan on top. Ruth had forgotten to fill the pan with water and came home to find that the burlap was dry; the milk that was fresh that morning had gone sour, and the butter had melted.

No, it had not been a good day.

Heck came in whistling and greeted Ruth cheerfully, hugging her from behind and burying his face in her hair. "How's Miz Whitleather?"

Ruth didn't reply.

"I brought you something," he said, tossing the turtle shell on the table in front of her.

She ignored the shell, pulling away from Heck to put a pan of biscuits in the oven.

"What's the matter?"

Ruth walked over to stand in front of him with her hands spread out for him to see.

"Look at my hands!" she commanded. "That's what's the matter. Look at them!"

Heck took her hands in his, turned them over and back, and then looked up with a question in his eyes.

"Do you know they're so rough that I ruined a pair of stockings on them? They hurt when I put them in hot water. Look at my hands!"

Heck stood for a moment, staring at the rough, red members. Then he turned without speaking and went out, returning with a dusty, square tin can he had retrieved from the shed.

He set it down on the table beside the tortoise shell. "Try some of that," he said. "It's good stuff."

It was good stuff. In later days, Ruth used it and found it was wonderful for chapped hands. Right then, when she saw that he had brought her Bag Balm, designed for cows' udders, she grew furious and screamed at him.

Heck, sitting on the bed and taking off his spurs, looked up in time to see the turtle shell come flying through the air toward him. He dodged to the right, instinctively putting up a hand to protect himself. That gesture was his undoing, for no sooner had the shell left her hand than Ruth picked up the can of Bag Balm and heaved it, too.

Her aim was poor, but his hand was in the air, and the heavy can caught his little finger, bending it back and snapping the bone.

Ruth hadn't seen the can hit his finger and so couldn't understand Heck's sudden pallor and the dash he made, practically bent double, to the door and outside. When he didn't reappear, she came to the door and looked through the screen. He was standing with his hand in the stock tank.

As she watched from the doorway, Heck lifted his hand from the water and looked at it. Then he went over to the unfinished house, returning a moment later with his carpenter's apron. Ruth held the screen open for him and saw that the little finger on his left hand was already swollen and tattooed with an ugly blue splotch where a blood vessel had popped.

"Oh, Heck!" she cried. "Oh, Baby, what have I done?"

He tossed the apron onto the table. "You want to get my carpenter's pencil out of there?" he asked. "We're gonna need some bandages. You got a rag you can tear up?"

She flew to find a flour sack and a pair of scissors. Using the pencil as a splint, she followed Heck's directions, binding it securely. Then she sat and looked mutely at him, her eyes making the apologies her lips couldn't form.

Heck tested the splint and nodded his satisfaction. Then he lifted his head and sniffed the air. "Is something burning?"

"My biscuits!" Ruth wailed. Grabbing a dishtowel, she opened the oven door and took out the pan of black lumps that had begun as sour milk biscuits. It was too much. She stood in front of the stove with the pan of smoking carbon in her hands, and the tears which she had been determined all day not to shed welled up and spilled over.

Heck silently took the pan from her, set it down on the table, and pulled her into his arms. That made matters worse, for what had been only tears before became almost uncontrollable sobs that went on and on.

Finally, Heck led her to a chair where he sat and pulled her onto his lap. She laid her head on his shoulder with her face pressed into his neck and strove for control as he whispered, "Hush, now. What can be so bad? It's all right, Baby Doll. Hush, now, and tell me what's the matter."

And so, she told him. Not about being ashamed but about needing more than the existence they had. "I can do it, Heck. You know I can, but I don't want to do it forever. There's more to life than fighting the weather and the bugs all the time. I've tried your life. Why won't you come and try mine?"

"That wasn't the deal we made, Darlin'."

"Deal? Do people who love each other make deals?"

"I don't know. It sounded like you were trying to make one right now."

"Maybe I was." She leaned back and looked at him. "If I was, what do you say?"

He kissed her on the cheek. "That I'm getting a cramp in my leg. Why don't you sit there, and let's talk this out?"

Ruth laughed a tiny laugh and moved to the other chair. He took her right hand in his right and laid his left hand clumsily over it, his wounded finger sticking out at an angle.

"It's like this, Darlin'. I'm a cowboy. I was a poor cowboy when I asked you to marry me. I never promised you more than that. I thought you were willing to stand by me and take things as they came."

"But don't you want to go places and do things and make something more of yourself than a cowboy?"

Heck released Ruth's hand and sat back in his chair, obviously considering. Finally, he said, "Let me ask you a question. Who was Henry David Thoreau's best friend?"

Her brow wrinkled. "What does that have to do with anything?"

"What was his name?" Heck asked patiently.

"I don't know his name," she said with an edge to her voice. "How should I know his name?"

"That's my point.

For a moment Ruth stared at Heck with hard eyes. Then they softened. "You're going to tell me one of your stories," she said with a faint smile. "I can tell."

He answered her smile with a small one of his own. "That's right. When Thoreau came of an age when all the young fellas usually set off for Europe to make what they called the 'grand tour,' he decided not to go. All his friends asked him how he was ever gonna be polished, how he was ever gonna amount to anything if he didn't travel to Europe. Do you know what he said?"

"I have a feeling I'm about to."

"He said, 'I shall travel widely in Concord.' Is there coffee on the stove?"

She laughed. "I'll believe he said he'd travel widely in Concord, but I don't believe he asked about coffee."

Heck grinned. "He didn't. That was me. We haven't had supper, if you will remember, and I thought I'd just have a cup of coffee to carry me through. No, don't get up. I'll get it and one for you, too."

Ruth watched him with red-rimmed eyes as he got the cups and poured them full.

"Now tell me," he said as he handed hers to her with his injured left hand, "what is the name of the fella who told Thoreau he'd never amount to anything if he didn't get out of town?"

"I don't know."

"So, would you agree that being widely traveled isn't necessary for someone to make something of himself?"

"I will agree that Thoreau wasn't born a cowboy," she said dryly. "If he qualified for the grand tour, I doubt he needed to 'make something of himself.'"

Heck took a sip of coffee. "All right, let's try this. I'm twenty-eight years old, but I've been working at my trade since I was fourteen. That's fourteen years I've got invested. I'm good at it. I'm good at working men, too. I've got the chance, right now, right here, to make a place for myself, a good, substantial place doing what I want to be doing, what I'm happy at, what I'm good at. I need my wife to stand by me in this and help me."

"Even if what makes you happy makes me unhappy?" Ruth's voice teetered on the edge of breaking.

Heck reached for her hand as he cleared his throat. "I didn't realize you were so unhappy." He looked away as he continued. "I know living here is hard, and I want to make the new place comfortable for you. I've even worked out how we can have indoor plumbing."

Ruth freed her hand, reached up, and turned his face, so she could see his eyes. A tear sat on his lower lash, and she wiped it away with her thumb. "Oh Baby Doll," she murmured. "I am so sorry."

Leaning forward, she kissed him. Gone for the moment was the discontent that had hung so heavily around her. "I'll try harder," she said.

He didn't answer. He simply stood and pulled her into his arms.

In the solidness of that shelter, she pressed her ear against his chest and listened to the hammering of his heart and the raggedness of his breathing. "I'll try," she whispered again, as if she needed reminding.

Chapter 38

RUTH CONTINUED TO spend a lot of time in town. Sometimes she came back in a good mood, full of energy and fun. Sometimes she was quiet and morose, dragging around to fix dinner and crawling into bed early with the dishes undone. She worked alongside Heck on the new place, listened to his plans and agreed or offered criticism, but he noticed she never made any plans, herself.

One afternoon, Heck was working on a trestle for the tank that was to supply water to the near-finished cabin. He had fashioned a leather splint that wrapped around his injured finger, holding it immobile and at the same time protecting it. Carpentry was only mildly awkward.

Standing by the belt that ran from the pump motor through the wall of the tin shack, Heck was hardly aware of the flapping as it ran by in one continual round or of the flywheel squeaking inside the house or of the occasional, erratic *kapow* of the old one-lunger.

All at once he heard the sound of a heavy object striking the corrugated tin just inside where he was standing. He walked around the house and opened the screen. Ruth was standing in the middle of the room with her hands on her hips. She shot him a defensive look.

Heck's eyes went to the wall behind the motor, to the dent in the tin, and to the cast-iron skillet on the floor. "Lost the fly swatter?"

"I was aiming at the motor. It's like waiting for the other shoe to drop. Drives me crazy."

Heck cocked his head to the side as he regarded his wife. "Are you feeling all right?"

"What do you mean?"

"I mean, um, are you well?"

"Do I look ill?"

"No. No, you look fine. I just wondered—" Heck, still standing in the doorway, took off his hat and raked his fingers through his hair.

"What did you wonder?" Ruth stood with her arms folded and one foot forward.

"Um. I was just thinking about how, sometimes, ladies have hard times when they're ..." Heck's voice trailed off.

Ruth blinked. "When they're what?"

Heck looked out the door behind him. If he was looking for reinforcements, none appeared. A slow blush spread over his face, and he looked down at his hat. "Ah, never mind. I think I'll ride out and check on that coyote trap I set last night."

He put on his hat and pulled the brim low. "I'll be back by dinner." He turned and strode toward the corral.

Ruth stared after him. She worked out the puzzle about the time she heard his pony's hooves pounding on the hard-packed earth beyond the windmill.

She laughed, ran to the door, and shouted, "I'm not pregnant," even though she knew he was too far away to hear. Still chuckling, she picked up the skillet and hung it on a nail by the sink. "Silly man," she said, smiling. "I guess we need to have a little talk."

When Heck returned, it was only to get his slicker, a blanket and a fresh horse. He paused at the door with his rifle and scabbard and told Ruth in terse sentences that the coyote had taken down a heifer that he had been doctoring for screwworms.

"How long will you be gone?" she asked, following him to the corral.

"As long as it takes." He swung into the saddle and looked down at her. "You be all right here alone tonight?"

Without answering, she grasped the denim of Heck's pant leg and put her forehead against his thigh. The horse shifted its weight and blew out a gusty breath, and she felt Heck's hand on her hair. "I'm sorry I've been such a witch," she said.

"Shhh. Don't talk like that. You be all right?"

She stepped back. "Yes. I'll be fine. Go get that coyote." She lifted her hand in farewell and watched as he rode around the corral and headed north, not moving until the only sign of his passage was a tiny plume of dust in the air. Then she went back into the house and played solitaire until it was too dark to see.

Heck returned the next morning. While he got the water tank completed, Ruth began painting cupboards in the new house. In the bustle of getting ready to move in, she never got around to having that little talk.

The new place was more comfortable and easier to keep clean. It even had running water. But the stove, when they moved it, became more reluctant to draw and consequently harder to start. The promised bathroom was still an empty room with outlines on the floor in chalk for tub, sink, and toilet.

Ruth would still have been ashamed to invite Bunny Ashton to visit.

One day she came home from town later than usual. Heck was due any time, and she was in a hurry to get supper started. After changing into a housedress, she tied on her apron, fumbling in her haste with the bow. She shoved some paper in the firebox with kindling on top, but, though the paper flared and burned, the wood wouldn't catch. She put in more paper, but the stove refused to draw.

Mentally cursing the stove, the house, and stubborn cowboys, Ruth pushed through the screen door and went to the shed where a fuel can was sitting with a battered tin cup beside it. She poured the cup half full and hurried in, emptying the entire contents over the wood. Picking up the box of matches, she broke the first one in her haste. Disgusted, she threw it unlit into the firebox and got another.

There was a nagging thought at the back of her mind, a sense that something was wrong, but it wasn't until she had let go of the second match and the tiny torch was dropping into the stove that she realized that she had grabbed the fuel for the gasoline pump and not the can of kerosene.

She could not call back the match.

Just before the explosion, there was time for her mind to work out what was going to happen, but there was no time to duck. Her ears caught and transmitted the sound of *whuuump*, but she didn't see the spraying of ashes and sticks and soot, for the back stove lid blew out at an angle and caught her on the temple, and she crumpled into a heap on the floor.

Heck rode in half an hour later. He saw that the car was there, but as he put his pony away, he saw no sign that Ruth was about. For a fleeting instant he wondered if she had left him as she had left Harlan, but he shied away from the disloyal thought and went about his evening chores.

Tossing hay to the horses he had in the corral, Heck was stopped dead in his tracks by the thought that maybe Ruth hadn't been playing bridge after all on all those days when she had dressed so carefully and stayed so long in town. Maybe she had been seeing some well-dressed, well-educated man. A man with money. A man who could give her a house in town.

Called back to the job at hand by his pony reaching over the fence and pulling the sweet-smelling hay from his hands, Heck pushed the thought away. But it was a persistent thought, intruding like an unwelcome salesman with a leering smile and a foot in the door.

The old range cow that they kept for milk shifted from one foot to another as Heck squatted by her and yanked on her teats, glancing over his shoulder every now and then at the house windows, vacant as an idiot's stare.

Heck turned out the cow and gave most of the milk to the calf that stuck its head through the slats of a little pen and bawled for its supper. Then he carried the milk bucket into the house, finally allowing himself to call Ruth's name as he opened the screen.

He knew instantly what had happened. Evidence of the explosion clung to the walls, coated the ceiling, and hung in the air. A gray-black blanket covered the inert form of the woman who lay with sable lashes closed against her pale cheeks and a dark blue bruise showing over one eye.

Flinging the milk bucket in the direction of the sink, Heck was at her side in a moment, kneeling, feeling at her wrist for reassurance. The pulse was there, but more than that, the warmth and firmness of living flesh kept him from giving in to the dark feelings and morbid images that ran rampant through his mind and breast, even as he picked her up and carried her to the car.

He drove like a madman to Hot Springs. Indeed, he must have been more than half crazy, for as they tore through the late afternoon stillness of the Jornada, he pulled his hat off his head. Glancing now at the heavens, now at the unconscious and wounded woman, and only occasionally at the road, Heck made a bargain with God.

Chapter 39

"SURELY YOU'RE NOT going to wear those boots!" Ruth sat on the bed in her nightgown, her hair tumbled around a face that was still too pale. She watched Heck lace up the second of a pair of heavy work boots.

"Well, yes, I am. What's wrong with them?"

"They make you look like Li'l Abner."

Heck stood up and tucked in his shirt. "Who's Little Abner?" He pulled his belt tight and fastened the buckle.

"He's a comic strip character. A big—I don't know what he is. He's a rustic."

Heck smiled and said lightly, "Well, so am I. So that's all right then; isn't it?"

"It's not all right that they're a dead man's boots. It gives me the willies to see you in them." Ruth shivered.

Heck chuckled. "Never mind, Darlin'. I'm grateful to Helen for giving them to me. I dang near broke my neck yesterday wearing my other boots. You want to have the willies, just come and watch me wearing cowboy boots while I'm climbing around a dragline." He grabbed his lunch bucket and hat and kissed his wife on the cheek. "There's Jimmy. See you tonight."

He was out the door, striding to meet his brother-in-law, who not only picked Heck up every morning but who also supervised him as he learned how to be an oiler on the dragline Jimmy operated.

Ruth lay back down. She had not fully recovered from the concussion that kept her at first unconscious, then disoriented and nauseous, and finally weak and lightheaded. She didn't completely understand how she came to be in Palomas in what was apparently her own home. It was as if the explosion had shattered the old existence she and Heck had shared. As yet, she hadn't scraped up the energy to discover what had been salvaged from the shards.

Heck didn't tell her about the promise he made on that grim ride into Hot Springs just after the accident. Didn't mention his vow to leave the ranch and move to town if Ruth pulled through, somehow equating what would make her happy with what would please God.

One of the hardest things he had ever done was to tell Ollie that he didn't want the position as foreman on his ranch. He had stood with his hat in his hands and said, "I hate it, Ollie, because I feel like I'm letting you down."

The gaunt old man had grunted and had fixed him with a baleful pale blue stare. "Ya hate it because you're lettin' yourself down," he snapped. "You and I both know you're a natural at workin' cattle and workin' men. I was glad to have you here with me. Thought that in time you'd take over. I'm sorry your little lady wasn't happy, was glad to think of her out in that little place you had built for her ..." His voice trailed off, and the eyes, grotesquely magnified by the thick lenses of his glasses, blinked, blinked. He wagged his head and said no more.

Heck shook hands with his old friend and drove back into town. Ollie's accusation was another in a series of events that bore little semblance to reality. It was as if someone else's wife was almost killed, as if someone else had renounced the freedom of the range, as if someone else had sold his fiddle because he needed money and couldn't play it anymore, anyway, since his little finger wouldn't bend properly. Heck Benham stood back as an onlooker and watched as a tall young man for whom cowboying was second nature—who wrangled and roped and branded and doctored almost by instinct—watched as he fumbled around among the heavy equipment that was constructing a huge clay dam across the Rio Grande. The first few days on the job had a nightmarish quality because he was so lost, and he felt of such little value. He couldn't even speak the language.

But Jimmy was patient and understanding and began to teach him, building upon Heck's mechanical experience. Jimmy didn't say much, but when he did, it was to the point and understandable.

"He's unbelievable," Heck said to Ruth one evening when she was well enough to come to the table for supper. "It's kind of fallen to him to start all the Cats in the morning."

"Cats!" she exclaimed. "What in the world are you doing with cats?"

Heck laughed and reached for a piece of cornbread. "Caterpillars. Bulldozers. Huge machines that have a blade in front and push dirt along. They have diesel engines, and to start a diesel, you have to first start a gas engine. They're all temperamental, and you have to baby them along and know just how each one likes to be treated, choking one, leaning the mixture out for another, listening for just the right sound before you try to start the diesel."

He paused, looking for the butter. She pushed it to him.

"Thanks. No one but Jimmy has the patience to mess with them. Every morning he goes early, and by the time the operators are there, the Cats are all up and running, and he's on the dragline starting his day. He's tried to show me how, so I can help him." Heck rubbed his thumb back and forth over his fingers. "I just don't have the feel of it. He's quite a guy."

Heck used the early morning time, while Jimmy was starting the Cats, to learn all he could about operating the big machines. He had no desire to spend much time as an oiler. His practice paid off about a month later when they needed someone to drive a Cat pulling a sheep's foot.

"A sheep's foot!" Ruth exclaimed when he told her he was now an operator. "Is that all right?"

"What do you mean?"

"Well, you're a cow man. I thought cowboys didn't have anything to do with sheep men. That must go for sheep's foots, too. Or, is it sheep's feet? How in the world do you speak of two of them?"

Heck tried to smile. Tried to speak lightly. But when he said, "I'm not a cowboy anymore," it didn't come out jaunty and unconcerned, as he intended. His voice was scarcely more than a whisper, and the words sounded bleak. He met her eyes, and though he wanted to explain, he couldn't find the words. To hide his feelings, he turned and walked outside into the night air.

Moving almost blindly through matte blackness under the giant cottonwoods, Heck turned by instinct onto the path up to where the schoolhouse and graveyard shared a moonlit eminence. Sitting on the school steps, leaning against the door, he smoked a cigarette and looked at the village below sitting in mottled, milky-blue light and navy shadow with the soft, rectangular gold of kerosene-lantern-lit windows glowing randomly here and there.

Heck was wise enough to know that his present mood would pass, that the wistfulness would fade. He sat and smoked, watched the river glistening in the moonlight beyond Palomas, listened to someone—Angel Armijo?—playing a guitar and singing, "La Golondrina."

When at last he made his way back down the hill, he was beginning to believe that he and Ruth would build a new life, taking some from his way and some from hers, making a hybrid marriage that blended the best of both cultures.

By high summer, Ruth was well. She and Heck and Jimmy and Lucy spent a lot of time together, going on picnics, swimming in the river, playing records on the wind-up Victrola that Bemis had in his store to lend. Sometimes they left Little Emory with Lucy's mama, but more often than not, he went along. He loved a party and was a social little being. All he needed was for someone to smile at him, and he did his best to entertain, flailing his arms and kicking his feet, grinning until his bright blue eyes were squeezed almost shut.

Little Emory was the darling of the whole village. Bemis loved to tend him while Lucy ran down to the post office. He held the little boy on his lap, allowing him to grab the elk's tooth that hung as a fob on his watch chain and use it as a teething ring. As the baby grew older, Bemis began to rearrange his store for the first time in twenty-five years, putting potentially harmful things up out of the way, so Little Emory could have free range as he scooted around on sturdy hands and knees among the salt blocks and bags of flour.

No one, save his own parents, loved Little Emory as much as Heck did. From the time the baby was six months old and could sit up by himself, Heck would come by three or four times a week in the evening to give him a ride to bed. Often Ruth came too, and they would all sit, visiting for a while in the dooryard that Lucy kept sprinkled and swept. When she said it was the baby's bedtime, and Heck stood up,

Little Emory would get excited, reaching up his arms and shouting jubilant syllables. Lucy would place him astride Heck's forearm, making sure that he held onto the thumb Heck stuck up for that purpose. Then, as Heck sang, "Strawberry Roan," Little Emory would ride a bucking bronc into his bed. The bronc would throw Little Emory, tumbling him off among the blankets, and Heck would tuck him in and sit holding a tiny hand in his, stroking it with his thumb, as he sang a night-herding song to lull the child to sleep.

One winter evening as Heck and Ruth were strolling over to Lucy's house to pop popcorn and play cards, the moon was bright and the schoolhouse on the hill was etched in gray upon the black background of night. Heck looked up at it and remembered the night in early summer when he sat on the schoolhouse steps and grieved because he wasn't a cowboy anymore.

You win a few; you lose a few, he thought to himself. Walking through the chilly night with his arm around his wife, he pictured one of his prizes, all done up in flannel pajamas, waiting for Uncle Heck to come and put him to bed.

Chapter 40

IT IS NOT to be supposed that half of a cowboy's monthly wages and the gain from selling a secondhand fiddle could provide much in the way of lodging.

After quitting Ollie Free's, Heck immediately went to work on the dam. He felt lucky to find a job so quickly and even luckier to be able to live in Palomas, so Mama and Lucy could look after Ruth while he was at work.

Bemis told Heck about the house. It wasn't much, Bemis said, but it was close by. Maybe he would be interested? Heck was, and he moved Ruth in immediately, making arrangements for Lucy to look in on her several times a day while he was gone.

It would have been simpler for all concerned to have stayed with his parents, but it set Heck's teeth on edge to have his father being courtly and solicitous and bringing flowers to Ruth. At age sixty, Nate Benham was still ruggedly handsome. A full moustache gave his face an austere look, but his smile changed austerity into a roguish recklessness that was quite beguiling. Weak as she was, Ruth had responded to the gallantry of the older cowboy as he bent his tall frame down and claimed a father-in-law's right to kiss her cheek.

Heck watched the smiles and murmured thanks Ruth offered in exchange for the desert flowers, carelessly picked yet so expertly proffered. Heck was the one who had thanked Mama for sacrificing one of her laying hens to be boiled up for broth, who washed bed linen on the washboard, and who emptied and scalded out the slop jar every morning.

Heck hated to go off and leave Ruth while she was barely able to get out of bed, but food and shelter are powerful motivating agents. He needed money to provide at least the basics, and that's about all that could be said about the tiny, two-room adobe structure that was their new home. It had the basic four walls and a roof. It was furnished with the basic bed, table and two chairs, and a cook stove. A path led to a "one-holer" in the back.

Just after Heck brought Ruth from his mother's, he sat on the bed beside her, holding her hand in his. She was pale from the exertion of clasping her arms around his neck as he carried her from house to car and then from car to house. There were great dark circles under her eyes, and the indigo bruise had turned purplish green. Heck watched as her eyes traveled around the bare cell that was the bedroom. As she looked through the door to the sad little room beyond, he said, "It's got running water."

Ruth eyed him speculatively.

"There's a pipe sticking up out in the yard with a handle on it," he explained. "You just work the handle up and down with one hand, and water runs right into the bucket that you're holding in the other."

She smiled faintly and murmured, "What will they think of next?"

Heck smoothed back her hair, looking tenderly down. She took his hand and turned it, so her lips touched his palm.

Then she closed her eyes to rest, and he tucked the borrowed bedclothes up under her chin and stole softly out.

After their move to Palomas, as Ruth lay in bed, she found out about the goodness of small town people. One by one, they dropped by to bring food, to donate household items, or to help. One brought a skillet, another a coffeepot. A third brought a washboard and a tub. A muslin sheet. A dishpan. A stack of dishtowels made of feed sacks. Luz Armijo, Angel's wife, came and scrubbed the place from top to bottom, muttering all the while about men who moved sick women into places that weren't fit for habitation. Bemis sent over canned fruit and juices to tempt Ruth to eat. Mrs. Armijo, Angel's mother, came each day to fetch Heck's dirty clothes and returned them later washed and ironed. Countless people sent in food or tended Little Emory, so Lucy could be free to feed Ruth, help her to the bathroom or simply keep her company.

With the passing of time, Ruth became stronger. As her body healed, her mind began processing all that had happened to her since she dropped that last match into the firebox at Hooper's Well. At first, she was depressed to think that the victory in weaning Heck from the range was negated by the living conditions at Palomas. As time went on and her natural resilience returned, she began to see that this could be just a way station, a whistle-stop that delayed arrival at the destination.

Patience and honey, she thought to herself. *California or bust*.

Ruth and Lucy became fast friends, spending much of the time together when their husbands were at work. They offered to clean Bemis's back room in exchange for a bolt of broadcloth that Lucy swore had been on his shelf for as long as she could remember. They parked Little Emory with Mama and tied their hair up in bandanas. Armed with brooms, mops, and soap, they threw open doors and windows and made a frontal attack, routing piles of debris, sacking and burning old catalogs, annihilating cobwebs.

They took the bolt of cloth to Lucy's. There was enough material for a dress for each and one for Mama with yards to spare for curtains or aprons. Jimmy moved Mama's treadle sewing machine over to their house, cleaned it, oiled it, and tightened the belt.

"Do you think," Ruth asked, "if I were to draw a picture of a dress, that you could figure out how to make it come out looking like the picture?"

"I don't know. I've copied dresses out of catalogs. That shouldn't be too much different from a drawing. We'll do Mama's first."

The dress turned out beautifully. Ruth had designed something that would hide the older lady's dowager's hump and compensate for a short waist.

"I can't believe it!" Lucy said as she watched her mother disappear into her bedroom to take off the dress. They had brought it over for a final fitting, but nothing else needed to be done. "I've never seen a dress look so good on Mama. The way you drew the pictures, it was easy to make it up. I can't wait to have you design one for me."

That was the beginning. Aprons and curtains were forgotten in the excitement of creation, and all of the material went into dresses. It didn't matter that they would both have two frocks of the same material. The important thing was that, together, they were doing something that neither could do alone. The bolt of ordinary broadcloth was made up into five extraordinary dresses. There was nothing of the homemade about them.

"Where did you learn to sew like that?" Ruth asked as she sat on the floor with a yardstick in her hand, marking a hem on Lucy's second dress. It was a good-looking shirtwaist with a skirt cut on the bias. Her question came out in a barely articulated nasal tone, the result of a mouthful of pins.

Lucy stood still, staring ahead as she answered. "I started sewing when I was ten. Mama taught me. I was making all my own clothes by the time I was twelve, but you should have seen them. Terrible. Check on the baby, will you?"

"You can talk, but don't breathe," Ruth cautioned. "It makes you move up and down. Now turn." She glanced over to where Little Emory was sitting on the floor, pulling quilt scraps out of a basket. "He's fine."

Lucy turned. "I had a Home Ec teacher in high school, Mrs. Simmons. We used to call her Mrs. Persimmons because she always looked so sour and was so hard to please. She had been a professional seamstress in Washington, D.C. Sewed for ambassadors' wives."

"What was she doing in Hot Springs? Turn."

"Her husband had tuberculosis. He was in the sanatorium up on the hill in town. She came and got a job teaching school to be near him and to pay for his care; I guess. After he died she just stayed on."

"Turn."

"I remember that I didn't want to take Home Ec. I thought that I knew how to sew, that she couldn't teach me anything, but it was required. It took me that whole first semester to realize that I'd better sit up and take notice because this was the opportunity of a lifetime."

Ruth took the pins out of her mouth. "There. It's finished. Turn clear around once more, so I can check and see that it's straight."

Lucy turned around slowly while Ruth held the yardstick upright, making sure that there would be no sags in the hem. She pushed herself back and leaned against the wall, looking critically at the dress.

Lucy undid the buttons and pulled the garment over her head. Dropping it in Ruth's lap, she picked up her housedress. "The thing about it is, you'll soon be able to do everything that I can, but I don't think I'll ever be able to do what you do." She paused to put on the gingham frock and close the zipper under her left arm. "I don't know how you can just look and know what will be right. Not just right for the person but for the fabric, too. And then, you sit down and draw a picture of it."

It was true. With one bolt of cloth, Ruth had learned how to achieve in fabric what she had conceived in her mind and recorded on paper. She wasn't expert. There was much she yet had to learn, but she understood broadcloth and how it lay and draped, what it would do and wouldn't do. She understood facing and interfacing, straight grain and bias, bound buttonholes and zippers, collars and cuffs.

When they were done and the material was gone, there was nothing left to do but talk about fashions, draw pictures, look at magazines, and wish for more fabric.

The lack of material to work with ignited an obsession in Ruth. She was driven, not only because she loved the designing process but because she had begun to believe that she had within herself not only a passport to California but perhaps the means to a fortune as well.

Ruth knew Heck had been lucky to work steadily through the Depression, but the change in their lifestyle that she had envisioned when she urged Heck to leave the ranch hadn't materialized. They were still without electricity, running water, or a telephone. They were still beating a path to the privy in back. And now, when she had discovered this gift, this marketable skill, she was stymied by the lack of money to buy the fabric to really become proficient.

When Monty Redmond mentioned at bridge club that she needed someone to come and help out at her dress shop, Ruth saw a solution to her immediate problem. She would work and earn money to buy more yard goods.

Monty Redmond was tall and angular with prominent clavicles and hair, once flaming red but now sandy silver, worn piled on top of her head. Monty dressed very smartly, playing down her bony neckline as shrewdly as she played bridge or ran her business. Her store in Hot Springs carried better dresses—nothing like the clothes Ruth had in her wardrobe in storage somewhere in town but certainly several cuts above what anyone in Palomas could afford.

Ruth started work the second week in October. She told Lucy that she wanted the money to be a surprise for Heck and asked her not to mention it. In reality, she had a feeling Heck would not approve, and she didn't want to risk telling him. Monty was delighted to have such a knowledgeable salesclerk and called Ruth the "Midas of Style," for, besides looking stylish herself, she was able to impart something of the same to the women who came to the shop. Ruth made far more money than any other clerk because the dresses that she selected for clients to try on were invariably flattering, and the accessories she suggested were usually purchased.

For three weeks, Ruth enjoyed herself hugely and made what she thought was quite a bit of money. She didn't expect to go undetected, but neither had she formed a plan about what she would do if Heck objected. Had she thought about it at all, she would have realized that keeping her employment a secret for three weeks in a town as small as Hot Springs was quite a feat.

Still, she was surprised when she emerged from the storeroom one day and saw Heck standing just inside the door of the shop. In his work clothes and Li'l Abner boots, he looked out of place among the mannequins. He removed his hat, but his eyes were flinty as he nodded to Monty and said quietly to Ruth, "I've come to take you home."

Ruth looked at Monty and cast up her eyes. "I'll have to go now. I'm sorry. I'll come in and talk to you tomorrow," she murmured. Then she picked up her purse and preceded her husband out the door.

They rode home in silence. Ruth managed to wait until they got inside the house before she exploded, but the delay did nothing to moderate either her voice or her feelings of ill usage.

The fact that Heck wouldn't tell her why he didn't want her clerking in a dress shop compounded the indignity Ruth felt when he told her she wouldn't be working for Miss Redmond anymore and then stood, wooden-faced, as she reacted. She was in fine form, detailing his lack of education, the menial work his mother did at home to earn money, and the fact that, like his mother, he had no ambition. Therefore he had failed to provide adequate housing.

Heck stood quietly until Ruth was through. Then, without a word, he left.

Heck went out to the dark little room attached to the house and got his saddle, blanket, and bridle. He slung the saddle over his shoulder and set off through the block to his parents' house where Emory's old cow pony, Shontie, was corralled.

Heck was grateful that Emory hadn't yet come to get his horse. Almost every week he managed to spend an hour or two riding across the river toward the mountains, where, in the solitude of the range, he could slough off the alien layers of noise and graceless supervision that gathered over his soul and threatened to suffocate him during the workweek.

Today, Heck needed time and space to recover from the verbal bloodletting in his kitchen. He was wounded, though he wouldn't show it in the set of his shoulders as he made his way to the corral where the old horse stood with lifted head and ears forward. But his face was rigid as he put on the bridle, and his hands trembled as he tightened the cinch.

As he was ready to swing into the saddle, Heck realized he was still in his work boots. "Ah, hell," he said under his breath. He stood with reins and saddle horn in his hand, trying to decide if he could face going home to change. Finally, he put one of the round-toed boots into the stirrup, swung his leg over, and turned Shontie's face to the Rio Grande.

Chapter 41

THE LITTLE HOUSE in Palomas where Ruth and Heck lived was one of the few that faced the river. Sitting at the table, they could see the line of cool green that marked the riverbank where cottonwoods, willows, and mesquites crowded and jostled, pressing like mothers at a bargain-basement sale on children's shoes.

The house had two rooms of living space, but it also had another room attached to the kitchen wall. Tiny and windowless, its only access was an outside door on the north. If the door was left open during the night and closed at sunrise, the room would stay cool and thus offer respite during siesta from the heat of the day.

There was an old cot set up in the room, and Heck had put his bedroll on it. As summer came on, he faithfully propped the door open during the night and closed it early in the morning, in case Ruth wanted to take advantage of the coolness he had hoarded for her. She preferred to use the daylight hours for something other than sleeping, but now and again, when the weather was scorching, and Little Emory was teething, Lucy would bring him over, so he could nap more comfortably. The only real use the room had was for storing Heck's saddle, which sat on a sawhorse just inside the door.

Once, on a hot and languid Sunday afternoon, Ruth persuaded Heck to come and lie with her in the darkness of the siesta room. The thick adobe walls denied the world, and for Heck it was a slow, sweet experience, a cool, quiet timeout in a week of hot, dry, dusty, teeth-grinding activity. The murmur of low love tones and the tingle of her fingertips tracing patterns on his back helped to erase the mental marks, the emotional wages of hours spent jerking and jolting on a roaring, clattering machine. The feel of Ruth's body next to his, fitting so well, concave and convex, the feel of her working with him to achieve the wonder of wonders in that cool blackness gave him a soaring, searing reason to endure. He could endure. He would.

They never used the little room for that purpose again, but "siesta" took on a new meaning in their vocabulary. Every now and then, to tease him, Ruth would use it in front of others in a perfectly innocent-sounding statement that was laden with erotic double meaning. She would watch Heck as she said it, and he would meet her eyes and know what she meant. Embarrassed, he would look away, lest he give himself away

Ruth loved Heck. Adored him. Couldn't imagine life without him. In her plans for leaving New Mexico for a better life, Ruth never thought of herself alone. Focusing on the comfort of electric lights, hot running water—any running water, for that matter—nice furnishings, household help—or barring that, a washing machine and electric iron— nice clothes, and adequate shopping, she was fuzzy about how Heck was to supply all those things once they arrived in California.

She believed in him, believed he could do anything he set his mind to. She was determined to roust him from his rustic niche, rather like a parent who says, "You'll thank me for this someday." Dedicated and single-minded, she was willing to take chances to attain her goal.

The chance she took in working for Monty Redmond ended with Heck heading out toward the Rio Grande after a monumental domestic scene. Standing at the kitchen window, she watched man and horse as they made their way down to the river. She was torn between remorse at having let her anger provoke her into saying what she had and dismay that Heck should have retreated to the open range.

She stared at the place where Heck and Shontie had disappeared into the willows and told herself that he knew she didn't mean all she said when she was angry. But her heart sank at the thought of him coming home silent and aloof.

Silent and aloof he was. They lived in cool courtesy for over a week, and then one evening things righted themselves.

Heck had bought an Aladdin Lamp, one that worked under pressure and burned a mantle, giving off a glow as bright as an incandescent bulb. He was seated at the kitchen table, studying by its light. His hair fell forward over his brow; he had a pencil in his hand, and he was whistling softly and tonelessly between his teeth. The whistling ceased as he underlined a passage and then moved the pencil under the phrase as he reread it. "That's as the crow flies," he muttered.

Ruth set a parcel down on the table and began picking with her fingernails at the knot in the string. "Did you say something?" Her voice was polite.

Heck pushed the book away and tipped his chair against the wall. "They must think we're a passel of idiots."

"Who?"

"Fellas who wrote this book." Without putting his chair down, he reached over and picked up the text to see who had written it. "A Mr. Alexander and a Mr. Davies."

"What are you reading?"

"Geometry." He tossed the book back on the table and fished in his pocket for his knife. Opening it, he handed it to Ruth, handle first. "Did you know that the shortest distance between two points is a straight line?"

She slipped the knife under the strings and cut them. "Of course. I took geometry in high school." She handed the knife back to Heck.

"Did you know it—about the shortest distance—before you took it in high school?" He tested the open blade with his thumb and then picked up his pencil and began to sharpen the point.

"I don't think I ever thought about it."

"Well, I have. Plenty of times, but I never knew I was thinking geometry." He tossed the pencil back on the table, closed his knife against his leg, and put it back in his pocket.

Ruth wound up the string and put it in a Mason jar on a shelf above the table. "Whatever possessed you to start on this?"

"Oh," Heck laced his hands behind his head, "I was talking to the project engineer the other day, asking how they knew how big to make the dam, and how they would know when they got it high enough and wide enough. I don't see them dragging something around to measure with. He started talking about triangulations and some such things like that, and I couldn't begin to understand what he was saying." Heck nodded toward the book. "I just wanted to be able to understand."

Ruth, struck by the wistful note in his voice, paused in the act of folding up the brown paper that had wrapped her package.

He met her eyes. "There's so much I don't understand."

She carefully finished folding the paper and put it in the woodbox for tinder. Then she sat down and rested both elbows on the table with her chin in her hands. "What don't you understand?"

Heck looked out the window, and she followed his gaze. The lamp glowed brightly and turned the windowpane into a mirror, but his voice sounded as dark as the night beyond. "Palomas is gonna disappear."

She blinked. "Beg pardon?"

"They already know it's gonna happen. Mr. Barrett told me. The seepage from the water in the lake'll melt the 'dobe houses." He turned from the window to face her and laughed a small, ironic laugh. "Isn't that something? It's gonna just disappear."

"When?"

"Seven, ten years, they say. Damn, but that's hard to think about!" He unlaced his fingers and shook his head, reaching for the round white tag hanging outside his shirt pocket. Spying the contents of Ruth's package, he asked, "What'cha got there?"

"Some material I bought in town." Unspoken was the rider, *with money I earned at Monty Redmond's.*

"Oh?"

"Yes." She sat back in her chair and folded her arms.

Heck looked up from the cigarette paper he was folding. "What'cha gonna do with it?" No irony, no challenge, just simple interest.

"It's just six weeks 'til Christmas. I thought I'd make something for your mother and something for Lucy."

Her words caught him with a lighted match halfway to his cigarette. He paused to look at her then applied the match and shook it out, tossing it into the woodbox. A slow smile spread over his face, crinkling the corners of his eyes. He dropped the front legs of his chair to the floor and leaned forward on his crossed arms. "I thought I'd like to make a rocking horse for Little Emory. One that'd stand about that high?" He marked the place with his hand above the floor. "I could make a little leather saddle and reins for it."

She answered his smile. "I could paint it for you. I could make him intelligent and friendly!" She pushed the material aside and retrieved the brown wrapping paper from the woodbox. Taking the newly-sharpened pencil, with quick strokes she began to draw a rocking horse.

That evening was as sweet and satisfying as any they had spent at Cottonwood Springs. Ruth made coffee, and they sat with their heads together, planning Little Emory's wooden steed and making a list of what they'd do for the rest of the family.

"I thought I'd make a quirt for Papa and one for Emory," Heck said. "Jimmy needs a fob for his pocket watch. I can make him one out of leather."

Ruth sketched the dresses she would make for Lucy and Mama and showed the material she had bought. The talk drifted to other things and finally petered out altogether.

Suddenly, Heck broke the silence. "Shoot, Baby Doll!" he said as he grabbed the list and scanned it again. "We forgot Carrie and the baby."

"Yes, we did," she said in dismay.

They both cast about in their minds for something appropriate.

"The baby's easy," she offered. "What do you do for a month-old child? I'll get some flannel and make a nightgown for him. But what about Carrie?" She eyed the dresses she had drawn on the brown paper and dismissed the idea. Carrie had two dresses. That would last her a lifetime.

"What you need to do is make her a pair of pants," Heck said. "Design a pair that'll make her look like a lady." His eyes danced. "That'll put you on your mettle!"

He didn't realize it and neither did she, but with that lighthearted challenge, he gave her her passage to California.

For the time being, though, she forgot California in the excitement of preparing for Christmas. As they worked industriously in the little Aladdin-lit kitchen, they would sometimes chat, but more often they were silent. Heck, his hands busy again with leather, began whistling and singing, and it struck Ruth that it had been months since she'd heard him sing anything but Little Emory's lullabies.

Christmas day was a kaleidoscope of shining eyes and happy faces as Ruth and Heck took their gifts around. Jimmy and Lucy loved their presents, but they were enchanted with the clever little rocking horse painted like an intelligent, friendly pinto pony with a mane made out of a mop head and with Lazy E branded on its rump. Heck put Little Emory in the saddle and rocked him back and forth. The little boy squealed in delight, flailing his arms and kicking his feet in excitement until he threatened to unseat himself.

Emory and Carrie were there with baby Jonathan when Ruth and Heck arrived at the senior Mama and Papa's, laden with packages. Mama's eyes grew misty when she unwrapped her dress, and Emory and Papa expressed thanks for the quirts, but the stunner of the afternoon was Carrie in her slacks. She tried them on and took an embarrassed turn around the kitchen where they were all sitting. Emory whistled, and Papa muttered something about silk purses into his coffee cup. Ruth caught Heck's eye, and he smiled and winked at her.

They ate Christmas dinner at Mama and Papa's, and then Heck and Ruth walked home, so they could exchange their gifts privately.

Ruth had labored long and in secret on a pastel drawing for Heck, a picture of their first little home at Cottonwood

Springs. She had captured the red of the cliffs that half encircled it and the blue-tinted shade cast by the giant cottonwood. Sun glinted off the creek as it flowed by, and she had drawn Bunny coming down the trail from the mesa above.

Heck was delighted with the drawing. He kissed her then took her by the hand and led her outside. The sunny afternoon was brisk as he walked her to the little siesta room. Pushing the door open, he revealed a sewing machine. It was a Singer. Not new but shiny nonetheless.

Heck's arm was about Ruth, and as he pulled her close and kissed her chestnut curls, he whispered, "Merry Christmas."

At that moment, she knew why the carols sing of joy.

Chapter 42

IN THE EARLY part of the twentieth century, an up-and-coming German woolen manufacturer was looking for a mordant that would bind dyes more tightly to wool. His company experimented successfully with a chemical that bore the formidable name p-aminobenzenesulfonamide. Apparently, it caused pigments in the dye to adhere to the protein in the wool.

No one remembers just how it happened, but the parent substance, sulfanilamide, came to the notice of scientists researching infectious diseases. It looked promising, and laboratories in England and the United States took up the work. By 1936, it was known that a group of sulfonamides had a profound effect in the treatment of many deadly diseases. Known as wonder drugs, they were used successfully against scarlet fever, rheumatic fever, meningitis, gonorrhea, and pneumonia. Doctors at the hospital of the Rockefeller Institute in New York City published accounts of a dramatic drop in the mortality rate when these drugs were used.

Dr. Colbin, the aged general practitioner who cared for the poor of Sierra County, subscribed to medical journals and read them faithfully. Two months before the evening that Jimmy Swank came looking for him, he found out about sulfapyridine and its effectiveness in treating pneumococcal pneumonia. But knowing a drug exists and having it in your medical bag are two different things.

There was no sulfapyridine available in New Mexico, no dramatic drop in the mortality rate in Sierra County, no wonder drug to save Little Emory as he burned with fever and struggled for breath.

Chapter 43

LITTLE EMORY DIED in the evening of January 6, a week before his first birthday.

Monday he had a runny nose. Tuesday he developed a cough and a fever. Wednesday night he was dead.

Mama had come over Wednesday morning. Lucy, worn out from tending a fussy baby through two nights, lay down when her mother insisted she do so. From the bed, she watched Mama mix flour, dry mustard, and water together to spread on a piece of flannel and put on the baby's chest. Lucy opened her eyes two hours later to find her putting tincture of benzoin in a kettle of steaming water she had set on the floor by the baby.

Lucy got up and helped Mama drape a sheet into a tent over the bed, so the sweet-smelling mist would drift up and aid the child's breathing.

At midafternoon, the baby's skin felt hot and dry. His cheeks, which had been flushed in the morning, were pale and bluish-looking. His eyes were unfocused and vacant.

Lucy was concerned about Little Emory's lethargy, about his fever and lack of response, but until Mama met Jimmy at the door as he got home from work and sent him to get Dr. Colbin, she was confident that the baby would get better. She leaned her forehead against the cool windowpane and watched as Mama walked out to the car with Jimmy. As her husband headed for town, Lucy's hopes faded away like the dust trail left by their Model T Ford.

Jimmy returned without the doctor, who was out delivering a baby and would come as soon as he could. Mama sent Jimmy next to tell Papa how things were and to ask Ruth to fix dinner for the family. Papa and Heck came immediately and stayed until all were ordered to go have supper. As soon as possible, they all returned to the tiny room behind Bemis's store where the baby lay, still alive.

They spoke little, sitting where they could find a place to perch, doing what they could to help. Lucy felt utterly powerless to fend off the destroying angel that was hovering around her little sunny boy.

The doctor came at eight o'clock, looking like a vulture in his black overcoat with the hump in his back and his head thrust forward. He spoke quietly and encouragingly, but his face was grave as he listened to the baby's chest. He told Lucy and Jimmy that their son had pneumonia. He assured them that Mrs. Benham was doing everything that could be done. The situation was serious, but you never knew. He had seen other babies this sick come through just fine. Glancing down, he saw the rosary that Lucy held in her hand. And yes, he said, be sure to pray.

Lucy prayed. Sitting in a chair next to her baby, her fingers told the beads and her lips moved silently as the minutes trudged by.

Ruth made coffee and took over the job of boiling water for the steam tent. Jimmy sat with one leg crossed over another, staring at his boot and rubbing his thumb slowly over the side of his index finger. Nate Benham, looking every one of his sixty years, sat on the bed with his forearms on his knees and his head in his hands.

Heck squatted on his heels where he could see through a crack in the tent. Golden hair, curling from the dampness, wreathed the baby's precious face like a halo. His sturdy limbs, so seldom still, lay quiet, with fingers lightly grasping the satin binding of his favorite blanket.

Unable to tolerate the inactivity, Heck stood and retrieved his coat and hat from the pile on the end of the bed. Ruth looked a question, but he shook his head and let himself out of the door.

The crisp coolness of the night came as a shock after the muggy sickroom atmosphere. Heck turned up his collar and dug his hands into the pockets of his coat, as if warmth could ward off despair. It wasn't possible—it was inconceivable— that life could go on without that child. There had to be something that someone could do, something more than mustard plasters and tincture of benzoin to fight the deadly, invisible hordes that invaded lungs and left no room for oxygen.

Grieving for what he knew was inevitable, distraught with his own impotence, Heck took off his hat and glanced up at the stars. "Lord ..." He searched for something to bargain with, something he could trade for the life of this boy. "Lord ..." Loath to ask for a favor without offering something in return, he felt there were things in his life that made it so he could not come empty-handed to petition God. As he stood bareheaded, looking at the nighttime sky and pondering, there came a high, keening wail, a sound as old as the earth, and Heck knew that he was too late.

He couldn't go back in. Turning his back on the sounds of Lucy's grief, he put on his hat and walked down the lane under the shelter of the cottonwoods.

Rounding the corner, he walked to his parents' house. Angling through the yard to the chicken coop behind, he could see Papa's garden tools hanging on the wall in the moonlight. He selected a shovel, put it over his shoulder, and headed back to the lane. Passing Ildefonso Armijo's house, he heard a voice calling from the shadows.

"*Amigo!*"

It was Angel Armijo, his childhood friend. Heck paused, turning to face the direction of Angel's voice.

"*Cómo está el niño?*" the voice asked.

"*Muerto.*" Funny that the action of lips and teeth should be so painful, that enunciation should hurt the throat and chest, make one short of breath, make one want to cry.

"*Lo pensemos. Nosotros lo sentimos.*"

Heck turned to go, but Angel called, "*Momentito.*" He stepped from the shadows, shovel in hand, and joined Heck in the lane.

They walked together in silence, pushing their shadows before them up the hill. When they reached the schoolhouse they stopped and looked down at the dark bulk of Bemis's store and at the two lighted windows of the little room built on back.

Angel sighed. "He was the sunshine in our village. Where do you bury the sun?" He turned and led the way around the schoolhouse to the graveyard beyond.

It was after midnight when they came down the hill. Heck parted from Angel at the bottom, shaking his hand and thanking him. Then he made his way to her door. His resolution almost failed him, but he pushed the door open and entered quietly. Everyone was gone but Lucy and Jimmy, sitting beside the body of their little boy.

Heck took off his hat and walked over to stand by the parents who seemed still in a state of shock. Heck touched Lucy's shoulder. Looking up, new tears started to her eyes.

"I'll sit with him for an hour or so if you want to get some sleep," Heck whispered.

Lucy shook her head, but Jimmy nodded and stood, pulling her to her feet and walking to the bed with his arm around her. They lay down in their clothes on top of the covers with Lucy wrapped in Jimmy's arms. Heck turned his chair to put his back toward them, so they could have some privacy, but he could not shut his ears to Lucy's whimpers and the muffled sound of Jimmy's sobs.

After a while, the sound of regular breathing told him they were asleep. Heck reached over and took one of Little Emory's hands, so cold, so different from before. As he held it, he stroked it with his thumb, and softly he began to sing.

Go slow little dogies, stop movin' around.

Chapter 44

NOTHING IN HER past experience prepared Ruth for seeing Little Emory die. She had buried her father and her mother, but each time, she had evaded a face-to-face confrontation with death. Despite countless bedside hours, helpless hours of sitting and waiting, it turned out that a physician's voice at the end of a telephone line informed her when each had "passed on." Two days later, she was taken in a limousine to a dimly lit chamber with understated décor, unobtrusive music, and a body bearing a faint resemblance to her parent lying in a silk-lined mahogany casket. Twice, Ruth sat in a curtained alcove while suitably somber men wheeled the body on well-oiled casters to the crematorium, and twice she visited the mausoleum, tapping in her high-heeled shoes behind a soft-soled guide to the place where the name of her kindred dead, etched in brass, had been fastened to the wall.

In moving to rural New Mexico Ruth had entered a place where there was no insulation against death. It came and sat next to you. It spent the night in your kitchen. It affected your vision and your speech, infected your dreams, tampered with your thought processes. There were no telephoned euphemisms, no soft-spoken professionals to take the body off your hands and dispose of it. The people of Palomas took care of their own.

The morning after Little Emory died, Ruth sat alone in her kitchen, smoking a cigarette and looking out at the river, wondering whether it were possible that last night could have been a bad dream.

Answering a soft knock at the door, Ruth was surprised to see her mother-in-law, haggard and hollow-eyed, dressed in a worn housedress with the ever-present apron anchored to her narrow bosom with two safety pins.

"Heck is still sleeping," Ruth whispered.

Mama nodded. "Lucy wants to bury him in this," she said softly, holding out the sailor suit that Lucy had been making for Little Emory's birthday. "She's in no shape to finish it. Could you?"

So it wasn't a dream.

Ruth said she could do the handwork and promised to have the garment at Lucy's inside of an hour.

She completed the project and arrived at the little room behind Bemis's store just as Ildefonso Armijo was leaving. He was a small man, spare and wiry, with dark eyes too large for his thin face. Taking off his hat, he nodded to Ruth. "For our sunny boy," he said, pointing with his hat toward the doorway.

Ruth returned his nod and slowly approached the screen, standing close enough to look through. She froze in horror at what she saw on the other side of the wire mesh. Ildefonso's offering, a small pine box, sat on the kitchen table. Mama had just spread a towel beside it and stood as if waiting while Lucy sat in the chair, cradling her dead baby in her arms.

Gazing down at him, Lucy pulled the blanket away from Little Emory's hand, lifted it, and spread it against her own. She kissed it and tucked it back in the blanket. After brushing the hair from his forehead and tracing the curve of an eyebrow, she gave the child to her waiting mother.

Ruth, shocked into silence and immobility, watched through the screen as the two women bathed Little Emory's body, washing and combing the golden hair and patting on talcum powder before they put on his undershirt and diaper.

Finally, Lucy looked up to see Ruth, still outside, clutching the sailor suit. She smiled faintly. "Thank you," she said. "I knew you wouldn't fail me." She stretched out her hand for the clothing, forcing Ruth to open the screen and enter.

Lucy must have noticed Ruth's averted gaze. "I didn't want to look at him, either," she said. "When Mama came and said we were going to bathe him, I thought I couldn't bear it. Then I remembered that I wouldn't see him again for a long time, and I thought it would be a shame if I were to miss this chance to see just how his little nose looks or how the hair curls right here."

As she touched the springy tendril, Lucy's voice tightened, and her eyes grew shiny with tears. "I know his spirit isn't here, but, he's still my baby. This is the last thing I'll be able to do for him. He was given to me to take care of, and this is a part of it. It's my job. I wouldn't allow anyone else to do it for me." The tears were streaming down her face now, but she managed to control her voice. "It's my job," she repeated as she smoothed down his undershirt. She laughed a small, shaky laugh. "He never would keep his undershirt tucked in."

Ruth felt as if she couldn't stay in that room one minute longer. She thrust the sailor suit at Lucy and fled, covering her mouth with one hand as she pushed the door open with the other. As the screen swung shut behind her, she heard Della say, "Let her go. She'll be all right."

Ruth arrived back at her house to find that Heck was up and gone. He had made coffee, and it sat on the back of the stove. She poured a cup and carried it with her as she prowled around the tiny house, feeling restless and unsafe and totally unable to complete any task.

She went into the bedroom and opened her sewing machine. Pulling back the curtain to let in more light, she sat down to mend a pair of Heck's Levi's. Hearing approaching footsteps, she looked up to see a tall figure dressed in a dark blue suit and black Stetson cutting through the lot toward their house. It was Heck.

Ruth stood in the doorway between the bedroom and kitchen as he entered the house. The white shirt and tie, the way that the suit fit with the pant legs just breaking over the pointed toes of his cowboy boots and beveling down over the high heels, the way he looked so at home in a three-piece suit, made her uncertain, and she frowned. "Heck?"

He set the new-looking Stetson on the table and went to pour a cup of coffee. "Yeah, Baby Doll?"

"I've never seen you dressed that way," she said.

He blew on his coffee to cool it. "This is my marryin' and buryin' suit," he explained. "I bought it when my grandpappy died. It's been at Mama's in the spare room wardrobe. Wasn't handy when I got married." He regarded her. "How're you doing?"

She leaned against the doorframe, trying to get her bearings in a day that had the warped, nightmarish feel of a carnival funhouse. First, she had seen her sister-in-law cuddling a dead baby, and then her husband, whom she had never seen in anything but Levi's, turned up looking like an El Paso lawyer.

She left the support of the doorway and drifted into his arms, closing her eyes, feeling him swing round to set his coffee down before he held her close, feeling the texture of blue serge against her cheek. "I don't know how I am," she said in reply. "I don't recognize myself. I don't know that I belong here."

"You belong here," he said quietly, kissing the crown of her head.

She didn't answer but stood in the circle of his arms, gathering silent comfort and putting off the time when she had to face what the day had to offer.

When she finally left the refuge of her husband's embrace and went with Heck to her in-laws', Ruth found that the day offered a continuation of the same slightly skewed unreality of the morning. Emory arrived with Preacher Lewis scrunched in next to Carrie, and a goat in the rumble seat. No one thought it strange that, because Carrie was unable to nurse the baby and Jonathan couldn't tolerate cow's milk, they would simply bring a goat with them when they had to be away from home.

There was a heavy, staring silence when Ruth announced that she wasn't going to the funeral. It went on and on, its length directly proportionate to the number of eyes bent upon her. She staunchly faced them down, raising her chin and clenching her hands until she heard Heck's quiet voice saying, "That's all right, Baby Doll. You'll be able to stay with Jonathan, so Carrie can go."

After the funeral, Ruth and Heck walked home, oblivious to the afternoon sunshine that made shirtsleeve weather of the January day. Their world was the hue of the stones that were piled on top of the new grave behind the schoolhouse. Heck went straight to the bedroom and tore off the suit as if it were a loathsome thing. Then he pulled on his Levi's and a work shirt and went to stand in front of the kitchen window with his hands in his back pockets and his weight on one leg. As he stared out at the river, Ruth knew he was thinking about saddling up Shontie and riding away.

"Take me with you," she said, and Heck looked at her as if surprised that she could read his thoughts.

They took a drive instead, going around by Cutter, across the flat, and up into the San Andres. Getting away from Palomas, away from the sight of Lucy looking around to check on her baby and then remembering where he was, away from Jimmy's silent stillness, made Ruth's spirits rise. She noticed the brilliance of the sun and rolled her window down to let the mildness of the day inside.

The blue-gray mountains loomed ahead, covered with the stubble of a scrubby forest like a three-day beard on an old man's face. Ruth smiled. "Remember the time you promised to take me up there, so I could see the Jornada?"

Heck raised one shoulder. "Seems like a long time ago. Back when I was young."

"You're still young."

He shook his head. "Today I feel ancient."

He drove to a place where they could park the car and walk to a rocky outcropping that offered not only a magnificent view of the Jornada but, also, a place to sit. So they sat, and Heck traced for her the spidery line of mesquite trees that marked the old Spanish Trail.

The sun was going down, and it started to get chilly, so Heck went back for the car blanket. He put it around Ruth's shoulders and sat next to her, wrapping himself in it as well.

"Where's Cutter?" she asked. He pointed, and she followed with her eyes. The light was bad, and she could see little, but she sat with her knees up and her arms folded around them, peering off into the distance. "Are you angry with me for not coming to the funeral?"

"I was surprised but not angry."

"I just couldn't bear to see them put him in a ... hole." The last word came out breathy and hardly voiced. Ruth cleared her throat and turned her head to look at Heck. "Burying is a barbaric practice. Why a hole? It's what you do with garbage, not with ..."

She couldn't finish. Suddenly the events of the night and day caught up with her, and she was weeping, making high-pitched, plaintive sounds into her knees as she sat hunched over, sobbing.

Heck stroked her hair and stroked her back and made soothing noises. He gathered her into his arms and lifted her into his lap, wrapping both his arms and the blanket around her.

When she had cried herself out, she felt him shift his weight and then felt his handkerchief in her hand. She blew her nose but stayed with her head on his shoulder.

Heck spoke, and his voice was husky. "The way I figure, burying is the way the good Lord provided. He made us from the earth, so we're going back to something familiar. We're protected from the heat of summer and the cold of winter and from the coyotes and all the things that would worry the body and scatter the bones. I don't know—I've heard poets talk about "Mother Earth." I think that's right. Mother Earth will hold Little Emory and keep him until Lucy gets him back."

She didn't speak but nodded against his shoulder, so he would know she heard him. They sat huddled together in the blanket as night closed down the Jornada

Heck was the one who broke the silence. "There was a family by the name of Cooper that lived this side of Cutter?" He paused, leaving the phrase hanging interrogatively to see if she were listening. She nodded again, and he went on.

"One day when I was about six, Mama and I went to visit them. I went out to play with the boy—he was going on twelve, I think. Seymour was his name." Heck paused again, and Ruth put her head back, so she could watch him tell the story.

"Seymour's mama had told him to get rid of some kittens. I think she thought he would drown them in the trough, but he had other ideas. He was gonna shoot them with the shotgun." Heck chuckled bleakly. "Only thing was, he only had one shell. He turned a bucket upside down and told me my job was to keep all those kittens up on the bucket while he stood ten feet away with the shotgun. He was gonna blast them as soon as I had 'em ready."

"What happened?" Shocked, Ruth's mental picture focused more on the shotgun than the kittens.

"Oh, Miz Cooper happened to look out the window and saw what was going on. She let out a shriek that would wake the dead and came flying out the door to put a stop to it."

"Thank heavens!"

"I often think ..." Heck began.

"Yes?"

"... that's like life. You're just trying to keep the cats up on the bucket and get out of the way before the shotgun goes off ..." His voice trailed away, and he was silent again.

"Has your leg gone to sleep?" Ruth asked presently.

"Yep. I wasn't gonna say anything, though."

"Here. I'll get off." She threw back the blanket and got to her feet.

He put up his hand. "Help me up, and I'll stomp the circulation back in." She took his hand and pulled him to his feet, and they stood watching a silver sliver of a moon rise above the Caballos.

Heck put his arm around Ruth's shoulders. "I was thinking I was doing pretty good at keeping my cats on the bucket. Then last night ..." He sighed and threw the blanket over his shoulder.

She put her arm around his waist and supported his weight on the sleepy-leg side as he hobbled back to the car.

Chapter 45

NOBODY IN PALOMAS called Arthur Bemis by his first name. Few even knew what his Christian name was. He had come to New Mexico in 1905 as a young man of independent means suffering from tuberculosis. When his lungs were clear, he didn't return to Rhode Island but looked instead for a business opportunity in this high, dry climate. He found a small general store for sale located in a tiny town, built all of adobe, with a population half Anglo, half Mexican.

There wasn't much that went on in Palomas that escaped Bemis. He watched Della Benham's homespun heroism in the little room behind his store as she fought for her grandbaby's life. That battle lost, he watched her put away her own grief and take charge, insisting that Lucy help lay the baby out for burial.

As Bemis dressed for Little Emory's funeral, he paused to pick up his watch and chain from the top of his dresser. Fingering the elk's tooth, he thought, *I'll buy a headstone. Something small so as not to embarrass the family but something so that his grave won't be lost.* But when he joined the family and friends on the hill, he found there was no need for a gravestone, for Heck and Angel had marked it forever: all the graves on the hill ran north and south, save Little Emory's. It ran east and west.

During the weeks that followed, Bemis watched from the window of his store as Lucy wore out the path to the graveyard. Daily, she went there to sit in the chilly wind and pray or weep or stare into space. She grew thinner, and the natural buoyancy that was the joy of all who knew her was gone. Bemis watched her and worried.

He worried, too, about Jimmy, the quiet one whose grief was unarticulated but intense. Jimmy didn't go to the graveyard, didn't speak of his dead son, didn't betray in misdirected anger his sense of loss. But more than once Bemis came around to check on him when Lucy was gone and found him sitting alone in the dark.

Bemis worried about Heck, once so lighthearted, who used to sing and laugh and tease. Now, he drifted quietly in and quietly out, walking like a man in pain, hunching one shoulder as if the hurt in his breast could be eased that way.

Bemis worried about Ruth but for another reason. She was driven by something besides grief. He didn't know what it was, but he knew that she wouldn't be satisfied to stay in Palomas for long.

Arthur Bemis may have been lax in the way he kept shop, may have been behind the times in the way he merchandised his wares, but when it came to doing clandestine good, he was shrewd, ambitious, sometimes devious, and if necessary, mendacious.

After a month of watching such intense sorrow, he decided that something must be done. He closed the store for a day and went to Las Cruces, arriving back home at suppertime. Jesús Armijo, oldest son of Angel and Luz, came whistling down the lane, and Bemis gave him a penny to go tell Heck and Ruth to come see him as soon as they could.

Chapter 46

RUTH AND HECK arrived about sundown. Bemis invited them in and offered them tea from a Wedgewood pot and Fig Newtons from a cookie tin. He sat back in his rocker with his cup in one hand and the saucer in the other and regarded the couple sitting expectantly in front of him. His round face broke into its customary smile, and he said, "You're wondering why I gave Jesús a penny to come get you when I could just as easily have walked to your house, eh?"

Ruth said nothing. The feel of bone china against her lips was surprisingly evocative. The smooth translucence, the feel of a saucer in her hand, the distinctive clink as she set down the cup were familiar and welcome. It was her first invitation to Bemis's house, and she examined the furnishings inherited from his well-to-do family back east. She hadn't been in such surroundings since she left Harlan.

Heck set his cup and saucer on a rosewood occasional table between him and Ruth. He extended his legs, crossed his arms and smiled. "The last time I was here for tea, Emory and Angel were with me. The next thing we knew we were standing in mud at the bottom of a twenty-foot hole."

Ruth sent him an inquiring look.

"We finished Mrs. Lindsey's well," Heck explained. "Some fellas took her money and left with the job half done."

Bemis nodded his head. "For knowing nothing about digging a well, you boys did all right, eh? When was that?"

"Before I went over to Henry Coughlin's the first time. I was sixteen years old."

Bemis took off his spectacles and polished them with his handkerchief. "Lucy would have been about five," he said as he held the glasses up at arm's length to look at the last of the daylight coming through the window. Satisfied, he restored them to his face and put his handkerchief away. He cleared his throat and sat with his fingers laced over his stomach. "Seems like yesterday to me," he murmured. Then, breaking out of his reverie, he unlaced his hands, slapped them down on his lap and stood up.

Ruth blinked at this sudden activity, but Heck simply looked up slantwise at him with a half-smile on his lips.

"Wait here, eh?" As the genial host backed toward a doorway, he held up both hands as if to make sure his guests wouldn't try to escape. Slipping into the next room, he returned a moment later with two bolts of black serge. He thumped them down on the rosewood table and then lit the lamp.

Ruth pulled the top bolt of cloth toward her and stroked the fabric, feeling the fineness of the weave. She looked up and saw Bemis's eyes twinkling.

Now," he said, "Lucy needs something to think about. Something to pull her thoughts away from—" He gestured in the direction of the graveyard with his thumb. "Only way I can think to do that is to touch her heart with something else. Eh? Eh?" He poked the black fabric for punctuation then sat down and folded his hands over his stomach again. "Friar Hollis, now, is walking around in tatters. Have you seen his habit?"

He glanced from one to the other, and both shook their heads. "Well, if it gets much worse, they'll be hauling him in front of the justice of the peace for indecency. Or vagrancy." He paused. "Well, it's not that bad, but Lucy needs to think that he's in dire need, eh?"

Ruth sat with a piece of the serge between her finger and thumb and gave Bemis a puzzled look. He looked back at her with his hands clasped over his paunch and a smile on his cherubic countenance. She turned to Heck for enlightenment.

"What he wants you to do," he explained, "is to go tell Lucy that Friar Hollis needs a new habit but you can't do it alone. You get her to help you make it."

"That's it?"

"That's it."

Ruth looked at Bemis, and he nodded. She counted the number of wraps on the bolt. "What about the extra fabric? It's not going to take this much."

"If you have something else that can get Lucy off that hillside, then use it for that. Otherwise, bring it back to the store."

"All right." Ruth laid her hand on top of the bolt of serge. "I'll do it."

Bemis beamed. "Wonderful!" He turned to take up his business with Heck. "I'd like to do a little horse trading with you."

"All right."

"I owe Doyle Gibson some money."

Heck's raised a skeptical eyebrow.

"True story," Bemis said. "Doyle helped someone out on my say-so, and I said I'd reimburse him. Now, Doyle's got a son. Son's got a horse, but the kid needs to be taught a thing or two about horses. Doyle said if you'd come over and spend some time with the horse and the son, we'd call it square."

Bemis stood up and took a flashlight down from a shelf and motioned for them to follow him outside. Heck stood and held his hand out in invitation for Ruth to come, too. She set the bolts on the table before preceding him out the door.

It was full dark outside, but Bemis lit their way to a large wooden crate with a jumble of metal pieces sticking out at odd angles. Ruth shifted impatiently, but Heck stood for a long time with his hands in his back pockets, staring at what seemed to be a pile of junk.

"Well I'll be damned," Heck said finally. "Is it all here?"

"The wheels are in the car still."

"Hell, Bemis. I'll go take care of Doyle's horse. You don't have to give me anything for that. Give this to Jimmy. I wouldn't even know where to begin."

"What is it?" Ruth asked.

"It's a motorcycle," Heck said. He was grinning. She could hear it in his voice.

"It's an Indian," Bemis said. "A 1929 model. Fellow who sold it to me said when you get it put back together, it should do 100 on the straightaway."

Heck shook his head in wonder. "How'd it get like this?" he asked.

"A fellow in Cruces had it. He was fixing something on it one day and left his tools lying around when he got finished. It was in a back shed, and he didn't notice that his nine-year-old son was being mighty quiet, eh? Good with his hands, that boy. Took it all apart. His daddy just put it in the box and got what he could for it. Said he didn't want to put temptation in the boy's way again."

Heck snorted.

Bemis went on. "If I give this to Jimmy, it will stay in the box while he sits in the dark and broods. If I trade it to you, and you ask him to help you put it together, he'll do it, eh?"

"You're a crafty old son-of-a-gun. Anybody ever tell you that?" Heck held out his hand. "All right. It's a deal."

They shook hands. As Ruth went inside to get the bolts of serge, she heard Bemis chuckling as he followed her in.

In succeeding days, Bemis watched Lucy going to her sister-in-law's instead of the graveyard first thing in the morning. He knew things were better when he stepped outside one day and called out, "So, you're on your way to Ruth's, eh?"

"Yes," Lucy called back, smiling at him. She raised the pile of black material she was carrying in her arms and added gaily, "It's getting to be a habit."

The two couples generally ate supper together at Ruth and Heck's house because the Swanks' kitchen table was covered with sprockets and gears. Once, Bemis walked around to see how things were going. Through the window, he could see both men standing silently, intently studying the pieces set out before them. Bemis knocked before he pushed the door open, and Heck turned to smile a greeting. "Did you have to have them take it completely apart, Bemis?"

Bemis threw up his hands, disclaiming any responsibility. "It was that way when I bought it!" he declared. And indeed it was. He wouldn't pay for the motorcycle until the man at the shop had completely dismantled it.

Chapter 47

THE HORSE THAT Doyle Gibson bought for his son was a spunky little buckskin mare, smart enough to take advantage of the fact that the Gibsons were town-bred and knew very little about horses.

Doyle's son, Randy, was ten years old, tall for his age but slight. He wasn't timid, but it was easy to be intimidated by a creature he could neither see over nor reach around and that outweighed him by at least 700 pounds.

Heck spent a month of Saturdays and several evenings in between, first with the horse and then with the horse and the boy. He found that in the familiar interaction with an intelligent pony there was release. In the act of helping an awkward boy grope toward confidence, there was healing. He talked to Randy about getting the mare to know and trust him and showed him the levers that could give even a wisp of a ten-year-old dominion over a horse of fifteen hands.

Doyle sometimes sat on the top rail of the corral and watched as Heck put the buckskin through her paces. He always asked if Heck would sell him his saddle, and Heck always replied that he could get one just like it from the Monkey Ward catalog.

After work during the week, and as they could on weekends, Heck spent many an hour letting Jimmy guide him as he had guided the boy. Piece by piece they put together the motorcycle that Bemis had brought from Las Cruces in the back of his car. The job was finished by the end of March, and Heck found that Bemis was right. It would do a hundred on the straightaway.

Bemis's other project seemed to have been successful, too. Lucy had agreed to help Ruth make the black serge into a habit for Friar Hollis, willingly treadling her way through the mountain of fabric piled on the table. Ruth called her Omar the Tentmaker, and they made dozens of jokes about the object of their industry: *If it doesn't fit, would you call it a bad habit? When he takes it off, is he getting out of the habit?*

Ruth and Lucy went together to deliver the finished article. They found the friar at home in the basement of St. Paul's Episcopal Church in Hot Springs. Lucy carried the package and Ruth knocked.

The good brother's round face under his medieval haircut showed first surprise and then delight at having visitors. He did not invite them in but directed them back up the basement steps and out to the tiny back lawn that owed its existence to his tender care. A crepe myrtle tree blossomed there, a splash of pink standing bravely above the postage stamp of just-greening lawn, both daring to be different in a dun-colored world. Friar Hollis asked the ladies to wait in the shade cast by the lacy blossoms while he brought out chairs for them.

Watching his retreating height and breadth, Ruth whispered, "Do you think we made it big enough?"

Lucy considered and nodded decisively. "I think it will be just right."

Friar Hollis seemed taken aback when they said they had something for him. He received the parcel wrapped in brown paper with a doubtful look. "You know I've taken a vow of poverty," he said.

Lucy leaned forward, a smile on her face. "I don't think this is against the rules."

Ruth found herself leaning forward, too, as the friar opened the package, lifted the garment by the shoulders, and held it up to see. Then he sat with the brown paper hanging down over his knees and his ham-like hands hidden in black serge as he turned his face away from the two women.

There was an uncomfortable moment of silence. Ruth looked at Lucy with raised brows. Lucy raised her shoulders in an I-don't-know expression. Ruth reached down to pick up her handbag and held it on her lap, but Friar Hollis cleared his throat and turned back around to face them.

"Do you believe in the goodness of God?" he asked softly, looking at Lucy.

There was a small pause.

"Bemis was the one who supplied the fabric," Ruth mentioned dryly. She looked over at Lucy, intending to share the small joke with her, but Lucy was gazing at her hands.

"I'll tell you about the goodness of God," said Friar Hollis. He leaned back in his chair and looked at the gray hills beyond town. "I took the vow of poverty willingly," he said. "I wanted to live as closely as possible to a life like that of Christ. As a Franciscan, I am commended to a life of 'poor and scanty' means." His great hand came up and spread itself across his breast. "Lucy, that is my joy. That is so easy!"

Lucy raised her eyes to look at him, but he was gazing again at the dry landscape that surrounded them.

"I didn't realize that poor and scanty meant more than what I could put in my belly or on my back."

Lucy frowned. "I don't understand."

"I'm from Portland," he said, "where the weather is temperate and the landscape is green—you've never seen so much green! And there's water—lots of water—in the sea and rivers and falling out of the sky."

"You miss the green," Lucy said.

The friar nodded. "I miss the green, but I miss the fellowship of my order, too. People who have a kinship with me in Christ, who understand ..." He felt for the wooden crucifix that hung from a chain around his neck. "I have been feeling very alone, lately. Very alone ..."

His words trailed off. Presently he sighed, a great, noisy clearing out of Franciscan lungs, and smiled, first at Ruth, for politeness, and then at Lucy because it was to Lucy that he was speaking. "My habit is disreputable. I have tried to repair it, but my fingers won't do the job." He held them up for inspection.

Ruth smiled at the thought of those great sausage-digits plying a needle.

"You have brought me a new habit, and I most earnestly thank you," Friar Hollis went on. "But now, let me tell you about the goodness of God. Today is my birthday."

They left shortly after that, and Lucy was silent most of the way home. As they approached the turnoff to Palomas, she finally spoke. "There's nothing else he could have accepted as a birthday present."

"The friar? So he said."

Lucy clasped her hands under her chin. "It was like God knew that he was feeling lost as a person and wanted to let him know he was loved and appreciated."

Ruth was amused. "So you're saying us giving him the habit was like God saying *Happy Birthday*?"

Apparently the irony was lost on Lucy because she nodded. "It made me feel that maybe God was watching over me, too. I know He's watching over Little Emory, but I've felt so alone. I don't feel so alone anymore."

Ruth drove the rest of the way in silence, not trusting herself to speak. Her throat felt tight, and she was afraid she'd embarrass herself by weeping.

The next day, as the habit was done and there was plenty of fabric left, Ruth suggested that she and Lucy design a line of women's slacks and see if they could market them.

"Are you serious? Who would buy them?" Lucy asked.

"Leave that to me. Will you help me?"

Lucy agreed. "But I'm not brave enough to cut them out of the serge to begin with," she said. "We need to make them up first in muslin. Only we don't have any muslin."

"Don't worry about that. I'll get the muslin."

And she did. Lucy asked her where she got the stack of R-monogrammed sheets, but Ruth only shook her head.

They were able to make eight pairs of serge slacks. Two were flowing and full like the beach pajamas made popular in California and featured in Vogue magazine. The others were straight-legged pants with variations. Some had high waists; others had yokes. Two pairs had pocket detail. One pair buttoned at the front like sailor pants. They made them to fit Ruth, and when the last hem was in, the last button sewed on, the last crease pressed, she took them and went to call on Monty Redmond.

Monty was enthusiastic and willing to do what she could to help. She made an appointment for Ruth with a man in El Paso and then sat down to give her some advice. "It's going to take money," she said. "You're going to have to invest in fabric and labels, probably in machines. You're going to have travel costs, and you're going to have to get a phone. Don't look for Nick Saunders to back you financially. He can introduce you to people who can help you, but you'll have to come to him with the resources to make use of his help."

Monty paused, and Ruth knew she was looking for a way to say that all she was willing to invest was an introduction. Ruth smiled and shook her head. "Don't worry. I've got some money."

The following Friday morning, Ruth waited until she heard the roar of Heck's motorcycle fade into the distance as he left for work. She then dressed for her journey. Even though she told herself that he had not specifically forbidden it, she had concealed the fact that she had gone to the place where Harlan's mother had warehoused her things and paid the storage for another quarter, so they wouldn't be given to charity as per Mrs. Reynolds' instructions.

Any sense of guilt that she might have felt was drowned in the pleasure of a new suit, hat, shoes, gloves—new to her at least because they had been so long in storage, and her life had been so different that she had forgotten about them.

Standing on the bed, so she could see the bottom half, Ruth checked herself one last time in the mirror. Satisfied, she stepped down and lifted a small cedar box from a shelf. She opened it and took out the tortoise shell that Heck had given her at Hooper's Well. Beneath it, the soapstone band that Heck carved for her and the diamond engagement ring that Harlan had given her lay side by side. She picked up the diamond, returned the shell, closed the box, and restored it to her shelf. Then she dropped the ring in her purse, picked up her case of samples, and went out of the house, closing the door securely behind her.

Lucy ran out and stood in the dooryard waving as Ruth drove by. "Good luck!" she shouted. Ruth tooted the horn and waved. Then she headed out to the highway.

When she hit the blacktop, she turned south to El Paso.

Chapter 48

NICHOLAS BOLIVAR SANDERS was the owner of Fashion House, a five-story department store in El Paso with sister stores in Tucson and Albuquerque. He was a handsome man, of medium build with a swarthy complexion. He had a wide brow and high cheekbones that were covered with a spider's web of wrinkles, the result of half a lifetime spent in the sun. His thatch of iron-gray hair was tamed by means of an expensive barber and a good hair dressing.

It was hard for stock boys and clerks to reconcile the stories that circulated through their sections with the well-dressed, well-spoken gentleman who was glimpsed every now and then as he toured through on inspection. Some said Mr. Sanders had helped a Mexican village stand off Pancho Villa. Others said that when Black Jack Kilmer tried to rob him as he passed through the Oscuros, Nick Sanders faced the bandit down and emerged with an ally among the outlaws.

All had more than a grain of truth to them. Orphaned at fifteen by the last renegade Apache in the United States, Nick had sold his legacy—the contents of a Conestoga wagon—and bought ribbons, bonnets, gloves, stockings, and other ladies' apparel and began riding from village to hamlet to outpost, selling pretty things to the women who lived far from civilization.

He was on the phone with his housewares manager one afternoon in late March, assuring him that pressure cookers were neither dangerous nor a fad, when his secretary came in and said that a Mrs. Benham was waiting to see him. He held up a finger and lifted his brows to detain her while he finished with Doubting Thomas.

"I got one for Cordelia last time I was in San Francisco. She swears she can do a pot roast in half the time." His voice was serious as he answered the concerns of the man who had just signed a receipt for twenty Presto cookers, but his eyes were crinkling at the corners. "That's fine then. I appreciate it." Nick Sanders hung up the phone and said, "He thinks women can't be trusted to operate a pressure cooker. What do you think, Trudy?"

Trudy had been with him for twenty years. "I think they'll sell like they're going out of style, and he'll decide that it was his idea to stock them."

"Probably so. Probably so. Shut the door, will you?"

Trudy swung the heavy oak door closed and stood with her back to the doorknob.

Nick Sanders sat leaning back in his chair, considering a pencil held at point and eraser with thumb and index finger of each hand. Looking up, he cocked his head and asked, "What do you think of our visitor from Hot Springs?" He pointed with the pencil at the door behind Trudy. "Mrs. Benham? Is she full of small-town confidence with stars in her eyes at being in the big city about to make her debut into the world of fashion?" Swiveling around, he turned to look out his fifth-floor window.

Without waiting for an answer, he went on, "How do I get myself into these things? I'm not interested in helping some eager young thing become a designer."

"You could certainly make the way easy for someone." Trudy's voice held a note of mild censure.

"I don't know about that." Nick considered. "I know a few people. I could make some introductions, open some doors, but the fact of the matter is ..." He swiveled back around. "... I don't want to. That's it in a nutshell." He fixed his secretary with a gently accusing stare and pointed his pencil at her. "Where were you when I needed you? You could have told Monty no. Or said I was out—gone to lunch. Or Hawaii. Or Timbuktu."

"Well, she's such an old friend, sir. I thought you'd want to do her a favor."

"I don't know what she was thinking! She's never been backward about telling anyone how the cow ate the cabbage. I can't see her sending some local girl up here with her home sewing—probably hanging out of a shopping bag—getting up her hopes." He opened his middle desk drawer, threw in the pencil, and pushed it shut. "What have I got out there, Trudy? Some dewy-eyed young thing who'll cry when I tell her she's come on a fool's errand? Or is it a plain-Jane steamroller, all pushy and ill-mannered?"

Trudy's eyes twinkled. "I didn't see a shopping bag."

"Monty said everything was in black serge but not to mind that. Is our Mrs. Benham one of those brooding bohemian types?"

"Shall I ask her to come in, and then you can see for yourself?"

"I don't know how I get myself into these things," he repeated under his breath. And then aloud in a let's-get-this-over-with tone, he said, "Yes, send her in, Trudy."

She nodded briskly and opened the door. "Will you come in, Mrs. Benham?"

Chapter 49

RUTH PAUSED IN the doorway, waiting to be introduced to the man who stood on the other side of the carpeted expanse. She had on her dove-gray suit with a pearl-gray silk blouse. Her accessories were black: patent leather shoes, kid gloves and a modified fedora with a low crown and a broad brim that dipped over her left eye. A black patent band box dangled from a strap she held in her left hand.

"Mr. Sanders, this is Mrs. Benham," said Trudy.

Ruth noted the flinty glance he sent his secretary as he said, "Thank you, Trudy. That will be all."

Trudy closed the door behind her with a decisive click. Nick Sanders stood behind his desk saying nothing.

Ruth lifted her eyebrows slightly and set her case down by the door. Then she began pulling off her gloves.

"How do you do?" she asked, holding out her hand to Nick Sanders.

She stood twenty feet away, and as he walked slowly toward her, the outer man—the polished, well-manicured exterior—struggled against being taken in by her appearance. *She has the look of a socialite,* the outer man warned. *She's taken a fancy to dabble in fashion, but she'll never stick to it. She doesn't know what it takes. Doesn't understand about the grueling work. At the first deadline, she'll decide she didn't want to do it and take up ceramics or do volunteer work. She's asking you to put your name on the line, vouch for a flash in the pan. Better stake your reputation on someone who's a stayer.*

As he walked toward her, her chin came up, and her eyes took on a luminous quality. The civilized voice in the corner of Nick Sanders brain redoubled its efforts, but he couldn't talk and listen, too, and it was his turn to speak. "How do you do," he said. As he took her hand, he felt the roughness of it, felt the calluses earned by living in Cottonwood Springs and Hooper's Well and Palomas.

It had been a while since Nick Sanders had shaken a hand that had the feel of Ruth's. In his early days as a peddler he had clasped thousands as he said hello or goodbye on the doorstep of a shanty in the middle of nowhere, in a mining camp tent perched on the side of a mountain, or in the dark, cool kitchen of an adobe house. He knew the strength of the southwest was in the hands of its women, in hands that felt like the one he was still holding in his own. The tactile sensation of her palm against his unleashed a thousand memories of a time and a place much less civilized than the one he was in now. A place and a time when sustaining life often depended on the kind of work that opened cracks on the fingers and raised calluses on the palms.

Nick Sanders looked at Ruth now with different eyes, and it was the inner man who spoke. It was the man who had traveled the dangerous trails of the southwest for twenty years who led her to a chair and pulled over another to sit beside her.

"Tell me, Mrs. Benham," he said. "What can I do for you?"

Chapter 50

WHEN EMORY AND Carrie signed the mortgage on their place, they figured that the two of them could work the ranch through the winter. That was before Carrie realized she was pregnant with Jonathan. There was no money to hire another hand, so they did the best they could. Emory pushed himself, working extra-long hours, and Carrie swaddled Jonathan in blankets and nestled him in a wooden crate on the car seat beside her. With the goat in the rumble seat, she bounced around the ranch, doing what she could to help. It wasn't the same as working full time, and they got further and further behind on things that needed to be done. Heck's offer to come out and help on weekends was gratefully accepted.

It was at about the same time that Ruth finished her business with Nick Saunders that Emory turned off the highway onto the gravel road leading to Palomas. Pulling up a few minutes later in front of Heck's house, he turned off the motor, honked the horn, and sat with his arm resting on the windowsill as Heck came out of the house carrying his chaps and spurs.

"I appreciate your help, *hermano*," Emory called, "but are you sure you're gonna need spurs to get the job done?"

"Afternoon, Emory." Heck stopped halfway around to the siesta room where his saddle was stored. "What'cha got in mind?" he asked, pushing his hat to the back of his head.

"Why, I thought you was comin' out to tend the young'un. Carrie says changin' the didey is about like flankin' a calf. You might need the chaps, but I don't believe the spurs are necessary."

Heck couldn't help grinning at the mental picture of Carrie McAlister hog-tying her baby to get a diaper on him. "I may not be as good a hand as Carrie, but I signed on as a cowboy, not a wet nurse. Besides, that goat doesn't like me."

All the way to the ranch, as the two brothers talked about family, friends and local news, Emory kept up the pretense that Heck had come out to babysit. Heck countered with an offer to teach the baby to suckle the goat, thereby dispensing with the need to milk and wash bottles.

They arrived at the ranch to find Jonathan having his usual evening fussy time, so while Carrie cared for him, Emory and Heck fried steak and made biscuits.

Heck was conscious that Carrie wasn't the housewife Ruth was. Her kitchen was ill-supplied and lacked the little grace notes--paint and Curtains and shelf paper--that made their own kitchen so pleasant. The house was cluttered with stacks of clothes, papers, books, harness, ledgers, vaccination and veterinarian supplies, plus all the paraphernalia that it takes to care for a baby. It was apparently piled according to some system, for Carrie found everything she needed for the baby and soon had him fed and put to bed.

Housewifery or no, by the time the three of them sat down for dinner, Heck could see there was a strong bond between his brother and this tall, redheaded woman. Carrie hadn't much of a sense of humor, and she responded to Emory's teasing with commonsense answers, but it was obvious that the singleness of purpose, the total trust, the sense of commitment they had for each other, were profound.

They all sat around the kitchen table after supper drinking coffee and remembering old times, but finally, Emory's yawns became so pronounced that Heck told him to go to bed before he had to be carried in.

Carrie rustled up two blankets and an extra pillow while Emory undid the latch to drop the back of the davenport. "There you go, Heck. See you in the morning."

"Good night, you two." Heck spread the blankets on the divan and lay wrapped in them, listening to the voices that came from the bedroom—Emory's hoarse questions and Carrie's placid replies. *She's not a beauty*, Heck thought, picturing her in his mind. Secure in her own domain, she moved with an easy strength. Astride a horse, she was even graceful, but around town women, she became clumsy and bashful. Heck compared her to Ruth and wondered at the reaction physical appearance invariably inspired. People were immediately drawn to Ruth because of her looks. They deferred to her and singled her out for favors. Carrie, on the other hand, unless she was working cattle, was discounted, dismissed, invisible. *How unfair*. Heck was proud of Emory for seeing the goodness and strength in Carrie.

Just before he drifted off to sleep, an impression flickered across Heck's consciousness, the thought that maybe he was guilty, too. Maybe he had dismissed Jonathan as not worthy of notice because his pale, skinny face and fretful manner were not pleasing like Little Emory's handsome, sunny countenance. The unease that swirled around in the wake of this fleeting idea gathered and began to solidify into a resolution, but sleep came and swept it away like dust bunnies in front of Mama's broom come spring cleaning time.

Saturday was a joyful day for Heck. The smell of greasewood and sage, the feel of the rope in his hands, the sound of his pony's hooves striking rock or swishing through sand, the creak of saddle leather. It all worked together to push back the darkness that had been following him as persistently as his own shadow.

All during January and most of February, he had lived in a dull depression where it seemed that his mind was wrapped in dingy quilt batting. Heck didn't suppose he'd ever lose the acute sense of loss he felt when he saw a towheaded toddler, but he was thinking more clearly now.

The motorcycle had helped. The wind whistling by seemed to blow the cobwebs from his brain. Slowly, he began to work through his loss, trying to sort out his relationship with God, to figure out where he stood and where God stood and why. He wondered why God would send a child who was so good—who was such a blessing to everyone who came near him—and then would take him home again after just a short year? Why would God cause such pain for Lucy and Jimmy, two of the best people who ever lived? There were times when Heck felt his kinship with God was in jeopardy. It was a kind of a shirttail kinship, but it had been earned by years spent pondering in the wilderness, and Heck was not willing to relinquish it.

It was midafternoon when he pulled his pony to a halt on the top of a knoll and searched the land below him for any Lazy E cattle. The sun was warm on his back, and he had spent the day riding the west half of Emory's range, mending fence, doctoring for screwworms and checking on the condition of Emory's herd. They had come through the winter well, and if the summer grass was good, he should have some nice looking two-year-olds to send to market in the fall. Heck's spirits soared each time he saw the round, red rumps of Emory's steers or as he watched the new little calves with their shiny white faces butting heads and leaping, full of health and vitality.

Heck turned in the saddle to look northward, raking the tan sweep of range with eyes crinkled at the corners. Back and forth he looked, back and forth, from the ridge where he sat his horse to the fence line that marched due south down the middle of the valley. About a half mile away, a fence coming from the west intersected the south-marching one. In the corner on this side, he could see a bunch of cattle standing with heads together and rumps fanned out to various points of the compass.

Heck sat for a moment, watching the cattle in the corner of the fence. "Well, I don't know, Dandy," he mused to his horse. "I don't think I like the look of that. Let's get on over and see what's going on." Dandy was willing, and Heck let him pick his way down off the knoll before urging him to a gentle lope.

Chapter 51

AS HE GOT closer, Heck could hear the bawling of a dozen cows. Slowing Dandy to a walk, Heck approached cautiously, trying to see what the trouble was. He stopped about a hundred feet away, searching for a reason for the bovine chorus.

It wasn't a dead cow or calf. If that had been the case, they would have been in a wide ring around the stricken animal. Instead, they seemed to be bunched up around a heifer in the center. As Heck watched, the heifer humped her back and put her head down. About the same time, the herd shifted, so Heck had a plain view of her back end. Something was sticking out from under her tail.

Heck relaxed in the saddle and reached for the tag that hung out of his pocket. "Well, Dandy fellow," he said as he fashioned a cigarette, "we'll just sit here and keep an eye on that old heifer. She may be all right; she may not." Heck watched with narrowed eyes as the cow stood with her head down, every now and then arching her back and straining. From the lack of movement in the two little hooves protruding from her back end, Heck could see that this new calf was making a difficult and protracted advent.

If the cow could manage on her own, it was best to let her be, but Heck knew that timing was important. He didn't know how long she had been standing there, trying to deliver, but once the calf was in the birth canal, if it was not out in an hour, the calf's head would start to swell, and then delivery became increasingly more difficult. If the calf died in the process, it would rot inside the cow, infection would set in, and the mother would die as well.

Heck finished his cigarette, pulled on his gloves and got his lariat. "Now then, Dandy," he said, "as far as I can see, she hasn't done anything at all. From the way all the other biddies are carrying on, I'd say she's in trouble. Let's see what you and I can do to help this old heifer along."

He shook out a loop and clicked his tongue, and Dandy began a sedate approach, gliding smoothly into the knot of cattle, careful not to agitate them by a sudden move. Heck easily settled a loop over the troubled heifer's horns and pulled it tight. He rode slowly to the corner fencepost, threw the rope around it, and, with the rope dallied around his saddle horn, he had Dandy exert continuous pressure to pull the cow up to the fencepost. Then Heck reined Dandy to the left, boxing the heifer in between the fence and the pony.

Dandy was Carrie's own horse, one that she had gentled and trained, and Heck had the utmost confidence in him. He knew that as long as there was a cow on the other end of the rope, Dandy wouldn't let the rope go slack until he had permission to do so.

Heck dismounted and praised his mount for doing such a good job. "She may chouse around a bit, but you just hold your ground. Yeah, you're a good pony."

Heck flapped his arms at the other cattle, and they bolted a short distance then turned to form up in ranks and look inquiringly at him. Standing with hands on his hips, Heck surveyed the heifer. "I don't know if we're going to manage this alone or not. I could do with a partner right now," he muttered.

The heifer watched Heck, showing white around the eye she turned on him. She tried to jerk her head up but was held fast by the rope around her horns.

"Easy, girl. Easy. Let's see what you got." Watching out for a lashing hoof, Heck walked carefully around to the back of the heifer. Just then, she humped her back and lifted her tail. The calf's hooves traveled a fraction of an inch farther into the air outside. Such a tiny gain for so much effort.

When the contraction had eased, Heck took off his gloves and put them in his back pocket. "So, are you gonna be a good girl and let me help you? If I can, that is." He rolled up his right sleeve. Checking the rope around the fencepost and then Dandy, he gingerly lifted the cow's tail.

The cow's only reaction was the wild eye turned back. Heartened, Heck stuck his hand up the vagina, following the legs until he came to the calf's shoulders and felt the calf's head. The nose seemed to have caught and turned the head back just enough to keep it from sliding smoothly through the birth canal. Heck hooked his fingers into the nostrils and pulled the head into the proper alignment, but with a sinking heart, he realized that it had already started to swell.

"Ah, hell," Heck said under his breath as he withdrew his hand and wiped it on his pants. The cow seemed to catch his mood and stirred uneasily. "Easy, girl," he soothed. "Easy"

He went to his saddle, got his piggin' string, and threw a double half hitch around the protruding legs just above the hooves. He had just pulled his gloves back on when he saw the heifer's muscles bunch again. Heck took a double loop of the piggin' string around his right hand and pulled for all he was worth. He was rewarded with two more inches of rust-colored legs.

During the time between contractions, Heck glanced again at Dandy to make sure he was doing his part.

Reassured, Heck fashioned a large loop on his end of the piggin' string, so he could pull with both hands. By then it was time, and he sat back on his heels to pull, gritting his teeth, straining, feeling the pressure clear up to the back of his eyes. This time, above the legs, he could see the tip of a white nose.

Heck dropped the loop and walked away with his hands on his hips, breathing deeply, getting set for round three in his fight for the life of this calf. When the next contraction came, he was ready, pulling with every ounce of strength he had. The force of his exertion rolled out in a great painful sound that made Dandy shift uneasily and made the onlooking cattle take to their heels in fright.

Heck was panting now. The sweat was running in rivulets down his cheeks, but he had earned two inches of nose. He took off his hat and wiped his face with the sleeve of his shirt. Then he backed up a pace and kicked a heel-hold in the dirt for himself. Flexing his hands open and closed, open and closed, he tried to get rid of the pain of the piggin' string digging into his palms. Then it was time to pull again.

As he pulled this time, Heck watched the vulva, despairing because, though the calf's muzzle poked through, it didn't seem that it would ever stretch far enough to allow the whole head to pass. He redoubled his efforts, summoning up a mighty pull for the last half of the contraction that allowed him the profit of the calf's eyes, which were closed. The tongue was sticking out of the side of the mouth, and the whole thing seemed pretty hopeless.

Heck again walked around, exercising his hands, breathing deeply, trying to think of some way to help this heifer with her first calf. Heck mentally raced through all his experiences and all the old calf-pulling stories he had heard, trying to think of some trick he might have forgotten. Nothing.

When the cow humped her back again, Heck whipped off his gloves and dropped them on the ground. Stepping up to the hindquarters, he slid his fingers under the edge of the opening, taut around the dead-looking face. Pulling outward with all his strength, he struggled to help enlarge the hole that nature was trying to cram the baby through. Again, he groaned with the effort of extending tissues that were already stretched tight.

The contraction was gone, and Heck relaxed. "I don't know about you, lady," he gasped as he patted the red rump, "but I'm glad for the breathers in between." He picked up his gloves and dusted them off against his pant leg. Then he put them on, wiped off his face again with his sleeve, and picked up the loop in the piggin' string. "Let 'er rip, old lady," he said wearily.

She did. The tail came up, and the back bowed, and Heck hauled back on his loop, pulling at the calf's legs, trying to get the head to pop through. "Come on, you white-faced hussy. Help me!"

He wasn't going to do it. Failure was a white nose and a tongue lolling grotesquely, and eyes shut because a tight ring of muscle was denying entrance to the world. Failure was a strong heifer with a dead calf that would turn into a putrid decaying mass and suck the health right out of her.

All of a sudden, Heck became angry—angry that he was put in the position of accepting death again. Angry to be impotent while Death pointed a bony finger and said carelessly, "That one." Rage and rebellion surged through him. He couldn't do anything about Little Emory. Little Emory was gone, but this—this was something he could do, and he would.

Somehow, the conflict took on a meaning beyond a weekend's stewardship over his brother's cattle. It became a duel between Heck and Death, and Heck summoned up strength he didn't know he had to fight for the Lazy E calf. The cords in Heck's neck stood out; the veins in his temples bulged. There was not a muscle in his body that was not called up, impressed to duty, drafted to serve in this desperate battle.

When the next contraction came, Heck tore off the piggin' string and dropped it on the ground. Heedless of the danger of breaking the calf's legs, he grabbed them up close to the shoulder and planted his foot against the cow's backside. He closed his eyes, as if the act of seeing would rob him of needed energy. Then he gritted his teeth and hauled back, holding inside himself the grunts and groans he had expended before, afraid to squander strength on anything but the task of dragging that calf out of the mother.

He opened his eyes to see that the calf's head was through. He was so surprised that he blinked, and it took a moment to realize that he had done the hardest part. The calf hung half out of the cow, partly covered by the membrane that had held it inside its aqueous world for the previous eleven months. The eyes were still closed, the tongue still blue and protruding. *Ah well, we'll save the cow anyway.*

The next contraction pushed the calf the rest of the way out, and it lay sprawled on the ground, half swathed in the membrane and mucous that still hung down from the cow's back end. Without hope, Heck picked a piece of grass from a nearby hillock and tickled inside the calf's nose. Nothing. He threw away the grass, a motion both weary and forlorn, and was leaning down to retrieve his piggin' string, when he heard a scrabbling sound beside him. Still bending down, he turned his head and found himself looking into the newly opened eyes of a game little calf that was already trying to get up on its forefeet.

"Yeeeeehaaaaaah!" All the sound that Heck kept within himself on the last desperate pull came out now in a joyful noise of celebration as he tossed first the piggin' string and then his hat in the air. "Yeeehaaah!" he yelled again, spreading his arms wide because he had nothing else to fling.

"Oh, Death," he shouted through cupped hands at the sky, "where is thy sting?" That felt so good he shouted again, "And thou art a bastard!" Which felt even better.

Called back to the business at hand by the lowing of the new mother, he picked up his hat and piggin' string. Mounting Dandy, he loosened the rope and freed his captive. The cow swung around and began sniffing the new arrival, licking him with her rough tongue, knocking him over just as he had wobbled himself into a precarious crouch.

Heck rode a ways away, coiling his lariat as he went. Then he pushed his hat to the back of his head and grinned as he sat and watched the comic scene before him. The mother bumbled around with the best of intentions, fussing and grooming the little red clown who was taking pratfalls and tottering around in his quest for an udder—something he knew was underneath, though fore or aft he wasn't entirely certain.

"That's the third time she's knocked him down," he told Dandy. "You'd think she'd figure out that he's more interested in finding the tit than having his hair combed. There. He found it. I guess you and I can go now. He'll be all right."

But he sat for a moment longer, watching the calf.

The little fellow was visibly stronger with each passing minute, and he lifted his head to butt his mother's stomach in the familiar nursing rite that reassured the cow and made Heck smile in satisfaction.

Reluctantly, Heck turned Dandy's face to the east. It was about five miles to the ranch house, and he needed to get a move on. The sun was low in the sky and the black shadow of horse and rider that went before him was elongated. Heck chuckled. "That's about as tall as I feel right now," he told Dandy.

As Heck rode, his mind returned to the struggle. He couldn't remember particulars. All he could remember clearly were the feelings. His mind played over the black despair, the hopelessness that he had felt, the absolute refusal to give up, and the jubilation of winning. He was within a mile of the ranch house, whistling as he rode, mentally putting it all into words, so he could tell Ruth, when suddenly he knew something he hadn't known before.

It was as if, simultaneously, someone had opened both his head and his breast and put the thought in his mind and the knowledge of its truth in his heart. It was an emotionally staggering experience, totally unfamiliar, and one for which he was completely unprepared.

He pulled on the reins, and Dandy stopped, shifting his weight and tossing his head as if to ask if that was what Heck really intended, so close to home. Heck pulled on the reins again to assure Dandy and then reached forward to pat the pony's neck. "Oh, Dandy," he said. "What a day this has been!"

Heck understood, finally, about Little Emory's death. Just a moment ago, the realization struck him that he had been looking at it all wrong. It wasn't that they had him *just* a year. It was that they had him at all. What if he had never known Little Emory? His birth had been a gift, something precious. Like a diamond. Does a fella grumble because a diamond is so small?

Heck understood that Little Emory would always be with him in memory, and that it was possible he would lose others equally dear. He saw that life was a series of beginnings and endings and that if one could learn to accept that, one could be happy.

Heck understood that all new life was precious in the potential it held, that Jonathan was a wellspring yet untapped, that his own sons who were yet to come would add to his own existence in a way that Little Emory or Jonathan never could. And he would be given the chance to be the kind of father that he had wanted his papa to be. It was the cycle of life. If you were going to inhabit the earth, you accepted that was the way it would be.

Heck must have sat for five minutes trying to put all these feelings into order in his mind, so he could think about them more fully. Unconsciously, he had taken off his hat, and as Dandy stirred again, hinting that it might be time to continue their journey home, Heck realized that he was holding it over his heart.

He felt silly and automatically looked around to see if anyone had caught him woolgathering in such a pose. There was no one in sight. He was just about to put his hat back on when the thought came that the calf-pulling experience and the subsequent feelings he had had about life and death were a gift, and maybe he should give thanks for it. He was uncomfortable with that thought, for it seemed too pious, too openly religious. So he set his hat square on his head and said, "Come on, Dandy, let's go home."

Dandy needed no urging and set off at a smart trot. But Heck pulled on the reins again before they had gone a hundred yards, and the horse had to stand again while Heck thought a minute.

It seemed so ungrateful not to say anything. Heck felt freer this afternoon than he had felt in a long time. He could not remember when he had felt so at peace, so sure of himself. Surely he ought to say thanks, just in case?

Heck took off his hat and looked at the sky. "Thanks, Lord," he said in his mind. Then he put his hat back on and clicked his tongue to Dandy, who eagerly set off for home.

The poor horse hadn't got fifty yards before he was stopped again. Heck was beset by a feeling that he had not adequately thanked God, and he didn't quite know what to do about it. He was not in the habit of praying, didn't really know how to go about it. He had seen his mother and Lucy at their prayers, and they knelt when they talked to God. He had the feeling that to do this properly he should kneel, and he was most unwilling to do so. But until he had this taken care of, he didn't feel that he could go on.

"Ah, hell," he breathed. Throwing his leg over, he dismounted. "I'll just be a minute, Dandy," he said as he patted the restive pony on the neck. "Just hold your horses."

"Hell," he said again. "That just shows the state I'm in, telling a horse to hold his horses."

Standing with the reins in his hand and his hands in his hips, Heck looked all around to make sure he was alone. He cleared his throat. "I don't know for sure what I'm doing," he announced to Dandy. He looked around again, but there was nothing but tobosa grass and greasewood all the way to the horizon. Taking a deep breath, Heck dropped to his knees and pulled off his hat. He closed his eyes and tried to think of the right words to say. He felt Dandy's breath in his hair and then felt the tug on the reins that he still held in his hand as the horse stepped away. Still no words came.

Finally, in desperation, Heck said, "Thank you, God, for letting me know." He opened his eyes to find Dandy's face close to his own. He hugged it to him with one hand. "I don't know if that was right," he said, "but I did it." He patted the pony's cheek and stood up. "And you know, I don't think I did too bad."

Chapter 52

WHILE HECK WAS riding across the west half of Emory's range, Ruth was on her way back from El Paso. The drive from that city to Hot Springs usually took around four and a half hours. Ruth made it in just under four, and all the way, her mind was spinning as fast as the wheels under her, laying plans and devising ways to justify them to her husband.

Monty Redmond had said Nick Sanders wouldn't back Ruth financially. Strictly speaking, that was true. However, as he and Ruth sat in his office talking about supplies and equipment she needed, Nick made several phone calls, and the next morning when Ruth went, first to the printer, then to the fabric warehouse, she found she had a line of credit and was a preferred customer.

Nick Sanders had also called a diamond merchant. His office was the last place Ruth visited before leaving El Paso just a little before noon. He was not usually open for business on Saturday and met her at the door, nodding a curt greeting while he fitted a key into the lock. He was small and neatly dressed with thin gray hair and gray eyes that gave little away. Opening the door into the bland cubicle that was his office, he set a straight-back chair for her in front of his desk while he took his own swivel chair on the other side.

"The ring?" he said, taking his jeweler's glass out of his pocket and screwing it into his eye. As Ruth handed it to him, she didn't really know what to expect since Harlan had sometimes bragged about things that weren't really true. This time, he had been right. The merchant told her with an economy of words that the diamond was flawless. He stated what it was worth and what he would give her for it. Since Nick Sanders had warned her that, given economic conditions, she could expect to get only a quarter of the stone's value, she accepted the offer, signed the proper document, and walked out of the office fifteen minutes after entering it with five hundred dollars cash in her patent leather purse.

When she reached the turnoff to Palomas, Ruth passed it without slowing and continued on to Hot Springs. She pulled up in front of Forsett Realty just as Mr. Forsett was getting ready to put the *closed* sign in the window.

Entering the office, Ruth eyed the rumpled figure before her, a middle-aged, pear-shaped shambles. He wore a gray double-breasted suit that was unbuttoned and hung all wrong because the pockets were full of tools. Ruth saw the end of a flashlight in one and what looked like a pair of pliers in another. She hesitated, wondering if another agent in town might look more promising.

Mr. Forsett put the sign on a shelf and declared that he was willing to stay late if he could help Mrs. Benham find just what she wanted.

A rental house? She was in luck. Old Mrs. Flint, who used to own the drugstore, just died, and the family was renting out her house. It was small but well-kept and had just been remodeled five years ago.

Ruth expressed interest in seeing the house and waited while Mr. Forsett fumbled around, untangling a bunch of keys, checking the white cardboard tag on the string of each as it came loose until he found the one he wanted.

She followed him outside and suppressed her annoyance as she waited for him to throw three empty Coke bottles and last week's newspaper into the back seat of his Buick touring car. After she was in and they were driving up the hill and past the sanatorium, as she listened to him suck absently on one of his teeth, Ruth began to wish she had looked for another agent.

Her irritation evaporated when they got to the house. Of red brick with a veranda extending clear across the front, it had a neat lawn surrounded by a white picket fence. An archway over the gate supported a climber rose that was already leafing out in red-tipped green.

"I have to tell you that your water bill will run you three dollars a month in the summer," Mr. Forsett confessed. "Takes a lot of water to keep a lawn from dying."

He got out and walked around to open her door. Leading the way to the gate, he opened it for her and followed up the walk and across the porch.

While he searched each pocket twice to find the key, she peeked through the front room window, noting the shiny hardwood floors, the sheer Priscilla curtains, the bright kitchen seen through an archway. Once inside, Mr. Forsett said magic words like two bedrooms, floor furnace, gas range, and hot water heater. Ruth felt that she had misjudged him.

They drove back to his office, so she could sign a rental agreement. He offered to find someone to move her things from storage into the house the following day and said he would arrange for utilities to be transferred into her name on Monday.

"Now, I don't know if you noticed, but there isn't a refrigerator in the kitchen," Mr. Forsett said. "If you would like, I could get Doyle Gibson to deliver one to you first thing Monday morning, and you can run by and take care of paying for it Tuesday after you're settled in. I don't suppose you want to use an icebox."

"No, I certainly don't," she said, snapping her handbag shut. She stood up and extended her hand. "Thank you so much, Mr. Forsett. It's been a pleasure doing business with you." Such was the force of a refrigerator and a hot water heater that she actually meant it.

Lucy was outside when Ruth drove by Bemis's store, so she stopped and talked through the window to her. Lucy thought she had just arrived from El Paso, and Ruth didn't tell her any different. She described the meeting with Nick Sanders and told Lucy how well their designs had been received.

"Really?" Lucy breathed. "Oh, Ruth! I would never have believed that it would be that easy."

"Well, we haven't done anything yet. Oh, the designs were good, but now we've got to do them in the right fabrics and see if we can produce them in quantity for a price that will sell. Either that or find someone who will buy our designs. We've got a lot of work ahead of us." She started the car.

"But he liked them? He thought we had a chance?"

"Yes, but he also said it wouldn't be easy. I've got some thinking to do and some other things I'm tied up with, but we'll get together in the middle of next week and talk seriously about what has to be done."

"That's fine. Is Heck staying out at Emory's tonight? Do you want to have supper with us?"

"No. I'm tired. I'm going home and going right to bed. Good night."

"Night." Lucy waved and stepped back so Ruth could drive on.

Ruth had spoken the truth when she said she was tired. She was hungry, too, and with petulant motions she built the fire, heated water, scrambled eggs for supper, prepared her bath. The simple chore of piling sticks on paper and lighting a match had never been so disagreeable before. Now that she was a day away from a real bathroom, the bucket of water had never been so heavy; the amount of water in the bottom of the tin tub had never been so meager. As she bathed and put on her nightgown, she decided she couldn't face dragging the tub to the dooryard. She would empty it in the morning.

She blew out the lamp and got into bed, but her mind wouldn't turn off. She lay shivering and thinking—about the house, about what Mr. Sanders had said, about what she needed to do tomorrow, about what she was going to do when Heck came home tomorrow night.

When she finally fell asleep, she had grotesque dreams in which she heard Heck calling her, but when she tried to reach him, she found she couldn't move. Finally, though her limbs were weighted with lead, she made her way to where he was only to find that it was Harlan, smirking at her and saying, "He's one of the, ah, hired hands; you know."

Ruth woke the next morning still wound tight, almost trembling with the effort of dealing with all the variables in her life at the moment. She dressed quickly in slacks, and taking some cleaning supplies, a change of clothes, and some toilet articles in a shopping bag, she drove into Hot Springs to the storage place.

Mr. Forsett was already there with a crew, loading things on the back of a Ford flatbed. Ruth took two boxes with her in the car to the new house and had barely unpacked them when Mr. Forsett arrived with the truck. She superintended the placing of the rugs, the chairs and sofa, the bedroom and dining room furniture. Then she requested that all the boxes be placed in the extra bedroom. She gave each of the men a dollar, and they left. Mr. Forsett stayed and helped her unpack, but at two o'clock, she persuaded him to take the empty boxes with him on the truck, thanked him, reminded him about the refrigerator, and pushed him out the door.

Alone at last, Ruth stood in the doorway and looked at the living room. It was a small room with white plastered walls, light and airy because of the windows on two sides. Her French Provincial sofa and side chairs fit nicely in it. The carpet was slate blue, and the rose-colored flowers on it picked up the claret hue of the sofa's upholstery and the light blue ceramic of the lamp on the walnut table. She closed her eyes and whispered, "God forgive me for wanting this so much," and then was surprised at herself for saying such a thing.

She took the shopping bag she had brought from Palomas into the bathroom and closed the door. *Blessed privacy!* She turned on the water and stripped off her clothes then remembered the bath mat. Opening the linen cupboard, she ran her hand over the burgundy stacks—bath towels, hand towels, and washcloths, with four bath mats besides. This was riches, indeed.

The water was so hot that it took her almost a minute to ease down in. She let the tub fill up to the overflow and then lay soaking as she looked around—at the ceramic tile on the floor and walls, at the mirrored medicine cabinet, at the towel racks and the toilet. *I shall stay in here until I'm wrinkled as a prune.* She giggled, knowing that would give away her secret. She let some water out, added more hot, and, when that cooled, did it again. Finally she decided she'd better get out, so she would be sure to be home when Heck returned.

Later, locking the door behind her, Ruth felt a reluctance to return to Palomas. She drove slowly, and as she parked in front of their old house, she looked at the adobe walls with the tiny windows, the ramshackle screen door, the privy out back. "He'll be glad in the end," she said.

She got out of the car and went into the dark little house. Rattling the stove lids as she built the fire, she said loudly to herself, "I'll spend tonight here, but it'll be the last time."

As she waited for Heck to come home, she tried to quiet the fluttering of her heart every time she heard a car approaching.

Chapter 53

SUNDAY HAD BEEN, to Heck's way of thinking, a near perfect day. The wind had been calm, the sky blue, and the high cirrus clouds reminded him of the wool that lay in long, silky streamers between the tines of Mama's carders. Heck had ridden one of Emory's horses that was only half broken, and the periodic tussles over who was boss added zest to a day that otherwise would have been almost too sweet.

"Do you want to leave your outfit here?" Emory asked as he was getting ready to take Heck home. "Then you could just ride your motorcycle out next Friday."

"I don't believe I will, Emory. I might want to take Shontie out during the week."

"Well, I tell ya. If you want to just come on out yourself, I've got an old saddle you can use. It's not as good as yours, but I bought it off a good cowboy."

"All right. I'll either have Ruth bring me out with my gear or come on out and use your saddle."

Heck threw his chaps and spurs in the rumble seat and his saddle on top of them, and the two brothers headed for Palomas. They spoke little. Heck was thinking of the things that he would have to share with Ruth: He would tell her about Carrie and Emory and how they were bravely working together trying to make a go of the ranch and how good he felt about being able to help them. He would tell her about what a fine horse Dandy was and how together he and Dandy had introduced a new little whiteface to the Jornada. And he'd tell her about what he figured out Saturday afternoon as he rode back to the ranch.

Emory broke in on his brother's thoughts. "Say, Heck, you plannin' on ridin' in the rodeo?"

"What rodeo?"

"The annual Hot Springs Fiesta rodeo, the first weekend in May."

"I didn't know Hot Springs had a fiesta, much less a rodeo."

"That's 'cause they never did before. This is the *first* annual one. The town fathers figger to drum up a little business. Most of the cattlemen are on the prod about it 'cause it's just before the spring work, and they don't want any of their hands busted up."

Heck didn't answer Emory's question. The sun was low in the sky, and he pulled his hat down to shade his eyes as he looked out the windshield at a notch in the Caballo Mountains. Palomas sat on the other side of that notch. Ruth would be waiting for him there.

Emory went on. "They can't tell the men not to go rodeoin' because the fellas from town have kicked in a lot of money. Some pretty good purses. Fifty, sixty dollars. You gonna ride?"

"You?"

"Hell, no. Oh, I'd like to, but about the time I busted somethin' Carrie'd have me home changin' didies and burpin' the young'un while she went out on the work, and I just can't take that chance. Now you—you just sit around all day pushin' pedals and pullin' levers. Coupla busted ribs wouldn't even slow you down."

Heck chuckled and looked out the window at the shadow cast by the bridge over the Rio Grande, a grotesque exaggeration, like a daddy longlegs spider crouching over the green water. Over the bridge then around the hills, down to Hot Springs, and then to Palomas. Twenty minutes and he'd be home.

"So, you gonna ride?"

"No."

"No? Why not? The way you ride you could make a hunnerd dollars! Maybe two."

"Yeah, well."

"If you can't come up with the entrance fee, I can stake ya."

"That's mighty kind of you, Emory, but I don't think I'll ride."

"Why the hell not? If you don't mind my askin'."

"But I do mind your asking." Heck was immediately contrite. "I'm sorry, *hermano*."

"Forget it."

"No, listen. It's not what you're asking. It's what I have to answer. I won't be rodeoin' because I promised Ruth I wouldn't."

"Aw, hell, Heck."

"Yeah."

They rode in silence until just before the turnoff to Palomas when Emory said, "I guess that's what gettin' married does. I'm not ridin' 'cause I'm afraid I'll be outta luck and hurt myself and lose the ranch. You're not ridin' 'cause she asked you not to. It's all tied up in bein' married and settlin' down."

Heck nodded slowly, but he knew that Emory knew there was a difference.

When Emory pulled up in front of the house, Heck asked him in, but Emory said he needed to get home, and as soon as Heck had his gear out of the back, he was gone. The sun was already down, and Heck could see the warm glow of the lamp in the window. He put his saddle away and carried his chaps and spurs in with him, feeling the tightness of anticipation in his throat as he opened the screen, turned the doorknob and pushed open the door.

Ruth was standing at the stove cooking dinner. She had on her gray chambray dress with an apron over it, and her hair was a chestnut cloud. She didn't smile at Heck but regarded him with luminous eyes, and the hand that had been stirring the gravy went to her breast.

It had been almost a year since he had been away from her—when he went out on the spring work with Ollie—and he had almost forgotten how good she was to come home to. Seeing her standing in the outer circle of the lamplight, with those splendid eyes in that beautiful face, he was suddenly unsure of himself. He rubbed his chin, aware that he hadn't shaved in two days.

Ruth smiled.

"Hello, Darlin'," he said.

"That's it? Just hello?"

"Well, no." He turned to hang up his hat and chaps and spurs and then strolled over to where she stood. Taking a hot pad from a nail, he pulled the gravy to the edge of the stove and then took her in his arms and gave her a long, gentle kiss.

"Mmmm," she said. "You're hungry. I can tell."

He nuzzled around in her hair, smelling the familiar fragrance. "You bet I am! But I want to bathe and shave first."

"No, I mean hungry here." She patted his stomach. "Otherwise you wouldn't have worried about the gravy."

"Shoot, Baby Doll, I just didn't want to be interrupted by you remembering you had to stir something."

"Well, let me go. I've got to check the biscuits."

"See what I mean? All right. I'll get the water on for baths."

"I've had mine," she said.

Heck busied himself pumping and carrying water. Ruth fed him, and he listened to her story about the trip to El Paso, looking up often to smile proudly as she told him about the meeting with Nick Sanders and the encouragement she had been given.

"I missed you," she said.

While she set the dishpan on the table, he dragged in the washtub and sluiced off the dust of the Jornada.

Afterward, clad only in a towel and getting ready to scrape off a two-day beard, he caught her reflection in the mirror, looking at him. Turning around, he saw her standing by the stove with the dishrag in her hand and an unmistakable message in her dark eyes that ignited the fire he had banked down 'til later that night. She put down the dishrag and untied her apron. Forgetting the stubble still on his jaw, he took a towel and wiped off a white streak of lather as he watched her drift toward him.

Chapter 54

THERE WAS A magpie that hung around their clothesline every night and did impressions. He could do a crow, an owl, and a blue jay, as well as the song of a whippoorwill. He would sit and go through his repertoire over and over until Heck would finally throw something at him. This night he waited until after the moon came up to begin.

Heck lay with Ruth next to him, her head on his shoulder and her arm across his chest, and listened to the magpie. "Well, I'll be damned." he said softly.

"Mmm?" Ruth's voice was languid, on the edge of sleep.

"He's doing a cricket."

There was a pause, and then Ruth murmured. "No he's not. That's a real cricket."

"No, listen ... see? He does the whippoorwill and then the cricket." He chuckled. "He's a nuisance, but you've got to admit he's got talent."

Heck lay looking at the patch of moonlight on the wall, feeling Ruth's shoulder in the hollow under his arm and the silky softness of her hair on his skin. He felt a breeze come through the open window and drew the blanket up over her bare shoulder.

"Are you awake?" he asked softly.

"Uh huh."

"I had something happen to me Saturday that I'd like to tell you about."

She didn't answer, but he felt the brush of her eyelashes against his chest. Blink, blink. She was listening.

So he told her. He started with the calf and told her what danger there was, and how he had despaired. He told about how steady Dandy was and how good the wild range heifer was to let him help her and how, working together, they finally got the calf out and how overjoyed he was when he turned around to find himself looking at a little white face with its long, white eyelashes.

He told her how that experience had somehow shifted things around in his mind, and he was able to think of Little Emory without hurting now. Slowly and quietly, he told her all the things he had learned that afternoon, ending up with the knowledge that he could be a good father to his own sons.

Blink, blink. The lashes fluttered again. She turned her head and asked, "Your sons? Have you got sons?"

Heck laughed softly. "No, Baby Doll, but if you'll oblige, I hope to soon."

"But didn't you know?" She drew back her head to look at him. "That's silly. Of course you knew!"

"Knew what? What did I know?"

"That I can't have children. Of course you knew!"

Heck couldn't answer because all of a sudden he couldn't breathe.

She sat up in bed and turned around, sitting cross-legged in the moonlight with the sheet pulled around her shoulders. "How could you not know? I haven't had a period since we married."

The sound of her voice seemed to be coming from far away, and a band of black around his vision was shutting out the moonlight.

"Heck?"

He forced himself to breathe, and the black band dissolved. "Yeah?"

"You don't know about women's menstrual periods? That once a month they—they bleed? That it's part of being able to have children?"

"No," he said softly. "I don't guess I do. There are lots of things about women that I don't know." He got up on one elbow and reached over to brush the hair back from her face. "How come you never told me?"

"I was going to. Out at Hooper's Well. But then you had to leave. And later, I got hurt."

He lay back down and closed his eyes.

"I really did think you knew." She touched his shoulder. "You know all about the breeding patterns of cattle. I thought you'd noticed I never had a period."

He rolled on his side. He couldn't look at her face, but he took her hand. "You're sure?"

"About what?"

"About not being able to have children."

"Oh, yes. The doctor said my womb is shriveled like a prune. It's a defect, like Hooter's harelip. Only mine is on the inside and doesn't show."

Heck didn't say anything. He pulled her hand under his cheek and tried to reconcile this new information with the world as he knew it yesterday. It was like trying to force a piece of a jigsaw puzzle into the wrong place. He was working so hard at trying to make it fit that he didn't hear what Ruth said.

"What?" he asked.

"I have something else to tell you," she repeated.

He raised his head. "Something else?"

She pulled her hand away. "I rented another house. In Hot Springs."

He rolled onto his back again.

She pulled the sheet tighter around her. "I have to have a telephone—Mr. Sanders is going to be calling me. And I need a place to sew. If this thing is going to go, we just have to have a bigger place. With electricity."

He took a moment to pull a pillow over and stuff it under his head. "Can we afford a bigger place? With electricity? How did you pay for it?"

Her chin came up. "I sold Harlan's ring."

He sucked in his breath. If she had said she cleared out the bank account or borrowed the money, that would have been a shock, but it wouldn't have hit him like a sock in the gut. He moved one arm across his chest, as if for protection.

"There's more, Heck. It's not a furnished house. I got my things out of storage and moved them in."

"You mean Harlan's things?"

"I mean my things."

Heck lay back on his pillow and regarded her.

Ruth sat in the moonlight with one shoulder bare, her hair a dark cloud, her eyes unreadable.

"Come to bed," he said quietly.

She didn't move.

"Come to bed," he said again. "We'll talk in the morning."

She lay down, though not nestled next to him as before. He sensed she might have been waiting for an invitation to come back over, but somehow he couldn't say the words.

She fell asleep still waiting. He lay awake staring into the night, thinking of kittens and buckets and shotguns.

Chapter 55

THERE IS SOMETHING about the night that magnifies suffering.

Daytime is sensible and pragmatic, full of a realistic light that snaps everything into focus. It has brazen colors and sharp images that crowd along the sensory paths, leaving scant room for dismal messages.

Night adds another dimension. When the sun is gone, so is perspective. Simple things become complex. Irritation tangles itself into an insoluble problem. Loneliness stretches like an evening shadow into utter desolation, and disappointment is a gaping hole through which a lifetime collection of dreams escapes like sand from a broken hourglass.

Another time, in different circumstances, the news that Ruth was barren would not have caused such hurt. But the dark desert stillness made Ruth's matter-of-fact tones sound like heartlessness as she spoke of her shriveled womb.

Had Ruth told Heck about her barrenness before he began to build up such hopes, before Little Emory died, before last Saturday, he would have been surprised, probably shocked, most certainly disappointed. Now, as he lay awake, staring into the night, listening to the even breathing of the woman beside him, he could not even think because of the pain in his head and in his heart.

Dimly, through the crush of his misery, Heck became aware of a sound nearby, high-pitched and eerie. Deep in his subconscious, some feral instinct quickened and pressed to know where it came from, what it was. The wind? An owl? A coyote?

About the time the question hit his conscious mind, Heck recognized the sound and realized with shame and surprise that what he heard was himself. He was whimpering. With that realization came the gut-wrenching remembrance of his own words to Ruth that day after the butterflies at Cottonwood Springs. *When the punishment is dealt to me, I hope I'm man enough not to whine.*

Never to have sons. Oh, dear God, not that.

Heck lay very still, as if by not moving he could keep the nausea that swept over him at bay. Sweating under the sheet and blanket, afraid to make the effort to throw them off lest he vomit, he closed his eyes and hoped he would not further disgrace himself by such weakness.

When he finally opened his eyes, the nausea had passed and the darkness around him had lightened. Morning was near. With relief, but slowly so as not to waken his wife, he crept out of bed. Picking up his clothes, he carried them to the other room, closing the door carefully behind him.

Heck lit the lamp and made a pot of coffee, dressing and shaving while he waited for it to perk. He drank the coffee as he put on his work boots, gulping what was left in the cup as soon as his laces were tied in his haste to get out into the open air.

Ruth was still asleep. He pushed open the bedroom door and looked at her. The face was familiar—the sweep of her brow, the dusky hair, the mouth with the full lower lip—but she seemed a stranger to him.

Heck walked over to the bed and sat on his heels. "Ruth," he said softly.

She opened her eyes slowly, fastening her gaze first on the white Bull Durham tag hanging from the left shirt pocket and next on his face. She frowned.

"I'm leaving," Heck said. As her eyes opened wide, he added, "I'll be back."

He took her hand and held it, running his thumb over the gold band on her ring finger. "I think I'll spend some time over at Emory's after work. He needs the help, and I need time to do some thinking."

"When will you be home?"

"Couple, three days, probably. There's coffee on the stove." He released her hand and stood up, aware that she followed him with her eyes. After collecting his cowboy boots from the corner and his hat from a nail, he went to stand in the doorway. "Where is home, by the way?"

"It's on the hill above town. Down past the sanatorium. Three thirty-five Silver Street."

"Three thirty-five."

"It's red brick."

"Red brick," Heck repeated. Then he nodded at Ruth as one would take leave of a stranger and was gone.

She heard him cross the other room and go out the door, and she sat up, so she could look out the window. In the murky early-morning light she saw him walk to where his cycle was parked and bend to put his boots and Stetson in the saddlebags. Then he swung his leg over, kick-starting the motorcycle with a quick thrust of his heel. He put on the goggles that had been hanging on the handlebars, and with a staccato roar, he was off.

Ruth sat alone in the ruins of the bed wondering whether to weep or to sing. She thought back over the events of last night, how Heck had rambled on about his day, how she had mentioned she couldn't have children, and how he was so surprised by that news that when she told him about the house in Hot Springs, he seemed barely to notice. All in all, he had taken it quite well. In fact, he seemed to care more about not having babies.

Throwing off the covers, Ruth swung her feet over the side. *I've got lots to do today. I'd better get at it.*

Humming to herself, she dressed quickly, so she could get last night's leftover dishes done and begin packing.

Chapter 56

HECK SHOWED UP Wednesday night at the house on Silver Street. It was after dark, and he approached silently, cutting the motorcycle engine half a block away and coasting into the driveway and around back where he parked the cycle by Ruth's green coupe. He sat for a moment, looking at the light spilling out of the kitchen window onto the lawn as he absently pulled off his goggles and hung them on the handlebar. Then he put down the kickstand and dismounted, strolling across the grass to stand just out of the rectangle of light and look up at the woman inside.

She was leaning against the counter with her back to the window, holding the telephone to her ear as she tipped her head back and ran her fingers through her hair. She turned, and Heck involuntarily stepped farther back into the shadows as he watched her draw her brows together in concentration.

He dragged his gaze away from her features, away from the intent expressions he had seen so many times, and surveyed his surroundings. The brick house was a mud-colored mass as it loomed beside him, solid and square. He was standing near the steps that led up to the back door, and he cautiously climbed them and looked through the small, square door-window. Just inside, banks of cupboards and coat hooks adorned the walls of a tiny anteroom off the kitchen.

Safe enough.

Suppressing the urge to knock first, Heck turned the knob and pushed open the door, quietly entering and closing the door behind him. He made hardly a sound, but Ruth must have felt his presence, for she turned to face him.

He took a step forward and leaned against the doorjamb with his hands in his pockets and his hair falling forward over his forehead, nodding slightly in response to the fingers she wiggled at him in a silent hello.

"Listen, Trudy," she said, "I've got to go now. Tell Nick I'll call first thing in the morning to talk to him. Yes, I understand. Thanks for calling on your own time. That's above and beyond; isn't it? No, I was over at my sister-in-law's. Thanks again. Talk to you tomorrow. Goodbye."

Ruth replaced the receiver onto its cradle, and she and Heck stood looking at each other for a moment. Then he glanced around the room, taking in the cupboards with the glossy white doors and drawers, the double sink with the hot and cold taps, the gas range, the new refrigerator, the frothy white curtains, the bank of switches on the wall to turn on the kitchen light, porch light, living room light.

Finally, his eyes came back to meet hers

Her chin came up, but her voice, when she spoke was breathless, "Well?"

He didn't quite shrug. It was more a dropping of his gaze, a cocking of his head, a tightening of his mouth. "I'm home," he said quietly.

I'm home. He knew she didn't realize what it cost him to say that. It was twenty miles from the dam site to Emory's. Heck could make it in fifteen minutes on his motorcycle. That was the only time from sunup till after sundown during the last three days that he had been still. All the while he was working he was thinking, pushing ideas around in his head as relentlessly as he pushed his body.

He hadn't even stopped to eat. Jimmy waited to sit with him at lunch, but Heck worked through his noon break, chewing on jerky and Carrie's leftover biscuits as he jolted and shook over the uneven clay surface. He wasn't ready to hear Ruth's name, and he was afraid Jimmy might say it.

Emory was surprised to see him Monday afternoon, but gladly gave him some chores. Emory had three windmills on his place. The two nearest were accessible by road, and Heck drove out on his cycle to service them. Emory wanted to make sure they were in good condition, so when he was out with the chuckwagon during the spring work, he wouldn't have to worry about his stock having water. Heck got back to the ranch house after dark and slept on the couch, rising early Tuesday morning to spend an hour shoeing horses before he headed back to work on the dam.

After work, Heck rode Dandy to the windmill farthest west, taking a blanket and a small coffeepot and spending the night there.

As he lay looking up at the immensity of the nighttime sky, he remembered a line from that old, ragged, black book he found in the bottom of the barrel in Bemis's storeroom. *I know that man is nothing, which thing I never had supposed.*

Heck chuckled in empathy with the unknown man who had written those lines. Had this man, like Heck, been so overwhelmed with problems that it seemed he and his afflictions were the most important thing in the world? And had he lain, as Heck was lying now, looking at a black and spangled universe of such depth and complexity that one could not begin to even comprehend the fact that it existed, much less understand it? "Sure whittles things down to size," he whispered to himself.

That's when Heck began to realize that it was not the judgment of God that had come upon him but simply the product of a choice he, Heck Benham, had made. God had not made Ruth barren to punish him. In choosing a woman with beauty and quickness of mind, with boundless energy and a whimsical nature, he had also chosen one with a useless womb.

It wasn't the judgment of God. Maybe it was justice. He didn't know. He'd have to think about that.

He remembered standing with Ruth on top of the hill above Palomas the day he had decided to marry her. What had he said to her? Something about, if you choose to disregard the laws—written or unwritten—then you choose the consequences. When he said that, he thought he knew what the consequences were. Now, lying under the immensity of this sky, Heck began to think that the true price wasn't discovered until the choice was made and the act accomplished.

He had taken a woman—a married woman—because he fell in love with her. Took her away from her husband. Now that man was dead. Heck had not meant for that to happen, but was it a result of his choice?

Heck laced his hands behind his head and pondered.

He had not married someone bred to the southwest, to the raising of cattle. He had chosen, instead, someone bred to town living. What, then, could he expect? Should he be surprised and angry when she would not pump water any longer? Should he be hurt because she wanted to live where she could have a telephone and electricity? Could he not have foreseen from the first that this was bound to happen? Emory had seen it, had tried to warn him with his little parable about Duchess and Headlight. Ah, well.

A shooting star flamed into view, its brilliant arc lasting only seconds before it was erased from existence, scraped away to nothingness against the atmosphere. *Funny that something as ethereal as the air could do such damage.*

All of a sudden, he was tired. He brought his arms down and wrapped the blanket up around his shoulders. His last conscious thought, after deciding that his problems would keep 'til the morrow, was a feeling of gratitude for the warm blanket that was around him and for the fresh breeze that blew across his face.

All day Wednesday—except for the time spent on his motorcycle rocketing between Emory's place and the dam site when inattention could have cost him his life—all day long, thoughts whirled around in Heck's mind. The vortex of that mental whirlpool was the vow he had made to a city-bred lady under a grape arbor one summer day in Kanab.

To have and to hold. As he operated the Cat, the cadence of its engine seemed to pick up the phrase. *To have and to hold, to have and to hold, to have and to hold.* The rattle and squeak of the sheep's foot had its own refrain as it followed. *For better or worse, for better or worse, for better or worse.* Heck couldn't get away from the sound. It ground away, wearying him with its repetition when he would have turned his thoughts elsewhere. *To have and to hold, for better or worse, to have and to hold, for better or worse.*

By the end of the day, Heck was worn down with it. As he climbed down from the machine, he was grateful as much for the silence as he was for the end of his labors. Jimmy joined him on the walk to the parking lot. Heck knew when Jimmy asked, "Want to come home for supper?" he was really asking, "How are you?"

He smiled at his friend's concern and said, "Thanks, Jimmy, I'm fine." He clapped him on the shoulder and waved goodbye. Jimmy stood silently by his car, watching Heck as he walked to his motorcycle and got on. He was still watching moments later as Heck roared out of sight.

Just before Palomas Creek empties into the Rio Grande, it slows down and bends around, creating a still pool about four feet deep and twenty feet across. There are cottonwood trees around the outside corner of the bend and cattails on the inside. There is grass and shade and coolness, quiet and solitude. It was there that Heck went after work, to lie on his stomach and smell the musty smell of the earth and the sweet smell of the cottonwoods, to stare into the water and try to see the future written there.

He saw a school of minnows feeding just below the surface. He saw a metallic-blue damselfly darting and hovering inches above. He saw a mud hen peep from the rushes just opposite him, but he caught not even a glimpse of the future.

Heck turned over and put his arm over his eyes, grateful for the quiet and the chance to rest. He had not realized that he was so tired. The day was still pleasantly warm, and it was so good to have nothing to do but lie here and relax. Without meaning to do so, he fell asleep.

It was well after sundown when Heck awoke, chilled and disoriented. Though it was night under the cottonwoods, the last blue light of a dying day was reflected on the pond, and he could see the dark, darting forms of swallows as they made their final sweep, skimming over the surface of the water. Heck sat up and leaned against one of the trees, building a cigarette to smoke while he gathered his thoughts.

"What's with you, *hombre*?" he muttered. "You've pretty much figured that you're gonna go on in. This is something you didn't plan on, but so was leaving Ollie's. You survived that. You can survive this."

When there was no more light for the pond to reflect, it became part of the dense black nightscape. Heck was aware of it, knowing it by touch the way a blind man reads Braille, for the feel of the air, heavy and moist and cool, told him that water was near. He could hear the bats now, their wings making a faint beating sound, their squeaky cries so high and short that the slightest noise would overlay them. It was time to go, but still Heck stayed.

"What'cha gonna do?" he asked by way of persuasion, "Let the marriage fall apart because what's better for her is worse for you? You've got to give a little to make a go of it, so what's keepin' you away? You scared of electricity?"

But he still didn't go.

It was hunger that finally moved him. He stumbled through the darkness to his motorcycle and rode into Hot Springs where he had enchiladas and sopapillas and black coffee at Felix's. The little restaurant was busy, and though he dawdled over his food, he could not in good conscience occupy the seat at the counter any longer. He paid his check and walked out into the night.

Up on the hill, past the sanatorium, she had said.

He found himself, not many minutes later, riding past the low, rambling structure where, for those afflicted with tuberculosis, the word *patient* was a double entendre.

Heck cut the engine and coasted. When he spied Ruth through a lighted window half a block away, something that felt like fear—or excitement—made a knot in his chest. It was still there as he stood on the service porch with his hands in his pockets leaning a shoulder against the doorframe, looking across the kitchen at her.

"Well?" she had asked.

And he had replied, "I'm home."

She offered him coffee from the pot that sat warming on the pilot light and pulled a chair out for him at the kitchen table. As they sat, she drew patterns on the tablecloth with her spoon, and he examined what he could see of the living room through the archway. Their eyes met occasionally; their smiles were tentative and faint.

Ruth offered to show Heck the rest of the house, and he politely accepted, nodding as she opened cupboards, turned on lights, pointed out features. He noted the mahogany hutch and matching table in the dining room, the mirror with the light above it in the bathroom, the spare room that already had her sewing machine and a cutout table set up in it.

As she turned to take him to the end of the hall, the knot in his chest tightened, and suddenly he knew what had kept him away. It wasn't a fear of electricity. It wasn't that he couldn't give a little for this woman who was coolly opening the door and inviting him into the bedroom. It was the sound of the cash register, *ka-ching, ka-ching*, still totting up the cost of the choice he made two years ago. Tonight he was to sleep in Harlan Reynolds's bed.

Chapter 57

A MONTH LATER, on his way home from work one afternoon, Heck met Heber Larson.

He first spied him from a mile away, a paramecium-sized dot floating in a blue pond that spread out over the roadway ahead. As he sped closer, the mirage faded, and the black dot grew and changed into a man trudging along the highway.

The man was tall with broad shoulders and a heavy-footed gait that marked him as a country boy even though he was wearing a white shirt and tie and carrying a suit coat over his arm.

Heck coasted up from behind and kept pace beside the stranger who kept plodding along, though he did turn and nod. Heck noted the short, sandy-colored hair with a cowlick in front, a generous sprinkling of freckles, and a space between the fellow's front teeth. Only his hazel eyes, keen and intelligent, rescued him from rustic caricature.

Heck spoke over the throbbing of his idling engine. "You get thrown off?"

"What?" The freckled face screwed up in puzzlement, but the long legs didn't stop.

Heck cut the engine and pushed the goggles up on his forehead. "I didn't see your outfit. You break down back a ways?"

The young man stopped and shook his head.

"What'cha doing way out here? Don't see too many salesmen riding their thumbs."

"I caught a ride out to the ..." Under the cowlick, the young stranger's brow furrowed in thought. He finally gave up, took a notebook from his shirt pocket, and consulted it. "... Coles. They said to come at five and stay to dinner, but when I got there, no one was home."

"Maybe they were out doing chores. If they were expecting you, they'll probably be back soon."

"I thought so, too. Hung around. Pretty soon this kid comes by to feed the stock. He says the family went to Cruces. Guess they forgot about me."

"Kid wouldn't give you a ride to town?"

"He didn't offer. I didn't ask."

"You want a ride?"

A gap-toothed smile flashed. "I sure do!"

Heck extended his hand. "Heck Benham."

The young man stuffed the notebook back in his pocket before he enthusiastically pumped Heck's hand and introduced himself. Then he shrugged on his suit coat and swung a long leg over to sit behind.

"Put your feet down there, like that," Heck advised. "Yeah. Now, hang on tight, and we'll be back in town in a couple a' minutes."

Heck replaced his goggles, started the engine, opened the throttle, and introduced a country boy to G-forces. They made the three miles to town in two minutes flat.

When Heck pulled up in front of the address he had been given, his passenger got off tentatively, as if mistrusting his legs to hold him. Wiping the palm of his hand on his pant leg, he offered it again to Heck and flashed a wan echo of his former smile as he said, "Thanks."

Heck looked at the white clapboard cottage in front of him. "This where you live?" he asked. "You related to the Hubbards?"

"No. I live out back." The young man pointed.

Heck looked past him at the dilapidated structure. "In the garage?"

Heber Larson shook his head. "Come and see."

Heck took off his goggles and hung them on the handlebars. Dismounting, he followed the figure in the rumpled suit down a path to a small lean-to attached to the back of the garage. Still following, Heck ducked under the low door lintel and entered a narrow, unlit room. Heber reached up to switch on the single forty-watt bulb hanging from the ceiling, and the ambience of the room lifted from dark and gloomy to dim and depressing.

Heck put his hands in his back pockets and looked around. Chair, cot, hot plate on a powder box.

"I had a companion," Heber explained, "but he got sick and had to be sent home. They haven't sent a replacement yet, and I couldn't afford anything better by myself."

"Shoot, Eldon," Heck said, "times are getting a bit better now. They should be paying you enough to get a decent place."

The younger man blinked. "Heber," he said.

"Beg pardon?"

"My name is Heber. Heber Larson."

"I could'a swore you said your name was Eldon Larson."

The younger man shook his head. "I said Elder Larson. I'm a missionary."

"Well, I'll be damned."

The missionary offered his hand again. "Thanks for the ride. It was, um, quite an experience."

Heck shook the proffered hand. "*De nada.* By the way," he said, glancing around for some evidence of food, "what were you gonna do for supper, since Miz Cole didn't feed you?"

Heber shrugged and spread his hands.

"Belt soup, eh?"

"Belt soup?"

Heck grinned. "Pull it a notch tighter. Fools the belly into thinking you've had a meal. Want to come have supper at our house?"

Heber only paused a moment before accepting, and soon they were back on the motorcycle, and he was holding on tight as they roared up the road that ran past the sanatorium. They parked behind the house, and he followed Heck up the walk to the back porch, laughing at the story of Bemis's first ride on the motorcycle.

As Heck opened the door, a delicious aroma rolled out and silenced all conversation. They passed through the service porch to the kitchen, and Heck opened the oven door to reveal a chicken, plump and brown, lying spraddle-legged in a baking pan with stuffing spilling out from between the drumsticks.

"Just like my mom used to make," Heber said reverently, closing his eyes for a long moment.

Heck picked up the coffeepot and glanced at his new friend who seemed fixated on the table, set for dinner with Ruth's bone china and sterling silverware. "Coffee?"

"What?" Heber turned to look at Heck and then looked back at the table. His Adam's apple moved as he swallowed. "Oh ...ah ... no. Listen, Heck. Your Missus isn't expecting me. I'll just go. I can walk back down."

"Nah. That's all right." Heck opened the fridge and looked inside. "Iced tea? Coca Cola?"

"No, listen. She's all ready and I'm ..." He pointed first to the table and then to the door and retreated to the service porch.

"We can set another place. Iced tea or Coke?" Heck held a bottle in one hand and an opener in the other.

"Coke." As he reached for the drink, it was almost pathetic how relieved he looked. The Coke was cold, and he drank half the bottle in the first pull.

Heck picked up his coffee and took a sip. "I imagine supper'll be pretty soon," he said as he strolled toward the archway. "It looks about ... oh, hello, ma'am." Heck paused and raised his cup in salute to someone in the other room. "Didn't know you were here."

The young man shifted uneasily. He swiftly downed the rest of the Coke, set the bottle on the counter, and edged toward the back door. "I'll just ..." He motioned toward the exit.

Heck took a sip of his coffee, regarding the person beyond over the rim of his cup. "I brought someone home to dinner."

It was at that moment that the Coke, hastily drunk, betrayed Heber Larson. The excess carbon dioxide escaped in a deep and resonant belch.

Heck sent only a brief glance the young man's way, but that glance noted flaming cheeks and hands covering his mouth. "He's a parson," Heck went on, conversationally to the person in the living room. He turned and smiled encouragingly at Heber. "Come and meet my wife."

Heber swallowed and balled his fists, his arms hanging at his side as he walked what must have been a mile to the archway. The blazing cheeks continued unabated as his eyes fell on the person who had created the delicious kitchen smells. Heck's wife wasn't round and plump and comfortably homey. She was sleek and cool and brittle. And gorgeous.

"This is Heber Larson," Heck said to Ruth. "He's a parson. Parson Larson." He smiled. "Parson, this is my wife, Ruth."

"How do you do?" Ruth's voice held no welcome. She did not smile.

Things went downhill from there. The young missionary seemed daunted by Ruth's looks, by her manners, dress, voice, and choice of words. She did nothing to set him at ease, and when she directed cool questions at him, his tongue tied itself in knots, and it seemed he could do no more than gabble beginning syllables in reply.

Heck saw that Parson was about to cut and run, so he hazed him into the corner of the kitchen and commanded him to sit down. Heck himself set the extra place and sat with Heber, smiling encouragement as Ruth carved the chicken and made gravy.

She set a plate of baked chicken and dressing, mashed potatoes and gravy in front of him. "And where did you go to divinity school?"

"Divinity?" Heber bent a blank and beseeching stare on Heck. "Like Christmas candy?"

"Where did you go to college?" Heck interpreted.

"Oh. I went a couple a' years to Weber State. Thank you, ma'am." Parson waited until all had been served and his hostess took a bite before he began.

Seeing that Parson was concentrating on his table manners, Heck asked Ruth, "How was your day?"

"Instructive," she answered.

"Oh?"

"Yes. I went to see Doyle Gibson about a matter of business. He said you and he had already made other arrangements."

Ruth's voice was smooth and matter-of-fact, but Heck knew from the look in her eyes and the set of her chin that she was angry.

"He's an easy man to deal with," he said. "I think Parson needs some more chicken."

It was true. Doyle was an easy man to deal with. He had reluctantly approached Heck when he met him in town, explaining that he understood that Miz Benham was going to come in first thing and pay for the fridge, but he hadn't seen her. Doyle had looked away from Heck's face and down at his own feet when he had said, "It's been almost a month now."

Heck admitted to Doyle that he couldn't come up with more than twenty dollars right then. Doyle said he'd be glad to take the twenty and Heck's saddle to boot in exchange for the refrigerator. They shook hands. Heck gave Doyle the money, and before the day was out, his saddle was in Doyle's tack shed. That was day before yesterday.

Heck watched in wry amusement as Ruth took Heber's plate to the stove and slashed at the chicken. He knew she was angry at herself for causing Heck to lose his saddle but able to express it only in attacking him. She speared several pieces of meat and thrust them onto Heber's plate, adding potatoes and gravy with decisive gestures, and setting it all in front of the young man so abruptly that his eyes widened. Heck got the idea that even if he hadn't been hungry, he wouldn't have dared to refuse a second portion.

On her way back to the table, Ruth picked up her silver cigarette case and lighter. She was wearing a set of beach pajamas of her own design, made of a clingy, creamy crepe that flowed to the floor. She sat, tucking one leg under her and crossing the other over. Leaning back in her chair, she opened the case, and drumming her fingers on the tablecloth as she considered, she used one of her long, well-manicured nails to lift out a cigarette. She snapped the case shut and tapped the end of the cigarette against it before lighting up with the silver lighter. As she inhaled, she put her head back, letting her chestnut curls fall down her back as she exhaled a cloud of smoke at the ceiling.

Heber Larson stared, a forkful of chicken halfway to his mouth.

Ruth regarded him from under her lashes. "Tell me, Parson. Have you been sent to the heathens in the wilds of New Mexico?" She took another drag on her cigarette.

"Um." Parson looked down at his plate. He set down his fork and wiped his mouth with his napkin. "Um."

"Yes?"

He folded his napkin and set it on the table as near as possible to how he found it, adjusting it twice to make it just so. Then he looked up at Ruth.

"I don't know anything about heathens, ma'am," Parson admitted. "I've been sent to the honest in heart." He stood. "I have an appointment in half an hour. Thank you so much for dinner. It was delicious. No—" He held up his hand to detain Heck. "I'll walk on down the hill. It'll help get my thoughts together."

"That's fine," Heck said, "I'll just see you to the door."

Parson walked around the table and thrust his hand out to Ruth, expressing again his thanks. Then he headed through the kitchen to the back door.

Heck followed him outside. "You'll go to hell for telling a lie, you know."

Parson smiled ruefully. "The only time I heard the word heathen was when I ran through Mrs. Farbinder's yard and she called me one. I figured I'd better go before I put my foot in it."

"You got something to eat for tomorrow?"

Parson flashed his spittin'-crack smile and offered his hand to Heck. "Don't worry. My money comes day after tomorrow. I won't starve before then."

"You're welcome here anytime."

"Thanks." Heber backed away from Heck and lifted his hand in farewell. Then he turned toward town, walking with a purposeful gait as if he really had someone waiting to hear what he had to say.

Chapter 58

HECK WAS LATE getting home Friday night. He had said he might work overtime, but it was full dark and Ruth had had to add water twice to the pot of beans simmering on the stove before she heard the roar of his motorcycle coming up the hill.

She was busy at work in her spare-room studio, and she stopped the wheel of her sewing machine with her hand to listen as he parked the cycle and strode to the back door. She heard him pause on the service porch to hang up his hat and again at the stove to pour a cup of coffee.

"I'm in here," she called and waited with a fluttering in her chest for him to come in.

They had spent a tenuous month together in the house on Silver Street. Things were not the same; there was no doubt about that. Heck spent as little time at home as possible, working extra hours at the dam or helping Emory out on the Lazy E.

Ruth didn't mind him working so much, as she was working long hours on her own projects. She did mind that their relationship was more hostess-guest than husband-wife. Heck was a pleasant companion. He seemed to be determined not to quarrel with her, but he held himself aloof. He smiled at her across the breakfast table in the morning, and his eyes followed her as she padded around in her nightgown at night. But he didn't hold her like he used to, didn't come up from behind to bury his face in her hair and squeeze her tight, didn't invite her to come and drift off to sleep in the circle of his arms.

Ruth had hoped that before today Heck would be comfortable here on Silver Street, that the old, easy intimacy would have returned. Tonight she had exciting news. Unbelievable news. But she didn't feel ready to tell Heck, didn't feel he was ready to hear about this. Things were happening a little too fast.

Heck stood in the doorway, leaning against the doorjamb with a cup of coffee in his hand.

She took the pins out of her mouth and smiled a welcome. "Hungry?"

"I could eat."

"Beans and tortillas all right?"

"You make the tortillas?"

She clipped a thread. "No. I didn't have time. I bought some down at the store."

"That's all right."

"Where've you been?" She held a piece of material under the light and examined a seam.

"Mr. Barrett had a couple a' things he wanted me to do, and then I went by to check on the parson."

"That hayseed. I don't know what you see in him."

"Oh, he's all right." Heck wandered into the room and over to a bunch of printed cards that were spread out over the cut-out table. "He and I've read some of the same books," he said. "We talk about breeding cattle and breaking horses, and every now and then we talk about God."

"Does he know you think God is a Mexican?"

"Oh, I mostly listen to what he has to say. What'cha got here?"

"That's my brand name. Do you like it?"

He held up one of the cards. It was an ecru-colored card with *miz whitleather* printed in stylized lowercase lettering. Very elegant. Very understated.

Heck stared at the card so long that she finally said, "It's been a while since you called me that."

He flicked the card back down on the table. "Want to come sit with me while I have supper?"

Her heart sank. He wouldn't even look at her. "Just let me sew this seam. Then I'll be in."

She joined him a few minutes later in the kitchen. As he ate his beans, she picked up a tortilla and chewed absently on it. "These aren't as good as mine."

"Nope," he agreed.

Silence.

"I'm working tomorrow," he said, finally.

"But tomorrow is—" She broke off, not wanting to have to remind him that it was her birthday. He looked at her expectantly. "—the rodeo," she finished.

"Yep. That's why I'm the one elected to go up to the quarry. Everyone else wants to go to the rodeo."

"Don't you want to go, too?"

"Oh, sure. But I'm glad for the extra money. Rent's due next week."

She smoothed a wrinkle out of the tablecloth. "Is it because you don't want to see Mike compete in the roping events? Lucy says he's riding Spook."

Heck didn't answer. He finished his beans and pushed his plate back. Sliding his chair away from the table, he crossed his legs and picked up his coffee cup. "Why don't you come with me?"

"Come to work with you?"

"Yep. I have to go up into the mountains. There's a dump truck up there that they want me to fix and bring down. We could take a picnic lunch and a blanket." He let the proposition hang in the air while he took a sip of coffee and watched her over the rim of the cup.

She met his eyes and read his intentions, and the fluttering in her breast increased. "Did you remember we have company coming for dinner and then we're going dancing?"

"It's just Lucy and Jimmy, isn't it? We'll go by in the morning and explain, tell them we'll meet them at Ashley's. We can have them to dinner next week."

Had he dwelt more on dalliance under the pines, or had he mentioned that he wanted to celebrate her birthday with a day spent alone together in the mountains, Ruth would have capitulated. Instead, he said, "I need someone to drive the pickup back down."

The words were like a douche of cold water. "No thanks," she said. "I have things I need to do tomorrow."

Heck shrugged and drank his coffee and didn't look at her.

Ruth sat for another minute, nervously shredding the tortilla she had been nibbling on, trying to gather courage to show Heck the letter that had come that morning from Los Angeles. When she stood, finally, she was surprised to find herself on her feet, because there had been no conscious decision made to rise.

She went and got the letter from her sewing room and brought it back with her. Feeling anything but careless, she carelessly dropped it on the table in front of Heck.

"This came for me today," she said.

While Heck studied the envelope, Ruth removed his plate and cleaned up the tortilla litter, watching him as she brushed the crumbs off the tablecloth into her hand and dumped them in the garbage.

"Read it," she prompted, sitting down opposite him again.

Heck gave her a searching look as he withdrew the single sheet of paper.

Ruth's fingers nervously drummed on the table as she waited for him to read the invitation so cordially extended. "Well?" she said when he finally looked up.

Heck tossed the letter back over in front of her then stood and poured himself another cup of coffee. Standing at the stove he gestured at the open letter with his coffee cup. "Who is he?" he asked.

"Just one of the top designers in America! He sells mostly in the west but in the best stores. I. Magnin, Neiman Marcus, like that. Nick told him about me, and he's interested in my line of women's slacks."

Heck looked at her a moment, and then a slow smile spread over his face. "Well, I'll be damned," he said softly. "That's really something."

"Yes! I've been so excited all day, but I was afraid to tell you. I was afraid you'd be angry."

"Hell, Darlin', why should I be angry? Isn't this what you've been planning on, why you spend all those hours treadling away in your sewing room?"

Ruth was up like quicksilver, throwing her arms around him, heedless of the coffee she spilled. "Yes it is! Yes! Yes! Yes!" She kissed him and hugged him tightly.

She felt Heck set his coffee cup down and lock his arms around her. Relief at having him smile about the letter and joy in the comfort of being in his arms made tears wet her lashes, and she spoke in a breathless whisper that showed how close to the ragged edge she had been. "I was so afraid you'd be dead set against moving to California that I was sick with worry."

"Beg pardon?"

"What?"

"You said something about moving to California."

Ruth still had her arms around Heck's neck and her cheek against his chest. She could feel the change in his body, could feel him tense and withdraw, even though his arms were still around her. She pulled away and looked up at him. "Well, yes."

"You're serious? California?" He let her go and leaned against the stove with his hands on the white enameled top behind him.

Her chin came up. "It's the chance of a lifetime." It made her angry that her voice had a tiny quaver to it. "I have to go to California to get that chance, and I am going. The question is, are you going with me?"

Heck walked over to the table and picked up the letter. He read through it again. "He didn't say anything about moving. He invited you to come talk to him. That's all."

"That's all I need. Don't you worry!"

"I thought you were gonna set up shop here. Use the spare room or find a bigger place. I thought you and Lucy—"

"Lucy doesn't want to do it. Jimmy is thinking about going to Oklahoma. Oklahoma! Can you imagine?"

"Yeah. Mr. Barrett's doing a job there and wants Jimmy to come with him. Wants me, too."

"He does? You never mentioned it."

"Didn't see any need to, since I don't plan to go."

"And you don't plan to go to California, either."

"No ma'am."

"But, why, Heck? It doesn't make sense. There are better jobs there than you have here. We don't have to live in the city. We'll get a place in the country. You can do so many things. It's a shame to bury yourself here! Come to California with me. Working together we could make lots of money. Lots of money!"

Heck sighed. He slowly folded the letter and put it back in its envelope. "Come and sit down," he said quietly.

"What?" Ruth was ready to bristle.

"Come and sit down. It feels like we're squaring off like a couple a' gamecocks. I don't want to fight with you. Let's talk."

He held a chair for Ruth to sit on and sat around the corner of the table from her, reaching out his hand for hers, holding it as he tried to think of what to say.

"You know, Darlin', there are things that you can read and learn, and there are things that other people can teach you. And there are some things that you can figure out for yourself. But every now and then, there comes something that you just know. You don't know how you know it. You just do. This is one of those things."

"I don't know what you're trying to say. What are you saying?"

"I'm saying, I know if I go to California with you, that that's the end of us. The end of you and me together."

Ruth jerked her hand away from Heck and sat bolt upright in her chair, holding the one hand cradled in the other as if she were afraid he would try to snatch it again. She gazed at him with dark eyes that were wide in disbelief and shiny because she was on the verge of tears. "Of all the dirty, rotten, lowdown tricks! That just about takes the cake."

"Beg pardon?"

"What a yellow, cowardly, backhanded sort of a trick!" She mimicked him, "I don't know how I know, but if we go to California that's the end of us." Her lip curled. "What utter nonsense. What drivel."

She stood, driven to activity by the rage boiling within her like geothermal pressure. Holding the back of her chair with hands clenched so tightly that the knuckles showed white, she asked, "Did you ever stop to think that if you try to bury me alive here in Sierra County that that's the end of us, too? I wouldn't say that this last month has been the happiest of my married life, but it's been the most comfortable. You'd better be careful about forcing me to choose between you and comfort, because a once-a-month offer of some fun on a blanket in the mountains doesn't get it with me, Bud."

Ruth picked up the envelope. "He wants to see me in three weeks. I'm leaving in two, with or without you."

Heck regarded her steadily for a moment and then said quietly, "All right."

There was nothing for Ruth to do but manage a dignified exit. She turned on her heel and sailed through the living room, down the hall, and into the bedroom, closing the door firmly behind her and leaning on it, not because she was afraid Heck would try to force his way in, but because her knees were suddenly weak.

When she heard the roar of his cycle, her throat constricted, and she clutched herself just under her breast, for it felt like someone was trying to cleave her in two.

Ruth heard Heck come in two hours later. The anger and heartbreak she had felt earlier had changed to a sense of ill-usage. Heck didn't care. If he cared he would either agree to come with her or insist that she not go. As she listened to him park the cycle and walk to the back door, she decided she would be just as cold as he was. Maybe she should lock the bedroom door. Except the bedroom door didn't have a lock. Scooting way over on her side of the bed, she prepared to breathe regularly in order to convince him she was asleep.

He didn't come into the bedroom.

She heard him lie down on the couch, and five minutes later she heard soft snoring.

Chapter 59

HECK WAS UP and gone Saturday morning before Ruth awoke. He left coffee made and sitting on the pilot light as he did every morning, but it earned him no gratitude from his wife. Not only had he neglected to even mention her birthday, but he had slept while she tossed and turned and wept and seethed. She could not forgive him his night's repose.

Morning left little time for reflection, however. Ruth had five hours' work mapped out for herself in her studio. By the time she took a break halfway through and drove to town to shop for dinner, some of the kinks had been eased out of her bent disposition. She splurged on a standing rib roast and stopped by the florist's for a dozen carnations. There was nothing like spending money to make a woman feel better.

By midafternoon, when the roast was in the oven and her studio work was done, when her bread was set for Parker House rolls, and the dining room table was resplendent with blue damask and sterling silver, Ruth was almost in charity with her husband again. *He's going to surprise me. He hasn't forgotten,* she thought. *He's bought me something special, and he's keeping it a secret until tonight.*

She even discounted his flat negative about California. *Didn't he say he wouldn't leave Ollie? Didn't he say we couldn't move to town? All I have to do is go, and he'll follow. I just had to have the determination to go through with it.* She put a record on the Victrola and began to dance to "Begin the Beguine." *What fun it will be to teach him about all the things that are available in the city—the restaurants, the theater, the social affairs. Heck will be quite the darling of society, with his tall good looks and his soft-spoken drawl.*

It was late afternoon when Ruth started listening for him. She paused, statue-like, as she was toweling off after her bath, but it was the neighbor's tin lizzy putt-putting by that she heard, not the throaty roar of Heck's motorcycle. By five o'clock he still hadn't come.

He's left his shopping to the last minute, she thought. *Just like a man!* Forgiving him this foible, she ran to the window with her heart thumping when she heard the cycle accelerating up the hill. But it wasn't Heck who turned down Silver Street. It wasn't even a motorcycle. It was a delivery truck coming to the sanatorium.

Ruth glanced at the clock. Lucy and Jimmy would be here in 45 minutes. *Where was Heck?*

She went into the kitchen and peeked at the roast. She turned over each of the potatoes and carrots that crowded around it, growing shiny and succulent. She checked her list, but all the preparations were complete, and there was nothing to do now but char the wicks on the candles and wait.

Conflicting emotions ebbed and flowed through her breast. Exasperation and anger surged and waned, followed by uneasiness. Maybe he wasn't going to come home tonight. But he stayed here last night, so he surely would come home tonight. He knew Jimmy and Lucy were coming for dinner. He would be home.

But where *was* the man?

Lucy and Jimmy arrived at six, full of news of the rodeo. The townspeople had gone all out and it was the biggest thing that had ever happened in Hot Springs. Mike had won a hundred dollars. Carrie and Emory had been there and were going to meet them at Ashley's at eight o'clock. Lucy had stopped by on the way and reserved a table for them.

The talk petered out, and they sat with great gaps of silence in the conversation. Their glances just about wore the numbers off the clock as each checked again and again.

Finally, at 6:30, Ruth decided to serve dinner. She hadn't told Lucy it was her birthday, thinking it would come out naturally as she showed off her present from Heck. Then the evening would turn into a birthday celebration.

Instead, dinner was a stilted affair. The food was excellent, but without Heck's leavening influence, the formal dining room and crystal wine glasses seemed oppressive to the guests. Ruth played hostess gracefully as she had been taught, but the conversation she made was as superficial as her smile, and the vacant chair at the head of the table was like a blight on the evening.

At eight o'clock, when Heck still had not come home, Ruth powdered her nose and ran a comb through her hair and said she'd go with Lucy and Jimmy. Lucy wrote a note to tell Heck to meet them at Ashley's, and the three of them—Jimmy silent, Lucy pensive, and Ruth feverishly gay—drove down the hill and to the edge of town where the band was tuning up in the ballroom of Ashley's night club.

Chapter 60

NONE OF THE things that Ruth imagined Heck might be doing as she stood at the window or glanced at the clock late Saturday afternoon approached the reality of his situation. He was not sulking out on the range. He was not shopping for a birthday present. He was careening down a mountainside, barely in control, thinking that if he had anything to do with it—if they both got down alive—Parson Larson might well join the ranks of missionary martyrs, done in by one of the heathens in the wilds of New Mexico.

Heck had gone by early in the morning to see if Parson wanted to ride up into the mountains with him. After being assured that they would only go as far as the dam site on the motorcycle, the missionary agreed.

The ride up to the quarry in the contractor's pickup had been pleasant. No one was working on Saturday, and there had been no worry about meeting traffic on the narrow dirt road. During the week, the solid granite was blasted and fractured and loaded into dump trucks to be hauled down and tumbled over the side of the clay dam. When the time came that the Rio Grande was to be turned back into its regular course, the hard gray covering would offer protection from the eroding forces of the river.

On weekdays, the dust hung heavy over the road to the quarry and upward progress had to be planned with an eye to turnouts, where ascending vehicles stopped to let fully loaded trucks rumble by. There was no dust today, no traffic. When Heck and Parson finally rolled down into the chunky amphitheater and parked by the solitary dump truck, they found the whole place silent and deserted.

All the way up the mountain the conversation had been about Sierra County. Heck had pointed out places on the valley floor below. He told Heber about the pool at the mouth of Palomas Creek and showed him the green clump of cottonwoods that marked its place. He pointed out Palomas, and told him about Bemis and the Armijo family.

When they got high enough to see across to the Diamond E range, Heck extended his arm out the window, tracing with his forefinger the north and south boundaries. He mentioned that this Monday was Cinco de Mayo and described what that meant to the Mexicans and what it meant to the cowboys. This was the first year since he was fourteen, he said, that he wouldn't be going out on the spring work the day after Cinco de Mayo.

As they pulled away from the sheer mountainside and cut through a high saddle pass, Heck shifted gears and looked over at his companion. "I've been thinking about the last time we talked and what you were telling me about the nature of God," he said. "There's a couple things I wanted to ask."

He voiced his questions, and as Parson tried to explain, Heck smiled to himself that such an ineloquent soul would feel the call to be a missionary. There was nothing wrong with the mind and heart of the young man—the mind was agile and the heart true. Somehow, the thoughts generated in those two members presented themselves in words that tumbled out in awkward disarray.

However ineloquent Parson might be, he certainly had staying power. He bent over the fender of the dump truck and spoke of the Godhead as Heck tinkered with the motor, pausing only to climb up into the cab upon request and press on the starter while Heck tried to get the motor to fire. He lay on the ground under the truck and spoke of repentance and forgiveness, handing tools to Heck who grimaced and grunted as he pulled on frozen bolts.

At noon they ate the jerky and tortillas Heck had brought and drank water from the water bag, cool and tasting of canvas. Parson spoke of grace and works.

As the sun waned, so did theological discussion. Heck glanced at the shadows and swore under his breath. He stood on the bumper and stared down at the mechanical puzzle beneath him, trying to plumb the mysteries of the internal combustion engine.

Heber Larson stood quietly waiting. When asked, he climbed into the cab again and pressed on the starter, but the only response was an unwilling groan and then silence. The battery was dead.

"Son of a—" Heck's epithet was drowned in the banging down of the hood. He picked up his tools, carried them to the pickup, and flung them in the back. Hauling out a chain, he dragged it to the dump truck. "You're gonna have to help me, Parson."

The young man climbed down from the cab. "Ah. Um."

"Back the pickup over here, will ya?"

"Back the pickup?"

"Yeah. We'll haul the truck down to the dam, and I'll get Jimmy to come out with me tomorrow and find out what's wrong." As Heck spoke, he was already fastening one end of the chain up under the dump truck. He stood with the other end in his hand and guided Parson as he backed the pickup slowly into position.

After the chain was hooked to both vehicles, Heck spoke through the window. "Just pull me over to where the road leaves the quarry, and we'll stop there and check the chain."

Heck climbed into the dump truck, slipped it into neutral, and waited for Parson to get going. Ahead, through the back window of the pickup cab, Heck could see young Parson's eyes watching him from the rearview mirror. They were wide with apprehension. Heck reached his arm out the window and made forward motions.

The pickup engine roared as Heber eased off on the clutch, and the chain grew taut. Slowly, the truck followed the yellow pickup across the quarry floor. Twice Parson must have become worried that he was going too fast, because the pickup slowed. The dump truck kept rolling and the line went slack. When Parson sped up and hit the end of the chain, there was a shuddering jerk.

They got to the edge of the quarry and stopped. Heck checked the chain and seemed satisfied. "Everything's fine," he said. "There's just one thing you need to remember, and that's to keep the chain tight at all times. If you go hitting the end of it when there's slack, you could bust it. But don't worry. You're doing fine."

Parson got in the pickup. Heck climbed back up into the dump truck, and they started rolling up out of the quarry. At first Parson crept along, but whenever he glanced up at the rearview mirror, Heck caught his eye and made forward motions, urging him to pick up some speed.

The road through the saddle was, for the most part, level, with a few hollows and hills. Heck braked on the first downgrade, but Parson didn't allow for the fact that the heavier truck would roll free downhill faster than his pickup would in second gear, and the chain went slack. When they got to the bottom and started up the rise on the other side, the chain tightened, the pickup shuddered, and Parson's eyes were large in the rearview mirror. Heck grinned and motioned him on.

By the time they made it through the saddle, Parson had learned to anticipate the dump truck on the downgrades, accelerating just slightly to keep the chain tight. He was driving with one elbow out of the window.

They left the saddle and began the descent down the side of the mountain. A steep rock wall was on one side of the road with a sheer drop on the other, and Heck realized he should have tempered his words to Parson about keeping the chain taut.

They had before them two miles of downgrade with no intervening upgrades. The younger man in the pickup drove jauntily along, making sure he kept pressure on the line, adding to the pull of gravity that, alone, in the course of two miles if unopposed, could make a thundering rocket out of the ungainly dump truck.

Heck rode with his foot on the brake, wishing he had an engine that worked, so he could gear down and not risk burning up his brakes. Surely, Parson would realize that he didn't need to be pulling right here. Heck waved his hand to try to get his attention and have him pull over to the side, but Parson wasn't watching. Along with the dust that boiled in through the open window came a snatch of song. Heck leaned his head out the window and hollered, but apparently the sound of the pickup engine, coupled with Parson's singing, drowned out Heck's voice.

He had to do something to slow down his tow car.

Forgetting that the battery was dead, Heck leaned on the horn. No response. No *beep, beep, beep* to get Heber Larson to look up and see Heck waving him over to the side of the road. A tight S-curve was coming up, and Heck pulled his arm back in to have both hands on the steering wheel. The muscles in his arms stood out as he hauled on the wheel, first to the right and then to the left, trying to judge a course that would keep him away from the rocky face of the mountain, and then from the drop-off on the other side.

Heck began sweating as he thought about the hairpin turns coming up. There were two of them before they reached the valley floor. Two tight, 180-degree turns. One of them had the apex of the curve against a solid stone wall. The other hung out over empty space.

The one saving thing was that the grade along the traverse between hairpin turns was long and gentle. Even so, with no horn to blow, no power to gear down with, and brakes that were fading, all Heck could do was stand on the brake pedal, wrench on the steering wheel and contemplate what he would do to Parson when they were finally at the bottom.

All the way along the straight grade, Heck had his arm out the window trying to get Parson's attention. As they approached the first curve, the one next to the rock wall, Heck pulled in his arm and cranked around on the wheel, feeling like the little boy on the end of the line playing Crack the Whip. Heck had the wheel as far to the left as it would go, and he strained to hold it there, watching the rocky face roll by in his right-hand mirror.

"Parson! You scummy dog breath!" Heck yelled. "Pull over, dammit!"

But Parson's elbow was once more out the window, and he was off down the traverse toward the right hand turn. His vehicle was having no trouble making the turns. He obviously had no idea that the larger, heavier truck might need to go slower down the hill.

Heck didn't even bother to try to signal him over. His right leg was beginning to ache from holding down the brake pedal as it sank farther and farther toward the floorboard.

Just before they hit the final turn, he lost his brakes altogether.

Heck swore and jerked on the emergency brake, holding it up with one hand as he worked to turn the steering wheel with the other. He hauled down on the wheel and held it in position with his left knee, let go and grabbed it back at the top, pulling it around again and again, hoping to get it turned in time, so the back wheels wouldn't slide over the bank on the outside of the curve.

As he sat, contorted, with the hand brake in one hand, the wheel in the other, his right foot pressed to the floor on the useless pedal and his left knee pressed against the steering wheel to help hold it around—as the smoke from the emergency brake burning up poured in with the dust—all Heck's frustrations, all his feelings of helplessness at being yanked willy-nilly down a mountainside solidified and focused on that elbow that was hanging out of the pickup window, with the sleeve unbuttoned and rolled up halfway.

"I'll rip that lily-white sleeve off," muttered Heck, glaring through the windshield. "I'll rip his whole arm off, beat him over the head with it. What can you expect from a farmer!"

He made it through the turn.

It was a straight shot to the bottom now. There was no danger of anything but plowing into the back of the pickup, which, because there was not a vestige of stopping power left to the dump truck, was a real possibility. Heck relaxed and started anticipating the moment when Parson would finally realize that he needed to be attending to the truck at the end of the chain behind him.

That moment came about a minute later. It was all Heck could have wished for. He saw the young man's eyes flicker in the rearview mirror, and the next moment, Parson turned all the way around to gaze, round-eyed and open-mouthed, out the back window as the dump truck thudded against the tailgate of the pickup. Parson's eyes traveled from the truck grill, looming as large as hell's gate, up to the driver grinning wickedly down at him, and he turned around and took off as if the devil himself were behind.

Unfortunately, Parson was shackled to his pursuer, and he hit the end of the chain with a teeth-jarring jerk twice before he managed to figure out that he couldn't outdistance the dump truck. By the time they reached the flat, Heck was so tickled about turning the tables on Parson that he forgot how mad he had been on the way down.

The young man slowed to a stop when they reached level ground. He stepped out of the pickup, but Heck leaned out the window and called to him, "Just keep on going. My wife's got company coming to dinner in an hour and she'll skin me alive if I'm late."

So Parson got back in, and they headed out on the final five miles to the dam site.

They made two of the five miles before the pickup had a flat tire. Parson bumped to a stop, and Heck climbed down to see what the matter was. "Oh well," he said, "at least it wasn't on the dump—" He broke off as he realized that there was no spare in the pickup.

After that mad descent down the mountain, Heck was emotionally used up, as empty as an arroyo in August. There was no reservoir of anger to surge forth and cause him to kick a tire or shake his fist at fate. He stood for a minute looking at the sun hovering just over the Caballos. Then he looked at his companion and smiled. "Care for an evening stroll?"

Parson, still a little limp from his final dash in front of the dump truck, could only stand with sagging shoulders, looking in mute disbelief at the flat gray stretch of gravel road that Heck was indicating. But when Heck struck out with his long, loose gait, Parson marched alongside, determinedly matching stride for stride.

They walked in silence for about a quarter of a mile. Then Parson shoved his hands deep in his pockets and sighed. "I, uh, was pretty scared back there," he said.

"Where?"

"Coming down, uh, that last grade. When you about ran over me."

"Yeah? Well, it doesn't hurt a fella to be scared ever' now and then. It's like salt on *frijoles*. Brings out the flavor. Makes you savor 'em."

"Yeah. I guess so."

They plodded on. Heck was doing his own bit of savoring, and his chuckle broke the silence periodically as he remembered the look on Parson's face, framed by the rear window of the pickup.

Parson interrupted him with a bleak question. "Do we walk back, too?"

"Nah. I've got the key to the shop. We'll get a spare and bring it out in another outfit."

"We'll have three trucks out here then. How're we going to get them all back?"

"We'll just have to make a couple a' trips to ferry trucks back. When we get the spare fixed and get chained up ready to go ..." Heck grinned and punched Parson lightly on the arm. "... you're in the dump truck."

Chapter 61

ASHLEY'S NIGHTCLUB WAS the only bar within seventy-five miles that had a dance floor. Dixie Ashley was proprietor, a hardworking, down-to-earth woman who liked people and had a soft spot for cowboys. She tolerated no roughhousing in her establishment.

The building itself was huge, a pink-stuccoed box standing alone on the edge of town. The bar and backbar that ran along the wall that divided the lounge from the ballroom came from an old boarded-up saloon in a ghost town up in the mountains. Made of a rich close-grained wood, it was ornately carved and at least thirty feet long. The backbar, all cupboards and shelves and beveled mirrors, was ten feet tall and did its imposing best to negate the effect of the tacky little clocks and lighted, bubbling beer signs that Dixie hung in any available space.

The dirty beige cinderblock walls of the ballroom were also adorned with a host of illuminated pictures and animated beer signs, all trailing extension cords that ran to the few electrical outlets and stacked up in multiple-plug units that would have sent any fire marshal into apoplexy.

There were two sets of French doors in the ballroom, one on the north wall, one on the south. They were strictly for ventilation as there were no patios inviting patrons to venture out into the night. The favored tables were the ones that sat in the flow of air between the two doors.

The tables, perhaps thirty of them, were arranged around the perimeter of the dance floor just inside a row of booths against the wall. The room could easily accommodate two hundred fifty people, and often did.

The bandstand was on the east end of the room, a small raised platform with a railing around it and a sad-eyed black plywood kitty sitting in front, ready to swallow the dimes and quarters that were offered in exchange for a special tune.

The lot the nightclub stood on sloped away to the east; consequently, the ballroom was four feet lower than the lounge. Just inside the entrance, above the hardwood expanse, was a railed landing where those who had just come in could stand and watch the dancers below before walking down the ramp to join them. Single girls would come in groups and sit in a horseshoe around a table—nobody wanted her back to the door. They laughed and chattered and pretended not to notice the single cowboys and construction workers who came to stand on the landing, leaning on the rail as they took stock of the pickings before descending to ask someone to dance or going back to the bar for another shot of courage.

Emory and Carrie were already there. When Ruth, Lucy and Jimmy arrived, they joined them at a table next to the open French door. Ruth ordered a Tom Collins and nursed it through the evening, glancing too often at the entrance and hating herself every time she did. *He can go to the devil! I don't need him to have a good time.* But she couldn't keep her eyes away from the door.

She didn't lack for partners. Alan Payne was first. As they circled the room in three-quarter time, he asked about Heck, expressing surprise that he hadn't been riding in the rodeo. Ruth said he had to work and agreed that he probably could have won money had he been there. After that, she danced with a cross section of townspeople, cattlemen, cowboys, and visiting dignitaries. She endured compliments from old gentlemen and brash young men, and she came to expect that if her partner knew Heck, she would have to give the reason he didn't ride in the rodeo.

During the ten o'clock intermission, Ruth saw a familiar figure on the landing, a slim, dark-haired cowboy leaning over with hands clasped and both forearms resting on the railing. He was laughing at something the fellow beside him had said and a dimple showed in his cheek. Ruth stared, and something quickened inside—a memory, perhaps, of things that no longer were. As the cowboy's eyes swept the room, they met hers and the smile faded. He looked at the table, at Jimmy on one side and Emory on the other, and knew that she was alone. Finally he nodded a greeting and looked away.

"There's ol' Mike," said Emory. "He won a hunnerd dollars today."

Ruth turned to him. "Do you think that Heck could have won money if he'd ridden in the rodeo?"

"Damn right!"

"So what is he doing, spending all day up in the mountains to make five or six dollars, when he can stay home and make a hundred?" She asked the question without heat. It was more of a playful question, a sign that she was unhurt by Heck's absence on her birthday, that she could speak lightly about the fact that he chose to work that particular Saturday.

She was totally unprepared for Emory's reaction.

Emory's jaw dropped and he stared at Ruth. Then he started to sputter, beginning a sentence and trailing off, starting another and finally lapsing into silence. He sat back in his chair, apparently noticing for the first time the four pair of eyes looking questioningly at him.

"Ah, hmm," he said, and waggled a thumb in Ruth's general direction. He cleared his throat. "Beg pardon, ma'am," he said to Ruth and, to the rest, "Never mind."

Lucy put her elbows on the table and propped her chin in her hands, looking from Emory to Ruth and back again.

"What's going on?" she asked. "Do you two have a secret?"

Emory said, "Yes," just as Ruth said, "No."

Lucy giggled and Jimmy smiled, and even Carrie looked mildly amused.

Ruth sent an inquisitive look at Emory, putting up her brows. "I beg your pardon," she said coolly, "but I must not be quite in the know."

"You know. About Heck not rodeoin'." Emory's whisper was audible to all.

"Yes?"

Emory looked desperately around, but Carrie and Jimmy had their eyes averted. Only Lucy was intent on what was being said, and she frowned in puzzlement.

Emory gave up. "You know. Heck isn't rodeoin' because you asked him not to. He promised he wouldn't."

Ruth stared. "You're joking!" she said. "Are you joking? You're making this up."

Emory shook his head emphatically. "Heck told me a couple, three weeks ago. Said you made him promise."

"Why that's absurd!" But just as the words left her mouth, Ruth remembered. The memory had been lost underneath the crush of twenty months, three moves, an accident, a death, Nick Sanders, and an invitation to California. It came back now, the memory of her wedding day. What had he said? *I love rodeoin', but I love you more.*

Ruth felt her cheeks getting hot. For something to do, she searched for her purse. When she had it in her hand and finally looked up, she found Lucy staring at her, wide-eyed.

"You didn't even remember," Lucy whispered.

Without answering, Ruth opened her handbag to see if her lipstick was there. She snapped it shut and rose. Jimmy automatically stood as she did. She felt them staring after her as she smoothly made her way through the crowd of people toward the ramp that went up to the lounge.

Mike had made it to the bottom of the ramp. He was leaning against the wall with a beer in his hand, listening to the story an older man was telling. Mike's head was cocked in an attitude of listening, but she was aware that his gaze followed her as she approached. She noted the sparkle in his brown eyes, and she wondered if he were laughing at her.

Her chin came up, and she walked past him up to the lounge where she took refuge in the ladies' room.

It wasn't much of a refuge. As dim as the ballroom, the air smelled of stale beer, stale smoke, and urine, and there was a hard-looking middle-aged lady standing unsteadily in front of the sink, peering at herself in the mirror. Ruth went into the stall, closed the door and sat on the closed lid of the toilet.

She looked at the knuckles of her hands clenched around her evening bag, and they were white. Consciously she relaxed them. That was better. Now. What was the problem? She had forgotten Heck's promise. Well, it had been reluctantly given—he'd just as well have broken it. Or asked to be released from it. He could go ahead and ride in the rodeo, for heaven's sake. She didn't care anymore. He could go and break his neck, for all she cared. That would be one problem solved, anyway.

The sound of faltering footsteps retreating, and the squeak-squeak of the swinging door told Ruth that she was alone. Wrinkling her nose in distaste, she looked around the stall at the lipstick prints dotting the grimy beige walls. She shivered. How anyone could put their mouth on that! Ugh.

So what to do? Go home. Better than that, go home and pack. Leave. Suddenly Ruth was excited. She didn't need any small-town, small-minded people looking down their noses at her. She'd show them. Why wait two weeks to leave? She could go tomorrow. No, not tomorrow. Too much to do. She'd have to ship some of her things. And the money in Harlan's account. She'd need that. The bank didn't open until Monday morning. That's fine. She'd leave Monday.

Ruth stood. As she opened the door, she caught sight of herself in the mirror beyond. Critically she surveyed herself. "You'll do," she thought, and walked out of the room.

Chapter 62

MIKE WAS NO longer at the bottom of the ramp. He was standing with both hands on the back of her chair, listening to something Emory was saying. She had intended to ask Jimmy for a ride home, but he was up dancing with Lucy. Ruth slipped through the chairs that had been left pushed out when their neighbors went to the dance floor and went to stand beside Mike, expecting him to seat her. Instead, he held out his hand, and the dimple flashed. "Dance, ma'am?"

As Ruth hesitated, he kept his hand extended. His eyes twinkled as he jerked his head toward the dance floor and coaxed, "C'mon."

Suddenly Ruth realized that this was Gretchen Hancott's cowboy, the one with the laughing eyes and the dimple. Well, if he was good enough for Gretchen, who was she to hold back? Answering his smile, she dropped her purse on the table and took his hand. He led her out to the dance floor and swept her away in a waltz.

Mike was a good dancer. He was not as tall as Heck, but he led as well and was as smooth. Ruth was conscious of his arm around her, of his cheek against her temple. She closed her eyes and smelled the familiar, dressed-up-cowboy smell of Lava soap and Old Spice, and something inside her relaxed and let go. It was so good to be held close, to feel a quickening breath by her ear, to dance, going round and round, two bodies acting as one. Without realizing it, the hand she had resting on Mike's shoulder slid to his collar, and her fingertips moved up to touch the nape of his neck. His arm tightened around her. She felt his head turn as he pressed his lips against her hair, and her thoughts beat in time with the music, *I don't care, I don't care, I don't care.*

When the dance was over, instead of taking Ruth back to her chair, Mike led her to the bandstand. Still holding her hand, he spoke a word to the piano player, dug in his pocket for a quarter and sent it spinning through the kitty's mouth. Then he turned back to Ruth, gathered her in, and they began to move to the slow, throbbing sounds of a plaintive song about love gone awry.

Dancing with her eyes closed, aware of nothing but the music, the soaring, exultant release inside herself, and the pure animal magnetism of the man she was dancing with, Ruth forgot to watch the door.

Heck stood on the landing for a moment and searched the slow-moving crowd as it eddied around beneath him. He spied Lucy first and winked at her as she and Jimmy slid smoothly by. Lucy's smile was a little forced. Looking beyond her, Heck could see why—his wife and his best friend were dancing in the shadows at the end of the room. Dancing as if they were alone. Dancing as if they were lovers.

Heck turned and walked out of the ballroom.

Instinctively, he headed toward support. He walked to the bar and leaned against it as his heart thundered against the walls of his chest. A snarl of conclusions and urges went spinning and backlashing around in his brain. Reason said wait and unravel. Things were not as they seemed. Instinct said there was a predator in his territory.

"Evenin', Heck." Danny the bartender set down a tray of glasses and began stacking them on the backbar.

Heck looked up to see who had addressed him and caught sight of his own stricken reflection in the mirror. He looked away and cleared his throat.

Danny picked up a towel and began drying glasses. "You win some money today?"

"Money?"

"In the rodeo."

"Oh, no. I didn't ride in the rodeo."

"Oh. That's too bad."

"Nah." Heck had to smile as he remembered his trip down the mountainside. "I didn't do any rodeoin' today, but I had one hell of a ride."

"Win any money?"

Heck thought of the three-mile walk in the darkness. "No, no money."

"What'll you have?"

"A Coke."

"And what?"

"Beg Pardon?"

"And what? What do you want in your Coke?"

"I'll take, let me see, one of those cherries."

"That's it?"

"Yep."

Danny blinked. "You go on the wagon, Heck?"

"I've got an appointment in the morning. Don't want to go with a hangover."

"Must be some appointment," Danny muttered as he poured the Coke over ice into a tall glass. He added a cherry and a swizzle stick and gave it to Heck with a doubtful expression.

"Don't worry, I've had one before," Heck said encouragingly. "I can handle it." He paid for the drink, saluted Danny with the glass and turned to walk back to the ballroom, grateful for the steadying effect of small talk with a bartender.

The band was playing "Cotton-eyed Joe." Heck scanned the dance floor. Lucy and Jimmy were dancing, as were Carrie and Emory, but Ruth was not on the floor. His eyes went clockwise around the room checking the tables and booths, looking for the familiar chestnut mane, the trim figure with the graceful carriage. He couldn't remember what she was wearing.

She was wearing a shimmery blue dress. He saw her just before she was swallowed up by the black hole on the south wall. She was holding someone's hand. Someone had led her, smiling, outside. No need to wonder who that someone was.

Mike hadn't spoken ten words to Ruth during the two dances they had together. When the band had struck up a livelier tune, he had led her back to her table and was just about to pull out her chair when a puff of a breeze came in through the door. Mike stared out at the darkness for a moment and then, instead of seating Ruth, he took her hand and coaxed again with a jerk of the head. "C'mon."

She had followed him out into the night.

"Where are we going?" Ruth's voice was light, just a little breathless. She knew where they were going.

"Careful," Mike said. "The ground's uneven."

"I can't see. It's so dark out here."

"Yeah. But it's cool, and look at the stars."

She looked up. "You cowboys really have a thing about stars, don't you?"

"Just the ones that know you." He pulled her to him and slipped an arm around her waist. "They remind us of your eyes."

"Ummm. Very pretty," Ruth murmured. She felt Mike's face next to hers, felt the pressure of his lips in her hair, felt the roughness of his chin as his lips moved to her cheek. She turned her face to him, lifting her mouth to his, and her hands slid up his arms, around his neck, completing the embrace.

Mike's mouth was warm on her own. Ruth closed her eyes and the imprint of the stars remained in her mind, swirling around like a galaxy tipped off-center.

"Evenin', Michael."

Ruth had her back to the French door. Locked as she was in Mike's arms, she could not turn around to see who spoke. But she recognized the quiet menace and knew it was her husband.

Mike looked up and chuckled. "Evenin', Heck." He bent his head and dropped another kiss lightly on Ruth's lips before he let her go.

Heck could hear her breathing. He stepped out of the doorway. "You're getting mighty careless about riding in country that's covered by another man's brand, Michael."

"Well, I tell ya, Heck. Wasn't no one ridin' night herd."

"Are you listening to me? We're talking about another man's brand."

"Well, in the normal course of affairs, we might be, but as I remember, another man's brand don't mean much to her. Seems like she took up with you when—"

Mike never got to finish the sentence. Heck was on him before he had time to blink. Whether Heck dealt that first punch in anger or in an effort to stop Mike from speaking something he did not want to hear, the effect was the same. Heck's fist connected solidly with Mike's chin and knocked him into a greasewood bush. Heck stumbled forward as the force of the blow carried through, but he gathered himself and turned to attack again even before Mike was standing.

Heck was savage. He was relentless. All the pent-up emotions of the last frustrating month had found release. Here was a target, something solid he could attack. Here was perfidy. Here was betrayal. Because he could not strike his wife, his friend must bear the full brunt of reprisal.

Heck was stone-cold sober. Mike wasn't drunk, but he'd reached the stage where he was reckless enough to romance a married woman and fight her husband. Mike's salvation was that there was no moon, and their sparring had taken them far enough away from the doorway that everything was pitch black. Heck could not see well enough for sobriety to weigh in his favor.

There was a lot of clumsy footwork, a lot of reeling through bushes, grunting and swearing. Mike caught Heck in the mouth with his elbow—an accident, but it made Heck see stars and drew blood. He stood still until the purple and green blotches receded from his vision and then called, "*Hombre?*"

"*Aquí.*"

Heck leapt toward the voice, taking Mike to the ground in a bear hug, rolling over with him until he could hold Mike down and sit over him. Careless of Mike's defensive blows to his stomach and chest, Heck took advantage of his longer reach to locate Mike's face with his left hand while he drew back with his right. He was going to rearrange that winsome smile, make it a little less attractive.

Instead, he was blinded by a flashlight pointed at his face and hauled off of Mike by two pairs of hands that fastened around his arms like hose clamps. Still down on his knees, he tried to jerk away, but they held him fast.

"Easy, *hermano*. Easy." Emory was on Heck's left, talking softly to him the way he'd talk to a mustang he was trying to gentle. Who was the other set of hose clamps? Heck lifted his left hand to block out the light that still glared in his eyes and saw Jimmy's worried face. Among the impressions that filtered through the darkness and pain and rage—impressions of people hovering, muttering, the crippling glare of Dixie's flashlight—among them all, the anxious look on the face of that stoical man was the thing that grabbed Heck and jerked him back to reality.

"It's all right," Heck said. "You can let me go. I'm through."

And he was. There wasn't an ounce of fight left in him. He felt hollow. Used up.

Dixie didn't argue with him when he said he'd walk around to the parking lot and go. Emory and Jimmy didn't try to detain him, either. He mumbled good bye and stumbled over to the wall, so he could use it as a guide through the darkness to the gravel lot in front.

Chapter 63

THE GLOW OF the neon sign on the front of the nightclub illuminated the parking lot. Approaching his car, Heck saw Ruth sitting with her hands grasping the steering wheel, staring straight ahead. He could read her mood from her posture, and he paused, not sure if he was up to squaring off with her.

She must have caught his movement in the corner of her eye because she turned and trapped him with a look.

Wondering what more was to happen to him that day, Heck gave up and made his way to the car. Opening the passenger door, he got in, but he kept his gaze averted. He would not look at her.

"The keys?" Her voice was cold.

He fished them from his pocket and held them out. Still, he couldn't look at her.

She snatched the keys from him with an exasperated noise and started the car. Grinding the gears, she tore out of the parking lot and sped toward home.

Heck sighed and closed his eyes, leaning his head back against the seat. He became aware of the warm, salty taste of blood and gingerly put a finger up to feel the cut at the corner of his mouth. He had never fought Mike before. They had always stood together against someone else. As he probed the torn lip, he was filled with a sadness that his life had changed to the point that he would attack his best friend in anger. It was such a great sadness that his throat constricted and he felt tears seep from under his closed lids. Embarrassed, he turned his face to the window, swallowing to get rid of the lump that threatened to strangle him.

He didn't realize they were home until Ruth turned off the engine. She left the lights on and sat for a moment regarding him. Then she picked up her bag. "Do you have anything to say?" The tone of her voice dared him to make an accusation.

Heck finally looked at her. Still leaning back against the seat, he rolled his head to the left and met her eyes.

Antipathy crackled in the air. Her hands were trembling.

He couldn't fight her right now. It was too painful. Wait until tomorrow when she'd calmed down. Then they'd talk it out. He closed his eyes and shook his head.

She turned off the lights and opened the door.

Heck spoke quietly. "Michael ..."

"What?"

He couldn't speak any louder. He was to weary for that. "Michael was my friend," he rasped. "I gave him my horse."

He was trying to express his sadness, but she must have taken it as an indictment. Her fury was like an electrical arc, almost visible in the darkness, leaping with her as she left the car, charging her voice as she turned to scream at him.

"You go to hell!"

Heck slumped back with his eyes closed and felt the force of the car door slamming shut. A moment later he heard, like echoes, the slamming of the back door and, faintly, the door to the bedroom being shut against him.

Chapter 64

HECK WAS AWAKENED by a tapping sound behind him, an erratic, metallic clicking that, by its mystery, dragged him from sleep. As he lay with his eyes closed, listening, he became aware of the grass prickling his hand. That was a new sensation, waking to the feel of grass. He had never spread his bedroll on a lawn before.

Click, click-click. There it was again. Lazily, Heck turned over and found that a raven had taken a fancy to his timepiece which lay face down a few feet away. He was a fine fellow, black and sleek and probably vain, for he cocked his head and fixed a black shoe-button eye on his own reflection. Then click, click-click, he pecked at the shiny silver disk, pausing again to cock his head.

It was morning. The sun was just coming up. The air was cool and fresh and still. This was a new beginning. A new chance. Heck lay and savored the prospect of a clean slate. *Lord*, he thought, *help me manage this thing all right*.

Funny how the earth spinning ninety degrees can alter a person's outlook. Last night, with everything falling apart to staves, Heck would not have been willing to wager money that the sun would rise at daybreak. But there it was, and his spirits rose with it.

He got up on an elbow and addressed the raven. "So, what do you have to say about the events of last night? Nevermore? Couldn't have said it better myself."

The raven took a tentative step away and bent his beady stare on Heck, who touched a finger to his lips. "Shhhhh," he said, and pointed to the bedroom window. "We'll let her sleep. I can be back before she's even had breakfast, and then we'll see."

Heck sat up and threw back his blanket. Startled, the bird flapped his wings and gained a foot of height before gliding to sanctuary at the corner of the house, his eye still on the watch.

Heck grinned at him and whispered, "Sorry," as he put the watch in his pocket. Then he picked up his dress boots and quietly entered the house. He set the boots down in the living room and went to the bathroom, closing the door softly behind himself before stripping to the waist to wash and shave. He eyed himself in the mirror. His lip had scabbed over at the corner and his jaw was sore. Other than a few odd bruises and scrapes, he wasn't too bad off.

Ruth was fast asleep when he stole into the bedroom. The curtains were drawn, and it was dusky inside, but he could see the dark shadows under her eyes and the white hankie she still clutched in her hand.

I shouldn'ta stayed outside last night, he thought. *Hell, I'd just as well a' been outside this last month. Wonder what I thought—that ol' Harlan's ghost was gonna spook me if I did anything in that bed? Well, that's another nevermore.* He pointed a finger at the sleeping woman. "You can count on it," he whispered.

Heck stood for a moment, gazing tenderly down at his wife. She was all softness; there was none of the sharp-edged brittleness of last night. "Ah, Baby Doll," he murmured. "Let's get this thing worked out."

At last he went to the closet. Taking down a fresh shirt, he picked up his work boots and carried them into the living room, where he finished dressing quickly and quietly. Then he went outside and put his bedroll away in the garage.

Checking his watch to make sure of the time, Heck took his goggles from the handle bars and hung them around his neck. He put up the kickstand and began pushing his cycle down the driveway and into the street. He puffed a bit, pushing the heavy machine up the incline past the sanatorium but didn't start the engine until he was well away from the house.

It was Sunday morning, and the streets were deserted. The sun was low and right in his eyes as he rode slowly, idling along, so the noise of his passing wouldn't disturb people still abed. As he squinted into the sun, trying to see the road, his mind kept returning to the picture of Ruth as he had just left her. That was the woman he married. How had she become the two-timing, screaming harridan she was last night? Heck shook his head, as if he could shake loose the memory. Was it because he said he wouldn't go to California?

The streets were still in shadow as he drove through town. Passing the assay office, he thought about the ring he had carved for Ruth out of soapstone. She hadn't wanted to change it for a gold ring, but he told her it was a fragile stone and would wear away after a while. So she put it away to keep and wore the wedding band he got her in Kanab. On down the street was the hardware store. He remembered when they had come in on her birthday to look at toilets and bath ... wait! Her birthday! With an awful sinking feeling, Heck remembered that Ruth's birthday was yesterday. He had completely forgotten.

Heck almost laughed out loud. Of course! He had forgotten her birthday. No wonder she was angry. No wonder she had taken up with Mike, let him kiss her. Knowing her, Heck understood.

He gunned the engine, and the cycle shot forward. No cryptographer laboring in wartime to crack a cipher—bearing the weight of lives lost with each day's delay, puzzling for weeks and months, muttering combinations instead of grace at meals—ever felt more elated when he finally discovered the key than Heck did at that moment.

"Yeeeehaw!" he shouted joyously over the roar of his motorcycle. He didn't care whose sleep was disturbed. The cipher was broken. He had the key.

He was swinging around the curve by Doyle Gibson's ice house where the upper and lower streets of Hot Springs converge. He blinked because he was facing full into the sun again, and it made his eyes water. Damn! How could he have forgotten her birthday? He'd been too focused on things that didn't really count, too worried about sitting on Harlan's couch and sleeping in Harlan's bed. He'd go back right now and tell her he was sorry. They could talk things out—

Ruth woke early. It wasn't the usual slow process, becoming aware of the world around by degrees until finally she surrendered to intruding reality. This morning, one moment she was asleep, the next moment she was awake and staring at the white Bull Durham tag that hung over the edge of the dresser, knowing that, in spite of the fact that his tobacco was still there, Heck wasn't, and their marriage was on the rocks.

She sat up and looked out the window. The motorcycle wasn't there. Staring at the empty driveway, she tried to think where Heck would be, but her mind seemed to be swathed in cotton wool and wouldn't work properly. She got out of bed and listlessly pulled her dressing gown over her shoulders, tying it around herself as she padded down the hall on her way to the kitchen. At the archway, she stopped suddenly and clutched the corner for support, because her knees had turned to jelly and would not hold her unaided.

Her gaze was fixed on the coffeepot sitting, unassembled, on the counter by the sink where she had put it last night.

"He's really gone," she whispered to herself. "And this time he's not coming back."

Dreaming of the glamour of California and threatening to go there alone was one thing. So was vowing she did not need Heck when she was beside herself with rage, but this was different. This was real, and Ruth was totally unstrung by the discovery that Heck had not left coffee sitting on the pilot light for her to wake up to.

"Oh, Lord. What have I done?" She stared vacantly at the symbol of what her life had become as it lay scattered and useless on the counter. She felt the pressure of tears welling around her eyes, and she cleared her throat, determined not to cry.

"Let's see," she said aloud. "I must dress."

She talked herself through a bath and getting dressed, breaking each task down into reachable goals, praising each accomplishment: "All right now, run the water in the bath tub. Good, good. That's good. Now, a towel. Set out a towel. That's right. Now, take off the robe. Hang up the robe. Good. Now, oh!"

The shirt that Heck had worn last night was hanging on the towel rack. Ruth picked it up and held it to her cheek. As she smelled his familiar scent, a wrenching tightness struck clear through to her soul. Her breast felt empty and wrung dry, and she could not get a breath. Sitting on the toilet, she buried her face in the shirt and the tears she had been working so hard to stave off came in torrents.

When she had cried herself out and the shuddering, gasping aftermath was over, Ruth sat up and began again in a voice that trembled but was resolute. "See if the water is warm. Not quite. Add more hot. That's right. Now, off with the nightgown. Put the shirt there beside it. Now, get in the tub. Good."

And so it went until she was completely dressed and groomed. As she was creeping down the hall toward the kitchen, someone walked by the front room window. For a heart-stopping moment, she thought it might be Heck, but a knock on the door routed that hope. Ruth was tempted to retreat to the bathroom and pretend no one was home, but she hesitated too long. A moment later, the caller leaned down to peek through the small window in the door and spied her. It was Parson.

When she made no move to answer the door, he knocked again. Still, she did not move.

Pushing the door open a ways, he poked his head through. "Morning, ma'am."

She bunched up the shirt she had been carrying and held it against her midriff, but she didn't greet him.

"Uh, I was just wondering. Is Heck here?"

She didn't answer, just kept staring at him until he obviously became uncomfortable.

"He, uh, was gonna, uh, come by and pick me up."

Silence.

"He was, um, we were going up to the pool at Palomas Creek. He was supposed to be by an hour—"

The ringing of the telephone cut into Parson's explanation. He glanced at the telephone as it rang sharply two shorts and a long, two shorts and a long.

"Ah, um, maybe it's him," he suggested. "That's your ring, isn't it?"

She looked from the telephone to Parson and back again, but still she did not move.

Parson opened the door wider and stepped inside. "Do you want me to answer it?"

She shook her head and went slowly to the phone. Still clutching the crumpled-up shirt with her left hand, she picked up the receiver with her right. "Hello," she said, but her voice was so whispery that she had to clear her throat and try again. "Hello."

As Parson anxiously watched, Ruth's eyes widened and flew to meet his.

"Who is it?" he asked.

The blood drained from her face and a bluish tinge appeared around her mouth. The dark crescents under her eyes deepened.

"Who is it?" he asked again.

She dropped the receiver down to rest on her shoulder, heedless of the sound that dribbled out, the sympathetic voice oozing over the wire, trying to smooth over the jagged edges of words like *concussion, hematoma, critical*.

"It's the hospital," she told Parson. "There's been an accident. Heck ..."

She couldn't say the words. Her eyes turned back and her hand went slack. The telephone tumbled to the floor and lay there spilling out details as Parson managed to catch her before she hit the floor.

Chapter 65

IT WAS ONE o'clock in the afternoon and Ruth was alone. She sat in a corner chair, trying to cool herself with a cardboard fan that was decorated in a Japanese motif and bore the inscription *Jones Funeral Home* on the handle in pseudo-Japanese script. Over the flapping fan she stared at Heck. *It's only when he's sleeping, when the sun-grins around his mouth and eyes are erased, that one notices how fine his profile is,* she thought.

It had been five hours since Parson brought her here, five hours since she stood on the veranda of the hospital with Parson's arm around her waist lest she faint again as Dr. Colbin gave his prognosis. The day was already unseasonably warm, but Ruth had been shivering as she listened to the kindly gentleman who spoke in the raspy tones of age.

"No hope," he had said.

He said no one knew why Heck had suddenly turned in front of an oncoming car. There was no way the driver could have kept from hitting him. Someone out early watering a lawn had seen the accident, had seen Heck somersaulting through the air to land on the curb. The back of his head was crushed, the doctor had said. The injury to his brain was massive, irreversible. There was no hope.

Parson had left an hour ago. Ruth could not let him go before then, for she had literally leaned on him for support as they followed the doctor's crooked figure down the hall past wards smelling of antiseptic to the small private room at the back of the hospital. Parson had kept one arm around her and one hand under her elbow as she stood with teeth chattering, looking at her husband lying in a coma from which he would never waken.

No hope.

She had pressed her cheek against Parson's chest and wept. Wept because Heck was leaving her, wept because she had parted from him in anger, wept because it was so unfair, because she could not live without him. As she cried, she heard the strangled sobs of the young man crying too. They stood by the bedside and clung together in sorrow, bereft because, though Heck slept not four feet away, there was no hope.

Finally Parson had insisted that she sit, and he sat next to her, gave her his handkerchief and took her hand. Trying to comfort her, he told the tale of their adventures coming down the mountain the day before. He told it so well that she managed a damp, shaky laugh, for she could see Heck in every line of his story. It steadied her somewhat, and finally she drew a ragged breath and let out a long-drawn sigh.

"He didn't make coffee this morning," she said. "I thought he had left me."

Parson had smiled at her and shook his head decisively. Heck loved her, he said. He was sure of that. He had taken his notebook from his pocket and asked if there were others that needed to know. Did she want him to bear the news?

She had looked blankly at him for a moment. She had forgotten that anyone else could be affected by what happened to Heck. Resting her hand on her forehead she paused to think. Then she picked up her purse and began to rummage inside. "I can't seem to find the car keys," she said, tearing up again.

"Oh. Uh, I still have them." Parson colored as he drew them from his pocket.

"Keep them," she said and told him how to get to Palomas. He was to tell Lucy about the accident and come right back. Lucy could tell the rest of the family.

Then he was gone, and she was left to the relentless buffetings of remorse. *If there really is a hell, I wonder if this is what it's like—to be penned up in a tiny, airless, colorless room, full of regret and no way to make it right.*

She begrudged every minute Parson was away. If she closed her eyes to block out the sight of her husband's inert form with the purple mask across his eyes where blood was pooling under the skin, seeping out from the massive wound inside his head, unwelcome memories of last night presented themselves to view. Ruth turned her head away each time the picture of herself and Mike intruded into her thoughts, as if by denying access to the memory she could erase the reality.

As the afternoon wore on and the shocky numbness of first knowledge wore off, Ruth's suffering increased. Sitting alone was torture, for there was nothing to fix her eyes on but Heck, nothing for her mind to do but dwell on things that might have been. She was so thankful to hear Parson's heavy tread and to see his reassuring, freckled face peek around the door that she stood and literally greeted him with open arms.

He was her good angel. As the family assembled, he greeted each in turn. After introducing himself, he told the story of the accident as he knew it. Ruth turned her white face and stricken eyes toward them, and they nodded. Except for that sober greeting, they kept to one side of the room and let her be. Last night must loom as uncomfortably in their memories as it did in hers.

Emory looked like he'd been gut-shot as he stood by his brother's bed. When Mama began sobbing he tried clumsily to comfort her, holding her to him and patting her head with the hand that still held his hat. "Oh Mama, don't cry. Don't cry," he begged in a hoarse whisper that trembled as if he himself were on the verge of tears.

Lucy stood by the bed and talked to Heck. She smoothed the hair back from his brow and spoke in a husky whisper. With tears streaming down her face, she said the things she had been too shy to say before—how she loved and looked up to him, how he had been the model for what she looked for in a husband. She thanked him for watching out for her as she was growing up and for teaching her to dance. "I know you're going to heaven," she said. "When you get there, will you kiss Little Emory for me? Tell him his mama loves him." Then, she could say no more and retreated to sit by the wall with Emory's arm around her.

At about ten o'clock, Dr. Colbin came by. He peeked into the room to make sure Ruth was all right and then stood in the hall talking to Emory and Lucy. She heard Emory ask, "How long?" She didn't catch the doctor's reply, but the phrases "tough cowboys" and "linger," came floating to her, and she snatched at the words, wondering if there was comfort in knowing that, even though there was no hope, he would not die quite yet.

Jimmy and Carrie had come no farther than the doorway, hovering uncomfortably before withdrawing to the waiting room where they sat silently staring at nothing.

Nate Benham, looking pale and ancient, had taken one brief, shattering look at his son and then had joined Jimmy and Carrie. He sat unmoving with his head in his hands until midnight, when the family finally went home.

Ruth was glad when they were gone, when she was left to watch with just Parson to keep her company. She smoked cigarettes and drank the coffee he brought her. Parson offered to get her something to eat, but she said no, she would rather that he talk to her instead.

So he did. He gazed at the man lying in the shadows across the room while he told her about Heck's spiritual quest, about the questions he asked, and the problems he posed. He spoke with respect about Heck's knowledge of the scriptures, about his incredibly wise, homemade philosophy.

As the night wore toward dawn, Ruth became more and more aware of a side of Heck she had never known. Finally, there was nothing left to talk about, and they both slept. Ruth leaned against the corner in ladylike slumber. Parson sprawled half out of his chair with his head back and his mouth open.

Ruth woke an hour later, at daybreak, and her heart stopped for a moment as she looked at Heck, for he was no longer breathing. She stood, and as she went to his bed a voice inside of her shouted, *No! No! No! Not yet!*

She wavered in confusion, wondering what to do, whom she should call, when his mouth opened and his chest heaved as he took a great, gasping breath. And then, as if nothing had happened, the regular rising and falling of normal respiration began again.

Weak from ebbing adrenaline, Ruth went back to her chair and waited for her heart to quiet. Knowing her husband was going to die had not prepared her for the actuality of his death. She sat and pondered about what life was going to be like without him. "I'd have gone and left him," she said to herself in wonder. "I'd have gone to California."

Parson slept until Mrs. Roberts, the starched and proper day nurse, asked them to leave, so she could do morning care for Heck. Glancing sleepily around, Parson stumbled out of the room and down the hall in Ruth's wake, following her out into the early morning air. He stood, yawning and scratching himself under the arm as he tried to recapture some of the purpose that had driven him yesterday.

Ruth smiled at him. "Do you still have the car keys?"

"Hmmm? Car keys?" He checked his pockets. "Yep."

"Let me see them."

He handed them to her, and she chose a key and held it up for him to see. "This is the house key. I want you to go have a bath and a nap. Get something to eat, too. Can you forage for yourself? Good. I'll watch until noon. Then, I want you to come and take over. There are some things I have to do, and I'd feel better if you were here with Heck."

"Do you think he'll ..." Parson didn't seem to be able to frame the words.

"I don't know. As Dr. Colbin said, he's a tough cowboy. Go on now, and come back at noon."

Obediently, he left. Ruth found a restroom and splashed water on her face. Then, she combed her hair and put on lipstick, and went to sit in the waiting room until Mrs. Roberts should allow her to return and bide by her stricken husband.

When the nurse signaled her to come back in, Ruth hesitated at the door. Heck lay as he had since she first saw him, quietly resting, breathing regularly. Except for that dark mask around his eyes and the unfamiliar surroundings--the green and white hardness of easily cleanable surfaces, the smell of carbolic hanging in the air, the high bed with its mechanical cranks and clipboard--except for that, she had seen him thus so many times before. Oh, for one more time to have him lying in her bed where she could raise up on an elbow and look down at his face in repose. *How we squander what we're given.*

She went to stand by the bed, running her hand over the coverlet to smooth out a wrinkle. It was hard to believe that it was her husband lying between these newly changed sheets.

Would Heck submit so tamely to death? He who had sat astride the explosive, killer brute-force of a wild mustang? He who had stayed in the path of a flash flood until the last possible moment to rescue her car—and his saddle? The corners of her mouth lifted a little and her eyes softened as she remembered him saying, "I set great store by that saddle"

Ruth strolled pensively back to her corner, settled into her chair, leaned her head back against the wall and began to think. At first, her mind worked busily at organizing the half-formed intentions of early morning, but the room got warmer, and her eyes got heavier. Before she was through with the afternoon's mental checklist, she drifted off to a deep and dreamless sleep.

Parson waked her gently, shaking her shoulder, softly calling her name. She opened her eyes, grimacing at the stiff neck she had earned from sleeping too long in the corner. She looked first at Heck, then at the anxious face hovering above her, then at her watch. It was just noon.

"Oh, thanks, Parson." Ruth blinked and sat for a minute, rubbing her neck and collecting her thoughts. Then, picking up her purse and taking the proffered car keys, she said, "I'm going to go have a bath and change. And I think I'll have something to eat." She managed a tiny smile. "I'm actually a little hungry."

She walked to the door and looked back at Heck. "I have another errand, too. I may be gone three hours. Can you stay?"

"As long as you like," he said.

"Thank you." She was off down the hall, jingling the keys absently. First, a bath, then lunch, then Doyle Gibson.

She checked at the sight of her mother-in-law and Lucy sitting in the waiting room. Mama had her work bag sitting on the floor, and she was darning a sock. As Ruth paused, Lucy opened her eyes and sat up straight.

"Oh, hello, Ruth."

"Why are you sitting out here?" Ruth asked.

"Oh, well, you know. We didn't want to disturb you. Didn't want to intrude."

"Don't be silly! How long have you been here?"

"Oh, a couple of hours. But—"

"We got here at nine," Mama stated, not looking up from her darning.

"Have you seen Heck?"

"We peeked in every now and then, and Dr. Colbin came by. We talked to him after he had been in."

"I seem to have slept through everything. Well, don't sit out here. Go on in and sit with Heck. I guess the doctor told you he's just the same?"

Lucy nodded. "Ruth, who is that fellow?"

"What fellow?"

"The one that just walked by, went down to your room. He was in there last night. Does he work at the hospital?"

Ruth smiled. "No, that's Parson. He's a friend of Heck's. Go in and talk to him. He spent all day yesterday ... what is today?"

"Today is Monday, the fifth of May. Cinco de Mayo."

"That's right. I've lost a day. Parson spent all day Saturday with Heck. Go ask him to tell you about it. It'll make you feel better." She jingled her keys. "I'm going to go have a bath and something to eat. I'll be back in a while." She sketched a goodbye wave that included both women. Lucy answered it, but Mama didn't look up. She kept stitching on the sock, a dark shroud on her darning egg, as if by closing the gaping heel-hole she could save her son.

Chapter 66

RUTH RETURNED AT a quarter to four. The sense of purpose she had enjoyed as she drove through the sunshine on her errands withered as she stepped through the door into the antiseptic air of the hospital. She dreaded the thought of sitting through another night, of having her eyes play tricks on her every time she looked to see if Heck was still breathing. She paused outside the half-opened door, not quite ready to take over the vigil.

Peeking through, she saw that Parson was standing by Heck.

"Any change?" she asked from the doorway.

"No. No change."

She came in to stand beside him. "Did Lucy and Mama go home?" she asked, looking not at him, but at her husband. She smoothed the coverlet again, though there had been no wrinkle made.

"They said they'd come back tonight. They had to go fix supper for the menfolks."

"You'd better go have some supper too."

Parson shook his head. "I'm not hungry," he said. "What can I do for you?"

"Just sit with me. Be here."

So he sat with her. Watching together, they had forged an easy companionship. Neither felt it necessary to make conversation to fill in the long, silent gaps. Parson read his scriptures, marking an occasional passage with a red pencil, looking up periodically to let his eyes rest on his friend or to smile encouragement at Ruth.

Ruth sat with her head leaned back against the wall. Answering his smile one time, she confessed, "I was mad at Heck that first time he brought you over. I don't even remember what about. It doesn't matter now, but I do recall I wasn't very cordial."

Parson blushed and looked away, shaking his head. "That's all right," he muttered.

"Funny, how life is," she murmured. The sun was setting, and sunlight coming through the window cut the space between her and Heck in two with a rosy shaft, as if the severing process were starting already. Ruth closed her eyes and summoned up memories of Cottonwood Springs.

The family came about dark and assumed the same positions they had occupied the night before. Nate, Jimmy, and Carrie sat in the waiting room. Mama, Emory, and Lucy occupied the wall at right angles to Ruth and Parson. They waited silently, knowing Heck was slipping away, understanding there was no hope, but totally unprepared for the finality of his exit.

At eleven o'clock, Emory gathered the family in the waiting room and persuaded them to go home. He would stay, he said. If there was any change, he would come and get them.

While Emory was sending the family home, Ruth was doing the same with Parson. "Emory will be here with me," she said. "I'll need you tomorrow. Go get some sleep."

Reluctantly he agreed, declining a ride home. "The walk will be good for me. Goodbye." He held out his hand, but she kissed him on the cheek instead.

Then there were just three of them in the room. Ruth and Emory sat in the wash of light from the table lamp and Heck occupied the shadows. They were all equally silent, equally still, until Ruth broke the silence.

"Emory."

Emory looked up, startled at the sound of her voice. "Ma'am?"

"Do you believe in life after death?"

Emory stared a moment. "I don't know, Ruth. Heck did. Mama does. And Preacher Lewis says so. I've never thought much about it, but those three have, and I'd stake my life on anything any of 'em would say."

"Parson talked to me last night about marriage lasting after death. What do you think about that?"

Emory just shrugged. He cleared his throat and shook his head, "All I know is, my brother's dyin'." He pulled his handkerchief out of his back pocket and blew his nose.

"I have Heck's saddle at the house," Ruth said. "I want you to take it and keep it for Jonathan."

"Jonathan?" Emory paused in the act of putting his handkerchief away.

"Yes. Listen to me, Emory. Heck told me one night that Jonathan was a wellspring, a source of future ..." She shook her head. "I don't know how he said it, but what he meant was that he wanted to be involved with your son as he grew up. I know he'd want Jonathan to have his saddle."

Ruth paused and waited while Emory dragged his handkerchief out again. He mopped his eyes and blew his nose and then sat with his elbows on his knees and his hands over his face.

"I loved Heck, Emory," Ruth said gently. "I didn't always show it, but I loved him."

She leaned back in the corner and closed her eyes. "Heck said something to me one time. It was after we left Ollie's and were living in Palomas. He said that sometimes you make choices that are wrong. And it's not just a mistake— you know what you're doing is wrong. He said that later on you can be sorry for what you've done. You can even be forgiven for what you've done ..." Tears seeped out from under her closed lashes, and she had to pause and wait for the tightness in her throat to ease. "But that doesn't ... that can't change ..." Ruth cleared her throat. "He said that even though you're sorry, even though you're forgiven, the consequences of your choices stand. You can't change them."

She took a great, ragged breath and slowly exhaled. "I didn't understand what he was talking about then, but now I do."

Emory didn't answer her.

She picked up her purse and went to stand in the shadows by Heck. Smoothing the hair back from his brow she said, "I'm going out for a while."

Emory wiped his eyes on his shirtsleeve. "But it's the middle of the night," he whispered.

"I'm just going to take a ride. I'll go crazy if I sit here doing nothing. I won't be long." Ruth touched Heck's hand lightly and went out the door.

The hall was a long, dark tunnel. The waiting room was a dusky cavern. Outside, the night was a cool black sea that flowed around her, obscured her vision, hid the little green coupe.

Ruth edged her way carefully to the street, walking slowly because of the meager light from the hospital porch. Feeling her way around the car, she found the door handle and got in. She turned on the lights, inserted the key with a shaking hand, and started the car.

Driving aimlessly, she followed the road that went by the river, crossing above town and heading toward Cutter. There was no moon, and the way seemed long and lonely. She passed the turnoff to Ollie's place and, on impulse, backed up and took it. She drove slowly, though the way was familiar. Her headlights picked out the windmill of Ollie's house when she was still a ways a way. The turnoff to Hooper's Well was somewhere along in here. "I won't torture myself by going down there," she thought, but she did.

Memories flooded back as she bumped over the gravel road. Somehow, they weren't the worrisome memories of blowing dust, chapped hands, and a stove that wouldn't light. The memories that rushed to meet her were warm and welcome. Heck up early and whistling as he made coffee, the magpie doing his shtick outside their window, the sound of Heck's spurs as he came home from a day out riding.

As she saw the outline of the new house in her headlights, she wondered what she'd say to the cowboy who was tending Hooper's Well, if she happened to wake him. Rolling into the yard, the place seemed deserted, and the front door stood ajar.

Ruth turned off the motor and climbed out of the car. She felt oddly comforted being here, though she didn't want to go inside the house. On impulse, she began gathering sagebrush, making a small pile where she and Heck used to sit in the cool of the evenings. That accomplished, she went back to the coupe and got her lighter and the car blanket. When she turned out the headlamps, the blackness seemed complete, but the tiny, flickering flame of her cigarette lighter guided her to the brush pile.

She lit it and sat for a long time on the car blanket, nursing the blaze and playing the weary, circular game of *What If*. Growing tired, she pulled the blanket around herself and lay down, resting her head upon her arms. Before the fire had burned down, she was asleep.

A jingling of spurs woke her. She lay with her eyes closed and listened to the familiar step, heard it pause beside her, felt the familiar hand upon her cheek. The roughness of the fingers, the calluses on the palm were just as she had always known them, and the sweet gentle voice that spoke to her was his. "It's morning, Darlin'. I'm going now. I've come to say goodbye."

"Goodbye," Ruth whispered and turned her face to kiss the palm of his hand. She opened her eyes to catch one last glimpse of that tall, lanky figure, but all she saw was open range and the gold-rimmed Caballos beyond.

As she sat up and looked around in the cold blue twilight, at the outlines of the pump shack and the hand-me-down house Heck had built her, she felt bereft.

His touch had been so real. His voice had been so true. How could it have been just a dream?

But it wasn't. At least the jingling sound was real, for there it was again. Ruth stood and searched through the brightening vista for the source of that sound. At last, she saw it.

What she heard was the jingling of the trace chains on Ollie Free's chuckwagon as his outfit moved out on the spring work.

Today was the sixth of May. The day after Cinco de Mayo.

ABOUT THE AUTHOR

A native of New Mexico and mother of seven, Liz Adair bloomed late as a writer—her first Spider Latham Mystery was published about the time AARP added her to their mailing list. Though she lived in green, moist, northwest Washington State for forty years, most of her books are set in the southwest.

Liz returned to high plateau country in 2012 when she and her husband, Derrill, moved to Kanab, Utah. "I love this area," Liz says. "I've decided to set all my future books in red rock country."

Look for a sequel to this book in July of 2016. The title will be *Return to Willow Canyon.*

If you enjoyed *Interlude at Cottonwood Springs*, please consider posting a review or rating on Amazon, Goodreads, Barnes and Noble, or Kobo. Reviews will help spread the word.

Also, feel free to email me with any comments or questions at writer.lizadair@gmail.com. I would love to hear from you.

For regular updates, sign up for my newsletter at http://www.sezlizadair.blogspot.com

OTHER BOOKS BY LIZ ADAIR

Trouble at the Red Pueblo, a Spider Latham Mystery set in Kanab

Amy's Star, a Spider Latham Christmas Story, in the anthology *A Christmas Village*

The Lodger, #1 in the Spider Latham mystery series

After Goliath, #2 in the Spider Latham mystery series

Snakewater Affair, #3 in the Spider Latham mystery series

The Mist of Quarry Harbor

Lucy Shook's Letters from Afghanistan

Cold River

Hidden Spring, a novella in the *Timeless Romance, Old West Collection*

www.ingramcontent.com/pod-product-compliance
Lightning Source LLC
Chambersburg PA
CBHW071638260626
47170CB00001B/153